Whispers IN THE MIND

CHARLTON CLAYES

iUniverse, Inc.
Bloomington

WHISPERS IN THE MIND

iUniverse books may be ordered through booksellers or by contacting:

iUniverse
1663 Liberty Drive
Bloomington, IN 47403
www.iuniverse.com
1-800-Authors (1-800-288-4677)

ISBN: 978-1-4759-7134-7 (sc)
ISBN: 978-1-4759-7135-4 (e)

Printed in the United States of America

iUniverse rev. date: 2/18/2013

"The trumpet does not more stun you
by its loudness,
than a whisper teases you
by its provoking inaudibility."

Charles Lamb,

"The Old and the New Schoolmaster,"
Essays of Elia (1823)

Obituary notice in the *Chicago Tribune*, dated 06 February 2012:

Dr. Lowell Vengtman, noted pioneer in the field of experimental psychology, died yesterday at the home of his niece, Dr. Nancy Vengtman Maxwell. He was 82 years old.

Dr. Vengtman was born in Boston, Massachusetts, on 14 December 1929 and studied psychology at Johns Hopkins University, where he took his PhD. in 1955. He taught at Johns Hopkins from 1955 to 1975 before entering private practice. During his time at Johns Hopkins, he developed radically new methods of treating mental illness. In his private practice, he established a number of resident facilities throughout the country in order to put his theories into practice. He continued his work until a tragic accident rendered him incapable of treating patients.

Dr. Vengtman was a brilliant lecturer and a prolific writer. Two of his books, *The Unquiet Mind* (1958) and *Journey into Darkness* (1969) are considered his seminal works and have won him a number of awards in the profession.

Lowell Vengtman was a life-long bachelor and is survived by several nephews and nieces. A memorial service will be held on 08 February at Delaney's Funeral Home in Aurora, Illinois. The eulogy will be delivered by Dr. Kenneth Maxwell.

DAY ONE:
Sunday, 07.06.1997
ORIENTATION

The first time I saw Melissa Waterman, she was talking to a dog.

At the time, I thought nothing of it. Such behavior was to be expected in the place she was at; it might have been more surprising if she had *not* been talking to the dog. Thus, in my innocence, I ignored the scene and continued on my way.

Where I was was the Vengtman Home for the Emotionally Disturbed (Illinois branch) -- one of a series of such institutions set up by the eminent Dr. Lowell Vengtman, a private sanitarium snuggled in what remained of the woodlands in Chicago's southwestern suburbs. The grounds covered ten acres and were dotted with stands of red oak, maple, and white pine; toward the back of the property, the undergrowth – mostly prairie grass and lilac bushes – grew wild, and little had been done to domesticate it. All of the landscaping efforts had been reserved for the "front yard," the acre or so between the main building and State Highway 31 which ran adjacent to the property. Here, the trees had been cleared out, the lilac bushes thinned, and the prairie grass replaced with a hybrid variety noted for its deep verdant color and its pest resistance. An asphalt drive led from the highway to the visitors' parking lot in a long, lazy arc; along both sides was a row of hedges which served as a "fence," effectively hiding the main building from curious passersby. A twelve-foot wrought-iron fence surrounded the entire property, interrupted at regular intervals by slender concrete pillars whose capstones had been carved in the form of lions' heads.

The land and buildings had originally belonged to a wealthy local manufacturer who treasured his privacy. Rumor had it that, during the heady days of the post-World-War-II economic recovery, the man had held wild sex parties for his friends and those political figures whom he wished to influence. One evening, one of the hordes of prostitutes hired for the pleasure of his guests took exception to the intentions of a well-oiled party-goer and, in the ensuing argument, stabbed him to death. The incident was hushed up by the local authorities (some of whom were allegedly already on the scene), but few parties were held thereafter. The manufacturer lived a long but hectic life and died relatively painlessly. After his death, his survivors squabbled over the estate, and his executor was forced to sell the property in order to satisfy all claimants. The main building had a brief career as an orphanage, an even briefer one as – of all things – a pizza parlor, and a lengthy one as a restaurant boasting of an Old-World ambience. During the recession of 1988-1991, the restaurant went bankrupt, and the property fell into disuse until Dr. Vengtman chose it for his newest Home.

As a former private residence, the main building was ideally suited for Dr. Vengtman's purposes. Built in the neo-Georgian style which enjoyed a short popularity in the post-war era, it contained twenty-three rooms distributed throughout three floors. Renovation had been kept to a minimum: the removal of a wall here, a partition of a room there. Each patient was afforded his/her own quarters, a necessary part of psychotherapy; rather than the patient sitting in a sterile environment, (s)he was treated amongst homey and comfortable surroundings. The two upper floors were given over to the patients. Maximum capacity was thirty individuals and, at the time I first went to work there, that capacity had long been reached; as soon as a room became available, a dozen or more individuals contested for it. Lowell Vengtman's reputation for successful treatment of mental disorders was such that there was always a long waiting list. The main floor housed offices, conference rooms, patients' common areas, dining and recreational facilities, and therapy rooms. This floor had required the least amount of renovation, as though the original owner had had some uncanny foreknowledge concerning the future use of his estate.

My introduction to the Great Man had come while I was a medical student at Rush-Presbyterian St. Luke's Hospital in Chicago. As the foremost authority in America on psychiatric medicine – his theory of chemically-induced mutation of brain cells as the cause of aberrant behavior is now taught in all the medical schools – he was in great demand as a guest lecturer. His lectures had been so spell-binding and so full of radical new insights into the workings of the human mind that I was persuaded during my third year of internship to specialize in the treatment of drug-induced psychotic behavior. Subsequently, I became a resident at R-PSL, treating drug addicts in Cook County who exhibited personality disorders, under Federal Medicaid auspices. Quite frankly, the job had not been what I had had in mind when I entered the field; day after day of looking into the glazed eyes and haunted and/or distrustful faces of the county's underclass (and smelling their boozy breath and unwashed bodies!) had led me to an eventual burn-out, and I craved a change of environment and a change of pace. Looking back, I supposed I laid myself open to accusations of cowardice and self-serving. At the time, I believed I could live with my decision to seek other employment.

That opportunity had presented itself during my third year of residency at R-PSL (1997). It literally fell into my lap. I had been taking lunch at the hospital's cafeteria (by the way, don't believe everything you hear about

4

hospital food!) when another resident, a striking redhead whom I had been pursuing unsuccessfully, deposited a flyer on my tray. The flyer was a general notice to all hospital administrators in the metropolitan area that a position for resident counselor had opened up at Dr. Vengtman's Illinois facility. The Vengtman Homes followed a pattern: he opened one in a certain location – the first had been in Harrisburg, Pennsylvania, in 1982 – oversaw its operations for a year, then turned it over to others so that he could re-locate and set up a new facility. The Illinois branch had been in operation for slightly over a year. I had read in the *Journal of the American Psychological Association* about a recent suicide by one of its staff and assumed this was the position to be filled.

In any event, my colleague thought I might be interested in the position (though I suspected afterwards that her "helpfulness" might have been a not-so-subtle hint that I was bordering on sexual harassment). She was right (about the job, not about the harassment!). This had been exactly the thing I was looking for, and I applied at once. The paperwork had been easy enough. It was the interview by Dr. Vengtman and the Home's Board of Trustees that proved to be an inquisition. Somehow, I managed to weather the agonizing ordeal and to put it behind me as I went through the motions of treating Chicago's wretched refuse longing to escape the miseries of their reality and succeeding only in living in a worse one. The happiest day of my life (or so I thought at the time) occurred when a letter of acceptance arrived in the mail. I gave R-PSL immediate notice.

The next four weeks were spent on the edge. I was too excited to think of much else except the prospect of working for Dr. Lowell Vengtman. I must confess that my current patients got short shrift during this period; quite possibly, I might have contributed to more than one relapse and/or overdose. In retrospect, it was not my finest hour. (I also stopped chasing my redheaded colleague, and I could have sworn that she was as upset about that as she had been about my alleged aggressiveness. Is it true, then, what they say about the chase being the most important part of the hunt?)

I was still nervous as I pulled into the driveway on the first day of my new employment. The lilac bushes were not in bloom since it was early July; yet, if they had been, I would not have noticed. As I cleared them, the first object that came into view was the impressive structure of the main building. The second thing was the "conversation" between Melissa Waterman and the dog, a dirty-looking, black-and-white wire terrier. Because both of them were sitting in the middle of the drive, I had to jam on my brakes to avoid running them over. Astonishingly, neither bothered to move out of the way, and the girl gave me only the most cursory of glances. I'm sure I uttered a few choice expressions under my breath as I weaved around the pair.

Though it was a Sunday afternoon, the grounds were crowded with people, either walking about or sitting on folding chairs, either conversing with others or remaining in self-absorbed isolation. The practiced medical eye can always distinguish between patients and non-patients; the former tend to be more animated (when they are aware of their surroundings at all), acting out their psychoses, while the latter – visitors of patients and the ubiquitous nurses (male and female) – attend to them with either the patience of Job or an air of boredom. As to the unusually heavy traffic, I later learned that Sundays were "free periods" in which the patients did not have to abide by the hour-by-hour schedule that characterized the rest of the week but could indulge in any activity which tickled their fancy (within reason!)

I drove past the visitors' parking lot and made straight for the smaller lot at the far side of the main building. My heart sank momentarily at the sight of all the late-model cars parked there. I was the not-so-proud owner of a 1990 Nissan Maxima (second-hand) on which I was still making payments. I supposed that, with the generous salary I'd be receiving from Dr. Vengtman, I'd be able to pay off the Nissan and my student loan and take my rightful place in this automotive hoi-polloi. And, speaking of places, I noted immediately that the Great Man had been expecting me; he had had a name-plate affixed to a parking stall – "Reserved for K. Maxwell." I beamed with pride at this small token of VIP status.

I marched through the front entrance and presented myself to the receptionist, a thin, slightly-graying, hawk-nosed woman whose starched whites hung loosely on her. To complete the avian quality of her face, her eyes kept darting from one side to another. She was your basically shy person who dislikes any attention at all. Why she had chosen to be a receptionist was a mystery; perhaps she had thought to lose herself in the anonymity of the job description. Her name-tag read "P. Oliphant," and the ring on her left hand identified her as "*Mrs.* Oliphant." I mentally chuckled at the last name as my twisted sense of humor came into play.

I've always had a problem remembering names. Five minutes after I've been introduced to someone, I forget his/her name. *Faces* I never forget; I can remember a face and the exact circumstances of meeting it years afterwards, even if I've only seen it once. Some anomaly in the

6

wiring of my brain is my only explanation. Therefore, I have had to resort to a mnemonic technique by which I have managed to avoid potentially embarrassing situations, e.g. meeting women with whom I wanted to make a better acquaintance. What I do is to pun the name. Puns have been part-and-parcel of the human condition since the dawn of Civilization, and they are all the more noticeable the cleverer they are. For me, then, Mrs. Oliphant became, mnemonically, "Mrs. *Elephant*," even though she hardly resembled her "namesake."

She bade me to have a seat while she announced me to Dr. Vengtman. I sat down in a plushly-appointed chair – none of that "reception-room furniture" here! – and browsed through the available periodicals. The magazines were three to four months old -- so much for the rejection of the Reception-Room Syndrome! (Does anyone actually read this stuff? Or is it just an affectation?) Happily, I had to wait no more than two minutes before I was ushered into The Presence.

Dr. Vengtman's office had once been the original owner's library and, in a sense, still was a library. Whatever the former occupant's tastes were, they had been replaced by the accumulated knowledge – theoretical and otherwise – of the very inexact science of psychology. One shelf contained the scant works of the pre-Freudian era; that is to say, the beginning of the world to the fourth quarter of the nineteenth century. One whole section was given over to the father of psycho-analysis and his disciples. There were sections on criminal psychology, child psychology, and sexual psychology. Works in English, German, French, Russian, Japanese abided here – some accompanied by translations, others not. And, of course, there was a shelf –full written by the Great Man himself, all modestly secluded in a far corner of the office. It was a marvelous collection, as complete as one could have made it; it might have been the perfect reference library, if one were so bold as to intrude upon the Director's privacy whenever his/her curiosity needed satisfying.

It was also anachronistic. At the close of the twentieth century, human beings were well-entrenched in the Age of the Computer. Few people bothered with *books*; everything was inscribed to compact discs, and anyone with a PC could access on-line whatever information (s)he required for research. Lowell Vengtman's private store of knowledge – stupendous as it was – was, in the long run, merely a personal idiosyncrasy and, for all practical purposes, a dying breed.

I had remembered Dr. Vengtman as a tall, gaunt individual with a shock of watery blond hair and a deep basso voice. The voice was still in command – the perfect lecturer's voice, guaranteed to draw in even the sleepiest student – but he was gaunter than ever, and his cheeks were sunken. His skin was pallid, and his hair had become completely white. And, perhaps it was my imagination, but I thought I detected weariness in his gray-green eyes and a stoop in his posture. Having seen so much of the worst side of humanity, he was probably entitled to a little weariness; after all, I was here because of my own disillusionment. I wondered idly then if, when I reached his age, I too would resemble someone with the weight of the world on his shoulders in the eyes of some up-and-coming Young Turk. If his eyes did not, his face smiled as he rose to greet me.

"Ah, Dr. Maxwell. I'm pleased to see you again." He strode purposefully around his desk and extended his hand. I took it. It felt like grabbing a dry twig. "Please be seated."

"Frankly, Dr. Vengtman," I responded nervously, "I'm surprised to be here. I didn't think I had made any sort of impression on you."

"Don't be modest, young man. You thoroughly grilled me when I lectured before you. How could anyone forget that?" He chuckled throatily. It sounded like a series of grunts. "It may interest you to know that I've followed your progress at Rush-Presbyterian. Your supervisors tell me you've used some unusual techniques in psychiatric medicine."

I'm sure I blushed at that point. I shouldn't have been behaving like a schoolboy; yet, this person was the established authority in his field, a consummate teacher, and the expert whom the world turned to for advice and consultation, and I was the merest acolyte, scarcely qualified to shine his shoes. And he was praising *me*!

"Really, sir, I was only following through on some ideas you had suggested in passing. *You're* the pioneer, not me."

"And someday, I suspect you'll be one yourself." He spread his hands. They were covered with large brown age spots. "Well, Dr. Maxwell, enough of this mutual admiration society, eh? You'll want a tour of the place before you get settled in. Tomorrow, I'll put you into harness, so to speak."

At the reception desk, he informed Mrs. Oliphant of his intentions and asked to be paged if a certain party called. She fluttered her hands over some paperwork and breathlessly signaled compliance. I could have sworn for a brief moment that she was more in awe of him than I was. No, not awe – more like...*adoration*.

We began the tour, logically enough, with the interview room. It had formerly been the downstairs parlor in the original layout, and some of the old furniture still remained. Oversized and stuffed sofas and chairs, coffee tables, brass lamps with glass mosaic shades, a side boy in one corner, an incongruous ottoman in another, a crystal chandelier – all the accoutrements of the well-to-do to make one's guests comfortable and at ease while enjoying an after-dinner brandy and an expensive cigar.

While the current "guests" in this Home were not allowed to have brandy or cigars or other substances which had put them here in the first place, they were afforded the comfort; part of the "beside manner" in dealing with emotionally disturbed people – and their emotionally wracked relatives – was to put everyone at ease. Here, there was no sterile, clinically-appearing doctor's office, but somebody's living room where one could sit down and have a nice friendly chat. With all parties relaxed, the prospective patient and the prospective sponsor could open up and give the interviewer a working idea of the problem at hand. At least, that was the theory. Given Lowell Vengtman's success rate, the theory seemed to be valid.

This sanitarium, like its predecessors in scattered parts of the country, catered to the more difficult cases of psychotic behavior, those that had baffled even the personnel of other private hospitals. The Vengtman Homes for the Emotionally Disturbed were, in essence, the "last resort" for those who sought a cure for their loved ones and had been unable to find it elsewhere. Many times, however, due to the Director's reputation, a Home had become the "first resort" as the supplicants bypassed the conventional facilities and immediately sought the aid of the Great Man.

Hence the interview room. Once a week, the supplicants came (by appointment only) and bared their souls (or as much of them as they dared) for the professional staff's inspection. Sometimes singly, sometimes in concert with his/her colleagues, a counselor poked and prodded and drew out answers to a hundred subtle questions. Only rarely did the Director participate in these discussions; he preferred to remain in the background and let his "troops" do their jobs unhindered. If the counselor was satisfied that no further preliminary information was obtainable, (s)he wrote up a detailed report; otherwise, future interviews were scheduled, and the supplicants went through the mill again. If, at that time, the counselor felt that the interviewees had finally been honest, then (s)he wrote his/her final report. All reports were discussed – in general terms so as to preserve the doctor/patient relationship – at the weekly staff meeting, and the merits of the supplicants "graded" as to acceptability for admission to the Home. This intensive screening was absolutely necessary since more people clamored to get in than the Home could accommodate.

There was, of course, the factor of "curability." If the staff believed that a prospective patient was beyond even the skill of Lowell Vengtman, then that person was simply turned away with the recommendation that (s)he be permanently placed in a state-run hospital to live out his/her days in isolation and/or sedation. If this sounds cruel, I'm sorry. The reality of psychotherapy is that some people cannot be cured, and there is little to be gained by pretending otherwise. Very few, I am happy to report, were ever turned away, although they did spend a long time on the waiting list.

Part of this screening process, I will say here, lay in the cost of treatment. Dr. Vengtman charged plenty for his services; therefore, only the well-heeled could afford to pay the price of admission. Unfortunately, mental illness is not limited to the upper classes, as I well knew. I had seen the other side of the coin of psychosis at R-PSL – the long parade of "street people," lost in a haze of drug and alcohol abuse. None of them could have afforded even a day's stay in a Vengtman Home but had to rely on Medicaid, funded by a Congress whose good will wavered (or so it seemed) with the seasons. I had debated long and hard over leaving them behind in favor of more conducive surroundings and rationalized my decision by telling myself that I could improve my psychotherapeutic skills if I were not always in a pressure cooker. If this also sounds cruel, I'm sorry. It's just another piece of reality. There was more mental illness in late twentieth-century America than there were professionals to deal with it. Screening, even financial screening, had to be done.

Our next stop was the medical records room where was kept a file on anyone who had been a patient in the Home. This all-inclusive policy was necessary to medical research; if a given patient exhibited similar symptoms as another, a file existed to provide information on the suitability of various treatments. Obviously, each case was unique and had to be approached as such. Yet, mental processes followed a "natural order" even as physical and physiological processes did, and it stood to reason that what worked for one patient might work for another (within certain parameters). In any event, no scrap of information was overlooked in this delicate field of study.

The files themselves were a marvel of co-ordination. Not only were they arranged alphabetically but also chronologically by month and year of admission. Colored tabs on each file referred to the type of disorder treated; some folders possessed more than one tab to indicate multiple problems which had to be treated separately. When a patient was discharged due to remittance of his/her disease, his/her folder was marked with a diagonal green line. A diagonal yellow line designated partial remittance and subsequent transfer to some other facility for completion of treatment. These instances were rare, and the backlog of people who wanted to get in was a factor in the staff's course of action. A diagonal red line meant the patient had died during residency – more often by cardiac arrest, though there had been a suicide or two. Happily, these instances were rare as well. It would hardly have done Lowell Vengtman's reputation any good to lose patients in large numbers!

The nurse presiding over this mountain of information was one Laura Petrie. I swear this was her name! The old "The Dick van Dyke Show" was before my time in its original run, but I had had occasion to watch it in re-runs during my lonely hours of internship at R-PSL (when I wasn't chasing the nurses!), and I thought the character of "Laura Petrie" was hopelessly naïve, even by the standards of the 1960's. *This* Laura Petrie, however, did not strike me as being the least bit naïve, and neither did she strike me as being the least bit friendly. Medium height, slender, with dish-water blonde hair, ink pools for eyes, and a pallid complexion, she sat rigidly in her chair as the Great Man introduced me, never smiling, never recognizing me as another human being. As she explained the procedure for accessing the files, she let me know in no uncertain terms just whose records room this was. I was not to open any file cabinet unless she was present, and I was to sign all files in and out no matter how long I needed them. She was meticulous and efficient to a fault, and I had never encountered such a no-nonsense type in an otherwise handsome woman. Mnemonically, I altered her name to "Nurse Petrified," for she was definitely a rock!

On the way to our next "port of call," we happened to pass by the large French doors that led out to the veranda on the side of the building opposite the parking lot. This area was used, more or less, as the original owner had used it – a place to entertain lightly one's guests, weather permitting. More often than not, the professional staff took their breaks there (one of the perks of being a specialist, don't you know?). I now had my second encounter with Melissa Waterman.

I judged her to be around seventeen or eighteen years of age, a tall, slender girl with auburn hair that fell to her waist in long, ropey tangles. A black plastic barrette had been set in place just above her forehead. Her skin was a creamy white and seemed almost to reflect the sunlight, so as to give her a slight glow. She was wearing a baggy gray sweatshirt with the "Grateful Dead" logo on it and a faded pair of jeans, but no shoes or socks. Wrapped around her left arm was a dirty pastel blue garter with white lace on both borders. This last item apparently had some personal meaning for her, and she wore it like a badge or an ID bracelet. The psychologist in me was naturally piqued, and I made a mental note to ask her about it in the near future.

Melissa's most compelling feature, however, was her eyes. Even at this distance, they resembled twin amethysts sparkling in the sunlight. In the fraction of a second when she turned in our direction, I had the eeriest feeling that she was looking right through me. Yet, she gave no indication that she was cognizant of either of us. The weird feeling quickly passed but nevertheless left me disturbed.

She sat cross-legged on the hard stones of the veranda, talking quietly to the terrier I had seen her with earlier. The dog hunkered on its haunches in rapt attention as if it were hanging on her every word. Occasionally, the girl would stop her chatter and cock her head in order to "hear" what the dog had to "say." The tableau had all the characteristics of an absorbing conversation between two long-time acquaintances. If Melissa was a patient here, then she was exhibiting the classic symptoms of personality-transference disorder, i.e. the invention of an imaginary friend in order to compensate for the inability to make real friends. Most children pass through this phase when they believe no one is paying them as much attention as they'd like; the psychosis occurs when the behavior is carried into adolescence and adulthood. Called unofficially the "Harvey Syndrome" (in reference to the old James Stewart film about a six-foot-tall, invisible rabbit), it is one of the less dangerous disorders and, if diagnosed early, easily treatable.

"Excuse me, Dr. Vengtman," I said, unable to contain my curiosity, "is that girl one of the patients?"

"Eh? Why, yes, she is. A rather unique case too."

"Do you allow the patients to have pets? I should think that would be risky."

"As a rule, no. You're quite right, Dr. Maxwell. Experience has demonstrated that many emotionally disturbed people tend to anthropomorphize animals, thus re-enforcing their psychoses. The dog must be a stray. I'll have it removed later."

"She seems to be enjoying its company, though, and acts as if she understands what it's 'saying.'"

"Um, yes. Melissa apparently has a rapport with animals. But, come along, Doctor. We've still much ground to cover."

During the remainder of my tour, I chanced to encounter two more of the staff, one professional, one non-professional. The doctor-patient ratio was, with my arrival, exactly one-to-five, an infinitely lighter load than I'd had at R-PSL. The five other counselors, I was soon to learn, were as varied a lot as one might find anywhere as far as personalities were concerned; yet, the Director had sought out their talents assiduously in order to address as wide a spectrum of psychiatric medicine as possible. The talents of the individual staffers might reflect particular interests, but the Director had blended them into a complementary whole and created an incisive psychiatric think-tank. To be a part of this team was a heady feeling – and a tall order for a relative novice – but I was determined to meet the challenge and make my mark. As I have already stated, my particular forte was drug-induced psychosis; there were four such patients in residence here, and Dr. Vengtman had hired me specifically to treat them. Of course, my duties were not limited to those four; as the junior member of the professional staff, I was expected to assist wherever I could, and I did have one out-of-field patient in my caseload to even the ratio.

One of the two encounters turned out to be with the Senior Counselor and therefore the number-two person on the professional staff. Dr. Harry Rauschenburg was, to put it charitably, *rotund*. The great silent-film comic, Fatty Arbuckle, was svelte by comparison. Dr. Rauschenburg had enormous jowls, and his jaw literally disappeared into them; his cheeks were like tiny balloons, and his eyes peered over them like two black buttons set in a pile of dough. Likewise, a tremendous paunch overwhelmed his chest and literally shook whenever he laughed (which was frequently). His arms and legs resembled huge sausages sticking out of his torso. How he was able to move about was a minor mystery; I would not have thought that anyone in this day and age – especially a *doctor* – would have allowed his glands to operate so wildly.

"Russian Bug" (in my mnemonic system) carried no particular privileges as Senior Counselor (he had come by the title only because he had been here the longest), except that, at staff meetings, he presided in the Director's absence. He was a person of enormous humor as well as girth; he loved to tell jokes (especially risqué ones), to make puns (especially bad ones), and – as I was to find out very shortly – to play practical jokes (the more outrageous, the better). It may be an old cliché, the "jolly fat man," but the Senior fit it to a "T."

When we met that first day, he stuck out a huge paw and gripped my hand like a vise. He shook it with exaggerated motions, all the while grinning and making happy noises. I tolerated the greeting as well as I could – I reckoned it was something I had better get used to – and thanked my lucky stars that he wasn't the hugging type. I don't think I would have survived that! He waxed enthusiastically about my "being part of the 'V-Team' ('V' for Vengtman)," gushed about my eminent qualifications, and allowed that I was "just going to love being here." I thanked him very much and extracted my hand from his grip.

Just as Dr. Vengtman was herding me toward the next stop on the tour, Dr. Rauschenburg offered me a stick of gum. I'm sure he was being as gracious as he could; he couldn't have known that I had recently given up smoking and was chewing gum to compensate for the nicotine habit. I popped the gum into my mouth and started chewing. Five seconds later, I was coughing and sputtering; my mouth was on fire, and my eyes were watering copiously. The Director chuckled throatily at my predicament. The Senior had pulled one of the oldest gags in existence by giving me *pepper* gum!

The other staffer I met near the end of the tour as the Director and I were returning to his office where he had some papers for me to sign. At Mrs. Oliphant's desk was a brick wall of a man. His muscles bulged and rippled beneath a uniform a size too small for him. He had a pudgy face, a broken nose, and gray eyes that seemed to mock you with every second of contact. He must have been a defensive lineman in a previous life and looked like he could take down two or three people at a time – just what a facility for the emotionally disturbed needed.

Dr. Vengtman introduced him as Clement, Senior Nurse at the Home and head nurse for the violent ward. Clement held out his hand; I gazed at his mocking eyes and his Cheshire-cat grin, tried to get my mental bearings, and took his hand reluctantly. The hand was cold and clammy, and I broke contact after a less-than-cordial handshake. My parents' generation used to talk about "good vibes" and "bad vibes" as a measure of one's personality. It may have been unprofessional and unsocial of me, but Nurse Clement fairly radiated "bad vibes," and I took an instant dislike to him.

As soon as I had completed the paperwork – the usual W-2 forms, life- and health-insurance forms, a release freeing the Home from all liability for violence perpetrated by a patient against a staff person, and a pledge not to conduct independent research without the Director's express written consent – Dr. Vengtman handed me the keys to my assigned cottage. I returned to the staff parking lot and grabbed two suitcases out of my car. I reckoned I'd need to make seven or eight more trips in order to wrestle all of my personal belongings into my new home.

The original owner had constructed six cottages at the back of the estate, nestled among the oaks and maples and pines. A well-worn footpath wound its way past all of them. The cottages had been intended for overnight guests and their "dates." While a good deal of partying took place in the main building – "group gropes," according to the local scuttlebutt – the real "action" occurred in private in these cottages. One might have seen similar structures at any motel; they were all identical to each other, inside and out. Outside, an A-frame, white with pastel yellow trim and blue-green shingles on the roof – the entrance in the exact center of the face of the unit between two equal-sized windows (the only other window was at the rear, off the bathroom, again in the exact center of the wall). Inside, a pastel-blue sofa-bed on one wall with bracketing side tables, a matching stuffed chair with another table next to it on the opposite wall, a five-drawer dresser in the left-rear corner, and a navy-blue wardrobe in the right-rear corner. The original owner hadn't bothered with modern entertainment devices (like radio or TV) – and his guests never asked for them – for he was providing other, more congenial "entertainment."

I should point out the one break in all this sameness: they all had names on the front doors, erotic names intended to enhance the "romantic" nature of their existence. These names had been painted on sign boards in graceful loops and curlicues which Dr. Vengtman had decided to leave intact for some mysterious reason. Perhaps he felt they might boost our own mental well-being and motivate us to greater effort in treating our patients. Be that as it may, the name on my cottage – the fourth down the line – was "Eros's Hideaway," as garish a title as I was likely to encounter – even for an experienced skirt-chaser like myself!

It wasn't the most luxurious accommodations I'd ever seen, but it beat the hell out of a cramped studio apartment in Chicago. And it was rent-free, part of the salary package. The Director had always insisted – due to the sensitive nature of his work – that his counselors be *resident* ones; thus, we were all on call twenty-four hours a day. In that respect, it was no different than being at R-PSL, except the pay was better. Still, for the privilege of working for the Great Man, I'd've slept in a tent!

The sun was just dipping toward the horizon when I was finished hauling all my belongings to my cottage and storing them in reasonably accessible places. Fortunately, I had brought with me my "student's bookcases" – four sagging two-by-fours and eight chipped cinder blocks – to accommodate my personal but much smaller "library." It went into the only space available, the front right corner. As I surveyed my new "kingdom," my stomach reminded me that I hadn't eaten since breakfast;

I'd been too busy packing to bother with lunch. I wondered idly if the dining room at the Home was still open. A check of the "Resident Counselor's Handbook" informed me that I was too late. Well, there were any number of take-out joints south of here, and I wasn't a prisoner confined to quarters for the duration.

As I trundled toward the staff parking lot, it occurred to me that, since this footpath wasn't lighted, it behooved me to tread carefully. Otherwise, I'd find myself walking into a tree or, worse, stepping into a hole and twisting an ankle or breaking a leg – a real horror for this city boy. I would also be wise in investing in a flashlight.

At cottage number two, I observed in the failing light the enormous frame of Harry Rauschenburg, standing in the door dressed only in a bathrobe and slippers. He was puffing away on a cigar, the size of which was proportionate to his own. In his other hand, he held a brandy snifter. I idly wondered if he had a liquor cabinet or if he stashed the stuff under the bed.

"Dr. Maxwell!" he boomed. "Hello, again."

"Good evening, Dr. Rauschenburg," I responded formally. I still had the taste of pepper gum in my mouth! "Relaxing after a busy day?"

"Indeed. Would you care for a brandy?"

"Ah, not right now, thanks. I'm off to get a bite to eat. I haven't had anything since breakfast."

"Perhaps when you return then."

"Perhaps. I might turn in early tonight so I'll be fresh for tomorrow. Must make a good impression the first day on the job, right?"

"Quite so, quite so. You'll also want to be refreshed for your initiation."

"My…'initiation'?" Instant suspicion dropped over me like a net. "What initiation?"

"You'll find out soon enough," he chuckled conspiratorially. "I shan't spoil the surprise."

"If you don't mind me saying so, but I thought I'd been 'initiated' earlier today."

"Hardly. That was just a bit of fun on my part. Nothing like what's in store for you."

"Um, well, thanks for the warning. Be seeing you."

If it had been his intention to induce a state of anxiety, he had succeeded. His cryptic remarks buzzed like a swarm of bees inside my head for the next couple of hours. What sort of "initiation" had my new colleagues in store for me? The possibilities were endless, of course. At R-PSL, for instance, all of the new interns were 'rushed" which, for the most part, meant that they were sent on fools' errands or involved in bogus medical "emergencies." Nothing hazardous, mind you – just a humiliating gag to remind one of his place in the general scheme of things. Then there were the "special celebrations" when one became a resident; one could expect horrendously embarrassing stunts that no one wanted to remember, least of all talk about. Since my own residency had not been all that long ago, the stunt my colleagues had contrived for me was still fresh in my mind. True to the tradition, I will not speak of it in any detail; suffice it to say that it had to do with necrophilia.... Could the staff at the Home cook up anything worse than that? It boggled the mind to think so.

My pre-occupation with the subject was so great that I drove straight through Aurora's "restaurant row" on North Lake Street (State Route 31 in that community) and was halfway to the central business district before I realized where I was and remembered what I was supposed to be doing. Cursing mightily, I doubled back, pulled into the local Taco Bell, ordered a couple of chicken burritos (with fries and a Coke), and hastened back to the Home.

By the time I returned, it was completely dark (except for the parking area), and the wooded section appeared to be a huge ink spot. The idea of a flashlight seemed wiser by the second. As I neared the woods, I spied two beacons of light shining intermittently through the trees. Someone was at home in numbers one and two. Number two was the Senior – still smoking cigars and drinking brandy? Whoever was in number one, I decided to make acquaintance with him/her as soon as humanly possible. The unmistakable strains of a Chopin etude wafted from that place and, despite my hunger, I slowed down to catch as much of it as I could. I have acquired all of Chopin's works on CD, and I have done my best "work" in the romance department to the stirring melodies of the Master Pianist. I like to think that a Chopin aficionado can't be all bad; in fact, we Chopin lovers form a unique brother- (and sister-) hood and feel no compunction in informing "lesser" mortals of their cultural shortcomings. With the etude filling my mind, I was quite unprepared for what happened next.

As I was approaching Harry's cottage (and wondering if I could pass by unnoticed), I heard a rustling sound behind me and to the side of the footpath. At first, I thought it was the wind in the trees; then I realized there was hardly any breeze to speak of. Something was moving through the undergrowth. I jerked around but saw nothing but the blackness of the woods. Even the footpath was an inky line. I stood very still, trying to penetrate – visually and audibly – the impenetrable. Presently, I wrote it off as imagination and continued on my way. I had taken no more than a few steps when I heard the sound again. This time, I pretended to ignore it until it came closer, then whirled around.

Close to the ground, two button-sized points of yellow punctuated the darkness, and they were steadily focused on me. An animal, I thought immediately. It had to be an animal, as curious about me as I was about it. What sort was it? It was hard to determine specific shapes in the pitch black. Possibly a raccoon – I recalled reading that raccoons liked to forage at night. They also liked to scavenge around human-occupied areas in hopes of a choice tidbit or two. Well, if Brother Raccoon was looking for a hand-out, he was in luck; I had some fries I could spare. I opened the take-out bag, fished out a couple of pieces, and flung them toward the yellow eyes. They neither flinched nor wavered from their steady gaze. The fries were ignored. Well, I thought, if the dude ain't interested in a freebie, the hell with him! By way of a taunt, I stuffed some fries in my own mouth and chewed noisily. See what you're missin', bro?

I moved on. Presently, I heard scurrying in the undergrowth again. I turned and spotted the same two yellow points of light. They were closer this time; the creature – whatever it was – was getting bolder. In a momentary panic, I wondered if it was rabid, then dismissed the notion. If it had been rabid, it would have attacked by now. Clearly, it was following me. But why? Had it finally accepted my "gift" and was looking for more? I suppose I could spare a couple more fries, but this would be the last freebie. I didn't want the creature to get the idea that it could drop by any damn time it pleased and expect a meal at my expense. I probably shouldn't have given it food in the first place. I tossed out a couple more pieces and continued on to my cottage. I heard the animal still dogging my heels.

Once inside, I put all thoughts of marauding animals out of my mind and dug into my chicken burritos ravenously. Yet, my new "friend" hadn't forgotten about me; I could still hear it prowling about, first on one side of the cottage, then the other. With no little annoyance, I got up, walked to the right-hand window, and peered surreptitiously through the lace curtains. The cottage's lights cast a white glow no more than three feet from the building; if anyone or anything came within that range, I would recognize him/it. Otherwise, he/it was invisible. I saw nothing in the nimbus of light. I even craned my neck at an awkward angle in order to catch a glimpse of whatever was out there. Still nothing. Brother Raccoon was fast becoming a pain in the butt. I gave up the attempt and went back to my burritos.

For the next couple of hours, all was quiet, and I decided to familiarize myself with the "house rules," particularly the many duties incumbent upon a resident (and junior) counselor. Some of these duties I knew well – too well, as far as I was concerned – as I'd had to perform them while an intern at R-PSL. Others were unique to the Home but no less disagreeable; they seemed to be beneath one's professional dignity. It was apparent that working for the Great Man required taking the bad with the good; and, for the money (and prestige) I was receiving, I supposed it was a small price to pay. Once I had paid my dues, however, I could seek a higher station, up to and including a Directorship of a Home, if and when a vacancy came open.

While I was dreaming my grand dream, I heard more scurrying outside. Brother Raccoon had returned, it seemed, to renew its efforts to secure another hand-out. Now, it was moving toward the rear of the building. Was it looking for a way inside? If so, it would find a big surprise waiting for it! I hurried into the bathroom, climbed onto the toilet, and peeked out the small ventilating window above it. The surprise was all mine, however, and I nearly fell off my perch. I spotted the yellow eyes with no trouble, glaring out of the darkness of the woods. But next to them was a pair of *amethyst* points of light! I strained my eyes in order to distinguish mammalian forms from plant forms. Nothing moved out there; the pairs of eyes simply remained immobile for long minutes. Then, in less time than it takes to think about it, they – whatever "they" were – were gone. The yellow and the amethyst winked out of existence, leaving the blackness behind.

I discovered I'd been holding my breath for the last few minutes, and I exhaled slowly even as I continued to stare out the window for any further signs of visitors. I had a chilling thought then: what if the creature had not been following me for a hand-out? What if it had been following me to give me, a newcomer to its territory, the once-over? It seemed like a far-fetched idea; on the other hand, with what little I knew about animal behavior (an elective in medical school), I couldn't dismiss the possibility out of hand. Whatever the answer, I experienced a most unsettling feeling, and it had nothing to do with the territorial imperative of raccoons.

Who or what had belonged to that *second* pair of eyes? I reckoned I knew the answer as soon as I had formed the question. It had to be Melissa Waterman. The real puzzle was why was *she* spying on me. Curiosity? It was as reasonable a guess as any, but there were other methods of satisfying curiosity than this clumsy attempt at espionage. Perhaps this was a part of Melissa's psychosis – a persecution complex – and she believed she could compensate by putting her "persecutors" under surveillance and thus reversing the roles. Yet, that possibility raised even more questions. I pulled out my mental list and made another entry, this one to re-enforce the previous one.

The burritos were now cold. It didn't make any difference anyway since I had lost my appetite. There was nothing left to do but hit the sack and be fresh for the morning.

DAY TWO:
Monday, 07.07.1997
INGRATIATION

I didn't wake up the next morning until eight o'clock – understandable, since I'd lain in bed wondering about my night visitors until well after midnight. Understandable, but not excusable. I'm one of those who seem to have an alarm clock built into his brain; if I have to be up at a certain hour, my "timer" never fails to wake me. Because my work day at R-PSL began at eight AM, I had been accustomed to rising no later than six o'clock, enough time to shake out the cobwebs, grab a bite of breakfast, and prepare myself for the onslaught of patients. This morning, however, the "alarm clock" had failed to ring, and I had overslept for two hours. Which meant that I had to scramble to make myself presentable and to get some breakfast before attending the Monday morning staff meeting at nine o'clock. It really wouldn't have done to be late the first day on the job!

It looked to be another typical Illinois summer day (thank God for air-conditioning!): sunny, hot, and humid. This wasn't Chicago by any means where the summers can be sheer hell, but the heat was still stifling. It wasn't sunny in the woods, of course; the sunlight filtered through the branches of the trees in streamers and ribbons and gave the place an ethereal quality such as one might observe in an early Renaissance painting. Admittedly, being a city boy who could count on one finger the number of times he'd been in the woods for any reason gave me a radically different point of view. Therefore, the ambience was more than ethereal; it was positively *alien*. Day or night, the woods seemed a world apart from the one with which I was familiar. At the time, though, I was quite unmindful of either ambience or ethereality. Like a certain white rabbit, I was late for a very important date, and I couldn't have cared less about the scenery.

I did make one penetrating observation on the way. As I quick-marched along the foot-path (and watched for holes in which I could twist my ankle), I spotted two familiar objects at the edge of the trail – the second pair of fries I'd tossed out to last night's marauding creature. I was startled to see them, but not so startled that I stopped to check them out. I did that further along when I spied the *first* pair still lying where I'd thrown them. I looked around reflexively in order to catch a glimpse of the animal, then caught and chided myself for being such a "dork." At least one of my questions had been answered: whatever it was out here hadn't been looking for a hand-out but had followed me for reasons known only to itself. That, of course, left only nine hundred and ninety-nine other questions unanswered, questions I couldn't begin to put into thought, least of all words. I shuddered, despite the growing heat of the day, and hurried on to the main building.

Though this particular Monday did not fall on the usual day of the month to begin a new job in the professions (either the first or the fifteen), neither of those days was a Monday in July of 1997, and Dr. Vengtman had wanted to throw me into the routine of the Home immediately in order to re-distribute the work-load as soon as possible. Staff meetings ordinarily ran until noon, depending on the length of the agenda. Sometimes, it did not run that long; and other times, it continued on into the afternoon. Always, however, it followed a set pattern.

The first item of business was the introduction of the current literature in the field. Usually, the Director (being the acknowledged leader) distributed copies of a monograph, a book excerpt, a magazine article, etc. which he thought germane to the operation of the Home for our perusal, but we could also submit literature from whatever source. After all had had a chance to study the material, we discussed it at the next meeting – the second item on the agenda – and judged its merits. If it proved to have some practical application for us, it was added to the Home's research library. Being a highly specialized facility, the Home of necessity had to be very selective in its counseling methods; malpractice in psychotherapy was just as common as it was in medicine, and we counselors were ever mindful of employing faulty techniques that might lead to a psychotic relapse and irreversible mental damage. While lawsuits were always a threat, our chief concern was the loss of credibility and of public confidence, not a few bucks out of our collective pockets. There was no greater blow to a doctor's practice than to be thought of as a quack. Thus, Lowell Vengtman held each of us to the same high standards he had long ago set for himself and made sure we were all grounded in proven psychotherapeutic techniques. Experimentation was encouraged, of course, but within certain parameters subject to general staff oversight. (I myself had written a monograph during my second year of residency, and I assumed it was the reason the Great Man had hired me.)

Oversight also characterized the third item of business. To the layman, it might seem odd that doctors would discuss their cases with their colleagues – the doctor-patient relationship and all that – but I can tell you it goes on all the time, more or less off the cuff. For the most part, doctors are unwilling to enter into such discussions because of professional jealousy; no one wants another to intrude upon his "territory" and to offer unsolicited advice. Consequently, when they do allude to their caseloads, the conversations are full of oblique language so as to disguise identities.

Dr. Vengtman had rejected this attitude as being counter-productive and taken the opposite approach.

At the Home, the conversations were institutionalized in the form of a round-table, and the staff was expected to participate fully. We were all specialists within the profession; each of us had our individual interests in and approaches to psychiatric medicine. Yet, Lowell Vengtman wanted only the best for his "customers," and that meant there was no room for professional jealousy; we were supposed to be a team and to behave like one. Hence, starting at the Director's left and going clockwise around the conference room, each of the staff provided an update on the progress of the treatment of all of the patients under his/her care. The patients' histories were discussed in a candid, dispassionate, and professional manner. After each individual report, a counselor received and responded to questions, observations, and/or suggestions from the others; this input was cordial and professional, and no attempt at belittlement of another's handling of his/her caseload was allowed. More often than not – and this was the Director's purpose behind this exercise – new insights stemming from diverse interests came to the fore. Precedence as well as expertise counted for much in these discussions. While I could not fully participate in this, my first staff meeting (I had not been given a caseload yet), still I felt an exhilaration merely by watching the others in their comradely give-and-take, and I counted myself extremely fortunate in having been "drafted" by this "team."

The next-to-the-last item on the agenda was given over to general announcements concerning the more mundane aspects of the Home. For example, Dr. Vengtman noted this day that the head cook was about to take his annual vacation starting on the following week and that the assistant cook would be in charge for the duration. Comic despair and loud groaning greeted this statement; the Senior wailed about three weeks of "wall-to-wall meatloaf." This part of the staff meeting took up very little time, for the group was anxious to get to the last item, and then off to lunch (if possible).

The last item – which I have called the "Blue Limerick Time" (or "BLT" – *not* to be confused with the sandwich!) – I will discuss shortly. Suffice it to say here that the staff participated in it with varying degrees of gusto.

I arrived at the parlor-cum-conference room barely two minutes before the appointed hour, hastily cramming some cold toast in my mouth, toast I'd managed to scavenge from the dining room to a chorus of disapproving stares from the kitchen staff who were trying to clean up. As I walked in, every eye turned to me and gave me a collective examination. Talk about self-consciousness! I found an empty chair near the disused fireplace and tried to disappear into it. Dr. Vengtman immediately brought the meeting to order.

"Good morning, ladies and gentlemen. We'll make a brief departure from our usual routine to welcome formally our new staff member, Dr. Kenneth Maxwell, late of Rush-Presbyterian St. Luke's Hospital." I smiled weakly by way of acknowledgement and swallowed the lump of toast that was still in my mouth. "Dr. Maxwell's field of expertise is drug-induced psychosis; his reputation goes before him, and I trust he will contribute significantly to our efforts. Dr. Maxwell, you've already met Dr. Rauschenburg. I'll introduce you to the remaining staff."

The first to be introduced was a wisp of a man, barely five-feet-five and small-boned. Dr. Dante Fingherelli had a trace of a New York City (specifically Queens) accent which he tried with little success to hide. When he was not speaking, he sat in his chair all bunched up as if he were afraid he'd fall apart if he relaxed one iota. He puckered his mouth into an "O" and peered out of squinting eyes. Despite his diminutive stature, he was exceedingly dapper and well-groomed. He wore a tailored three-piece, gray-pin-striped suit, a solid navy-blue silk tie, and black wingtip shoes with white tassels. His thinning hair was neatly combed, and not a hair was out of place. A thin, razor-cut moustache adorned his upper lip and looked like he had drawn it on with a marking pen. On both of his manicured pinkies, he sported enormous diamond rings. I judged that he spent as much time primping himself as the fictional detective, Hercule Poirot. Mnemonically, he became "Dainty Fingers."

The second individual was Dr. Fingherelli's opposite in every way. Dr. Lambert McIntosh was as lanky and raw-boned as they came, and I suspected that he suffered from a touch of acromegalia. A full six-feet-six with a long horse's face, short-cropped sandy hair, and watery blue eyes, he literally sprawled in his chair, dangling one leg over the arm. Whereas Dante was a natty dresser, Dr. McIntosh seemed to have acquired his wardrobe (if it could be dignified by that term) from the local Goodwill outlet. Nothing fit him; everything hung from his huge, angular frame loosely, and he kept tugging at various places in order to keep his clothes from bunching up on him. He stared at the ceiling perpetually, even when he spoke, and seldom made eye contact with anyone. Additionally, he had the annoying habit of wrinkling his nose – clearly the longest proboscis

I had ever seen on a human being – at the oddest moments. Naturally, I had to call him "Mac the Nose."

The third staffer was Dr. Madeleine Chantrier, as different from her male colleagues as an apple is from rutabaga. A petite, frail-looking woman in her late thirties or early forties, she radiated shyness almost palpably when attention was directed her way. She tended to blush frequently and to rub her hands against her legs repeatedly. She wore her reddish-brown hair in a bun which accented a narrow face and an equally narrow nose. Clothes-wise, she preferred full-sleeved blouses and ankle-length skirts in pastel colors. It was her 'little girl" aura which charmed me, however. She had pale green eyes that crinkled when she allowed herself to smile and pouty lips that suggested a paradoxical impishness. And then there was her marvelous French accent in soft, purring tones which I could have listened to all day. My mnemonic for her was perhaps a cruel jest in this light – "Mad Chanteuse."

When the last member of the group was introduced, I forgot about the others immediately. Dr. Nancy Vengtman, the Great Man's niece, was a statuesque brunette whose six-foot-two body made her a stand-out in any crowd. I must confess that I have a weakness for tall women. I fancy myself a connoisseur of the female form, and I've had my share of women since puberty; but, there has always been something about tall women which attracts me more than the general run. Tall women strike me as being self-possessed, self-assured, and self-confident. And they may be self-conscious as well – tall women are still an oddity in this society – but they don't seem to show it outwardly. Rather, tall women stride through the world as if they own it, and such an attitude has had an aphrodisiacal effect on me.

As it did at that moment. Dr. Vengtman the Younger sat in her chair as a queen might – regally – and regarded me coolly. Her shoulder-length hair fell partly over her face in the manner affected by the 1940's actress, Veronica Lake. She too wore a three-piece suit, hers with blue-and-white pinstripes, accompanied by a lavender blouse, indigo tie, and white bucks. To complete (and complement) the picture, she sported a white carnation in her lapel. It was lust at first sight, I can tell you, and I was determined to mount a campaign to woo her at my earliest opportunity. I felt no need to mnemonicize her name; I was not likely to forget it!

"I'd like to thank you," I said when all the introductions had been made, "for having the confidence in me to allow me to work with you." I hoped I wasn't laying it on *too* thick, although it was somewhat reflective of my true feelings. "I'll try to maintain that confidence at all times."

"I'm sure you will, Dr. Maxwell," the Director assured me. "Now, without further ado, we'll get to the regular business."

I have had a long-time habit of taking copious notes, no matter what the occasion. Call it a compulsion, but I believe no comment ought to be overlooked if it has even the remotest bearing on the subject under discussion; a chance remark – as I had alluded to Dr. Vengtman the day before – might take on great importance later on in different circumstances. So, I was seldom without the familiar yellow, legal-sized notepad. In medical school, I had been known as the "Mad Scribbler"; I'd had occasion to fill up two entire notepads in a single day, although one was the average. I had brought this habit with me to the Home, and the minute the Director began to speak, I had my pen poised to write. While my own part in this first staff meeting was necessarily minimal, I did manage to ask a few pertinent questions concerning the Vengtman approach to psychotherapy.

I will not attempt to set down a full account of that meeting, only an excerpt which I think represented the way the staff operated. It afforded me an immediate opportunity to assess the genius of Lowell Vengtman in the choosing of his subordinates (and, as a corollary, learn his professional opinion of me). During Dr. Fingherelli's report, he mentioned he was having difficulty in establishing a rapport with one of his patients, a young woman referred to only as "Anna K.," who suffered from recurring lapses into autism, apparently due to a childhood trauma.

> DF ("Dainty Fingers"): "Da damnable t'ing of dese episodes is dat dey ah not indicative of true autism, but rat'er of manic-depression. Yet, not dat eit'er. If da episodes were one oh da ot'er, my course of action would be clearer."

> RB ("Russian Bug"): "Have you tested for true autism then?"

> DF: "Of course, Harry. I haven't lost my wits entirely. When Anna displayed her foist episode, I followed da procedure suggested by Novotny and Blas five years ago. She only tested positive in two o' dem; in da ot'ers, dere were no conclusive results."

> RB: "And the manic-depression?"

MN ("Mac the Nose"): "Wait a minute! Wait a minute! This doesn't sound like manic-depression to me. I'm seeing avoidant personality disorder here."

DF: "Do yez t'ink so, Bertie? I can't agree. Da wit'drawal factor is too severe."

VE ("Vengtman the Elder"): "How about *schizoid* personality then, Dante?"

DF: "No, no, not autistic enough. Damn! I hate to t'ink I've discovered a *new* mental disohder. Dat would mean having to experiment wit' all da known t'erapeutic techniques, by trial and error, never knowing whet'er I'm close to a solution oh not."

RB: "But, there *is* manic-depression involved?"

DF: "Um, well, it's a symptom, yes, but not a majah one."

MS ("Mad Scribbler"): "Excuse me, please. I realize I'm the new boy here, but I'd like to ask a question."

VE: "By all means, Dr. Maxwell. Feel free to jump in as you see fit."

MS: "Thank you, sir. Dr. Fingherelli, have you examined any, uh, environmental factors?"

DF: "'Environmental factors'? Whatevah do yez mean, Dr. Maxwell? Do yez t'ink Anna is being affected by...*air pollution*?" [General laughter around the room.]

MS: "Well, I wouldn't rule that out if there weren't any other explanation. No, what I'm referring to is Anna's *social* environment. Has she had any conflicts with another patient – or with a staff member?"

DF: "Ah, I see your pernt. I'll look into dat."

VY ("Vengtman the Younger"): "Are you suggesting that Anna has a deep-rooted fear of someone in the Home, Dr. Maxwell?"

MS: "I'm not suggesting anything of the sort, Dr. Vengtman. I'm just throwing out a possible avenue of exploration to the problem. I tend to agree with Dr. McIntosh; there is avoidant personality disorder at work here, but the cause seems to be something you – I mean, *we* haven't yet considered."

MN: "And that unknown cause mimics autism? Hmmm, a distinct possibility."

As it turned out, this particular session ran late and, promptly at noon, the Director called a halt to the proceedings, cutting short a vigorous exchange between RB and MN almost in mid-sentence. At a pre-arranged signal (I supposed), one of the kitchen staff wheeled in a serving cart and parked it near the side boy. If he was nothing else, Lowell Vengtman was a model of efficiency. No need to retire to the dining room, then return here, possibly losing our train of thought. We would have a leisurely lunch in a homey atmosphere and not waste time and energy. As soon as the server had laid out the dishes and uncovered the largest tray, the aroma of beef Stroganoff hit me like a hammer. My mouth watered instantly. I must've licked my chops, for I caught the Director looking my way with a mischievous grin on his face. I don't believe I can ever get enough beef Stroganoff, especially when it's prepared correctly (with sherry). I might have stormed the buffet if I had not remembered my manners and allowed my seniors to serve themselves first. As soon as we had all gone through the line and returned to our seats, Dr. Vengtman the Elder raised his glass of claret (from his own private stock, no less!).

"To our newest member – may he live long and prosper!"

I gaped at him in surprise. I'd never have taken the Great Man for a "Star Trek" fan!"

"Hear, hear!" the Senior wheezed and downed his glass in a single gulp.

"For your information, Dr. Maxwell," the Director remarked casually, "we've been spying on you. Otherwise, we wouldn't have known your favorite dish is beef Stroganoff."

"You prepared this just for me? I – I don't know what to say."

"Then say nothing, dear boy," Dr. Rauschenburg chuckled. "Eat and enjoy."

If this was the "initiation" which I had been promised, then it was the best one I'd ever had. After getting over my bout of embarrassment at being spotlighted, I attacked my lunch with gusto and savored every bite. Having missed breakfast put a sharp edge on my appetite. Periodically, out of the corner of my eye, I noted Nancy Vengtman scrutinizing me; when we chanced to make eye contact, an impish smile similar to her uncle's briefly played across her lips in imitation of the Mona Lisa. Was that a family trait, or did she effect the gesture to let everyone know whose niece she was? A pretty puzzle, that. Yet, it did not diminish my desire to woo her at my earliest opportunity. That would be an initiation worthy of the name!

All too soon, our delicious repast concluded. The kitchen staff returned to take away the dishes (what would they do with the left-overs, I wanted to ask but constrained myself to avoid embarrassing myself again), and the Director called us back to order. We picked up almost exactly where we had left off with RB and MN resuming their debate concerning one of the latter's patients. The round-table ran its course, ending with a few brief recommendations from the Director. He then smiled wryly.

"Whose turn is it today, Harry?"

"If memory serves me correctly – and it usually does – our dear Maddie has the floor."

"Very good. Madeleine?"

I swear the woman turned as red as the claret as she got to her feet. The others gazed at her expectantly with varying degrees of bemusement. Naturally, I was thrown into consternation. Whatever was about to take place, it seemed to be part of the routine, not to be shirked; and, apparently, I would have a "turn" at it in the near future. Judging by the Senior's merriment, I suspected one of his practical jokes. Dr. Chantrier took a moment to compose herself, all the while rubbing her legs, then pulled a piece of paper out of the pocket of her skirt and began to read from it in her lilting French accent.

> "Zere once was a flashair from 'Ong Kong
> Who exposed an exceedingly large dong.
> When asked if she 'ad been
> Offended by ze scene,
> Ze victim said, 'Oh, yes, it was all Wong."

Having said her piece, she quickly sat down and stared at her lap. A nervous tic developed under her left eye.

Personally, I was flabbergasted, and I nearly dropped my notepad on the floor. I was no stranger to "locker room" talk, having engaged in a bit of it myself during the time I had been involved in athletics; and, while it might have become risky business in this era of feminist self-assertion and sexual-harassment awareness, it still existed in die-hard pockets of resistance. In some "enlightened" settings, women even bantered with men in the same scatological manner – sauce for the goose, etc., etc. (Truth to tell, I've always believed that women have always engaged in "locker room" talk themselves, describing men in much the same way we did them.) But to hear such talk in a supposedly professional setting – why, it boggled the mind!

I cast a glance around the room. Dr. Vengtman's lips were pursed as if he were in deep thought. Drs. Rauschenburg and Fingherelli were smiling broadly, while Dr. MacIntosh rubbed his jaw. To my utter shock, the other Dr. Vengtman – lovely, luscious Nancy! – gave me a saucy wink. The only one who was disturbed (besides me, that is) was the limerick deliverer herself; yet, beyond her embarrassment, she did not appear to be overwrought or angry for having been put through her ordeal. Though this seemed to be SOP for these meetings, I was damned if I could fathom the purpose. And, since I was the "new boy," I was hardly in a position to criticize.

"You've worked in a pun this time, Maddie," the Senior appraised. "You're improving."

"And," added Dr. Fingherelli, "yez're picking up American slang."

"Still needs work on the cadence, though," Dr. MacIntosh observed.

"Oh, *bosh*, Bertie!" Dr. Vengtman the Younger exclaimed. "It was well within accepted parameters."

Dr. MacIntosh spread his oversized hands in a conciliatory gesture.

"I will say," Dr. Chantrier spoke in her own defense, "zat it is becoming easiair to create zese little…ditties. I am still 'aving trouble wis ze *propriety* of zem, but at least I can appreciate your vote of confidence."

"Hear, hear!" the Senior declared, rapping his knuckles on the end table next to him.

"Well spoken, Madeleine," the Director said at last. "If no one else has anything to add, then this session is concluded. Dr. Maxwell, if you'll meet me in the medical-records room in an hour, I'll give you your assignments."

When he had departed, my new colleagues descended upon me to greet me more informally.

"Pleased to see you jump right into the discussion," the Senior enthused. "Shows initiative."

He stuck out a huge paw for a handshake. I took it – and quickly withdrew. He had done it to me again! This time with another old gag: a "joy buzzer." He and the others laughed uproariously, and my ears burned. Dr. MacIntosh then acquainted me with an old Scottish adage: "Fool me once, shame on you; fool me twice, shame on *me*." Ah, well, what's an initiation without a gag or two?

"I think I'm going to have a very interesting time here," I remarked as I flexed my fingers. "If I survive, that is. I seem to have provided you with a fresh victim."

"Oh, this is nothing, Ken," the Senior said with a chuckle. "May I call you 'Ken'? Once you've had your initiation, things will really be interesting."

"You mean, this wasn't it. But, I thought…"

"Still in the future, dear boy. And, I will tell you that the rest of us are taking bets on when it happens."

I wrinkled my nose in annoyance. This was getting to be damned peculiar. It was bad enough to be the butt of petty jokes. Now I was to be thrown into the middle of some intrigue which – judging from the sense of humor already exhibited by this group – could entail anything under the sun. I shuddered to think what more was in store for me if these people were so crass as to make book on it.

"Thanks for the warning, Dr. Rauschenburg. I –"

"Call me 'Harry.'"

"Harry. I can't wait until this ordeal is over."

"Oh, I think you'll find it most enjoyable. Well, I'm off. Toodle-oo."

Dr. Vengtman the Younger sidled up to me and offered her hand. I tingled all over at the contact, and I tried to put a little extra into the handshake. She broke off quickly, however, and frowned briefly. That was not a good sign; I'd wanted to start off our relationship on the right foot.

"I didn't realize you were an 'environmentalist,' Dr. Maxwell," she said by way of making conversation. "From your background, I'd have thought you were more of a 'reactionist.'"

"I am. But, no one else was raising the possibility, so I did. And, please, you must call me 'Ken.'"

"Must I? All right – Ken."

"And can I call you 'Nancy'? I certainly wouldn't want to confuse you with your uncle."

She laughed throatily. Even her laugh was seductive.

"If I ever thought you might do that, I'd have to reserve a room for you here. But, I'm 'Nan' to my friends."

"I certainly hope I can be your friend," I responded with a seductive touch of my own.

She fixed me with an expression I'd seen on the face of the Chief Resident at R-PSL the time I had asked about scheduled breaks. That was not a good sign either. If I weren't careful, I'd be out in the cold with this woman, and I'd never know why.

"We'll see. Excuse me now. We have a sanitarium to run."

The other three wished me well in their turn and in their own fashion. I told Dr. Chantrier I sympathized with her and that I'd been just as embarrassed by her "recital" as she was. She thanked me politely and hurried away. Dr. MacIntosh hoped we could discuss the subject of avoidant personality disorder in more detail in the near future. I assured him I would make some time for such a discussion. I really didn't care about the topic one way or the other; still, it couldn't hurt to score a few points here and there, because one never knew when they'd come in handy. Dr. Fingherelli unexpectedly asked me if I'd like to borrow his copy of Isaac Asimov's collection of "dirty" limericks in order to get some ideas for my turn at "recital." I thanked him for his help, and he scurried away, leaving me alone with a rush of bewildering and conflicting thoughts.

I had told Harry that working with this group would be an adventure, and not just from a professional point of view. That was true enough; each of my new colleagues – with the possible exception of the Director – had shown that they were quite prepared to drag me into their quirkiness whenever and wherever the spirit moved them. I could understand the need to blow off a little steam once in a while – psychiatric work can be a pressure cooker at times – and I had pulled a few pranks of my own in my day. But one might have expected more than juvenile pranks from such a distinguished ensemble. And Dr. Vengtman the Elder seemed inclined to give them a free hand in this regard, so he was not going to be any refuge from their shenanigans. So, there wasn't a damned thing I could do about it – short of resigning and putting as much distance between me and the

Home as I could. But, give up a plum job like this, just because my nose was out of joint for a short while? No way, Jose!

It occurred to me afterwards that, during the round-table discussion of case histories, no one had mentioned Melissa Waterman. If she were a patient as Dr. Vengtman had intimated, why hadn't her emotional disorder been discussed? What was the nature of her illness? And just whose patient was she anyway? It was a minor mystery, to be sure, but I was in no position to pursue it; as the "new boy," I could hardly charge in where I was not supposed to go. Clearly, the girl's case history had been deliberately withheld for a good reason – why else would a man like Lowell Vengtman be so discreet? – and I must not be seen prying into someone else's affairs. Still, my curiosity being what it was, I was full of questions and, once I had established myself at the Home, I could finagle a few answers out of my colleagues.

On the other hand, if Melissa continued to spy on me, as I believed she was doing, then I was obliged to report her to the Director. If her behavior was connected to her illness, I would not be doing her any favors by ignoring it. Spying out a stranger was possibly a symptom of paranoid personality disorder, and the sooner it was brought to someone's attention, the better for all concerned. And I might learn her story in the end and have my curiosity satisfied that way.

That, however, was for another day. I had an appointment to keep and my own patients to worry about.

I arrived in the medical-records room before Dr. Vengtman did and found myself under scrutiny again, this time by the redoubtable Nurse Petrie. When I explained why I was there (and somehow I felt compelled to do so, though I was under no obligation), she responded with an icy stare that might have paralyzed a Gorgon. In no uncertain terms, she let me know that she didn't care to have anyone loitering about her records room. If anyone had any business there, well and good; otherwise, stay the hell out! My attempts at small talk were met with stony silence at best or an occasional contemptuous *hmmm* at worst. Despite her obvious attractiveness, she displayed all the personality of a brick wall. I couldn't imagine climbing into bed with her; it would be like having sex with a statue.

Finally, the Director came to my rescue. He gave Petrie a list of names and requested the appropriate files. Quickly and efficiently, she located all five and laid them on the counter. When I attempted to pick them up, she drew them back and wordlessly handed me the sign-out sheet. With a bit

35

of grousing under my breath concerning the disposition of bureaucratic red tape, I dutifully filled in the date and time of the requisition, the file numbers, and my name. I noted that there was a seventy-two-hour time limit on sign-outs and idly wondered what would happen to me if I exceeded the limit. I could picture Petrie breaking down my door, brandishing a club, and demanding that I surrender her files immediately or suffer the consequences. It was with great relief when I departed the Ice Kingdom and was on my way toward sunnier climes.

"Study those histories carefully," the Director advised as we returned to his office, "and apply your own experiences and research to them. Perhaps you'll succeed where your predecessor could not. Tomorrow morning, I'll introduce you to your new patients."

"Thank you, sir. I'll give it my all."

"I'd expect nothing less, Doctor."

I hesitated to broach the subject uppermost in my mind for fear of appearing – well, less than enthusiastic about my new work environment. My curiosity, however, was a more powerful force.

"Excuse me, Dr. Vengtman. Far be it for me to tell you how to run your Home, but I have to know one thing."

He eyed me with bemusement.

"Only *one* thing, young man?"

"Well, lots of things, I guess, but one in particular."

"And that is?"

"The last item on the agenda of the staff meeting – just what was that all about anyway?"

Another wry smile from him.

"Were you offended, Doctor?"

"Wel-l-l, 'offended' is not in my dictionary. Let's say I was *shocked*. Dirty limericks are the last thing I'd expect here. I'd sooner expect Dr. Rauschenburg to take up ballet."

He stared off into the distance for a moment, choosing his reply carefully. It was one of his more common traits. Some people assumed that, by these long pauses, he had become bored with the conversation and was rudely letting the other party know he was through talking. This was not the case as I can attest from personal experience; the Great Man had his ways of dismissing you, but a long silence was not one of them. He still had points to make and simply wished to make them in the most succinct manner possible.

"You're aware," he said at last, "that the nature of our work here is more serious than, say, at a state institution – this because we take the most difficult cases." I nodded in agreement. "Then, you should also know that the stress which accrues to the profession in general is proportionally higher. Therefore, a more unique mechanism for relieving that stress is called for, one more…unorthodox, shall we say? I permit Harry his little pranks because, one, they're harmless and, two, they provide everyone with a quick laugh. As for the limericks, Doctor, it may surprise you that my niece suggested that little exercise."

I *was* surprised. In fact, I goggled at this revelation. If anyone other than the Director had made it, I would have dismissed it out of hand. Who would have suspected that a classic beauty like Nancy Vengtman could harbor a dirty mind?

"She has a weird sense of humor, that girl," Dr. Vengtman continued. "And I can tell you that she didn't get it from *my* side of the family. In any event, the limericks serve two purposes; one, they take our minds off the depressing business that occurs here and, two, they act as self-therapy by forcing us to confront our own socio-sexual hang-ups. Does that answer your question, Dr. Maxwell?"

"Yes, sir, though…"

"You're wondering if you'll be required to participate." I nodded again. "It's strictly voluntary, despite appearances. No one will fault you if you choose to decline." He looked at me strangely. "Your predecessor declined, claiming it was a waste of time. While I hesitate to make a correlation between that attitude and his subsequent behavior, one cannot help but wonder how matters might have turned out had he joined in the fun. And, I think you may find yourself drawn in in spite of your reservations."

"Well, I wouldn't think of disappointing the group. I have a 'weird' sense of humor myself. I just needed to clear up the matter. Thank you, sir."

"You're welcome. I'll see you tomorrow morning then."

And that's how the Great Man dismisses you – directly, without fanfare!

I headed to the veranda to study my new caseload. After a quick scan of the files, I began to make some preliminary observations. First, three of the five individuals were referrals; that is, they had originally been treated at other facilities and brought here when said treatment proved to be ineffective. I concluded that they would probably be my greatest challenges. The other two were "originals," brought to the Home directly by relatives/guardians. Second, two of the files, both referrals, were tagged with two colored tabs, i.e. multiple disorders (extremely great challenges!). Third, four of the five – two of the referrals and both originals – fell into my field of expertise, drug-induced psychosis. The fifth, the other referral, was my "fair share" of the Home's total caseload. And, lastly, four of the five lived in the metropolitan Chicago area; the other one came from DeKalb, a good forty miles west of the Home. All, of course, came from well-to-do families who had spared no expense to find a cure for the mental illness displayed by their loved ones (although, in my more cynical moments, I felt that no expense was spared in order to hide the family skeletons and avoid possible scandal).

The one common thread in these cases was that all of them had been the patients of my predecessor, the late Dr. Mathias Hinkelman, whose suicide earlier in the year had left the opening I was filling. In effect, I was "inheriting" his caseload. What was odd about the files – though, at first, I dismissed it as mere co-incidence – was that all of the patients had evidenced some progressive improvement in their behavior patterns to one degree or another and then showed a sudden relapse. And, now that I thought about it, the relapse corresponded to the time period – according to the news item in the *Journal of the American Psychological Association* – when Dr. Hinkelman himself had gone mad prior to his suicide. That sent a shiver up my spine. What had happened to him that he should lose not only his patients but also himself? Another mystery for the future.

While I was lost in thought, I had the eerie feeling that I was not alone. Abruptly, I turned in my seat. Melissa Waterman was standing next to me, gazing at me serenely. How long she had been there was anyone's guess; she moved as quietly and gracefully as a cat. Seeing her was quite a shock, and I nearly dropped my files on the ground.

If she was cognizant of the surprise she had sprung on me, she did not indicate it. Rather, she exhibited a warm, personable smile as if she were glad to see me. Up close, I noted that she possessed an open face, though her nose and mouth were unusually small, giving her a slightly elfin appearance. As I have said before, however, it was her *eyes* which riveted me – those compelling amethyst eyes deep set in their sockets so that she seemed to look at you from the bottom of a well. They possessed a laser-like quality and, if she hadn't been smiling at me, I would have believed she was mentally dissecting me.

Then again, maybe she was!

"Hello, Dr. Maxwell," she spoke with a voice like the tinkling of bells. "How are you?"

I was still too stunned to reply immediately. Besides, how did she know my name? We'd never been introduced. Perhaps she had asked around about the "new boy" or overheard my name being mentioned by some staff person – either of which might explain why she had chosen to spy on me the night before; she wanted to check me out and see if I measured up to the Home's expectations. I didn't dare ask her directly because, not knowing her medical history, I could have precipitated a psychotic episode and undone whatever progress in her treatment her counselor may have accomplished. Best then to remain neutral – and cordial – until I knew the whole story. Presently, I found my tongue.

"Hello, there. Melissa, isn't it?"

"Yes, Doctor."

She continued to penetrate my being with her gaze. To say the least, it was very unnerving. Suddenly, my mind was filled with an image in slow motion of a flower opening its petals to the sun. A second and a third image of flowers burst forth – meadows full of them wavering in a gentle breeze -- and washed over me in a warm rush of air. I think I shook my head in wonder then, for the physical reaction served to break the connection between my brain and the unknown source of the images. I caught my breath and squirmed in my chair. Beads of perspiration dotted my forehead. Quickly, I checked my bearings to see if I were still in Illinois on the grounds of the Vengtman Home for the Emotionally Disturbed.

What a fantastic vision that had been! How had I come to see it? Had there been, after all, a bit too much sherry in the beef Stroganoff? Or something else that Harry had slipped in? I sighed deeply.

All this while, Melissa maintained her scrutiny of me.

"I like you, Dr. Maxwell."

Again, I was taken aback. Instant personality analysis at first encounter? I supposed it was possible. Hadn't I taken an instant dislike to Nurse Clement? Ordinarily, one should study a person in depth before casting judgment upon him. Be that as it may, Melissa had rendered her own judgment based on – what? A chance meeting (or had it been *chance*?) and some espionage? Her opinion was, of course, flattering, though I might disagree with her "methodology."

"Why, thank you, Melissa. I…like you too."

"You're a nice man. I hope you stay here forever."

With that, she skipped off toward the northwestern section of the estate and some unknown errand. Her last words left me in a state of bemusement. I was going to have to disappoint her. I had no intention of staying here *forever*; I had every intention of staying only as long as it took to acquire enough experience to move on to other environments and other challenges. Obviously, the girl had spoken hyperbolically, making simplistic analyses and guileless assessments common to younger children. Tomorrow, she might have a different opinion. Unfortunately, this brief encounter had afforded me no insight into her problems (beyond the possibility of marginal mental retardation), though it had served to increase my curiosity about her.

As soon as I had collected my wits, I made my way back to my cottage and immersed myself fully in the files. As a matter of routine, I usually gave a file a quick preliminary scan (which I had already done), then put it aside to mull over the salient parts; later, I re-read it with greater attention to the details. The oddity I had noted in the first reading, however, prompted me to skip the "mulling" stage and go directly to the details. I re-read all five files, word for word, sometimes back-tracking and re-reading certain phrases and sentences or even a whole paragraph aloud in order to grasp the writer's intent. I hoped not only to gain an insight into Mathias Hinkelman's methodology but also to discover a clue as to why he had chosen destruction rather than counseling for himself. Inadvertently, he may have left such a clue in his commentary on his patients' progress (or lack of it); if so, I wanted to find it and prevent his fate from befalling some other doctor (including me!).

Whereas all of the patients had begun to open up and to discuss freely their problems, abruptly, they became "sullen, morose, withdrawn, near-paranoid" (Hinkelman's words). It was as if all five had experienced the same trauma at the same time, a trauma which affected them equally. What were the odds against that? I decided to pay less attention to the patients' statements and more to Hinkelman's choice of words. Did he start to go mad as a result of this experience, or had his own madness triggered their relapse? One clue: his sentence structure devolved from the complete, compound form to an incomplete, simple one; and, toward the next-to-the-last page of each file, the sentences were mere strings of words, suggesting a mind which had lost its grasp of language structure. I found it most disheartening. Though I had never met the man, I could empathize because, in this line of work, it was all too easy for anyone – even the most skilled of counselors – to lose his way. The loss of a colleague, especially to suicide, was always an occasion for sober reflection.

By the time I had thoroughly committed those files to memory, the sun had set, and my stomach was grumbling. Once again, I had missed the scheduled meal service and was forced to go for take-out. That was a distasteful thought for more than one reason. In the first place, Man does not live by fast-food alone; he requires something more nutritionally balanced. In the second place, what fast-food joint could possibly deliver the equal of the superb lunch I'd had? I supposed I could have gone to one of the more respectable restaurants – I hadn't tried one this far out of Chicago – but I hated to go into one without a lady on my arm. In the end, I went to a pizza parlor and ordered a large pepperoni-and-green-pepper to go.

Before retiring that evening, on a hunch, I peeked out the front window. Sure enough, I spotted a pair of yellow eyes peering out of the dark of the woods. My "old friend" had taken up his post right on schedule. I searched the area more intently but saw no sign of *amethyst* eyes. I shrugged. Maybe Melissa had already been here while I was busy feeding my face. *C'est la vie*, as they say on the South Side.

Just as a token of good-will, I left a slice of left-over pizza on the front stoop.

DAY THREE:
Tuesday, 07.08.1997
INAUGURATION

I made sure my "alarm clock" woke me up at the proper hour. No more missing breakfast for me!

At seven-thirty sharp, I sauntered into the staff dining room. The aroma of scrambled eggs, bacon, hash-brown potatoes, oatmeal, and coffee filled my nostrils, and I went straight to the serving counter and helped myself. Even though I had eaten three-fourths of a large pizza the night before, I still felt famished; whether it was the idea of a freshly-cooked meal or the sense of intrigue and mystery I was experiencing, I couldn't have said, but whatever it was prompted me to heap my plate with a double portion of everything.

Two others were already dining: Harry and Nan. Boldly, I took a seat opposite the latter. I glanced surreptitiously at their trays. It's an old habit of mine. As a boy, I'd heard that "you are what you eat"; and, since then, I have tried to verify the truth of the statement. Nan was eating lightly – a bowl of oatmeal, two slices of cinnamon toast, and a glass of orange juice. One might have thought a woman of her stature might have had a heartier appetite. Perhaps she was saving herself for lunch or dinner. I goggled in amazement, however, when I examined the Senior's plate, and I quickly understood how he had become as large as he was. I have a reasonably healthy appetite; playing football and basketball in college (I had had a choice of trying out for a professional team or becoming a doctor) necessitated a large intake of food. On the other hand, eating to excess was counterproductive, and I always watched my weight. Obviously, Harry did not share my concern; he loved food, and lots of it. He seemed to have taken *triple* portions of everything, and he was steadily shoveling it in. Except he did pause briefly to flash me one of his patented cheery smiles as I sat down.

"Good morning, Ken! Lovely day, eh?"

"Morning, Harry. Sure is. I'm looking forward to getting into harness."

"Fine, fine," he said and went back to his trench-work.

"And a good morning to *you*," I addressed Nan.

"Hello, Ken," she replied in a semi-seductive tone. She peered at me oddly. "You look like hell. Didn't you sleep well last night?"

"Thank you for your appraisal," I replied wryly. "As a matter of fact, no, I didn't. I was studying the files of my new patients, and I lost track of time."

"My, my, such dedication."

"The new boy has to make a good impression, right?"

"Very true. And perhaps your efforts will pay off in the end."

"I certainly hope so – in more ways than one."

Inasmuch as I would have liked to continue this playful cat-and-mouse conversation, I did have other things on my mind, and there was no time like the present to find answers to the burning questions that were sizzling my brain.

"It seems I've inherited my caseload from Mathias Hinkelman. Did either of you know him well?"

If I'd stated that I had supported Patrick Buchanan in last year's presidential election, I don't think I could have elicited a stonier silence than at that moment. Nan nervously poked at her oatmeal, eyes downcast; Harry stared off into the distance and chewed more slowly. Only the occasional noise from the kitchen penetrated that gloomy atmosphere. I seemed to have hit a sensitive nerve, but I was determined to see the matter through.

"Look, all I know about what happened is what I read in the *Journal*. Somehow, it's gotten under my skin, and I really would like to know more about him."

More silence. Nan glanced at Harry with a "shall-we-tell-him-or-shouldn't-we" expression. Harry actually stopped his gorging and stared a hole through me. I returned his gaze coolly. Presently, he set down his knife and fork and took a deep breath.

"Mathias was a friend, and a damned good doctor. His cure-rate was well above the norm. Not as high as that of Himself, of course – that's a goal we all strive toward – but admirable. And he was as sane as they came. Why he did away with himself, even *I* can't tell you." He spread his hands. "It was all so – so damned…*eerie*!"

"'Eerie'? How so?"

"There was no discernible cause for his erratic behavior, no text-book case which even remotely applied to the situation. It was as if someone had – well, as if someone had thrown sand in his gears, so to speak."

"An interesting way to put it, but I have to agree. When I read his observations in the files, I thought I was witnessing a Jekyll-and-Hyde transformation. Once the change occurred, the end came quickly."

Tears formed at the corners of Harry's eyes. He wiped them away with the back of his hand.

"Too true, too true," he said hoarsely. "Now, if it's all the same to you, Dr. Maxwell, I'd like to drop the subject. Later, perhaps, I'll be in a more receptive mood."

"Sure. Anytime. Sorry I upset you, man."

His appetite obviously ruined, Harry heaved himself to his feet and clumped out of the dining room, leaving his tray still half full on the table. I rubbed my jaw in chagrin.

"Well, I guess I opened up a real can of worms."

"You'll have to excuse Harry. The scuttlebutt was that he and Dr. Hinkelman were close – *very* close, if you know what I mean."

I nodded knowingly. There were as many gay people in this profession as there were in any other. It was just a fact of life. Not too long ago, the profession had actually considered homosexuality a "mental disorder" and approached it accordingly. The consensus these days is that it is a quirk of biology, a mix-up in the genetic code, and therefore not treatable in the conventional sense. Blacks had a hell of a time proving that their different biology didn't make them "inferior" too. I had no problem with Harry's sexual orientation as long as he had none with mine.

"Can you shed some light on this mystery, Nan?"

"Sorry, Ken. Dr. Hinkelman killed himself shortly after I began work here. I never had a chance to get acquainted, and the others were in too much of a shock afterwards to talk about him. I haven't thought much about the matter – until you brought it up."

"You think I should drop it?"

"It doesn't matter what I think. You seem to have gotten an itch you need to scratch, and you're not going to quit until it is scratched."

"Well, thank you for that instant analysis, Doctor Vengtman. But, as wild as it sounds, what happened to Hinkelman is linked to his treatment of his patients. Before I can understand their problems, I need to find out about his."

"You sound like a man on a mission, Ken."

"Yeah, I guess I am." I took a deep breath. "Speaking of 'missions,' I'm on another one a bit more personal. I've spent the last two nights eating dinner by myself, a situation I don't relish at all. Any chance of you joining me tonight? I know a place on Ogden Avenue in Downers Grove that serves out-of-this-world ribs."

Now, she propped her elbows on the table, rested her chin on folded hands, and gazed at me beguilingly. Mona Lisa couldn't have done a better job of smiling enigmatically. I felt myself tingle all over again.

"You certainly didn't waste any time on that score, did you? The answer, however, is no."

"Oh. There's someone else?"

"No, there's no one else. It's not that I wouldn't like to go out with you, Ken. It's just that you haven't been…initiated yet – at least, I don't think you haven't."

"That business again? Harry has made reference to it a couple of times, but he didn't elaborate."

"And I won't either. You'll know you've been initiated when it happens."

"And after that, we can get together?"

Another smirk.

"Ask me again after it happens."

I took the rest of my breakfast in frustrated silence. I'd been at the Home only a day-and-a-half, and already I'd found myself embroiled in *three* separate mysteries, solutions to which I apparently had to find on my own. All those murder mysteries I'd consumed in my days as an intern and a resident at R-PSL couldn't help me here since there weren't any corpses lying about with obscure clues for the discerning detective. The only death that I knew about had been a certified suicide; and there weren't any damned clues attached to it, obscure or otherwise!

As much as it was physically possible, the patients' quarters were categorized by types of disorder. That is, all of the manic-depressives were put in one bloc of rooms, the paranoids in another, the schizophrenics in a third, etc., etc. Not too surprisingly, the various sections were color-coded – stripes painted on the walls – to reflect the tabs on the files; once one familiarized oneself with the system, he would know exactly where he was at all times -- handy in case of emergencies. The coding also saved time in traveling from one patient to another. Personally, I thought this was taking efficient organization a bit too far; people of like dysfunctions absorbing each other's problems and adding fuel to their own struck me as being counter-productive. (On the other hand, one might argue that the same result would occur with a random mix.) The rationale for the present system was that a given patient might perceive another as having a bigger problem than himself and thus be encouraged to be more optimistic. When all is said and done, the lack of self-esteem was usually at the root of all mental disorders. In any event, it was not my place to re-organize the Great Man's operation. I was here to learn. If and when I had achieved his rate of successful cure, then I could run the show any way I pleased.

One other observation on organization: those who exhibited violent tendencies were housed on the uppermost floor in the farthest corner of the building. The "violent ward" was naturally coded black. Sound baffling had been incorporated into the floor and walls so that the noise of vented frustrations would not disturb the other patients. Also, more male nurses were assigned to that floor, two for each room.

My caseload (and everybody else's, I was sure) was scattered over the two residential floors. Since the Home was a reconverted mansion, there were no elevators, only broad staircases. One got his exercise in short order (whether he wanted it or not!) going up and down two flights of stairs several times a day. That the original plush carpeting had been left intact helped the feet immensely. As it happened, only two of my patients were on the second floor; the others were on the third, including one in the "violent ward." As the Director introduced them to me one by one, I mentally set down my own route for making my rounds.

Fred K. (I tend to avoid pseudonyms) was a product of Lake Shore Drive in Chicago, i.e. his family was filthy rich, having made their bundle through extensive real-estate holdings. It was safe to say that anyone in Fred's family could have bought the Home several times over and not put any sizeable dent in his bank account. Being fabulously wealthy, however, did not give Fred immunity from mental illness; on the contrary, it may have caused his disorder. At age twenty-two, he'd had a long history of drug abuse, beginning in middle school. Whichever drug of the moment his peer group was experimenting with – cocaine, phencyclidine piperdine (PCP, a.k.a. "angel dust"), mescaline, marijuana, 3,4-methylenodioxymethamphetamine (MDMA, a.k.a. "ecstasy") – Fred was right in the thick of things. He not only had legal entanglements (which his family's money and influence had effectively ameliorated) but also psycho-social problems, the chief of which was a failure to maintain cordial relations with anyone. He quarreled over the least little thing, defied any symbol of authority, and refused to co-operate in any project, great or small. He had a history of school expulsions, fines, terms of incarceration in "reform school," and futile attempts at rehabilitation through group therapy. Yet, sociopathy was the least of his symptoms, for Fred had gone one step too far and settled on peyote as his drug of choice.

It was a moot point why he had chosen this particular hallucinogen to play with, but his use (or abuse) of it had led to a rather unusual consequence. Without being overly melodramatic about it, Fred had become a "werewolf." That is to say, he believed himself to be a wolf in both mind and body; at any moment, the "transformation" could occur, and he would display the classic form of lycanthropy – removing all of his clothing, crouching on the floor on all fours, and occasionally howling plaintively in reaction to his alleged "captivity." He did not, of course, sprout fangs and body hair and become bloodthirsty as depicted in the old horror films, and the appearance of the full moon had nothing to do with his disorder. Apparently, during one of his hallucinogenic episodes, he had imagined himself as a wolf, and the notion so intrigued him that he progressed into a permanent psychosis. Fred K. was still a sociopath, but his illness had taken on a most curious form.

He was in his "human" form when I was introduced to him, although he did insist that I sit on the floor because it was "more comfortable." Rule #1 in psychotherapy: always put the patient at ease. Physically, he was your average young man, just under six feet in height, of medium build, a shock of unruly dishwater-blond hair, green-gray eyes that alternated between friendliness and fear, and a nervous tic at the corner of his right eye (which may or may not have been associated with his disorder). Emotionally, he was sometimes petulant, sometimes introspective, always defensive; during my initial visitation, he seldom remained still but fidgeted constantly and let his attention wander. Sad to say, I'd seen his kind before on the streets of Chicago and in the clinic at R-PSL. The hallucinogenic factor was not new either, but I hadn't seen it quite so pronounced as in Fred's case.

Fred was one of the "originals." His family had committed him to the Home immediately after his latest episode of "wolf" behavior made the ten o'clock news on a Chicago TV station. No amount of money could have kept the incident under wraps that time, and so his parents had had to come to grips with reality. Under Dr. Hinkelman's care, the young man was provided with the "standard treatment." (I have used quotation marks here deliberately because I wish to point out that the expression refers to what is acceptable in psychiatric medicine. It is *not* acceptable to me, and I have argued the point endlessly.) Fred was given, over the space of several weeks, a series of anti-psychotic drugs to combat his lycanthropic hallucinations; when one type failed to do the trick, another one was tried. I had three objections to this approach: (1) these particular drugs all had unfortunate side-effects, requiring other drugs to combat them; (2) use of one drug to treat the symptoms of a disorder originally produced by another drug is contradictory; and (3) too much reliance on drugs defeats the purpose of psychotherapy. Shortcuts lead only to short-term solutions; they don't address the root cause of mental illness which is buried deep within the psyche and must be exposed, and disposed, by the patient himself. In the present instance, Fred was suffering from a mild form of akathasia as well as his lycanthropy, due to the anti-psychotic drugs he was being given, which explained his restlessness.

On the plus side, however, Dr. Hinkelman seemed to have broken through Fred's defenses (if only temporarily) and to establish something of a rapport with him. And it was a weird sort of rapport too. Hinkelman had convinced his patient that *he* was a wolf as well and that he was seeking to join a "pack" for the purpose of mutual protection. Where he had come up with this arcane idea was anybody's guess – *my* medical school had never taught us to identify with the patient for fear of compounding the problem – but it had seemed to have worked in this case. Little by little, Fred had come to accept Hinkelman's "pack" status and follow him on a trail toward a pseudo-anthropomorphism. The hallucinations became less and less frequent, and the akathasia less and less pronounced. Drug use was decreased accordingly.

Then the bottom fell out, as the inexplicable episode that led Mathias Hinkelman to his own dementia brought this unique experiment to a screeching halt. It was all there in the files I had so meticulously studied: page after page of optimistic commentary on Fred's progress, giving way to disjointed remarks. As the counselor went mad, the patient relapsed back into full lycanthropic mode. And that was how things stood currently.

I had no clear idea about where to start. Naturally, I was quite reluctant to become a "wolf" myself; what had worked for my predecessor might not necessarily work for me. I had the impression that Hinkelman had neglected to mention a key ingredient in his "formula," and I was damned if I knew how to discover it. I'd have to start from scratch and play it entirely by ear. But, first, I needed to get a personal feel for Fred's illness.

"How've you been, Fred?" I inquired as soon as we had hunkered down on the floor.

He shrugged noncommittally.

"I won't pretend that it's going to be easy for you to work with another doctor, but I hope that in time you'll see me as much of a friend as Dr. Hinkelman."

"Mathias was a pack-brother," Fred replied moodily. "You aren't."

"I understand. I won't intrude upon the, uh, pack. I just want to, uh, observe and to learn."

"Learn what?" he snapped.

"The nature of the pack, the functions of each member, your obligations to it. That sort of thing."

"Why?"

"I, uh, feel *compelled* to know these things. Have you –"

Before I could finish the question, a low animalistic sound issued from the back of Fred's throat, and he quickly went to all fours. Dr. Vengtman and I tensed ourselves to make a run for the door and/or to call out for a male nurse. The "wolf-man" began crawling back and forth in front of us, eyeing us with great suspicion. Had he been a real wolf, I could well imagine that he was close to baring his teeth in the presence of a threatening creature. Fortunately, it did not come to that; his episode was short-lived. He ceased his crawling, jumped onto a chair, and curled up, peering warily at us.

"Go away!" he rasped.

"All right, Fred. But, I'll be back tomorrow to talk some more. I still want to learn."

He shrugged again.

"A rather promising beginning, Doctor," the Director remarked as soon as we had departed. "He didn't reject you outright."

"No, he didn't. I'm going to follow up on Dr. Hinkelman's example – up to a point, that is – and attempt to win his confidence by being curious about his perceived 'pack.' It's risky, I know, but I have little else to work with. Besides, I once heard some prominent individual say that the only effective way to defeat a psychosis was from the inside."

"Hmmm. So I did. Well, then, Dr. Maxwell, I expect to hear an interesting report from you at the next staff meeting."

"Yes, sir." I paused, debating with myself over broaching the subject uppermost in my mind. "Speaking of Dr. Hinkelman, what sort of person was he? The reason I ask is that part of the confidence-gaining I hope to achieve is predicated on who and what he was."

Dr. Vengtman fell into one of his lengthy silences. I could almost hear the mental gears clash and grind. Then:

"What do you know of him so far?"

"Only that he seemed to take a most unorthodox approach to psychotherapy. And it seemed to work until he, uh..."

"I chose Mathias because he *was* unorthodox. In fact, all of you are here because of your unique approaches to psychiatric medicine. I'm sure the idea of being on the cutting edge hasn't been lost on you, Doctor. Mathias's specialty wasn't substance-abuse-as-a-causative-factor, but he did recognize the relationship, and I allowed him free rein. As you've surmised, he had some small success.

"I knew him as a shy, reserved individual, not the sort to be in the center of things at social gatherings, telling one humorous story after another. Rather, he chose his relationships carefully. Perhaps, because of his own reservations, he felt empathy with his patients and was therefore able to ingratiate himself easier."

"I, uh, know about his relationship with Harry too."

"Um, that came later, just before he ...became ill. I doubt homosexuality had anything to do with it, though."

"I didn't mean to suggest otherwise, sir."

"Of course not. Whatever else Mathias Hinkelman was, he was not the sort to wear his emotions on his sleeve. He worked diligently and never succumbed to despair – until the end, that is."

He moved off quickly, and I guessed that he wished to speak no more on this subject. I didn't press the issue. I had all the time in the world to play detective.

Her family was not as wealthy as Fred's was, but Georgina W. had not lacked for creature comforts. The only daughter of a restaurateur in Berwyn, she had married a local banker and moved up the social ladder a couple of rungs; and, because her husband had been twenty years her senior, many eyebrows had been raised, the epithet "gold-digger" having been bandied about from time to time. It was safe to say that the couple was, in current slang, "yuppies," and they made all the usual social events. It was a heady life-style for a former middle-class girl – perhaps too heady. Like others in her new social circle, Georgina began to experiment with the drug-of-choice of the well-heeled – cocaine – snorting a line or two nearly every day; even when she had no "excuse" to snort, she did so because "coke makes me relax." A doting husband ignored her habit until he was forced to recognize it.

About three years into the marriage, there was a child. Georgina was, naturally, both nervous and elated, since her husband had made no secret of the fact that he wanted an heir. She made every attempt to play the part of a good mother, but the role deepened her dependency on cocaine. Then tragedy struck; the child, at age four, accidentally drowned in the backyard swimming pool at a time when Georgina was snorting a line. She became an instant emotional wreck, blaming herself for the child's death and refusing to believe anything to the contrary. She quickly switched to "crack," the concentrated form of cocaine.

The combination of substance abuse and emotional trauma induced in her the form of schizophrenia known as "perception disorder." She was not a true schizophrenic as that disorder is produced strictly by psycho-social trauma; yet, the symptoms were the same, and she had to be treated as if she were one. Her illness manifested itself as auditory hallucinations. In short, she "heard voices," just as Joan of Arc did. The voice she heard was not that of God, however, but that of her dead son; usually, it criticized her life-style but, occasionally, it provided "guidance." It was a classic delusion, made all the more terrifying by having had some foundation in a real event. Whenever Georgina heard the voice, she fell into a hysterical fit, followed by self-flagellation, in an effort to punish herself for not having been a good mother. Flagellation took the form of face-slapping or banging the head against the wall or both. No blood was ever drawn; she had not yet reached the stage where she wished to injure herself severely, only to feel enough pain to "atone" for her "sins."

Happily, I did not have to witness any flagellation during my initial visitation, although Georgina did unfocus her eyes at one point as if she were listening to someone else far away. By anyone's standard, she was an attractive woman: reddish-blond hair; green eyes (a bit too widely spaced, I thought); full, sensuous lips that always threatened to pout; a buxom but high-waisted figure. She sighed constantly and fluttered thin hands, nervous habits carried over from her pre-drug days. During our talk, she huddled up on the bed, her arms wrapped around her legs and her chin resting on her knees. She spoke in a whisper, and I had to strain to listen.

She was a "referral" from the state hospital in Elgin (north of the Home on Highway 31). Reluctantly, her husband had committed her to that institution as her psychosis deepened. The state's doctors, however, found no means of "bringing her out" and recommended that she be transferred to the Home. As her schizophrenic tendencies had been drug-oriented, the cocaine habit was attacked first by prescribing – as the state had done – tricyclic antidepressants. In addition, in a novel approach to the problem, Dr. Hinkelman assumed the identity of an alleged "witness" to the drowning and conducted three-way "conversations" between the patient, the deceased, and himself. Despite warnings against this tactic by other staff members, he gradually intruded upon Georgina's subconscious and influenced her attitudes; over the course of several months, the chemical residue of the cocaine was purged from her body, and the voices she heard not spoken by Hinkleman came to her less and less frequently. Frankly, I had to marvel at his success, but what really perplexed me was how he had intended to extrude *himself* from the scenario once he had brought his patient out of her psychosis. If he had a plan, it had died with him. Georgina returned to her former "relationship" with her dead child.

I was no more eager to assume the persona of a witness to tragedy than I was to play the part of a wolf, even if Hinkleman had had some degree of success with this approach. I might have considered myself a "radical" when it came to unique treatment of mental illness, but at least I attempted to provide some rational basis for my methodology. Hinkelman's "solutions" (if that's what they were) seemed to have come out of left field. One supposes that "inspiration" plays a part now and then and the counselor takes an intuitive leap into unknown territory. The evidence for intuition is strictly anecdotal – I could add my own experiences to the list – and one can accept it according to one's personal inclination.

"Hello, Georgina," I greeted her. I noted the shallowness of her cheeks and added: "Have you been eating enough?"

"No. Lewis says I eat too much. He says I should go on a diet."

"Lewis?"

"My son. He's always criticizing me." She sighed deeply. "He's right, of course. I've always had a weight problem. All those parties I went to, all that rich, fattening food."

"Surely you don't get that sort of thing here?"

"Lewis says it's still too much. He says I ought to cut out one meal a day."

"Well, we can discuss that later. I'd like to know more about Lewis."

She stared up at the ceiling, her head cocked in attention to some invisible speaker. Several minutes passed. Apparently, she had forgotten we were there, and Dr. Vengtman signaled me to leave. As I started toward the door, Georgina finally spoke up.

"Lewis says you eat too much too."

Then she fell silent again.

"I wonder," I remarked out in the hallway, "why Hinkelman didn't mention anorexia nervosa in his analysis. Perhaps she developed it when he was…removed from the 'relationship' he had created."

"Quite correct, Doctor. Loss of someone close is a prime cause of eating disorders. Odd though that it took so long to develop."

"Well, I intend to get to the bottom of it. So far, it's been quite a 'legacy' Hinkelman left me."

The Director must have agreed with me for he chose not to comment this time.

Not all of the people in my specialty suffered as a result of ingesting illicit drugs. They were only the tip of a large iceberg, visible only because of the nature of the drugs involved; since the narcotic substances were the most volatile (from a chemical stand-point), those who used/abused them were affected in highly dramatic – and unpredictable – fashion. The bulk of those who might fall under my purview tended to react to the so-called "legal" drugs, a host of which were available to Twentieth-Century Man (and Woman) – alcohol, nicotine, prescription and over-the-counter pharmaceuticals, and the like. All of the "legals" had their peculiar side-effects, according to an individual user's unique metabolism, and, in a note of irony, some of them acquired still other drugs to combat the ill effects. It was the most vicious of vicious circles, and it was natural that someone like me who had seen the worst side of drug use should reject them as much as the "illegals." To my mind, they were only the opposite side of a very bad coin.

Somewhere along human development, mankind had been duped into believing that a chemical fix was the ticket out of a life of misery and stress and anxiety, and it gulped pills and capsules and powders and fluids by the ton in order to rise above the real world. I called this desire the "Feel-Good Syndrome" (though my colleagues simply referred to the more neutral term, "drug culture"). My views were not popular, to say the least, especially in those circles where drug therapy superseded psychotherapy; yet, none of the advocates of the former approach hadn't had to watch the parade of human wreckage as a result of drug abuse, legal or otherwise. I would have gladly put myself out of a job in exchange for a drug-free society.

A case in point was Terry M. from nearby Aurora, a middle-class advertising executive who spent his days (and part of his nights) thinking up catchy ad copy for local businesses. Despite his middle age, he possessed a rather muscular physique, the result of weight-training and body-building in his youth. He had not a trace of gray in his reddish-brown hair nor any seams or wrinkles in his face. He pierced one with steely gray eyes in the manner of a prison guard regarding an inmate. Though he shunned "illegal" drugs like the plague, never smoked, and only occasionally took a social drink, because of the stressful nature of the advertising business, he had suffered from migraine headaches and relied on pain-relievers and tranquilizers to calm the demons. These, however, did not affect him adversely (except to the degree that he became yet another statistic in the "Feel-Good Syndrome"). Terry's real problem stemmed from his participating in one of those never-ending "clinical tests" which used hundreds of ordinary (and unsuspecting) people to judge the validity of some new drug or another. He had had a couple of strokes (due to stress), and his physician had decided he was an ideal candidate to test a new drug (which I can't name here because I would open myself to a libel suit) which allegedly alleviated damage to the heart by strengthening the heart wall. Subsequently, he had to sign a release absolving the manufacturer of the drug, the clinic where it was administered, and the personnel who administered it from any and all liability as a result from his participation in the test. Predictably (from my point of view), there were casualties; one of them was Terry, who joined the ranks of the psychotic.

He now believed himself to be a Great American Writer (along the lines of his former occupation), and he had become fixated on the idea that he was the re-incarnation of Edgar Allen Poe. Sometimes known as "delusions of grandeur," his illness was more properly known as "narcissistic personality disorder." He was hypersensitive to criticism, claiming that he was misunderstood and that no one would publish his writing because they were all "incompetent fools." (It may or may not have been a coincidence, but my research suggested that the real Poe also suffered from this disorder, probably as a result of his alcoholism and opiate ingestion.) Because of this fixation, Terry had memorized large quantities of Poe's own works and, with little or no prompting at all, would quote at length a poem or short story, often dramatically. While he was either pontificating against the "incompetent fools" of the publishing industry or reciting his "latest work," he alternated in mood between petulance and sullenness.

According to Hinkelman, Terry's delusions reflected his failure to achieve what he believed was "greatness" in real life and so led him to achieve it in a fantasy world. The "standard" treatment had been a daily injection of lithium in order to stabilize the mood swings. On the psychotherapeutic side, Hinkelman had resorted to yet another role-playing game specifically designed to empathize with the patient's sense of being a "lost soul." To this end, he had become a "raven," the same raven (for those who are unfamiliar with Poe's works) which sat atop a bust of Pallas in the poem of the same name, bedeviling the narrator. Except, he said a lot more than "Nevermore!" in his conversations; *his* raven nagged the "wannabe Great American Writer" at every turn and challenged him to put up or shut up. This was not the approach recommended by the book. Rule #2 in psychotherapy: build up the patient's self-esteem and give him the strength to face his fears. Yet, my predecessor had had a modicum of success, and before his own downfall, progressed to the point where Terry was becoming doubtful of Poe's "influence" over him and hoping to make it on his own. His patient's relapse sunk him deeper into his psychosis, and now he was more bitter than ever toward an allegedly uncaring and incompetent publishing world.

When Dr. Vengtman and I entered Terry's room, he was hunched over the bedside table, scribbling on a sheet of paper (a stack of obsolete medical forms printed on only one side courtesy of Mrs. Oliphant, also a Poe fan) and muttering to himself. I say "scribbling" because sheet after sheet had been filled with disjointed sentences, nonsense words, and just plain gibberish which he believed was his "latest work." As soon as he filled the sheet he had been working on and casually tossed it aside, he looked up at us and calmly recited the first stanza from "The Raven."

"This," he explained before I had a chance to introduce myself, "is the inspiration for my latest novel." Here, he gestured at the pile of paper sitting on the floor underneath the table. "In it, I tell the story -- Oh, but I won't reveal the plot to *you*. You'll steal it and rob me of my due."

"You needn't worry," I re-assured him. "I'm a terrible writer. No one would publish anything I wrote."

"Perhaps, perhaps not. Those bastards in the publishing houses wouldn't know good literature if it bit them on the ass. They'll publish *trash* instead and send *me* rejection slips!"

"What's their main objection?" I inquired, sensing an opportunity to do a bit of psycho-analysis.

"Would you believe 'plagiarism'? Those horses' asses had the gall to claim they'd read my work before, submitted by other writers. The idea!"

Whereupon he launched into another recitation – in appropriately sepulchral tones – of the opening scene from "The Fall of the House of Usher." When he had finished, he turned to his "writing" again and ignored us completely.

"As complete a personality transference as I've ever seen," I commented shortly afterward. "I'm surprised he hasn't altered his appearance yet to match Poe's."

"Now you understand why I needed a specialist with your background, Dr. Maxwell. These drug-oriented psychoses pose the greatest challenge to psychiatric medicine."

The challenge, I was rapidly learning, was hardly limited to the profession itself. It threatened to tax the abilities of the practitioners. I was beginning to see why Hinkelman had gone mad; not having been trained specifically to treat this category of patient, he had probably found himself at one impasse after another. Despite his limited success in remission of symptoms, he hadn't been able to sustain and build upon it, and the house of cards he had elaborately constructed soon collapsed under its own weight of fantasies.

How would I fare in picking up his pieces? I'd soon know once I had entered into serious dialogues with these disturbed people. I had mixed feelings on that score: awed by the monumental task ahead of me, but eager to get my feet wet.

Another victim of a prescription carelessly administered was Matthew J., an otherwise sprightly old gentleman with powder-blue, twinkling eyes, a thick thatch of snow-white hair, and a wiry body that still had some good years left in it. He was the lone patient from outside the metropolitan area where he had lived all of his life; he'd been a newspaper reporter in DeKalb most of that time but finished his career as a city-desk editor before retiring four years ago. One might say that he was the epitome of the "good life" in twentieth-century America: meaningful work; a loving family; many good friends; and community recognition. He had no particular vices (outside of betting on the horses at Arlington Park once a month) and showed himself as an exemplary role model to younger generations.

Unfortunately, Matt was not able to live out his years in peace. Somehow, he had contracted Parkinson's disease, a dopamine-depleting illness which resulted in depression. His physician had prescribed a monoamine oxidase inhibitor which negated the depression but replaced it with a mild form of schizophrenia. His form of schizophrenia was "formal thought disorder." Matt now believed himself to be invisible and, if he removed all of his clothing, to be free from prying eyes. Unlike Georgina, who had the potential for harming herself (if not others), he was completely harmless. It was just that his habit of walking around in the nude had upset the sensibilities of his neighbors. Eventually, they had insisted that his family "do something" about him. He was another referral from Elgin.

According to Hinkelman's notes, Matt was such a borderline case that he was reluctant to treat him beyond restricting his movements. The old fellow was suffering enough – Parkinson's disease had advanced so far that Matt required massive doses of MAOI's – and, if one harmless delusion ameliorated his suffering, why not let him indulge in it? In the end, our Hippocratic Oath not to do harm had won the day, and Hinkelman had embarked upon another novel technique. He fought fire with fire, as it were, by persuading Matt that he had developed a sort of "radar" that allowed him to "detect" solid objects even if he couldn't "see" them with his eyes. By this method, the patient became accustomed to the idea that he could be "seen." Apparently, it had been Hinkelman's intention to spread the "radar power" to others and thus to demonstrate to Matt that he had nothing to fear from being visible. Despite the radical nature of the approach, I had to agree and wondered how things would have turned out had Hinkelman not self-destructed.

When I was introduced to Matt, Dr. Vengtman was prescient enough to ask him if he'd put some clothes on "so we can see you." The old man complied readily enough and greeted us both as if there was nothing wrong with him, physically or mentally. I found him to be a rather engaging individual, full of little anecdotes and shrewd observations about the people he'd known; given the fact that he had been a newspaperman, I'd have been greatly surprised if he was ignorant of the human condition. At one point, I idly wondered just who was psycho-analyzing whom here! I also suspected that some of his remarks probably were exaggerations in order to pull the wool over the listener's eyes – a common trait of the gregarious person.

"So, Dr. Maxwell," Matt said in a clear, crisp voice, "you're my new shrink, eh? Well, like I told the other fellow – Hinkelman, was it? – I'm not the least bit crazy. It's just that other people don't understand things the way I do."

"How would you convince them otherwise?"

"Ha! Now, there's the corker! Reminds me of the time I went out on my first reporting assignment." For the next ten minutes, he regaled us with an astonishingly detailed account of an incident that had to have occurred more than thirty years ago. His ability to recall events seemed to belie the fact that he was a victim of Parkinson's disease. "After that," he concluded, "I learned to watch my step, no matter what I did or where I did it."

"I should imagine," I murmured, anxious to leave and see my last patient. "I think I'd like to discuss that further the next time I see – I mean, *visit* you."

"Sure thing, Doc. My door's always open to bright young fellas like yourself. Stop by anytime."

I departed, shaking my head in amazement. I felt as if I'd just left the college advisor's office after having received a pat on the head for

Whispers in the Mind

my diligent efforts. Beside me, noting the expression on my face, Dr. Vengtman chuckled heartily.

"Nothing like a good come-uppance, eh, Doctor?"

"That's for sure."

In sharp contrast to the others, Ray W. was a study in "sadistic personality disorder." A product of the Bridgeport community (also home to the then mayor) in Chicago, he was my "gratuitous" patient; that is, his psychosis had nothing to do with drug abuse, but he had been assigned to me in order to balance the caseload at the Home. He was also my "violent ward" case (each of the staff had one so as not to overburden anyone), and for good reason. He represented a textbook example of how *not* to raise a child; both parents had been alcoholics, and the father was physically and psychologically abusive. When the latter was killed in a barroom brawl, the mother took up with a man who possessed no better temperament or habits. The boyfriend eventually beat the mother to death in a fit of jealousy and put Ray in the hospital. From there, it had been one foster home after another; no family had desired to keep him for any length of time due to his streak of cruel and destructive behavior. The abuse received from those stronger than he was transmitted to those weaker than he – beginning with cruelty to animals whereby he would torture cats and dogs and often kill them in gruesome fashion.

As he grew older, he bullied his classmates and inflicted as much pain and humiliation upon them as he could on a daily basis. Inevitably, his antisocial behavior led to trouble with the law. As an adolescent, Ray joined – and eventually took leadership of – a street gang and engaged in mayhem on a major scale; thereafter, he was in and out of the St. Charles School for Boys (where he continued to be the bully). Upon reaching the age of majority, he quickly "graduated" to the Cook County Jail for various assaults and batteries. In a fit of exasperation, an unusually liberal-minded judge "sentenced" him to Elgin for psychiatric evaluation (though it might have been too late by that time to have had any effect on him); and, when that effort proved to be fruitless, the judge authorized transfer to the Home.

Ray was around the same age as Fred, though he was much stockier in build. He had jet-black, unruly hair, dark brown eyes, and a swarthy complexion; his boyish good looks reminded me of a larger version of "Beaver Cleaver" – a deceptive mask. Consistent with sadistic personality disorder, he was fascinated with weapons of all sorts but especially with the firearms of the "Old West." He had been drawn to the famous (or infamous, as the case may be) outlaws of that period and knew every detail of their short, sordid lives; his favorite individual was William H. Bonney – aka "Billy the Kid" – with whom he identified personally, often expressing a desire to take part in a "shoot-out on Main Street."

In my subsequent research, I discovered that Hinkleman had specialized in treating psychopathic/sociopathic behavior. Thus, he had spent a great deal of his time at the Home in an attempt to break through to the underlying causes of Ray's illness. This did not mean, however, that he had been more conventional in his approach than he had been elsewhere. On the contrary, he feigned an interest in the moral leadership of the Old West and presented himself as an itinerant preacher; and, while he sidestepped any mention of the lawmen of the day (particularly Pat Garrett, the Kid's ex-friend who had gunned him down early one morning), he debated morality for hours on end in the manner of the times. According to Hinkelman's notes, Ray was beginning to have doubts about the path he had taken over the years and was thinking about "reforming." Naturally, Hinkelman's demise had sent him into a tailspin, and he was again his old swaggering, antisocial self.

Ray glared at both of us with undisguised suspicion and distrust as we walked in, more so in my case because he was more accustomed to the Director's presence (the "Mayor of this wide spot in the road," in Ray's world-view). When Dr. Vengtman introduced me, he deliberately addressed the young man as "Kid" at which I had to frown. I still had a great reluctance to role-play in anybody's fantasy.

"Howdy," came the noncommittal response. "Set yerself down a spell. Ain't got nothin' to offer ya. This here's a *dry* town." He glanced to one side. "Them damn temperance people!"

"Other than that, are you comfortable?" I asked by way of ingratiating myself.

He started to crack his knuckles, one by one. The sound of displaced joints was quite audible. The cracking was a sure sign of nervousness; and, though I was careful not to show it, it made *me* nervous as well. After he had ministered to one hand, he answered my question.

"Hell, one jail's as comfortable as the next. At least the grub is tolerable." He grinned abruptly and leaned forward in a gesture of confidentiality. "Could use a woman, though."

I supposed he had meant to shock me, but I wasn't shocked in the least. Rather, I could sympathize with him. I merely grinned back.

"Afraid I can't do anything there, my man. Maybe later."

"Yeah." Now he looked me up and down. "So, yer the new preacher, huh? Gonna preach to me like the last one? Him 'n' me got along all right, but I don't cotton to preachers as a rule. Ain't none of 'em ya kin trust – always got sumpin to hide."

"I hope I can change your mind on that score."

Ray shrugged and looked away again. He began to crack the knuckles of his other hand. We took that as our cue to leave. In the hallway, I gazed at Dr. Vengtman for a long moment. He waited me out. Then:

"Cold. Emotionless. Dispassionate. The mark of a sadist, all right. I'll have fun with this one."

"I'm sure you'll be up to the task, Doctor." He checked his watch. "You'll excuse me now. I have an appointment in Oak Park in an hour. And you have other duties to attend to."

That was true enough. One might have thought that we of the professional staff would have had much free time on our hands once we had made our rounds. Not so. Counseling our patients on an individual basis was our principal, but not our only, business; we were also required to oversee and/or participate in various group activities. My orientation being at an end, I now had to earn my keep. In the present moment, I had been scheduled for infirmary duty in order to provide first-aid as needed. For the time spent in orientation, I had been given temporary grace by switching hours with another of the staff.

I was not in any great hurry because my new caseload had filled my head with a truckload of questions, half-formed observations, and conflicting ideas on where and how to begin treatment. And, now that I had seen the fruits of his labor, the mystery of Mathias Hinkelman had deepened. He would be a tough act to follow, and I wasn't too keen on following it.

While I was "pondering weak and weary" (as Terry M. might have expressed it), I unconsciously stepped through a set of French doors which led to a balcony overlooking the front yard. Originally, this section of the building had been a guest bedroom, and the guests were afforded a pleasant view on a moon-lit night. With the remodeling, old walls had been replaced with new ones, and the French doors were now at the end of a short hallway. I gazed out at a scene of mildly frenzied activity; the arts-and-crafts period had been moved outdoors that day, and the patients and non-professional staff were busy moving easels, palettes, brushes, and paints into position.

I also observed another little scene which so fascinated me that I forgot about everything else. Sauntering toward the main building from the direction of the wooded area was Melissa Waterman. Her ambling gait reminded me of a younger child who had no particular place to go to or to be at but had all the time in the world to let its impulsive nature take it wherever it will. Melissa seemed to be totally devoid of care and completely oblivious to her surroundings – not zombie-like by any means, simply withdrawn into herself and aware of only some internal world. Yet, I doubted that was the case, for she was engaged in a very distinct externality. And, if I hadn't seen it with my own eyes, I wouldn't have believed it possible.

Surrounding her was a flock of squirrels, the common brown variety. Six or seven of them scampered along at her feet, and one actually perched on her shoulder. She was feeding the latter creature by hand while the others had to be content with whatever she tossed their way. What she was feeding them was indeterminate – nuts, seeds, or fruit – but they gobbled it up as if they hadn't eaten in a week. Frankly, I was amazed. Squirrels normally shied away from humans; only through long, painstaking, Pavlovian methods could you get one to eat from your hand. Melissa had won over more than half a dozen and led them about like pets.

"Damnedest thing you ever saw, huh, Doctor?" a gruff voice spoke behind me.

I whirled in surprise and came face to face with Senior Nurse Clement. I gazed into his mocking eyes and his Cheshire-cat grin, trying to recover my mental bearings. Huge he was, but he moved very quietly!

"Uh, yes, it is. You'd think she had those animals *trained*."

"Uh-huh. Them damned squirrels trust her implicitly."

"Tell me, Nurse Clement, does Melissa have the freedom of the grounds?"

"As far as I know, she does. Don't do nobody no harm, though."

"Do you know whose patient she is?"

"Nope. Nobody ever told me. Don't much care either."

"I see. Well, thanks for your time."

"Any time, Doctor. See ya around."

I had temporarily forgotten about Melissa and the mystery she posed, having become absorbed in the conundrum of the late Dr. Mathias Hinkelman and his "street theater" approach to psychotherapy. Now, she was back in my consciousness to remind me that there were other puzzles to solve. I glanced out the French doors again. She was disappearing around the back of the building, her coterie of squirrels merrily dogging her heels. If it weren't for the fact that I had to report to the infirmary, I would have been tempted to follow her and see where she went and what she did there.

On the other hand, maybe I wouldn't have *wanted* to know.

DAY FOUR:
Wednesday, 07.09.1997
INOCULATION

The following morning, I awoke earlier than usual for two reasons, only one of which had to do with my employment.

The reason which did not was the fact that I had too much on my mind to wait for the alarm to go off. "Too much" included the strange dream I'd had. In it, I had been tied to a pole as a horde of squirrels danced around me on their hind legs. And they all had amethyst eyes! While they circled me, they chattered away in an unknown language in the rhythm of a limerick. I was laughing loudly even as I struggled to free myself. When the head squirrel – I knew he was the leader because he was wearing a doctor's smock and clutching a hypodermic in one paw – approached me to stuff peanuts into my mouth, I woke up in a cold sweat.

Every psycho-analyst who ever wrote on the subject has had his/her theory of dream-interpretation. By and large, they generally agree that dreams are the brain's method of sorting out or coping with social conflicts; the *how* and the *why* are where one professional disagrees with another. Frightening dreams are associated with post-traumatic distress; some unresolved problem has caused the mind to display symbolically the scene of the trauma over and over again until the problem is dealt with. I will admit here that I myself have had two recurring types of dreams, neither of which is a nightmare *per se* but, because of their repetitive nature, nevertheless represent unresolved conflicts in my life. The first is what I call my "hometown" dreams in which I am walking about in familiar neighborhoods (I seem to walk a lot in my dreams – which is another matter altogether). Yet the scene is not exactly the same as the one I have actually seen; there is usually either a building or other structure missing or another one in place of the real one. No one has been able to explain to me why this type of dream occurs. The second type is my "school" dreams wherein I find myself in a classroom or a hall full of lockers. I've been told that this type represents my dissatisfaction with a current situation and a need/desire to change my environment. None of my dreams, however, have been so compelling as to force me into wakefulness – the mark of post-traumatic stress disorder – until now.

The dream had been so off-the-wall that it left me deeply disturbed. Obviously, I'd had a lot on my mind lately, and my brain had been hard-pressed to deal with it. Nothing traumatic, mind you, just…*weird*. All of the elements of the dream were familiar enough, but their juxtaposition formed another minor mystery. I reckoned that I had better solve the backlog – and soon – or I was going to have similar "night visitors" in the future.

The work-related reason for waking up early (a glance at the clock told me that the alarm was due to go off in a half an hour) was another of the tedious little duties the staff were required to perform. It goes without saying that mentally ill people behave unpredictably. Their medication (if any is administered at all) may wear off, or some incident/person may trigger an adverse response; whatever the reason, all group activities had to be supervised by a professional staff member in case of an emergency. One hoped, of course, there wouldn't be any; but, in this line of work, one had to expect the unexpected. At the Vengtman Home for the Emotionally Disturbed, all monitoring duties were rotated daily in alphabetical order. Since there were several types of monitoring to perform, one found him/herself on one list or another; and, if one were "lucky," (s)he might find him/herself on *two* lists on the same day (after all, there were only six of us). Our ever-cheerful Senior Counselor had charge of making up the lists (in consultation with the Director), and he tried his best not to "double up" anyone – even if it meant having someone switch with another and pull the same duty two days in a row. Schedules were posted the week prior in order to allow the staff to re-arrange their counseling sessions accordingly, and there were penalties for inexcusable absences (though no one ever discussed those in public). The staff was allowed to cut deals with each other on a *quid pro quo* basis.

One of the primary group activities was dining. In addition to the staff room, the Home possessed a larger area (formerly the servants' quarters without separating walls) where the patients took their meals cafeteria-style, unless they were physically unable to do so. This was the only instance where a staff member ate with the patients instead of with his colleagues.

So, I reported to the dining room shortly after sunrise to confer with the head cook about the breakfast menu (a task I'd have to repeat twice more that day). Why the conference? Certain patients could not eat certain foods, because either some foods would react adversely with their medication or they would remind them of the traumatic experiences which led them to their psychoses. Most of this "mother-henning" fell to the gaggle of nurses (male and female) who herded the patients along, but the meal monitor also needed to be alert to any potential flare-ups. It was a standard precaution, but it made the task no less tedious. (On the other hand, it would have been better to be bored stiff than to find oneself in the middle of a food fight by thirty mental cases!) Consequently, some of the offerings (the patients always had several selections from which to choose) were – if you can believe it – color-coded to denote their prohibition to certain patients. I had to make sure the codes were in their proper places.

All meals were prepared from scratch – a rare thing in this age of pre-packaged food. Lowell Vengtman always insisted that part of patient therapy was a wholesome meal, nutritionally balanced, devoid of all the excessive fat, sugar, salt, and artificial additives which characterized late twentieth-century American diets. He had been a casual acquaintance of the late Dr. Linus Pauling (who had died three years previously), the Nobel laureate physicist who, in his later years, had turned to promoting vitamin C as a cure-all for various illnesses. Dr. Pauling's forceful testimony persuaded the Director to reject the packaged "junk food" in favor of fresh food, especially fruits and vegetables. Several medical studies had suggested that fresh food was able to ameliorate *physical* ailments, and Dr. Vengtman reasoned that they ought to work as well on *mental* ailments. A healthy body – and, by extension, a healthy brain – ought to produce a healthy mind. Having grown up poor, I had spent the major part of my life eating, well, *crap*. It wasn't until I began to participate in sports that I came around to learning the value of nutritional diets. Later, at R-PSL, watching a steady parade of overweight people in the emergency room suffering from strokes and coronaries added more fuel to the argument. (I should point out that, in the world of psychiatric medicine, the Vengtman Homes were unique in this approach; whether their patients were responding to this "treatment" had yet to be proved since no empirical data had been published.)

After conferring with the head cook – a rail-thin type with wispy strands of hair slicked over a balding head and a scraggly goatee that looked as if some animal had been grazing it – I served myself (orange juice, oatmeal, and milk) and sat at a table near the dining-room entrance where I had a clear view of the entire area. For some reason, my selection wasn't sufficient to stave off the hunger pangs, and I went back for a refill (to the raised eyes of one of the serving-line personnel). I no sooner had returned to my table when the "first shift" shuffled through the door.

All meals were served in two forty-five-minute periods. In the first place, the schedule lessened the strain on the kitchen staff; having to serve fifteen people, getting a breather, then serving the remainder was much easier than dealing with all thirty at once. In the second place, it also lessened the strain on the nursing staff (and the monitor!), one half of whom ate while the other half watched their charges. Only the meal monitor had to sit through both periods. And, in the third place, it lessened tensions between patients. Sociologists had begun to take the view that overcrowding contributed a great deal to the stress and strain of urban life, that a less-dense population mix will reduce aggravation, hostility, and violent reactions. My own childhood could have served as a text-book case. Thus, the patients at the Home did not have to knock elbows with each other any more than they absolutely had to. Neither did they have to look at the same faces, day after day, for, like everything else here, they too were "rotated." In their case, however, they drew lots – a white marble for the first meal period, a black one for the second period – prior to breakfast each day.

Obviously, these random combinations had their drawbacks – to wit, once in a while, you'd have two patients in close proximity who didn't particularly care for each other. In these cases, the meal monitor had to step in and act as "referee," re-arranging the seating so that the potential antagonists were greatly separated from each other. Thankfully, my very first meal period passed with no major incidents. There was one minor one, though; old Matt, my "invisible man," became upset when he thought too many people were staring at him and he decided to become "invisible" again by taking off his clothes. Clement, the Senior Nurse, talked him out of his rash decision by offering to stand between him and everybody else and blocking their view. That seemed to satisfy him.

Melissa slinked in toward the end of the "second shift." I say "slinked" deliberately, because she behaved as if she had no business being there and wished to grab a bite to eat as unobtrusively as possible. When she came through the door, she halted and scanned the room carefully. Our eyes met briefly at which time she gave me a shy smile and hurriedly looked away. Having scrutinized the population, she eased over to the serving line, ramrod stiff and eyes straight ahead. I observed that, when others in the room – patients and nurses alike – spotted her, they stopped whatever they were doing and watched her as warily as a bird does a cat. The sudden silence was thick enough to cut with a knife, and one could imagine that something dramatic was about to happen. Melissa paid no attention to anyone else, however, but took a glass of milk and an apple, found a table in the corner (opposite my own position as it happened), and sat on the chair cross-legged.

While she ate – nibbled actually – she stared out the window at the lawn that stretched toward the woods. Was she, I wondered, thinking about her furry friends? Were *they* waiting for her to put in an appearance? I was almost tempted to go to the window and see if they were gathering nearby, and I had to literally shake that notion out of my head. At the end of the meal period, she waited until the other patients had exited, then darted out herself, her "breakfast" only half consumed.

Inasmuch as I would like to have followed her and find out what she did with her time, I had my own patients to tend to. We professional staff were allowed wide latitude in the treatment process – as long as we produced results – and we had much discretion in scheduling therapy sessions, administering of drugs, visitation privileges, participation in recreational activities, and so on. There was one hard and fast rule, however: we had to see our patients at least three times a week; more visits were optional. As far as I was concerned, three times a week was a luxury. After seeing a dozen (or more) persons every day at R-PSL, often for no longer than half an hour at a time, I had barely gotten to know any of them on even a *last*-name basis. Now that I had all sorts of time on my hands (relatively speaking) and a light caseload, I decided to schedule *daily* sessions for my patients, two in the morning and three in the afternoon, in random order so that none of them could anticipate me and rehearse their remarks. From one sheet of my ubiquitous notepad, I created five slips of paper and wrote one name on each slip. I turned the slips over, shuffled them around, and selected one. By this very unscientific method, my first "port of call" was Georgina, the haunted mother.

Before I looked in on her, I had to grease the wheels of bureaucracy. Bureaucracy has been around for as long as humans have been organized into societies; and the more complex the society, the greater (and more intricate) the bureaucracy. It has ever been a necessary evil and has flourished especially well in this so-called "Age of Information" since its chief function is to pass pieces of paper from one place to another. Even with computerization, bureaucracy exists, simply by adapting to the new technology. At the Home, we all had to pay our tribute to the Great God of Paper-shuffling. Specifically, when the staff was called upon to monitor any group activity, they were required to file a report, listing who was present and what activity was involved and noting (in detail) any unusual incidents (if any) and the responses to them. I duly made my entries on the form provided as tersely as I could. I had no idea what would become of this report or what purpose it served; only the Director (and God!) knew for sure. But, orders was orders (as the sergeant says), and I reported to Mrs. Oliphant with all deliberate speed. She accepted the form as if it were the latest version of some tabloid, tossed it into her "In" basket, and thanked me sweetly. On the way out, I encountered Dante Fingherelli entering.

"Good morning, Ken," he greeted me cheerfully. "How are yez today?"

"As well as anyone who pulls meal-monitor duty. Happily, everything went smoothly. How are you, Dante?"

"Ah, well, dat depends on *you*."

"Excuse me?"

"I mean, have yez been…initiated yet?"

I eyed him suspiciously. He had an almost child-like expectant look on his face.

"No one will tell me what this 'initiation' is all about, so I can't tell you if I've been initiated or not. Why do you want to know?"

Now he looked sheepish, and he tugged nervously on his bowtie.

"Well, yez know we've formed a pool around da event. We each contribute fifty dollahs and pick da night we t'ink it will happen. I picked last night."

I glared at him then. I hadn't thought much of the idea when I first heard about it, and I still didn't. Some mysterious ritual performed by persons unknown on an unspecified date upon an involuntary subject – and my new colleagues, whom I had known for all of two days, were taking bets on it. What gall! I felt like telling one and all just exactly what I thought about the business. As far as I knew, they were playing one big joke on me (I saw Harry Rauschenburg's fingerprints all over this one).

"You lose, Jack," I growled. "Excuse me. I got business to take care of."

And I stalked off.

I still did not go directly to Georgina's room. Not in the mood I was in at that moment. One does not provide the best therapy when one is in need of it himself. "Physician, heal thyself" still holds true. I would have been in danger of transferring my own innermost feelings to my patients and thus compounding their psychoses. So, I walked around the grounds to let off steam.

I have already mentioned the lilac bushes lining the driveway. Now, I'll mention the flower beds that line the fence adjacent to the highway. While the lilacs had been part of the original estate, the flower beds had been installed at the direction of Lowell Vengtman, who had had the novel idea (one of many, I was beginning to realize) that brightly-colored flora soothed the savage breast just as surely as music (and there was that as well). To this end, he had had planted extensive plots of various species, covering an area about five hundred square yards; the place looked like a smaller version of the Morton Arboretum – azaleas, carnations, lilies, chrysanthemums, roses, violets (Illinois' state flower!), peonies, rhododendrons, tulips, sunflowers, and many others which I didn't readily recognize – all in a variety of colors. The Director had a gardener in three times a week to maintain the plots. That day was his first visit of the week, and I observed him for a few minutes, pruning, weeding, and aerating the soil in the plot given over to the roses. A portly, graying black man, he seemed quite at home there, sweating and fussing over his charges. He spied me watching him, flashed a huge, toothy grin, and returned to his labors. The combination of seeing so much glorious color in one spot and the gardener's obvious pleasure in his work served to lift my own spirits. I felt…refreshed, restored, and rejuvenated.

Georgina was crocheting when I looked in on her. She had crocheted before coming to the Home – had, in fact, been doing so since childhood – and Mathias Hinkelman had encouraged her to continue the hobby. Whatever she had created before her decline into mental illness may or may not have been great works of art, but they certainly weren't now by any stretch of the imagination. Her disordered mind, while combating both the residual effects of her cocaine habit (plus the drugs given to her here) and the delusion of hearing the voice of her dead child, had produced variations of the same repetitive theme. Instead of crocheting sweaters or shawls or antimacassars or other useful pieces, she devoted her talent and energy to churning out, factory-style, a string of samplers; some were monochromatic, others were multi-colored, but all were of equal dimension and contained without deviation the same number of strands of material. And all were monogrammed with the letter "L" (for Lewis, her son's name). The "L" might be large or small, block or script, color-complementary, or clashing with the background, but it represented the only distinguishing mark to an otherwise nondescript piece of cloth. The sampler on which she was currently working was typical: an indigo background with a violet scrolled "L." Hinkelman had hoped (according to his notes) to direct Georgina toward more constructive forms; with his demise, she had reverted to primitivism. It was up to me to lead her back out.

She greeted me perfunctorily and continued to crochet. Occasionally, she would nod her head and murmur something inaudibly. I presumed she was having another "conversation" with Lewis. I sat down and waited her out. Without warning, she slapped herself hard across one cheek, then the other. I tensed, ready to jump in and prevent her from doing serious harm to herself, but allowed her to play out her little drama. If I were going to have any effect on this woman, I needed to know more about what had gone on between her and Hinkelman; treatment, whether I approved of it or not, began and ended with that relationship, and I could not hope to succeed by walking an unknown path. I picked up one of her samplers at random, a maroon-and-black one with a curly cued "L."

"This is quite remarkable, Georgina. How long did it take you to complete it?"

She set aside the sampler she'd been working on. Sighing heavily, she peered at the one in my hand.

"A couple of days, I think," she replied in a small voice. "I don't remember."

"I see you prefer the same motif – or variations of it. Have you tried any others?"

"No. Lewis likes this one. I have to make him happy. I'm his mother, you know."

"Uh-huh. Have you ever done anything else?"

"Oh, yes. I did some marvelous things when I was in high school. I even" – she actually blushed at this point – "won an award for one of my antimacassars."

"That's wonderful! I'd like to see it."

"Sorry, Doctor. I gave it to my mother for her birthday."

"Oh. Well, do you think you could make another one for me?"

She fell silent for a long moment. Then:

"Lewis is suspicious of you, Dr. Maxwell. He wants to know where Dr. Hinkelman is."

I had planned on leading the conversation in this direction. To gain information on Hinkelman's methodology, I had to question not only his colleagues but also his patients. It had occurred to me that the latter might prove to be a better source since they had been witness to his approach on a daily basis. I just had to press the right buttons. Inadvertently, Georgina had given me an opening.

"Do *you* know where Dr. Hinkelman is?"

A long pause. Then, in a whisper:

"Yes."

"But Lewis doesn't know."

"No. I haven't told him yet. He's too young to understand such things."

"Really? Or do you think *you'd* be upset if he knew?"

"I don't know what you mean."

"Tell me, Georgina, what was Dr. Hinkelman like?"

Another pause. She picked up the sampler she'd set aside and traced the "L" with a finger.

"He reminded me of Lewis," she said at last. "Shy. Quiet. He always" -- She bolted upright and covered her face with her hands. "Oh, God! Is that why he went away? Because he was – was like Lewis?"

"What do you think?"

"I remember now, six weeks before he went away, when he and I were talking about me leaving the Home because – because Lewis wasn't talking to me anymore. Then something happened – he never said what, but I heard it had something to do with another resident – and he started to believe *he* was Lewis. It was all very confusing."

Alarm bells started going off in my head. The files I'd scoured all pointed to the same glaring fact: Mathias Hinkelman had begun to go mad *six weeks* before he'd killed himself. I could have pinpointed the exact day just by comparing notes in each dossier. And now, Georgina had corroborated that fact – in her own distorted way – adding another tantalizing piece to the puzzle.

"This…other resident – were any names mentioned?"

"I don't remember. I – Hush, dear. I'm talking to Dr. Maxwell." To me: "Lewis thinks I'm talking too much again. He wants you to leave now."

Rule #3 of psychotherapy: never push the patient beyond what he can reasonably handle. And rule #4: encourage him to walk there on his own.

"Very well, Georgina. But, I'll be back tomorrow. I want to know more about what you and Dr. Hinkelman talked about."

This new piece to the growing puzzle struck me as being a complete mystery in itself. Some unknown person had been interfering with Hinkelman's work. Who? Patient or staff? And how did he – or she – interfere? More ominously: had this interference been a factor in Hinkelman's going over the edge? Admittedly, we professionals are not immune to mental illness just because we are professionals; it sometimes happens – and Hinkelman was very much a case in point – that a doctor will succumb to the stress and strain of the job. (I imagine it might have happened to me if I had remained at R-PSL much longer.) Yet, of all people, we ought to recognize the warning signs when they appear. Why hadn't Hinkelman sought out counseling when he realized what was happening to him. He had realized it too; his notations in the files clearly demonstrated that fact. Had the causative factor been so overwhelming that he was helpless to fight it? I suppressed a shudder. Who could have done such a thing? And why? Did I really want to know?

Next on my schedule was Fred the lycanthrope, but he was in a surly mood and refused to speak to me. After repeated attempts to pry him out of his shell, all I could get from him was a series of deep, guttural growls. Eventually, I gave up and left, giving Nurse Clement instructions to keep a sharp eye on him for the rest of the day.

With better than an hour to kill before I had to report to the dining room again, I decided to check out the Home's medical-reference library. Instead of a cavernous room lined with row upon row of dusty old books and bound newspapers and magazines, reading tables and study nooks, and the ubiquitous librarian's station, this library was entirely computerized, a room next to, and approximately the same size as, the medical-records room. It consisted of six small rectangular tables – three on each of the side walls – on which VGA monitors, key boards, and printers sat. Each of the staff had his/her own station which (logically enough) corresponded to the number on our cottages.

The monitors were plugged into the mainframe down in the basement. With it, one could call up a wealth of information – full texts of papers and addresses read before the annual meetings of the American Psychological Association and the American Medical Association, articles and essays from their respective *Journals*, newspaper and (general) magazine articles, book reviews, and whatever else the staff thought should be included – from one database or another (depending on the nature of the material), all entered on a daily basis by Nurse Petrie (when she was not jealously guarding her precious records). The databases went back twenty years (by no sheer co-incidence the length of time the Vengtman Homes had been in existence), and the interested person could browse for a month and still scan but a fraction of the library's contents. For anyone who wished to conduct a bit of research or to keep abreast of the latest thinking in the field, the contents rivaled any of those maintained by a major university. Lowell Vengtman made sure his people were well-informed.

When I entered the room, I observed only one other person there: Madeleine Chantrier. As she seemed to be quite absorbed in her work, I did not disturb her – professional courtesy and all that – but went straight to my own station and sat down on a plush ergonomic chair each table possessed. I switched on, and the unit immediately asked for a password. It may seem strange that security measures were required in a reference library (no state secrets here!); the rationale, I had been told during my orientation, was to prevent unauthorized persons from accessing and misusing the databases. I had been hard-pressed to understand how anyone could "misuse" material (s)he could obtain simply by subscribing to various periodicals; but, as I have said, I was low man on the totem pole, and I had to play the game by the established rules. That did not prevent me, however, from having a little fun with the computer. The password I had chosen was "Emperor Jones," a private joke.

Upon gaining access, I called up the main menu. I had four options: recall specific author, recall specific subject, recall all cross-references to a file, and print. The sub-menu for the first three options listed eight categories of material; following each heading was a brief description of the subjects covered in the category – a handy thing for those (like me) who were new to the system and wanted to know what was where. I didn't need a "map" at this time. I was looking for anything published by Mathias Hinkelman; if he had been published, his writings might give me a clue to his thinking. Thus, I went straight to option #1 and typed in Hinkelman's name where indicated. A fifteen-second delay followed while the computer searched for the requested material. Presently, the information began to scroll across the monitor's screen.

Whatever else the man may have been, he had not been a prolific essayist. He was, on the other hand, a prolific book reviewer; I counted more than two dozen different entries in that category. In addition, there were two addresses he had delivered before the APA, the first a year before his death, the second two months before. Now I went through the laborious task of calling up the material and requesting hard copies; I even asked for the book reviews because it had been my experience that no reviewer ever passed up a chance to inject his personal opinions into his critiques. By the time I had finished, I had a small stack of paper in front of me.

I also had Dr. Chantrier at my side, her mouth pursed in wonder. I looked up at her and flashed my best smile.

"Good morning, Maddie. How are you?"

"*Bon jour*, Ken," she trilled in her marvelous accent. "I am well, zank you. I see you are not wasting any time in using ze library."

"Nope. Got to do my homework, or the teacher'll make me stay after school."

She laughed, throatily and unrestrainedly, reminding me of a young girl at play. In that instant, I idly wondered what it would be like to make love to an older woman. I had always had this preconception of the accessibility of French women; and, it was rumored, the older and thus the more experienced one of them was, the better the sex. I hadn't any real hope of testing that theory, but I certainly couldn't discount the possibility out of hand. She wasn't wearing any wedding bands; so, either she was divorced or she had never been married. On the other hand, that did not necessarily have anything to do with her sex life.

"And what sort of ''omework' are you doing?"

"I've got Mathias Hinkelman's old caseload. I'm looking for some clues about his methodology to see if I can adapt it to my own."

At the mention of Hinkelman's name, the smile on her face and in her eyes vanished, and she blanched. Muttering something in French, she crossed herself a couple of times.

"My pardon, Ken," she murmured upon seeing the look of consternation on my face. "Mat'ias' deas is still disturbing to me, even now. It was a tragic loss."

"Did you know him well?"

Now she smiled sadly.

"We were lovairs for a time before he… I 'ave bose fond and bittair memories."

"I'm sorry. I didn't mean to pry."

"It is all in ze past now. When you have time, I will discuss it wis you more fully."

With that, she was gone, leaving me with several dozen additional questions bouncing around in my head, not the least of which was the exact nature of Hinkelman's sexual orientation. What would Sherlock Holmes have made of this new information? Would he have thrown up his hands in frustration and have no more to do with the case? Or would he have pursued doggedly until he had the answers? Maybe the Great Detective had had the luxury of picking and choosing his cases, but I didn't. I had gotten in too far to back off now; I had to see my "case" through to the bitter end.

The conversation with Maddie had put me off my schedule, and I had to hotfoot it to the dining room in order to confer with the head cook. He didn't take too kindly to my throwing him off *his* schedule and let me know about it by being especially curt. My profuse apologies had little mollifying effect. If I hadn't been at fault, I might have been tempted to dunk his head in the soup vat and let him suck up the noodles in the chicken-noodle soup through his nose! We concluded our business in rapid order after which I grabbed a tossed salad and a bowl of soup and took my place near the entrance. And just in time too – the first "shift" was beginning to pile in.

Old Matt caught my eye and waved cheerfully. I returned his greeting. I hoped there would be no repeat of the commotion he had caused at breakfast, and I noticed that Nurse Clement was keeping watch on him too. When the Senior Nurse spotted me watching him, he just smirked. I grimaced with annoyance. Just what in the hell was that all about? In a sudden flash of inspiration, it occurred to me that perhaps some (or all) of the non-professional staff were cognizant of my forthcoming "initiation" and that they had a lottery of their own. Was the upcoming night Clement's pick, and was he anticipating a big pay-off? As eager as I was to discover what was in my future, I hoped he was a big *loser.*

As I poked at my salad and soup, I scanned the Hinkelman material, in chronological order so that I might discover a pattern of evolution in his thinking. Only rarely do people change their minds on any subject once they have settled on a position; the counter-argument must be so overwhelming as to cause a reversal. The common course is to accumulate new "evidence" in order to justify old ideas and to dismiss whatever does not fit into the mold. I myself had changed my mind about a subject only once, and that in the face of tremendous social conditioning. Having grown up in an atmosphere of violence and despair where human life was regarded cheaply, I had accepted the prevailing view on capital punishment ("fry 'em all!"). After entering medical school, however, and seeing the problem from the other side, I began to have my doubts and to really study the issue in a more rational frame of mind. And, now, I hold that the death penalty does not do what its advocates claim it does, that the causes of violent crime are rooted deep inside our psyches – individual and collective – and that only a massive campaign of re-education and a battery of social services will render capital punishment obsolete.

Even in the medical/psychological professions, one will find the mossbacks, those who insist on doing things "by the book," i.e. the way things have always been done, and consider innovation as if it were the plague. For innovation to be accepted, it must be immensely successful. That was why Lowell Vengtman was a giant amongst his peers; he had pioneered, and he had succeeded. No one could speak against him. And, since his employees shared the Great Man's notoriety and had his imprimatur, they were also in a "state of grace" and were allowed to pursue their own innovative ideas. No one could speak against us – unless we failed to prove ourselves. Then we were out on our ears!

Mathias Hinkelman had been experimenting with psychotherapeutic techniques. He too had worked in a clinic before joining the Home, except he seemed to have stumbled into the treatment of drug-oriented psychosis quite by accident. It may have been that his unfamiliarity with the territory had induced him to try untested methods. His first published work was a scathing review of a book by – of all people! – Lowell Vengtman on the history of isotropic drugs. The review was, on the surface, a real hatchet job (I thought), full of nitpicking and personal interpretations of facts and rhetorical questions concerning the author's sources; such a poison piece might have been written by a first-year med student who was envious of his betters. The question which bugged me was why Dr. Vengtman had hired this fellow to work for him. I had no doubt that the Great Man knew of the review and should have had nothing to do with its writer. Apparently, he had read between the lines and seen some promise (as I suppose he had in me). Perhaps I was missing something because of my professional regard for the Director. I made a mental note to reserve judgment until I had read the entire body of work.

I was about to move on to the next piece (also a book review) when I became aware of someone standing nearby. I looked up and peered into a pair of amethyst eyes. Hastily, I glanced around and discovered that the second "shift" was entering the dining room. I had been so absorbed in that first book review that I had lost all track of time. And my soup was now tepid!

Without any invitation on my part, Melissa sat down opposite me and fixed me with an intense stare, oblivious to the attention she was drawing from the other people in the room. The mesmerizing effect of her eyes took hold of me again, and I wondered what visions would rush into my mind this time. Subconsciously, I tried to resist but could not. All around, staff and patients alike registered expressions of concern or bemusement or disgust or outright fear. One of the female nurses, a heavy-set person who resembled Cher Bono on steroids, rumbled toward us, determination writ all over her face. I waved her off without really looking at her – I couldn't tear myself away from those awesome amethyst eyes! – and in such a manner that provoked an indignant reaction. The nurse halted, took two more hesitant steps, and halted again. She huffed and backtracked to her original position.

Thankfully, Melissa broke off eye contact when the dining room door opened and admitted a couple of stragglers. Quickly, I focused on my salad in order to recoup my mental equilibrium. Relief lasted only a few seconds. The girl riveted her attention on me again.

"Dr. Maxwell," she said in a low, conspiratorial voice, "I have to speak with you, but I haven't much time."

"All right. But, first tell me how you came by my name. We hadn't been introduced. Did someone on the staff tell you?"

Her face became even more pixie-ish, and her amethyst eyes gleamed mischievously. I had the distinct impression she was enjoying a little joke at my expense.

"In a manner of speaking, yes. A robin overheard one of the nurses mentioning your name, and it told me."

"A...*robin?*"

She was yanking my chain, of course! Even if she loved animals and surrounded herself with them – even if she had some talent in training them *en masse* – she was no female Dr. Doolittle. Humans do "talk" to animals, but it's not the *speech* that the latter understand; rather, it's the *sounds* associated with physical gestures and/or facial expressions that they learn. Anyone who has read Pavlov and Skinner knows this.

Melissa reacted to my obvious skepticism in a manner suggesting she was dealing with a simpleton. Instantly, there came into my mind an image of galaxies and nebulas and globular clusters and clouds of gas and dust. All were spinning and whirling and colliding in kaleidoscopic fashion. Two elliptical galaxies, mutually attracted by gravity, pirouetted about each other and merged – great gouts of energy flared up where matter touched matter and both tore apart – forming a large spiral galaxy. The image faded away as quickly as it had come, and I found myself perspiring heavily. My napkin was a soggy mess after I had wiped my face.

"I have a...gift," said Melissa, ignoring my distress, "that lets me talk to animals. I don't expect you to believe me, but right now, I don't care." She chewed her lip a second and glanced again at the door. Her voice became a whisper. "I've come to warn you."

"Warn me? About what?"

"About Dr. Vengtman. He's –"

She broke off her sentence and stared apprehensively at the open door. Her face was now ashen. I pivoted in my chair and spotted the Director standing there. He seemed uncharacteristically grim and elicited from the staff and the patients the same range of emotional responses that Melissa had only moments before.

"Melissa, dear," he muttered. "So, this is where you've gotten to. Good afternoon, Dr. Maxwell."

"Good afternoon, sir. Uh, won't you join us?"

"Thank you, no. It's time for this young lady's counseling session."

Melissa said nothing but stared resolutely at the table.

"Come along, my dear, and leave Dr. Maxwell to his lunch – and his duties."

Was it my imagination, or had he put a slight emphasis on the words "his duties" as an implication that I was not attending to them by conversing with Melissa? Dr. Vengtman appeared to be piqued for some reason; perhaps he was having a bad hair day. It happens to the best of us.

In any event, the girl stood up and moved away from the table without a word. Before exiting, however, she tossed me a soulful, pleading look that nearly stopped my heart – both figuratively and literally. My breath caught in my throat and, in one wild moment, I was gripped by a desire to prevent the Director from taking her to God-knew-where. I restrained myself on the grounds of professionalism and of simple face-saving. I was not prepared just yet to throw away my career because of the imaginings of a patient.

Dr. Vengtman turned to follow Melissa out. I made a quick decision to stop him – not to prevent some "tragedy" but to satisfy my burgeoning curiosity.

"Excuse me, sir."

He turned back. His face was as rigid as a rock.

"Yes?"

His voice was as somber as a tomb, and I momentarily had doubts about being so direct.

"I don't believe Melissa was mentioned at yesterday's staff meeting. Who is counseling her?"

He eyed me sternly. Suddenly, I felt like the schoolboy who has just been caught smoking in the bathroom; and, for a hot minute, I thought he was going to give me a tongue-lashing then and there. Out of the corner of my eye, I observed that all attention had riveted upon us, that the whole room was tensed for – what? Had they seen Lowell Vengtman in a dark mood before, and had they seen him reprimand someone in public? The act did not jibe with the Lowell Vengtman I knew – or the one I thought I knew – but perhaps these people in their odd way knew him better than I. I braced myself for the storm-to-come. Thankfully, it did not come.

"I would have told you eventually, Dr. Maxwell," he said at last in a completely emotionless tone, "since you are now a member of the staff here. But, since you insist on knowing now, I will tell you now. Melissa is a special case at the Home – her…problem is not open to discussion – and therefore she is not subject to the normal routine. She's under my special care, and that is all you need to know. I must ask for your co-operation in this matter."

"Yes, sir. I'll be discreet."

"Thank you, Doctor. Enjoy your lunch."

And that was that. I intended to be discreet all right, though not in the manner as the Director had hoped for. My curiosity, far from being satisfied, had just risen a couple of notches, and I was determined to find out all I could about Melissa Waterman, past and present. That included getting her medical records at my earliest opportunity which, in turn, meant inventing an excuse for the redoubtable Nurse Petrie in order to allay any suspicions her paranoid mind might harbor. She viewed everyone as an intruder upon her domain, and only a dire need was one's sole excuse for entering it.

The remainder of the lunch period passed without further incident, and I headed for the grounds. I had an hour to kill before my afternoon rounds, and I wanted to read the rest of Hinkelman's writings in relative peace. Somewhere in my past, I picked up the bad habit of reading on the fly; perhaps I had done so at R-PSL where reading on the fly was a necessity. In any event, I had my mind on Hinkelman and not on my surroundings. Consequently, I ran into Nan – literally. Ordinarily, I would not have minded a slow-motion collision with a prime sample of feminine pulchritude; and I would've used the opportunity to be extremely "clumsy" and do a bit of surreptitious groping. Since my mind *was* elsewhere, all I could do was mumble some sort of apology like an idiot. She regarded me with no small amount of amusement which made me feel even more foolish. What a way to start off a relationship!

"Pre-occupation is an occupational hazard, Ken, but I wouldn't have thought you'd been here long enough to acquire it. An old habit, hmm?"

"I'm afraid so, Nan. But this time, it's because of the extraordinary experience I've just had."

I then related in detail everything that had occurred between Melissa and me and tried to describe the psychological atmosphere which had surrounded the encounter. Nan scrutinized me with ill-disguised skepticism (not that I could have blamed her – I might have reacted the same way if our positions had been reversed); and, while her scrutiny was not as intense as Melissa's, I still felt like a specimen under glass.

"And you believed her?" was her only comment when I had finished.

"Of course not. But you have to admit that it was a weird experience. She seemed sincere, and she exhibited genuine fear."

"Obviously, paranoia is part of her psychosis."

"For sure."

There followed an awkward silence. I wanted to pursue another matter, and I didn't know how to lead into it.

"Is there something else on your mind, Ken?" she supplied the lead-in.

"Uh, yeah. It's about my 'initiation.'"

"Has it happened yet?"

Did she seem anxious about it? I hoped so.

"I can't say, because I still don't know what's supposed to happen. But, look, you said you wouldn't go out with me until it did. What if it never happens? Where does that leave us?"

"Dangling in the wind, I suppose. Don't worry, though. It *will* happen. I can practically guarantee it."

"How long did you have to wait before it happened?"

She stared off in the distance, and her brow furled as if in deep thought. Then:

"Not long – a couple of days, I think."

"Was it a pleasant experience? Or painful?"

"It was…interesting. I can't say anymore about it though; it'll spoil your surprise. Look, I have an appointment now. We'll talk later. Oh, and thanks for telling me about your habitual daze. I'll recognize the symptoms in the future and take precautions."

I retreated to the "arboretum" and sat down on an upside-down bucket the elderly gardener had left behind. He was nowhere to be seen, and I assumed he was elsewhere on the grounds. The bucket was as uncomfortable a seat as they came, but at least, I was alone to do some serious thinking.

Hinkelman's initial book review had been followed by four others – all equally as vitriolic – before he wrote his first monograph. All of the reviews had been published in the *Journal of the American Psychological Association*; someone on the editorial staff apparently thought his hatchet jobs were so worthwhile that he was allowed to vent his spleen as often as he wanted. Not alone did Lowell Vengtman feel Hinkelman's ire, but several other distinguished individuals (including one of my old professors) had had their books savaged. One in particular, Dr. Emil Razumov's curious work,

Radiopsychology: The New Science of the Mind had been ripped apart almost page by page as "fantasy," "unprofessionalism," and "an insult to scientific methodology." I can't say that I had put much credence in the notorious Russian parapsychologist's ideas – his was a strange journey into unknown territory – but no one deserved the treatment Hinkelman had given him. Then and there, I wished I could have met my predecessor, discussed his views with him, and learn just what in the hell was his problem that he felt obliged to bad-mouth his peers (and his betters!) at every turn. If he had thought to be the "conscience" of the profession and goad everyone into improving themselves, he had sure gone about it the wrong way. Hadn't he ever heard of "positive" and "negative" re-enforcement? That is basic behaviorism – works every time!

After reading the string of reviews, I still hadn't a clue as to Hinkelman's personal philosophy, only what he didn't like – which seemed to be everything. My head was beginning to hurt from absorbing so much negativism, so I set the stack of papers aside and contemplated the flowers. As it happened, I had parked myself near the bed of chrysanthemums. The gardener had been rather imaginative in the lay-out; he had created a giant spiral array in which each loop was a different color, as close to the order of the colors of the rainbow as he could get with the available varieties. Clearly, he had spent a good deal of time planning it all out. On a whim, I eased myself off the bucket, strolled over to the outer loop of the spiral, bent over, and sniffed one of the blossoms. Its heady aroma filled my nostrils and my head, and I felt somewhat light-headed. I inhaled deeply a second time.

"Y'all lahk mah babies, son?"

I straightened up and whirled around in surprise. The gardener stood there with a colossal grin on his face. Most of his teeth were yellowed and crooked (and a couple were missing altogether), but they did not detract from his obvious glee at catching someone red-handed in admiring his handiwork. His face was cracked and seamed, and I judged him to be in his sixties. He had a hose coiled about one shoulder and a rake over the other one. I smiled nervously and marveled at how quietly he'd been to get the drop on me.

"Yes, sir. I haven't seen this many flowers in one place for a long time."

He looked me up and down, and I had the distinct impression that he was also looking at me inside and out!

"Humph! Y'all mus' be a Chicago boy fum de looks o' ya. Chicago boys don' see nuffin but dirty streets an' empty lots."

"Well, that depends on what part of Chicago you're talking about."

"Ah'm talkin' 'bout the paht you come fum, son. Ah kin tell by de way y'all hold yo'self." He broke out in another huge grin. "But, don' mahnd me. Ah ain't prejudiced 'ginst Chicago boys. Useta be one mahself. Ah reckon y'all are de new doctor Ah heered about."

"Yes, sir. Maxwell – Kenneth Maxwell."

I stuck out my hand. He took it in a large, sweaty one and shook it vigorously. There was immense strength in his grip, and I imagined he had seen his share of the hard life.

"Doctor Maxwell, eh? A big step up fo' ya. Ah reckon y'all deserve it too. Ah'm Benjamin Cutter. Jus' call me 'Ben.' An' drop dat 'sir' shit. Ah ain't bin a 'sir' in mah lahf, an' Ah don' intend to be one now."

"All right – Ben. How long have you been a gardener?"

"All mah lahf, it seems. Useta work in de steel mills 'fore dey went belly up. Done odd jobs after dat. Still doin' 'em, really. 'Cept yo' Dr. Vengtman pays me more'n Ah'd git fer de same work some'ers else. He wanted flowers – an' lots of 'em – an' he was willin' to pay me extra fer tendin' to de details."

"That sounds like the Director, all right. And from the looks of things, I'd say he got his money's worth."

"Ah'll take dat as a compliment."

"I meant it as one. But, tell me, Ben, don't you have any problems with animals digging up the flower beds? Being so close to the woods, I mean."

"Son, lemme tell ya, Ah had all *so'ts* o' troubles – de birds and de squirrels 'specially. Always comin' 'round and eatin' mah seeds an' bulbs. Mah pore babies looked awful, an' Ah lahk to quit de job more'n oncet."

"What changed your mind?"

"Now, dat's de damnedest thing. Ah wuz complainin' to dat whaht girl what's always hangin' 'round, an' –"

"Excuse me. 'White girl'?" He described Melissa Waterman to a "T." "Melissa's a patient here."

"*No shit?*" the old man exclaimed, his eyes bugging out in surprise. "Coulda fooled me. She *'pears* lahk she got all her mahbles. Well, anyways, Ah complained to her 'bout de damage to mah pore babies, an' she sez she'll take care of it. Ah thought she wuz jus' funnin' an old man and' di'n't pay no nevermahnd." His eyes narrowed in deep thought. "'Cept, de very nex' day – wouldja believe? – Ah di'n't see no mo' animals in de yahd at all. Dat whaht girl wuz as good as her word. If she did have anyfing to do wif it, dat is."

Under the circumstances, I might have dismissed this tale as the fanciful ramblings of an old man who couldn't recognize co-incidence if it bit him. Yet, after having been at the Home only three days and already witnessing some strange events myself, I was not sure that "co-incidence" was playing a large part here. Something mighty weird was going on, and it had all the marks of willful, deliberate action. Just exactly what that action was, who was behind it, and why it was being done was beyond my comprehension, and I really didn't want to speculate until I had a few facts under my belt. I could have let my imagination run wild, I supposed, but no one would have believed my conclusions unless I had solid proof.

Since I still had my afternoon rounds ahead of me (and the evening meal to monitor), I thanked old Ben for his time and returned to the main building. All the way back, however, I visualized Melissa in the woods with all of her little friends gathered around her, sternly lecturing them about not damaging the flower beds, and the animals agreeing to leave them alone. I shook my head vigorously. That sort of thinking was guaranteed to net me a "reservation" in Dr. Lowell Vengtman's "country resort." I possessed a good-sized imagination (left over from my childhood in Chicago), but I still knew what was real and what was not (or so I thought at the time). Imagining things and pretending they were real was why I and others like me had full-time jobs. It happened because too many people used *too much* imagination!

DAY FIVE:
Thursday, 07.10.1997
DEPRECIATION

The best laid plans of mice and men, etc., etc.

No sooner than I had devised a schedule of rounds which I could easily handle than another of those damnable monitoring duties popped up to throw a monkey wrench into the works.

It being a Thursday, it was Delivery Day. Dr. Vengtman had made arrangements with a medical-supply house in Chicago and an office-supply store in Aurora to deliver all of the Home's non-pharmaceutical needs on Thursday mornings; and he had done the same thing with a pharmaceutical-supply house in Chicago for Thursday afternoons. Yet, because no *specific* time had been contracted for, the duty person was obliged to make him/herself available at an instant's notice. Whatever (s)he was doing, (s)he was expected to come running when Mrs. Oliphant announced the arrival of the delivery trucks over the PA system. Presence of a professional staff person was not absolutely necessary for the morning delivery. This was part of the Senior Nurse's job: to receive all such shipments and to maintain a running inventory. The doctor merely provided "quality control," i.e. making sure all containers had been properly packed and checking for broken seals which might lead to injury and/or contamination. The job was a bore-and-a-half, but the Director insisted upon crossing all the "t's" and dotting all the "i's" when it came to health care.

Attention to detail was definitely absolutely necessary for the afternoon delivery. The non-professional staff was not expected to be responsible for the transfer of drugs and for their quality; only a doctor was, and (s)he had to inspect each and every container and determine that the contents were what they were supposed to be. Any slip-ups in this department could lead to serious injury and/or death, and the Home (and its personnel) could face civil-liability suits and/or criminal-negligence charges. In the end, the reputation of the Home (and its personnel) would be irreparably damaged.

Though this particular duty occurred only once a week, the "new boy" had been lucky enough to pull it his first week on the job. I imagined that my colleagues were quite thrilled when Dr. Vengtman announced his hiring of me; during the interim between the disability of Mathias Hinkelman and my arrival, the duty rosters must have been horrific, one's workload having jumped twenty per cent. They all must have heaved a collective sigh of relief at the prospect of returning to a "normal" routine. It occurred to me, while on my way to breakfast, that piling up of monitoring duty on my shoulders might be the "initiation" at which everyone had hinted. On the other hand, the fact that everyone and his brother was taking bets on its taking place suggested that the "initiation" was a one-time affair rather than any adjustment in the work schedule – unless they were all waiting to see if and when I would collapse from nervous exhaustion! Well, they were out of luck on that score. While monitoring was the pits and I'd rather be listening to punk-rock 24/7, none of it was beyond my training to perform (I'd had plenty of "OJT" at R-PSL), and neither was it physically taxing.

When I entered the staff dining room, I discovered that all but one were already chowing down. The absentee was Nan, the meal monitor for the day. Once I had served myself (ham, eggs, hashed browns, coffee), Harry waved me over. I supposed he wanted to sound me out about his favorite topic, manic-depression. I wasn't looking forward to such a discussion at this time of the day; but, I hadn't really seen much of him since the staff meeting, and I needed to touch base with all of my colleagues at least once during the rest of the week (and with one of them *all* the time!). Warily, I trudged over to his table and sat down opposite him. Frankly, he looked like Death warmed over; his huge jowls appeared to have drooped even more, his skin had a sallow cast to it, and his eyes were very blood-shot.

"Too much hair of the dog last night," he declared when he saw the look of concern on my face. "My German ancestors would disown me if they thought I couldn't hold my liquor." He took a long gulp of coffee. Some of it dribbled down his chins. "What's your favorite drink, Ken?"

"I grew up in a neighborhood where beer was as common as water, but I never cared much for the stuff. I drank it because everyone else did. Lately, though, I've developed a taste for anything with rum in it."

"Rum, eh? Well, we'll have to do the town some night – drink rum until it runs out our ears."

I couldn't say I was looking forward to that event any more than a prolonged discussion about manic-depression. Drinking to excess had been an acceptable behavior in my old neighborhood, but (I am happy to say) I had grown out of my old neighborhood. I didn't mind bending the elbow once in a while, but my new outlook on life required a new set of rules. Be that as it may, I was forming the opinion that Harry might have a drinking problem. Whether he had reached the stage where either he had a psychological dependency on alcohol or he just liked to go on a binge now and then was beside the point; he exhibited all the symptoms of an alcoholic. Still, it wasn't my place to dictate his social habits so long as he showed up for work on time. If, on the other hand, his drinking interfered with his work performance, then it behooved me (or anyone else on the professional staff), both as a humanitarian and as a doctor, to step in and urge him to seek counseling. Quite possibly, he could wind up as a patient in his own workplace; and I, the drug-oriented psychosis specialist, would be expected to cure him!

"Well, maybe. I'm still learning the ropes here. Once I get into the routine, then..."

"Okey-dokey, Ken." He took another slug of coffee, slurping loudly. I averted my eyes in embarrassment. He peered at me over the rim of his cup. "By the by, you didn't get lucky last night, did you?"

"Excuse me?"

"A roll in the hay. A little nookie. A piece of ass."

"I know what you mean, man. What I don't know is why you're asking. It's hardly the thing to be talking about at the breakfast table." *And it wouldn't be any of your damned business in the first place*, I added silently.

"Sorry to be so direct, but you know about our pool. I picked last night."

I glared at him for the longest time, the wheels in my head spinning like crazy. Whether Harry was aware of it or not, he had let slip an important clue concerning the nature of my upcoming "initiation." Apparently, it involved sex; I was supposed to have sex with persons unknown before a "winner" in the staff lottery could be declared. But, sex with anyone or with a particular person? I now recalled my conversation with Nan, who had become quite distant when I asked her if she had been "initiated." Now I understood why – not that it helped me score points with her. Was I expected to go around and ask all the females if they'd like to service me? (I'd soon be out on my ear in no time fast – or in jail – if I ever tried that stunt!) Or was I supposed to take the first one who propositioned me? Damn whoever had thought up that stupid game!

"Sorry, Harry," I replied as evenly as I could. "I'm still a virgin."

"Oh, I doubt that very much. Here, maybe, not in the wider world." He checked his watch. "Ah, well, I've got to oversee the exercise period. See you later, Ken."

For the first of my morning rounds, the "luck of the draw" fell to Ray W. (a.k.a. "Billy the Kid"). I entered cautiously because, according to the medical log kept by the Senior Nurse, Ray had had a violent seizure during the night wherein he banged on the walls, kicked the furniture, and cursed all of the floor nurses in obscene fashion. He had been sedated by the doctor-on-call (Bertie), and that was the end of that. The log did not, and could not, explain *why* Ray had thrown a tantrum (not his first episode, according to his file); that was for his counselor, i.e. me, to determine. I didn't have a clue as to what I might be walking into, and so I instructed the assistant head floor nurse to unlock the door and stand by in case of an emergency. In the back of my mind, I wondered where Clement was; this was supposed to be *his* job, not his assistant's.

I observed Ray huddled up at one end of the bed. A tray sat untouched on the bedside table. He seemed to be sufficiently calm at the moment; otherwise his breakfast might have decorated the walls. Still, there was no guarantee that he would remain calm or that he would attempt to decorate the walls with *me*. He glowered at me out of lazy eyes that reminded me of Robert Mitchum in *Cape Fear* – not exactly a pleasant analogy!

"Howdy, preacher," he drawled. "Come to pay yer respects?"

"Howdy, Ray. Yes, I –"

"Name's '*Billy*,' preacher!" he growled, straightening up so quickly that I thought he might leap off the bed at me. "Ah dunno no 'Ray,'"

"Billy, then," I acceded. "Mind if I sit down?"

He shrugged. I took a seat midway between the bed and the door. If he were to have a recurrence of last night, I wanted at least a two-step head start. Once comfortable, I assumed the half-smile all psychotherapists (and all preachers, for that matter) wear, an affectation denoting both a concern for the patient and an allaying of his suspicions. Although I hated to role-play, I was more or less forced into it, no thanks to Hinkelman, who had been slavish about role-playing. Play along, I decided, and look for a way to exit the part, hopefully taking the patient with you.

"Well, Billy, I heard there was a...ruckus in town last night."

He grinned crookedly.

"Yeah. Some o' the boys got drunk and started sumpin they couldn't finish. Ah got 'em straightened out real quick."

"You personally? Where was the, uh, sheriff?"

"Fuck the sheriff! He's so damn corrupt, he don't want to dirty his hands with the 'riff-raff,' as he calls us. *All* them sumbitches what call themselves 'city fathers' are corrupt. Ain't none of 'em worth a goddam. 'Scuse mah French, preacher, but that's the way it is here."

"I...see. When you say 'city fathers,' just exactly who do you mean?"

"Ever' mother's son who carries a title, that's who. On the take, all of 'em."

At least Ray's internal logic was consistent. As a kid growing up on the streets and being involved in gangs, he had had his share of run-ins with law-enforcement and criminal-justice officials. He could hardly have had a benevolent view of any of them. Here was a classic case of guilt-transference, from oneself in order not to hold oneself in low esteem to a cold, impersonal authority-figure structure which failed to "understand" the individual and which wished to stifle his "freedom of expression" and "freedom of association," thus reducing his sense of worth in the eyes of his peers. Charges of "corruption" and "double-dealing" naturally flowed like water in such a mind-set, and Ray was obeying the dictates of this self-imposed blueprint to the letter.

"An interesting idea, Ra – Billy. You know, I have a title too. Do you think *I'm* corrupt?"

Now, he looked sheepish as if he had realized he might have gone too far in his accusations. He stared at the floor and scratched his head.

"Nah," he murmured. "Ah guess not. You ain't interested in money, are ya?"

"Only that which I earn."

"Thought so." A pause. "T'other preacher, he wuzn't neither."

Oh, really?

As much as I wanted to pursue Ray's antagonism toward authority and his refusal to assume responsibility for his own actions, I wasn't about to waste an opportunity to get another opinion on Mathias Hinkelman. There would be plenty of time for the other matter.

"Uh, Preacher Mathias was one of the few good men in town, then?"

"Yeah. He di'n't like the way the city fathers ran the town any more'n Ah did."

Suddenly, he leaped to his feet. The action took me by surprise momentarily, and I flinched. Recovering quickly, I suppressed my alarm, thereby avoiding triggering another violent episode. Inwardly, however, I calculated my options and measured the distance to the door. As nonchalantly as I could, I slipped my hand into a pocket of my smock and gripped the "panic button." The "panic button" was simply a transmitter which sent a signal to the nurse's station, alerting one and all to an emergency situation. The professional and senior non-professional staff all carried one as a matter of course. Each transmitter operated on a different frequency; when the signal was received, one knew instantly who had sent it. And, because we counselors ordinarily appraised the head floor nurse where we were while on the floor, response time to the alarm was kept to a minimum.

As it happened, Ray did not throw a tantrum but moved stealthily to the door and pressed his ear to it. Satisfied that no one else was listening to our conversation, he padded back to the bed, sat down on the edge, and assumed a posture of confidentiality. I removed my hand from my pocket.

"Kin Ah tell ya sumpin in private, preacher?"

"Speaking as, uh, a man of the cloth, I can assure you that anything you say will be treated in strictest confidence."

"OK. Well, whut Ah I wanna tell ya is" – he looked back at the door – "ya oughta watch yer back around here."

"And why is that?"

"'Cause they killed Preacher Mathias."

There are conspiracy theories, and there are conspiracy theories. Live long enough, and one will hear them all. Who ordered the assassinations of Lincoln and Kennedy and Dr. King? What is the Trilateral Commission's real agenda? Who really kidnapped Lindbergh's baby? Who was behind the Oklahoma City bombing? The list is endless; everyone has had his own pet theory. I had even read a few years back that Napoleon might not have died of natural causes but had been poisoned so that he could not escape captivity a second time and cause more mischief. Dark hints of conspiracy always surround the (often violent) death of some well-known figure; and the fewer the facts concerning the event, the grander the conspiracy is. Particularly where assassination is concerned, human beings prefer the mythos rather than the mundane.

Conspiracy theories, from the viewpoint of psychology, are born out of a sense of powerlessness and/or helplessness in the individual, and rather than admit to a lack of knowledge, one will indulge in a little I-know-something-you-don't in order to puff up the ego. And this is in the so-called "normal" world where otherwise sensible people who get up in the morning, go to work, come home, go to bed, and live their lives routinely from day to day harbor secret (and usually erroneous) ideas about Life's Great Mysteries, never once thinking of investigating the truth for themselves.

During my tenure at R-PSL, where life was far from normal, I had learned to listen to conspiracy theories with only half an ear, dismissing them as part of the drug-oriented psychosis (which they often were) of the patient. I supposed that I would have to listen to more of the same wild ramblings at the Home for precisely the same reasons. In fact, hadn't Georgina spoken in just such terms during my initial visit? And wasn't Melissa about to "warn" me of yet another sinister plot (this one concerning Dr. Vengtman, of all people!)? So, I shouldn't have been too surprised by Ray's startling comment.

And, yet, I was surprised. My breath actually caught in my throat, and my heart actually skipped a beat. Why now and not before? I think it must have had something to do with a bit of conspiracy-theorizing on my part (albeit on a sub-conscious level). I was beginning to think that Mathias Hinkelman was not the suicidal type; his angry book reviews suggested exasperation with things-as-they-are and a desire to re-order the profession rather than despair and a desire to end it all. Besides, the madness that led to his self-destruction had come upon him relatively suddenly. That is not a symptom of the suicidal mind; the impulse requires a long period to incubate and hatch. It is, perhaps, a mistake to use the word "impulse" at all. Like other mental illnesses, the desire to self-destruct is a matter of evolution and accumulation and a growing sense of powerlessness and helplessness that can only be halted by death. In Hinkelman's case, something – or *someone* – had driven him mad almost overnight. What – or who – had been responsible remained a mystery at this point, but it was now too compelling to drop and walk away from. There was always the possibility that I was reading too much into otherwise psychotic babbling, but I suddenly became very interested in what Ray had to say.

"Who are 'they'?"

"The mayor, the sheriff, the town council – all the damned corrupt people."

"How do you know all this?"

He scowled deeply.

"Ya think Ah'm loco too, doncha? Yeah. Preacher Mathias, he di'n't believe me neither at first – until it wuz too late. Ah heard 'em plot aginst 'im. They said they'd fix it so's he had to leave town in disgrace. Well, he left town all right – in a box. Pore bastard. Wuzn't whut they had in mind, but it suited 'em all the same."

"Do they suspect you know about their plot?"

"Mebbe. Ah dunno. Ah'd jus' watch mah step, if Ah wuz you."

He said nothing more after that, despite my efforts to elicit more details. On the surface, everything he had said so far was sheer paranoia, and I would have expected it from one who distrusted and resisted all forms of authority. Yet, the psychotic individual speaks a sort of Truth; he simply cannot express it in real terms. Instead, he resorts to symbolism and metaphor because they are more psychologically comfortable for him. The key then to unlocking the closed doors of his mind and revealing the *real* Truth is understanding the nature of the analogies and translating them into meaningful singularities. Ray suspected – as I was beginning to – that Hinkelman's death was *involuntary* suicide but, in his current state of mind, could not grasp the concept objectively. On the positive side, however, he felt obligated to warn me about some perceived threat to me in connection with the previous event. Which meant he trusted me – not entirely, of course, since I was still the "new boy" in town -- but enough to confide in me. Half of any counselor's job is to win the trust of the patient; it is a sure sign that the patient recognizes the need for, and a desire to seek, help for his illness. I had just taken a very important first step with Ray.

On my way to my other morning appointment, the Dreaded Call came for me. In one respect, I hated the huge imposition that it represented, and I wished there could have been a way around it; in another, I was thankful that it had arrived while I was "in between" patients. Otherwise, it would have been really inconvenient to have had to break off in mid-session! Heaving a great sigh, I headed for Mrs. Oliphant's desk for the necessary key and paperwork.

The "supply room" wasn't actually a room at all. Rather, it was the garage behind the old mansion, which had been converted into a storage area. There was no other place on the grounds in which to stockpile the large amount of supplies – medical and otherwise – required to keep the Home functioning. And there had been much concern for a secure and environmentally safe place for the various pharmaceuticals on the premises; above all else; these needed a system of controls to prevent abuse and/or degradation.

The garage, a three-car building (as befitted the original owner), had been remodeled into four cubicles and the entire front wall, including the slide-up doors, replaced by a solid frontispiece with three separate doorways. The first cubicle contained nothing but office and housekeeping supplies and possessed only a minimal security system, i.e. a padlock. Only the Director, Mrs. Oliphant, Nurse Petrie, and Nurse Clement had keys to open it. The second cubicle held ordinary medical supplies (bandages, splints, blankets, sheets, bedpans, etc.) which were the nuts and bolts of a quasi-hospital setting. This too had minimal security, and only the Director, the Senior Counselor, and Nurse Clement had keys to the lock. The third and fourth cubicles (which shared a door) harbored the pharmaceuticals; the former was refrigerated while the latter was not. Here, the outer door was secured by two differently configured dead-bolt locks, and each cubicle was similarly bolted. The Director had a key for one configuration, and Nurse Clement had one for the other; none of the doors could be unlocked without both individuals (or their assigns) being present. I, of course, was the Director's "assign" for that day, and I had to sign out his key at the office. This arrangement would not deter your average urban thug looking for drugs to ingest and/or sell, and so there was also a silent alarm linked to the county sheriff's office. Proper unlocking of the dead-bolts prevented the alarm from going off, and *improper* "unlocking" summoned a squad car immediately!

When I arrived at the "supply room," I saw (besides the delivery-van driver) a small-framed black female nurse in her late twenties whom I recognized as the first-floor head nurse. She wore her hair pulled back in a bun and had applied a great deal of rouge to her face. In another setting, she might have been considered attractive; here, she looked as out of place as a hooker. She watched me approach with all the enthusiasm of a rape victim toward her attacker. Personally, I didn't care just then about her mental state; I simply wanted to get this boring business over with so that I could go back to the *real* work at hand. Also, I was annoyed by the fact that Clement, whose job it was to be here, was not present but had shoved the responsibility onto this nervous Nellie.

"Good morning, Nurse" – I quickly glanced at her name tag – "Michaels," I said starchily.

"Good morning, Doctor," she replied just as stiffly.

We were going to get on famously!

"Where's Clement?"

"I don't know. He called my station earlier and asked me to cover for him. One of the other nurses even delivered his key to me."

"Huh! So, he's Mr. Bad-ass today."

"If you say so, Doctor."

"Well, let's get this over with."

Since this delivery van was the non-pharmaceutical-medical supply one from Chicago, we unlocked door number two. While we were doing so, two blue jays that had been perched on the roof began squawking – in protest, I had to assume, of our disturbing them. I paid them no attention and turned to the van driver. The fellow couldn't have been more than eighteen at the most. He had dark hair and a swarthy, pock-marked complexion. He walked with a stoop that suggested he might have practiced it all of his life. Dull, listless, gray-green eyes hovered over a perpetual frown. His idea of oral hygiene was apparently limited to a toothpick; his teeth were yellowed beyond belief, and I smelled garlic on his breath. Where, I wondered idly, had his employer dug him up? And why? I had thought I had left his sort behind in Chicago; but, in this "age of the global economy," where one had to scramble just to survive, I reckoned that his type was everywhere. He was, paradoxically, neatly dressed in a company shirt and slacks – and an expensive pair of Nikes! Go figure!

I accepted the invoice from him and looked it over. Heavy on the first-aid items – nothing unusual there since they were always in great demand. One item on the computerized form fairly jumped out at me: a gross of specimen bottles. The Home did not have a pathology lab – we usually relied on local hospitals – but weekly urine samples for drug-screening were still taken. As the driver hauled out cartons from the van, Nurse Michaels opened them and called out their contents to me. I repeated everything she said and checked it off the invoice. After I had signed for the delivery as being correct, the driver gave me a copy, jumped back into his vehicle, and roared away in a tire-squealing hurry.

That was the easy part. Now Michaels and I had to put all the stuff in their proper places. All the while, I noted that she was eyeing me as covertly as she could and biting her lip. Obviously, she was not comfortable here, but whether it was the last-minute task or me – or both – I couldn't say. I tried to ignore her nervousness and concentrated on logging the delivery on the inventory form on a clipboard which hung on a nail just inside the door. Everything that went in or out of this building was posted, item by item; at the end of the month, the Senior Nurse would work up a Monthly Inventory List, based upon the individual entries. The Monthly List went into the inventory-control program of the Home's computer where it was reconciled with orders placed and invoices received. Once reconciled, the Monthly List became part of the Master List, a running total of all supplies on hand. When we were finished, we both initialed the sheet, locked up, and walked back to the main building in stony silence. Michaels kept her distance but still eyed me warily. I merely grimaced and let it go at that. Far be it for me to push myself on someone – she might holler "sexual harassment"!

I returned the key and the Home's copy of the invoice to Mrs. Oliphant. The former went into a key cabinet (locked), and the latter into the ubiquitous "IN" basket on her desk. She thanked me kindly and returned to whatever she had been doing. Before departing, I asked:

"Say, have you seen Nurse Clement? He seems to be missing."

"No, I haven't, Dr. Maxwell. Would you like to have him paged?"

"Uh, that's not necessary. I was just curious as to his whereabouts."

"Now that I think of it, he's not the only one missing. One of the new nurses reported for work this morning, but no one's seen her for the past hour."

"A couple of truants, huh? What's the punishment for that?"

"A verbal warning the first time, a written reprimand the second time, suspension without pay the third time, and finally dismissal."

"A no-nonsense policy. Who does the warning, reprimanding, suspending, and dismissing?"

"The Senior Nurse," she replied with a grin.

"But, he's missing too. Who disciplines *him*?"

"Dr. Vengtman, of course. He's ultimately responsible for discipline and morale."

"So he is. Well, thanks for the information, Mrs. Ele – Mrs. Oliphant. If I see either of our AWOL's, I'll let them know they're in deep doo-doo."

I started to climb the stairs to the second floor to make my other morning appointment when I experienced the same tingling sensation I had two days before. Instinctively, I turned around. Behind me, as quiet as ever, was Melissa Waterman. Had she been "waiting in ambush" for me? Or was this simply a co-incidental encounter? I was beginning to believe that nothing about this girl could remotely qualify as "co-incidental"; she seemed to have a knack for knowing where everyone in the Home was at any given moment. And, somehow, she had singled me out for special attention.

"Hello, Melissa," I greeted her neutrally.

"Hello, Dr. Maxwell. I hear you're looking for Nurse Clement."

I stared at her in disbelief.

"How did you know that? Wait! Let me guess. A 'robin' told you, right?"

"No," she responded with a straight face, "it was a blue jay this time." Now I recalled having seen such a bird on the roof of the garage-*cum*-supply room, squawking its head off. "She overheard you asking Nurse Michaels about Clement." Now she smiled at my look of incredulity, then frowned. "I know where he is."

"Oh? And were you going to tell me?"

"Yes. He's a horrible man, and I want to see him punished."

"And why is that?"

"He does…bad things to women. He's probably doing them right now. That's why he's missing."

"So, where is he?"

"In the basement. He's got a cot set up behind the furnace. That's where he does the…bad things."

"You've seen him do these…'bad things'?"

"Lots of times. Never with the same woman twice in a row. Like he's got a schedule or something."

"Well, I'll certainly check it out. We can't have someone disappearing anytime he wants to, can we? Thank you for the information, Melissa."

I turned to resume my climb.

"Doctor Maxwell."

"Yes? Was there something else?"

"I still have to tell you about –"

She chopped off her sentence and paled. Chugging down the stairs, puffing and wheezing from all the weight he was carrying, was Harry. As soon as he spotted us, he pulled up and goggled. Why, I hadn't the foggiest notion; perhaps it was "taboo" to talk to Melissa. If so, no one had told me. Without a directive to the contrary, I believed I could talk to anyone I pleased, even if the conversation was beyond my comprehension. Melissa gazed at me pleadingly, then dashed down the stairs and rounded a corner. The Senior raised an eyebrow at me.

"Hum, I seem to have interrupted something, Ken."

"Nothing to write home about, Harry. I think the girl is lonely and needs someone to talk to. Since I'm new here, she seems to be testing my ability to listen."

"P'rhaps. I'm sure you've found her rather…unusual."

"'Unusual' hardly comes close to describing her."

"Indeed. Well, carry on, Doctor."

I had the distinct feeling that the Senior preferred that I didn't talk to Melissa (beyond the amenities, that is) and that, if I did engage in extended conversation, it would be cause for alarm in the rest of the staff. The Director himself had appeared upset to find the two of us together. And Nan had tried to downplay the situation. What were they all afraid of? That Melissa, who claimed to "know" where everybody was at all times, might reveal their deepest, darkest secrets? I always felt uneasy around her, but I'd scarcely credit the feeling to any blackmailing ability she might possess. No, there was another factor at work here, a factor which filled my colleagues with extreme anxiety.

Be that as it may, I had other fish to fry. I'd have to solve my co-workers' problems some other day.

Everyone knows about Murphy's Law: if anything can go wrong, it will go wrong. What is lesser known, however, is a specific corollary to that rule: if Kenneth Maxwell's daily routine can be disrupted, it will be disrupted.

The delivery of pharmaceuticals out of Chicago came earlier than usual – right in the middle of lunch, in fact. It was a "light day," according to the delivery person -- a short fellow with curly blond hair and a large beer belly -- and he was ahead of his normal schedule. As I approached the garage, on a hunch, I scanned the area for robins or blue jays or any other creature which might be acting as Melissa's "eyes" and "ears." Though I didn't put any credence in this notion, I thought perhaps, by making more careful observations, I could trip her up and force her to face whatever fantasies she had concocted. I saw no birds this time, but there was one of the ubiquitous squirrels scampering across the lawn. I made a mental note to remember that one – its size, coloring, and method of scampering.

I also spied Nurse Clement trudging this way. Wherever he had been, he'd had a longer road to travel than I had, and he was quick-marching in order to avoid any delays. We more or less arrived at the same time and nodded curtly to each other. Wordlessly, we opened door number three and took charge of the shipment.

I would like to state at this point, knowing full well that I may be breaking a confidence, that the Vengtman Home for the Emotionally Disturbed kept a supply of addictive drugs on the premises. Most of it was morphine and sodium pentathol used to alleviate pain; while they were prescribed sparingly and only as a last resort, they were part and parcel of the treatment certain patients received. There were other drugs which could be addictive if misused – the anti-psychotic ones come readily to mind – but morphine and sodium pentathol caused the most concern. Obviously, Dr. Vengtman had to be licensed to possess and to administer any of these substances and to be highly accountable for them. Equally obviously, he did not advertise their presence or use in order to discourage would-be thieves or would-be patients looking for a steady "fix." I should also point out that there is now no danger of thievery and/or misuse of these drugs because the new Director rejected their use as valid tools for psychotherapy and had them removed.

No morphine or sodium pentathol were part of that day's shipment, but our supply of anti-psychotic drugs had now been replenished. As with the non-pharmaceuticals, Clement and I carefully checked each container and made the usual notations before we accepted delivery. Thereafter, we quickly stored those items which needed to be refrigerated (the same anti-psychotics, as it happened) and secured the area. All the while neither

Clement nor I uttered one word that was not related to the task at hand. Personally, I wouldn't have had it any other way; he was still giving off "bad vibes," and the less socializing I did with him, the better I felt.

Yet, I have never been known to let sleeping dogs lie if those dogs were in my way. In this particular instance, I wanted to know where he had been during the morning delivery when he should have been at the garage doing his job. When I asked him (politely, of course), he peered at me in a surly, none-of-your-fucking-business sort of way. And, I must admit, I gave him an in-your-face look myself.

"I had other business to attend to, *Doctor*. It couldn't wait."

"Uh-huh. And did this 'business' take place in the basement?"

He stiffened as if he had touched a live wire, and his face turned beet red.

"I dunno know what you mean."

"That's not what I hear."

Now his face became a mask of rage, and he clenched his fists a few times. He was a big, powerful-looking man, and he probably could have given as good as he got. I wasn't exactly a wimp, though; growing up on the mean streets of Chicago tended to toughen a person. I had been in more brawls than I cared to count, losing some, winning some, and I believed I could hold my own with anyone who wanted to test me. Naturally, I had no desire to go one-on-one with Clement in the present circumstances – it wouldn't have been *professional* of me – but I braced myself just to be on the safe side. He did not attack, however, but simply glared at me with feral eyes.

"You been here four fuckin' days, and already you think you know ever' fuckin' thing. I been a nurse sixteen *years*, and I worked hard to get where I am. I ain't gonna let some fuckin' punk like you fuck things up for me. If I was you, *Doctor*, I'd keep my fuckin' nose outa what didn't concern me."

"Is that a threat, *Nurse*?"

"You c'n take it any way you fuckin' like."

He pivoted and stalked off.

Let it never be said that Mrs. Maxwell's son didn't rush in where both fools and angels fear to tread. If one were to read between the lines, then Clement had clearly implicated himself in some shady dealings by his defensiveness; threats to nosy persons notwithstanding, he had reacted to a leading question exactly as a guilty person would have and hadn't realized he'd been manipulated. I suppose now that it was a shameful thing to have done – we doctors ought to be pinnacles of ethical behavior – yet it had produced results. Clement was hiding something, and I was going to discover what it was. Not necessarily for Melissa's sake, who abhorred him for reasons of her own, but for my sake who believed that the best defense against his implied threat was to catch him in the act of whatever it was he was involved in and to toss out a counter-threat. A bit foolhardy, perhaps, but the element of surprise would be on my side.

As I started back to the main building, I was shocked to spy the aforementioned squirrel sitting on its haunches at the edge of the driveway, eyeing me steadily. How long it had been there was anybody's guess; if it had "witnessed" the confrontation between Clement and me, then it would have a fine tale to "report" to Melissa. I was further shocked to see that it was not alone. Two other squirrels flanked it, also sitting on their haunches and staring me down. It might have been a comical sight if not for the fact that they symbolized one of the two great Mysteries surrounding the Home and that they were behaving decidedly in a most un-squirrel-like manner. Since I couldn't control their behavior, I was forced to accept their presence as a "fact of life." So, I waved to them cheerfully and went about my business. (And, no, I did not look back to learn if they were waving to *me*, though I couldn't have ruled out that possibility!)

Because of my interrupted lunch, I had a few minutes to spare and decided I'd check out Melissa's claim about Clement. Thus, rather than re-entering the main building by the front door, I took the shorter route through the kitchen entrance, startling the kitchen staff no end. The head cook was particularly miffed by this invasion of his domain; he said nothing but stared a hole in me every step of the way. I just ignored them all, passed through, and came out into a short hallway at the end of which (opposite the kitchen door) was the access to the basement. I quickly scanned the area to make sure the coast was clear, carefully opened the door, and slipped through. There was light switch just inside, and I flicked it on.

Whatever other remodeling Lowell Vengtman had had done on this former mansion, it hadn't included the basement. The stairway before me appeared to have been the original one – weathered, well-worn two-by-fours that actually creaked as I gingerly stepped on them. And, while some effort had been made to keep the area relatively free of grime and debris, little else suggested that the hand of Man had been working hard down here in the recent past. Support beams – as worn as the stairs – formed a vertical jungle while, above, a maze of air ducts, gas and water pipes, and electrical conduits created a horizontal one. It reminded me of the old tenement building in which I had been raised as a child; I had avoided some of the pain and misery of living in poverty by roaming through the bowels of the once-elegant apartment complex and conducting exciting (to me) explorations into unknown territory. This basement wasn't quite as cluttered as my old one, although I saw a large stack of file cases against one wall – old medical records, I assumed.

The furnace sat to the right of the stairway, just off-center of the basement itself. I made directly for it, though I had to stoop as I walked. This basement hadn't been constructed to accommodate a six-foot-five former basketball player; the least inattention to what I was doing resulted in whacking my head against a duct or a pipe. (And, in fact, I did manage to whack myself – not once, not twice, but *five* times – as I tried to look in all directions at once.) The furnace was the one concession to modernity down here. What once had been a coal-burner had been replaced by a gas-burner; its sharp, clean lines and shiny metal plating contrasted markedly with the basement's "décor." As I passed by it, I spotted the markings on the floor where the old one used to be.

And just on the other side, I discovered that Melissa had told me some truth. A cot squatted between two support pillars, an old Army-surplus type which had seen better days. Nearby was an empty wooden crate standing on end; it held a half empty pack of cigarettes, a matchbook with only two matches left, a whiskey bottle with perhaps three shots remaining, and two plastic cups with whiskey dregs. I sniffed at the bottle and wrinkled my nose; whoever had bought it certainly had poor taste in liquor. Even the cigarettes were generic! The cot showed indications of recent use, and it was a sure bet that the party responsible for its being here would return in the near future. It was also a sure bet that *I* would return to shut down this little operation at my earliest opportunity. I didn't care if Clement screwed every nurse here, but he could damned well do it on his own time and in his own place. This was a sanitarium, after all, not some whorehouse!

From now on, I intended to keep a close eye on Clement. If I saw him head for the basement, I'd follow him in order to catch him in the act. I needed proof of his activities to take to the Director; I couldn't very well make an argument solely on the strength of Melissa Waterman's word. I'd look like an idiot. Of course, there would be an element of personal risk involved, since Clement would not be standing idly by while I blew the whistle on him. But, I would cross that bridge when I got to it. The important thing was *getting* to the bridge. Having seen what I came down here to see, I made my way back to the more "civilized" parts of the Home (but not before cracking my head a few more times!). It was time for my appointment with Matthew J., a.k.a. the "Invisible Man."

Matt was not the most kempt person in the world. He was as likely to drop an item on the floor as put it in its proper place. Sometimes he would pick up something and drop it off somewhere else for no discernible reason at all. Most of his clothing and personal belongings were strewn about his room; wherever a surface existed to put something on, something was put there (often many somethings). That included the largest surface available, i.e. the floor, and, more likely than not, one had to wade through the piles as carefully as a soldier through a minefield. Matt hadn't always been this sloppy; in fact, according to his file, he had once been a very tidy person. Parkinson's disease had progressively eroded his ability to remember to pick up after himself. The disease was now in its second stage, and only the drugs he was given prevented it from eating at him at a faster rate.

When I walked into this "jungle," I found the old man on the bed, completely naked (as was his usual habit), reading a paperback Western novel. As much as I hated to do it, I pretended not to see him.

"Good afternoon, Matt."

"Hiya, Doc. How's it hangin'?"

"Um, do you think you could put something on? I feel foolish talking to thin air."

"Sure thing. You young people need all the reassurances you can get in these troubled times."

He slid off the bed and knelt on all fours, his butt up in the air and his paunch hanging like a cow's udder. It was a ludicrous sight and, for an instant, I wished he really was an invisible man. He rummaged under the bed and produced an orange-and-blue stocking cap sporting the logo of the Chicago Bears. He plopped the cap on his head and pulled it down around his ears. He looked so absurd that it took a great effort for me not to laugh out loud.

"There. How's that, Doc?"

"Much better, thank you. I, uh, thought you were over by the table."

"Close, but no cigar." He resumed his place on the bed and peered at me from under the pulled-down cap. "Whattaya want to talk about today?"

Curing him of his fantasies should have been uppermost in my mind, but it wasn't. I was still determined to learn why my predecessor had treated his patients as he had. So far, I had received two very different views of him (three, if one counted Fred's wolf-pack references). I might as well hear from the rest of his/my patients.

"Tell me about Dr. Hinkelman. Did he and you get along?"

The old man leaned back against the head board and stared at the ceiling for a moment. Then:

"I guess I knew him as well as anyone. Stand-offish type, as I recall. Oh, he'd talk your ear off once he got going, but getting him started was the trick. He seemed almost afraid to speak his mind."

That certainly did not correspond to the Mathias Hinkelman of the *written* word. On paper, he was not afraid to render his opinions on any subject under the sun. Perhaps his inflammatory prose had been a compensation for a speech defect; many of the world's great writers suffered that way – e.g. Plato stuttered. Still, a glib tongue is not necessary for psycho-analysis, but a good ear is; knowing what questions to ask is as important as being able to ask them.

"Had he always been like that?"

"Yeah. He spent almost as much time in small talk as in trying to convince me I wasn't invisible. I think I know what you're going to ask next. He got quieter toward the end, and sometimes he'd just walk in and spend the hour staring out the window. Must've had a lot on his mind, but there wasn't much I could do. *He* was the shrink, not me!"

"How do you feel about his death?"

"It was a damned shame. You young people oughtn't to think about suicide so much. Life isn't so black that you need to check out early."

"Uh-huh. Yet, something forced him over the edge. I want to find out what."

"Good luck. You might talk to that French pastry, Dr. Chantrier. The word was that they had a thing for each other before he went bonkers."

"So I've heard."

He leaned forward and leered.

"Speaking of pastry, I saw you talking to the young Dr. Vengtman the other day. I'd like to get close to her myself. She's got a great set of knockers."

What a dirty old man!

"Oh, really? I hadn't noticed."

An eyebrow shot up.

"You can't be serious, Doc. How could anybody *not* notice? That's one foxy lady. If I were a few years younger…" He began to stroke his penis with his forefinger. I found it most disconcerting, and I had difficulty maintaining the ruse of his invisibility. "I guess," he continued, "that she couldn't handle an invisible man, could she?"

"Uh, no. There'd be problems with, uh, logistics."

"'Logistics'? Ha-ha-ha! That's rich, son! Logistics, yeah. She'd feel it go in, but she wouldn't *see* it."

By now, he was fully erect, and I expected him to start masturbating. I hoped he'd resist the temptation, of course, if only on the grounds of courtesy to one's guests. Even if you think you're invisible, you ought to play the good host. Having no desire to fuel the sexual fantasies of a dirty – and psychotic – old man aside, I was forming a few fantasies of my own concerning "logistics" with the young Dr. Vengtman which posed too much of a distraction. Matt, however, was on a pornographic roll and didn't want to change the subject.

"One woman I'd want to stay invisible to is that Nurse Petrie. Now, there's an icicle for you." Despite my growing discomfort, I found myself nodding in agreement. "What you want to do is come up behind her and do her doggie-style. It would serve her right too."

Personally, I wouldn't have cared to "do" Nurse Petrie in any fashion – not even in the dark, on a deserted island, with both of us blindfolded. But that was neither here nor there. This conversation was going nowhere fast, and I had to steer Matt toward some safer topic. To this day, I still don't know why I asked him the question I did. Inspiration, desperation, or just plain perverseness – take your pick – but the idea popped into my head amidst a cluster of bursting balloons.

"How would you 'do' Melissa Waterman?"

He bolted upright, his eyes wide with fright. His erection disappeared instantly.

"Melissa!" he screeched. "*God damn it, Doc!* Why'd you have to mention her?"

"Just a random question, Matt," I replied evenly. "Do you have a problem with Melissa?"

"You could say that." He licked suddenly dry lips. In a low voice: "*She's the only one who can see me!*"

This stunning admission opened up a whole new realm of possibilities. Matt's psychosis was predicated on the notion that no one could see him unless he chose to be "seen," that he could go about and do whatever he wanted undetected (a power, I might add, to which many – sane or otherwise – aspire). On the face of it, his mental state suggested a deep-rooted desire to engage in unconventional behavior without fear of criticism or reprisal; since he had been a solid, respectable member of his community before Parkinson's disease overtook him, he undoubtedly wished he could just cut loose once in a while and throw inhibition out the window. He also displayed agoraphobic tendencies, reacting hostilely to the outside world and employing an irrational means of hiding from it. My lone, innocent question had thrown his carefully constructed façade for a loop. What was really interesting, however – from a professional standpoint – was that he had finally recognized (inadvertently) the existence of his problem. For, if he could admit that at least one human being could see him, he might be persuaded that others could too; by gradually knocking holes in his "invisibility" thesis, he would come to understand that he had nothing to fear from the outside world. It cannot be emphasized too strongly that self-realization is the first step toward a solution of a given mental disorder. Now I had a hook upon which to hang my therapeutic hat.

"Are you sure about that?"

"Damn straight! What's worse, she looks at me like she's seeing into my very soul. She's not human, I tell you!"

"When did you first realize she could see you?"

He relaxed now, his reporter's mind kicking into action. I noted, however, that his skin was still mostly goose-bumps.

"Let's see. I had my suspicions the second day I was here. I was out on the grounds, getting a tan, when I saw her playing with a bunch of squirrels. Damnedest thing too – it looked like she was *talking* to them and they were *listening*. I thought she looked my way, but I wasn't positive. The next day, I did know, because she came right up to me and *called me by my name.*"

A sudden chill crept up my spine. I knew that feeling well, though I doubted that Melissa had taken Matt into her confidence and revealed her "source" of information. That might have deepened his psychosis even further.

"The *second* day? And you've been here – what? -- two years now?"

"Yeah, a little over two years. Doc, is she a…*witch*?"

"Do you think she's a witch? Do you think she's cast a spell which can cancel out your invisibility?"

"It sure looks that way. What'll I do?"

"What do you want to do?"

"I want to stay invisible. But, if she can see me, then maybe others can too."

Aha! The very path I wished him to take. From the way he was fidgeting with the bed clothes, I realized he was at a crisis point. Best not to push him any further but to leave him to ponder his situation on his own for a while. I now had my foot in the door, so to speak; I could prod him gradually toward the ultimate goal in future sessions. Still, one comment he had made needed to be followed through then and there.

"Tell me, Matt, do you know how long Melissa has been here?"

"The scuttlebutt is that she was here when the Home first opened its doors. What's that got to do with anything?"

"I'm not sure. Perhaps it might help your peace of mind if I found out a little more about her."

A little white lie, to be sure, but a necessary one. I was grasping at straws here, and any information, trivial or otherwise, could be pivotal.

"Good luck, Doc," the old man said sourly. "Just watch out for those damned squirrels of hers. I swear she's got them trained for some devilish reason."

I took my leave of Matt then, satisfied that I had made considerable progress so soon out of the gate. I had also gotten a piece of corroborative evidence to be filed away in my mental "Mathias Hinkelman dossier." So far, everyone I had questioned more or less described him as basically a shy person, to the point of moodiness. Yet, the Hinkelman who wrote fire-breathing book reviews and monographs and play-acted in a most unorthodox fashion was a different person altogether. During his tenure at the Home, he had undergone a radical personality shift. Actually, he had undergone *two* of them, the second being his plunge into madness and suicide. I felt that, if I kept probing long enough, sooner or later I'd arrive at the truth of the matter.

There was one caveat, however. Suppose whatever – or whoever – had been responsible for Hinkelman's demise moved to block my investigation or even to send me on the same self-destructive path. It was a scary proposition; yet, I hadn't gotten as far as I had by being a wimp. I could take care of myself, if it came to that. Besides, I needed to play this hand I'd been dealt, come hell or high water.

DAY SIX:
Friday, 07.11.1997
CONFRONTATION

Serendipity is defined as a "fortuitous accident."

That's the only way I can describe the amazing discovery I made after waking up on a Friday morning. I awoke early, not because I was eager to rush into my work routine but because I was obliged to pull meal-monitor duty again. It hadn't been my turn so soon – I thought I had a couple more days – but Harry had knocked on my door late the night before and claimed that Dante was down with a summer cold and would I please cover for him. I supposed I could have refused (although on what grounds, I couldn't imagine), but I had the distinct impression that the Senior believed refusals were not an option for "junior" staff. So, I had agreed (and, in the back of my mind, noted that Dante owed me one).

For some reason, the previous day's exertions had fatigued me more than I realized, and I found it difficult to come fully awake. Consequently, I fumbled at my clothes, hoping I was putting them on in the right order. That's when my keys slid out of my pants pocket and disappeared into the gap between the arm and the frame of the sofa-bed. Employing some choice expressions retained from my days on the streets, I re-retracted the bed frame halfway out of its enclosure and peered underneath. My keys were clearly visible.

And so was another object I had never seen before simply because it had never occurred to me to snoop under the furniture. It appeared to be a book of some sort, approximately five inches by eight, standing upright against the backboard. I stretched my arm underneath the frame and brushed the object with my fingers. A bit more exertion, and I could just grasp the thing between my thumb and forefinger. Yet, it refused to come away easily, and I discovered why by running my fingers over its surface. Someone had *taped* it to the board! Clearly, this had not been a case of carelessness but of deliberate secretion. As if I hadn't mysteries enough to "entertain" me, here was another one I really didn't need.

I checked my watch. I had no time to spare right now for investigating this book further. I'd have to come back before lunch and retrieve it then. Hastily slipping on my smock, I dashed out the door, only to observe Maddie coming down the path. I waited for her to catch up with me, then walked with her to the main building.

"You're up early," I remarked disingenuously.

"I did not sleep much last night. Dante's cottage is next to mine. And he kept me up wis his incessant coughing."

"Harry told me about his condition. That's why *I'm* up early. I have to fill in for him as meal monitor."

She regarded me with a touch of sadness mixed with bemusement.

"*Mon pouvre* Dr. Maxwell. So new, yet so quickly srown to ze wolves."

I chuckled. I might not have expressed my situation in precisely those terms; I think a meat-grinder would have been more apropos. At that moment, however, I was not awake enough to do more than accept her sympathy in the proper spirit.

"Ah, well, I've survived worse than this as an intern. It's all part of the job."

"You may suffair even more," she murmured.

"Excuse me?"

"*Pardonez moi*, Ken. I was…sinking out loud."

She then lapsed into silence. I wondered if this were a good time to ask her about her relationship with Hinkelman again. I ought to take my opportunities when they presented themselves; yet, I had to avoid appearing overly inquisitive. Be casual, I advised myself.

"Is there any more you can tell me about Mathias, Maddie – professionally, that is?"

She remained silent for another minute. Then:

"I did not know 'im very well eizair professionally or personally. I do know zat, shortly aftair we began our affair, 'e became more and more wisdrawn. Lovairs we might 'ave been, but zere was a part of him zat shut even me out. By mushual agreement, we stopped seeing each ozzair socially.

"Zen, he 'ad 'is – 'ow can I put it? – 'is 'fling' wis 'arry. I 'ave nevair understood zat. Mat'ias nevair ex'ibited 'omosexual tendencies during our time togezzair; zat was not ze reason we went our separate ways. Somesing else troubled 'im. What, I cannot say." She laid a hand lightly on my arm and sent out a plea with her eyes. "If you learn ze trus, *mon ami*, I would like to know, if only for my own peace of mind."

"Of course. I didn't know Hinkelman at all, but I feel a loss too."

We parted company at the dining room entrance, she going to the staff dining area, I to the kitchen to confer with the head cook (who turned out to be as affable as ever). Afterwards, I served myself (cream of wheat, OJ, and toast) and took my customary place near the entrance. My first "tour of duty" had perhaps lulled me into a false sense of security by having been relatively uneventful. I had just settled down for what I hoped would be more of the same when the flare-up occurred.

I say "flare-up," but what it really was was a good old-fashioned food-fight. Unfortunately, this one did not involve over-enthusiastic, underdeveloped youths with too much free time on their hands. It would not have been so disastrous otherwise. What triggered the incident was that two of the patients got into a snit over a piece of toast; both, apparently, had reached for the same piece at the same time, and what might ordinarily have been a moment of apology and/or retreat by either party turned into a perception of intrusion by both. The psychotic mind, tending to magnify and to exaggerate, overreacts to the slightest gesture or word and provides its own momentum toward nasty behavior.

Since one of the "aggrieved" parties in this incident was my patient, Ray, who had a history of violent impulses, one expected trouble. The other party, one Arthur L. (under Nan's care) with bipolar personality disorder, decided to be manic at that moment and accused Ray of stealing *his* food. Ray hotly denied it and made a counter-charge in a similar vein. Whereupon Arthur picked up a handful of toast and flung it at Ray's head. Ray retaliated with an outburst of profanity and a hostile step toward Arthur. This and the reaction by the other patients snapped me out of my reverie; I looked up just in time to witness Ray scoop up a handful of scrambled eggs and shove it in Arthur's face. I leaped to my feet and steamed toward the serving line, the Black Bag in hand; on the way, I signaled the senior nurse on duty and got him to handle Arthur while I tried my hand at subduing Ray. That proved to be a big mistake, because Arthur, not one to be deterred, had been in the process of letting fly with a handful of cream of wheat and thus caught me in the back of the head instead. I ignored this assault as best I could and stared Ray down. He glared at me even as he hefted yet another load of scrambled eggs. I was only vaguely aware of the SNOD behind me attempting to restrain Arthur.

"*He* started it, preacher," Ray whined. "He shoulda got his fuckin' toast when he had the chance, 'steada waitin' 'til the last fuckin' minute."

"Does his rudeness justify yours, Billy?"

He did not reply but peered at the eggs in his hand, now turning cold. Was he debating whether to throw them after all? If so, at whom?

"Why are you wasting time on the likes of him?" I pressed. "He's not important. We both know what's really at stake here, don't we?"

"Yeah, but…"

"No 'buts,' Billy. If we're going to clean up this town, we're going to have to be smart about it, right?"

"I guess so."

"Now, apologize to Arthur."

His ire ignited, and his nostrils flared.

"*Shit, no!*"

"Apologize," I said firmly, "or you won't be able to count on my help."

He mumbled something under his breath, turned to Arthur, and mumbled a quasi-apology. The latter still looked defiant. I faced him and gave *him* a hard stare.

"Your turn, Arthur. Apologize."

Arthur was clearly in no more of a mood than Ray to admit error, and he glared at me fiercely. If he were still in his manic stage, I'd have to sedate him, something *I* wasn't in a mood to do. As I started to open the Black Bag, Arthur suddenly blanched with sudden fright. At the time, I believed his reaction was due to a combination of a realization of my intentions and of simple intimidation of a five-foot-six individual by a six-foot-five one. Now, I know better. In any event, the fire went out of him, and he stammered an apology to no one in particular. I signaled the nurses to escort both of them back to their rooms so that they could clean themselves up before being allowed to return and finish their breakfasts.

By this time, the head cook had put in his own appearance after learning of the commotion from one of his servers. He was ready to chew nails at the sight of the food scraps on the floor. And, when I casually informed him that, pursuant to the public-health regulations of the State of Illinois, all of the food on the serving line which had been involved in the food-fight would have to be removed, disposed of, and replaced with fresh supplies, he was definitely not a happy camper but was ready to chew railroad spikes. Frankly, I didn't care if he fell over from apoplexy. The cream of wheat on my back was beginning to harden, and I was ready for a quick shower myself. I had no time to argue with disgruntled non-professionals. I turned away from him and requested one of the nurses to wipe the mess off me. The head cook stalked back to the kitchen, muttering imprecations by the ton.

As I returned to my table, I discovered Melissa sitting there, elbows propped up and her chin resting on her hands. She regarded me dreamily yet could have been thinking the direst of thoughts. I didn't know whether to be flattered or frightened.

"Good morning, Melissa," I greeted her once I had sat down. I peered at my cooling bowl of cream of wheat with sudden disgust; having been "christened" with the stuff seemed to have dulled my appetite. "Have you been here long?"

"Long enough," she murmured.

"Long enough for what?"

"Long enough to see you stand up to those two. They both would have hit you if I – uh, if you had shown fear." Her amethyst eyes bore twin holes through me, and I idly wondered what sort of "visions" I'd see this time. "You aren't afraid of anything, are you? I knew I was right about you."

"I'm pleased I meet with your approval, Melissa," I responded dryly, secretly happy but apprehensive over her snap assessment. "As for being afraid, where I come from, that's not an option, if you want to survive."

"Yes, I sense that. You must've felt the same way when Clement bad-mouthed you yesterday."

So, her squirrels had "reported" to her after all!

"Speaking of Clement, I saw that little set-up down in the basement. It looked like it had been used recently. Still, there's no evidence to link him with it."

"He's been there! I have…sources of information."

"So you say. But, I'll need to catch him with his pants down, so to speak."

She fell silent then. I excused myself to dump the cold cream of wheat in the garbage and to grab a bowl of granola (yes, the Director had thoughtfully included so-called "health food" in his menus). When I returned, Melissa was staring at the ceiling moodily. Abruptly, she focused on me. I braced myself for a mental onslaught. Happily, it didn't come, but gazing into those amethyst eyes was perhaps attack enough.

"Dr. Vengtman is the one you should fear," she stated without preamble. "He's…an *evil* man." I did nothing to hide my incredulity. "I know how that sounds, but it's true. He…uses people."

"Melissa, you can't mean that. Dr. Vengtman has a world-wide reputation. He may be gruff at times, but that doesn't mean he's *evil*."

"Oh, Dr. Maxwell, if you only knew."

"Suppose you tell me then."

Now she squirmed on her chair and wrung her hands. A tickling sensation played at the base of my skull. If she were having an anxiety attack, I had to be very alert. If, on the other hand, she was just play-acting in order to gain my sympathy, she was doing a damned good job of it! I was surprised the table was still in one piece, the way she was staring a hole in it. Finally, in a small voice:

"I'm not crazy."

"No one said you were. Confused, maybe. Look, Melissa, I know the Director. He's a good, kind man."

"I've know him a lot longer than you have, Ken" – she bit her lip – "I

121

mean, Dr. Maxwell. I've seen his…dark side. He didn't earn his reputation on his own merits. He's taken credit for what others did."

As much as I would have liked to continue this intriguing conversation – none of which even skirted reality – it ended with the "changing of the shifts." When the second group marched in, Melissa bolted upright, looking around wildly as if she had just realized where she was and what she was doing. Without any goodbyes, she darted through the door, nearly colliding with Clement in the process. Their eyes locked briefly. Contempt was writ large on the girl's face, while he registered momentary panic. Melissa pushed by him, and a potential confrontation faded into oblivion.

My monitor's report was necessarily longer this time. In addition to the usual statistics, I was required to include in as much detail as possible any unusual incidents. So, after all of the patients had been ushered off to their recreational activities and while the kitchen staff cleaned the dining room around me (grumbling to themselves, no doubt, at the obstacle I presented), I described the food-fight in the "Incidents" section of the form, even as the hardened, crusty cream of wheat residue on the back of my head and neck began to create an itch. (When I scratched, crumbs trickled under my shirt collar and down my back and made me even more uncomfortable!)

SOP required that incident reports be copied as many times as patients involved. The original was filed in the main office, and the copies went to the patients' counselors to be included in their medical records. These reports were as much a part of a patient's program of recovery as a counselor's diagnoses, because they tended to criticize current treatment and suggest the necessity of alternate methods. Since I was going to get a copy myself (for Ray's file), I decided to tailor the report to my own needs; also, since a copy was going to Nan, I didn't want to alienate her by being unduly critical of Arthur's behavior. Instead, I attempted to assign equal blame (within the bounds of objectivity, of course) to both parties.

I delivered the report to Mrs. Oliphant's desk, only to find someone else in her chair. A thin, sad-eyed female nurse with dishwater-blond hair and a habit of brushing her hair away from her face – one Nurse Blakely, according to her name-tag – told me nervously (why did the damned nurses find me so intimidating?) that Mrs. Oliphant was a devout Jew and that, instead of risking not being able to get home by sunset on Friday evenings, she had arranged with the Director to take the whole day off and work Sundays instead. Live and learn, I thought; she didn't look Jewish to me. But, what did a street kid like me know? I turned in my report, received my own copy, and departed to take a much needed shower.

Enter serendipity.

While I was relaxing afterward, I turned my attention to the book taped to the inside of the sofa-bed. I pulled the bed away from the wall, bent down, and heaved upward. The sofa tipped over and landed on its back, exposing a dust-ball-and-cobweb-filled undercarriage to plain sight (who had charge of house-keeping around here?). I reached down and tore off the Scotch tape holding the book.

To my great surprise, it was not just any old book. It was a journal, meticulously kept. While the exterior was covered with cobwebs, the interior was clean and white, the pages still flexible, which meant that it had not been under the sofa-bed for long. The author had taken pains to keep this record in spotless condition and intended that someone should find it and read it. Yet, why hide it in the first place? Had he feared that it might fall into the "wrong" hands? And, if so, whose hands might they have been? Here was a new mystery to add to the growing number.

I opened to the first page and recognized the precise but crabbed handwriting at once, having seen it often enough in the files of my new patients. It was Mathias Hinkelman's! In one of those colossal co-incidences that occur throughout human history, I had not only "inherited" his caseload, but also his cottage. And now, I had his journal – perhaps the last thing he had ever written. To say I was ecstatic is a great understatement. I could scarcely contain my anticipation at what I might find within those pages.

The first entry was dated August 10, 1996. I made a quick mental calculation based upon my reading of the notations in the files; the date was approximately four months before the onset of Hinkelman's mental breakdown. And now I asked myself: were there other journals before this one? If so, where were they? I made a mental note to search the cottage thoroughly before too much time passed.

The first sentence of that first page fairly leaped out at me and threatened to tear my eyes out of their sockets.

"Melissa is jealous!"

The statement spoke volumes. Apparently, Hinkelman had had some sort of relationship with Melissa Waterman; and, if my own experiences were any guide, she had attached herself to him arbitrarily. Had she also told him that he was a "good man" and that she hoped he would stay at the Home "forever"? Without really knowing absolutely what had occurred nearly a year ago, I could nevertheless make an intuitive leap and conclude that somehow Hinkelman had not lived up to her expectations – whatever the hell *they* were – and that she had succumbed to Shakespeare's "green-eyed monster."

The entry continued:

> Almost from the moment I began my employment here, she mooned over me and followed me everywhere I went. At first, like any red-blooded American male, I found her attractive and was flattered by the attention; later on, however, her adolescent infatuation became quite embarrassing. God knows Dr. Vengtman had given me any number of stern looks, though he will not speak of the matter, even in private.
>
> Bluntly speaking, there is something not quite right about Melissa – the way she looks at a person is nothing short of *eerie* – but what it is I can't put my finger on. I keep telling myself that she will get over her crush on me and find someone else to annoy.
>
> In any event, I really don't have much time to spend analyzing her. I'm making such enormous progress with my patients that I can scarcely wait until the next sessions with them. I'm still unsure of how I'm accomplishing these miracles. I've had moments of inspiration almost every day; and, while the methodology seems bizarre (how much criticism have I had to endure from my co-workers?), it has produced results, and that's all that counts. For example, I have nearly persuaded old Matt that he really isn't invisible, and Georgina no longer talks to her dead son. The others are not quite as far along the road to recovery, but they show promising signs.
>
> My love life has improved too. If only those clowns at Johns Hopkins could see me now – the nerd who couldn't even look a woman in the eyes, much less ask her for a date. True, Maddie is several years older than me, but she has opened up marvelous vistas to me. I feel like I'm on top of the world whenever I'm with her!
>
> Unfortunately, Melissa found out about us, and she's

consumed by jealousy. I can tell by the way she looks at
Maddie – especially when we're together.

Well, she is just going to have to get over it. I need my
space as much as the next person, and I intend to get it.

A-men! I said silently.

What an astounding revelation this had been. And had it been
Hinkelman's reason for such elaborate precautions? Did he really believe
that Melissa would learn of his journal and become enraged by his candid
remarks? I knew well the unearthly effect she had on people (if indeed
she was responsible for the disturbing visions I'd had); I knew too that
she could frighten an old man nearly out of his psychosis, and I knew she
could cause momentary panic in a steely-eyed fellow like Clement. What
else could she do? What, I wondered – with no small trepidation! – would
happen if I were to lose "favor" in her sight? Would she try to make life
miserable for me by spreading ugly rumors similar to the one about Lowell
Vengtman she had been attempting to foist upon me? Another leap of
intuition: was Hinkelman's breakdown the result of some evil whispering
campaign which no amount of denial could derail? "Hell hath no fury like
a woman scorned." How about a scorned *witch*, to use Matt's evaluation
of Melissa Waterman?

This journal was yet another piece in the puzzle I was working on
-- a giant piece, to be sure, but still not enough for me to draw any solid
conclusions. I had to keep digging, to keep making a nuisance of myself
until the truth was finally revealed. I suspected that the truth – whatever
it turned out to be – was not going to be pretty. Still I wasn't about to let
go of this bone I had in hand; at the very least, I owed it to Hinkelman to
redeem his reputation (such as it was).

As compelling as this journal was, I had no more time then to read
further. I'd have to wait until after business hours. For good measure, I
stashed it where I had found it. Perhaps it was a foolish thing to do, but I
had the nagging feeling that continued secrecy was essential.

My first call that day was Terry, the frustrated writer who had assumed
the persona of Edgar Allan Poe. He was sitting at the table scribbling away,
pausing now and then to stare out the window. On my previous visits,
there had been a pile of crumpled-up sheets of paper on the floor, the
result of a fickle Muse and increased frustration. Now, however, no pile of
discards greeted me; instead, a pile of neatly stacked sheets lay to one side
of the table, the product of a writer who has finally been inspired and writes

for as long as Inspiration tarries. In addition, Terry was humming some pleasant ditty, increasing the pitch and tempo in parallel with movements of his hand. All in all, I had never seen him more cheerful, and I casually remarked on his mood.

"Good morning, Doctor!" he enthused, reluctantly setting aside his pen. "Yes, I'm in fine fettle today. Queer thing about that too. The idea for this story" – he gestured at the stack of sheets – "came to me in a dream last night. I couldn't wait to get started on it."

"That's very interesting. Have you ever had other inspirational dreams?"

"Occasionally, but not as brilliant as this one." He leaned toward me and lowered his voice. "This story is sure to gain me the recognition I deserve."

"I'm happy for you, Terry. I'd ask to read it, but I know you creative types have a superstition about others viewing a work-in-progress."

"True. I did make one exception, though. I came to trust Dr. Hinkelman enough to read my stuff and offer constructive criticism."

I suppressed a derisive laugh. I'd read quite a bit of my predecessor's "constructive criticism" in the past day and a half, and I wondered what sort of reviews he'd given Terry who was obviously no more than a hack writer whose greatest achievement was some clever advertising slogans appearing on television or in magazines only to sink into a well-deserved oblivion as someone else's "work of art" replaced it in the minds of a jaded public. If I knew Hinkelman at all, he would have had a grand time tearing into "inspired" writing with a sneer tucked into every phrase. On the other hand, that had been the Old Hinkelman, for I was reminded that the consensus here at the Home was that he had presented a different persona altogether. Perhaps he had mellowed in the interim and been a "kinder, gentler person" (to quote a former President). I saw an opportunity to obtain another piece of the puzzle.

"And did his criticism prove to be helpful?"

"Um, not at first. As time went on, he began to take a greater interest in my career and made a number of good suggestions." He paused to eye me woefully, then picked up his pen and doodled on the sheet of paper before him. Finally: "After he…left us, it was touch-and-go. My Muse was harder to hear."

"But you've gotten a new story line today."

"Yes. After all this time, the Muse is back."

He smiled broadly, leaned back in his chair, and gazed at the ceiling as if searching for something. Without warning, he started to recite Poe's "The Bells."

> "Hear the mellow wedding bells –
>   Golden Bells!
> What a world of happiness their harmony foretells!
>   Through the balmy air of night
>   How they ring out their delight! –
> From the molten golden notes,
>   And all in tune,
>   What a liquid ditty floats
> To the turtle-dove that listens, while she gloats
>   On the moon!
>   Oh, from out the sounding cells,
> What a gush of euphony voluminously wells!
>   How it swells!
>   How it dwells!
>   On the future – how it tells
>   Of the rapture that impels
> To the swinging and the ringing
>   Of the bells, bells, bells –
>   Of the bells, bells, bells, bells,
>   Bells, bells, bells –
> To the rhyming and the chiming of the bells!"

In clear, stentorious tones, he projected all the rhythm and harmony of this most musical of the poet's output. Frankly, I was enthralled as Terry recited it perfectly, all the while gesturing dramatically as he spoke; wherever he had come by this talent, he had been wasting it in the advertising business. A long silence followed as he regarded me pensively. If he was hoping for praise, I decided to give him some. I nodded in approval. He nodded in acknowledgement, the author accepting the adulation of his audience with magnanimity!

"That was one of my better efforts," he stated flatly. "Dr. Hinkelman especially was taken with it."

"Tell me, Terry, what do you think happened to him at the end?"

He rose from his chair, walked over to the window, and peered out. Though his jaw was set, I noticed a nervous tic at the right corner of his mouth. I speculated that I might have ventured into dangerous territory.

I had no idea what had been their relationship – beyond the "writer" and the 'reviewer" – since Hinkelman's notations in Terry's file provided only a clinical analysis and not a personal one. Many people deny death – particularly when it strikes near to home – and seek some other explanation for a loved one's absence from the world. (E.g. Georgina believed that her son was not dead but existed on a different plane of reality.) Terry may have sublimated Hinkelman's suicide because what had led up to it had been unacceptable to his frame of mind, and thus he had pushed it deep into his subconscious where it would be "harmless." My asking him to recall it to the conscious level could therefore have re-enforced his psychosis. Presently, he turned back toward me and asked:

"Do you recall the story I wrote last year, the one about the man who believed he had been insulted and walled up the insulter in his cellar?"

I admit that my tastes in literature are limited, but I can't help what I like. If Agatha Christie didn't write the story to which he referred, then I didn't know it. (Later, I learned that the story was "The Cask of Amontillado," one of Poe's earlier tales of horror.) I had to resort to another little white lie in order to facilitate this conversation and keep Terry on an upbeat note.

"Well, that's something like what happened in Dr. Hinkelman's case. He said something to one of the other patients that didn't go over too well, and that's when his problems began. Before, he had given me good reviews; afterwards, he thought my stuff was" – he took a deep breath as a cloud passed across his face – "*trash*. We argued constantly until…"

In his own way, Terry had corroborated Hinkelman's own assessment which he had set down in his patients' files while he was still lucid. Though he had enjoyed fantastic success in leading his charges toward rationality, ultimately he had lost ground until he himself became a patient. Did he know what – or who – was responsible for those reversals of fortune? Was that why he had hidden the journal – because the answers were so off-the-wall that no one would believe him? I had to finish reading his journal before I learned the truth. In the meantime, I could pry one more piece of information out of "Mr. Poe."

"Another patient? Which one?"

He returned to the window and searched the grounds in order to assure himself that he wouldn't be overheard. I thought it was an absurd notion since we were on the second floor; but, when he finally spoke, I began to have my doubts. He came away from the window, drew his chair close to mine, and said in a hushed voice:

"You won't believe this, but the word is that it was that strange girl who keeps wandering all over the place."

"Melissa?"

"Yes. She used to follow Dr. Hinkelman like a puppy. Then they had some sort of falling out – I don't know the details – and he started to have his problems."

Confirmation!

It was all beginning to fall into place now. A teenaged crush gone sour had led to the worst sort of jealousy: a vicious, vindictive campaign of rumor and innuendo. No wonder Hinkelman had gone mad. Who could possibly combat smear tactics without losing a part of himself in the process? And, in his case, the smears must have been colossal, for he had lost all of himself irrevocably. I made a mental note to be more cautious around Melissa; I didn't want her doing to me what she had done to Hinkelman.

Now that I had the *who* and the *why*, all I needed was the *how*, and I could lay this mystery to rest. The *how*, I believed, perhaps stemmed from the reason Melissa was a patient here; her emotional balance (whatever it was) had colored her attitudes toward everyone she met and subsequently her behavior in their presence. To learn more about the girl, I simply had to get my hands on her file – which meant invading the domain of the Ice Maiden. What excuse could I give her for wanting a file not in my caseload? Nurse Petrie had already made it clear that my being a doctor didn't cut any slack with her; if I had no valid reason for being in the records room, she would toss me out on my ear like some *common* person! That little venture had to wait, however, since I was running late on my other business.

The lunch period ran fairly smoothly, though I sensed some tension in the air. Everyone – staff and patients – gave me covert glances when they thought I wasn't looking. I took my own lunch and pretended to read a file; but, I watched out of the corner of my eye, and I saw them. What were they feeling? Fear? Envy? Apprehension? It was hard to say for, as soon as I "accidentally" shifted my gaze someone's way, (s)he turned away, and I could not get a full "read." Obviously, the tension was a result of what had occurred at breakfast. All – especially Arthur – seemed to be seeing me in a new light (or so I believed at the time), and they were keeping their distance (psychologically speaking). More importantly, they were treading lightly, lest they incur my wrath again!

In some respects, this attitude was welcome. It meant that I would no longer be treated as the "new boy" but as a full, functioning member of the staff; there would be no questioning of my directives or appealing them to a "higher authority" and no more sneering, disdainful remarks and expressions, such as I had received at R-PSL. On the other hand, I felt that a wall had been erected between me and them, and I could no longer engage in small talk or swap jokes or ask after the welfare of their families. Consequently, my role as counselor could have been diminished.

The exception to this change of attitude was Nurse Clement, and I was not too surprised by his continued surliness. Evidently, he had not been overly impressed by my handling of the morning's flare-up and wasted no time in demonstrating his disdain for my "refereeing" talent. Not with words did he put me down, however, but with defiance in his eyes and facial expressions. He made no effort to disguise his contempt for either my person or my "authority." It is a sad fact about human beings that such behavior exists, and one wonders if it can ever be avoided or at least mitigated. Clearly, psychology has a long way to go before fully understanding human behavior. In any event, I ignored Clement as best I could and went about my monitoring. If he could have been "solved" at all, it would have had to wait until a later date.

I departed the dining room as soon as feasible and made my way to the medical-records room. I still hadn't thought of what to tell Nurse Petrie. As it happened, the place was deserted; either Petrie was taking a late lunch or answering Nature's call or running an errand. I called out her name a couple of times just to be sure I had the room to myself. How long, however, was another question. Therefore, it behooved me to conduct my "research" as quickly as possible. My task was hampered by the fact that I knew next to nothing about Melissa Waterman; especially, I did not know when she had been admitted. I was thus forced to look for her file the hard way – one file drawer at a time. Happily, because of the efficiency of the filing system, I did not have to fumble about haphazardly but could work through the months and years methodically. Purely arbitrarily, I began with the files for August 1996 – when Hinkelman had begun his journal – and worked backwards. Midway through "1994," I was halted dead in my tracks by an arctic voice.

"May I help you, Doctor?"

My luck had just run out!

I quietly and deliberately closed the file drawer I'd been ransacking, slowly and tremulously turned around, and confronted the rigid form of Nurse Petrie. Her face was an ice sculpture, pale, immobile, and passionless.

Only her eyes – black narrow slits out of which a lethal gleam oozed – evinced any sign of life. Her cool, calculating regard of me sent shivers up and down my spine. I may have been a professional with a degree to prove it; but, at that moment, I appeared to be a little boy who had just been caught sneaking a peek into the girls' bathroom. Petrie just stood there staring at me for what seemed like centuries, not saying another word, as if she were waiting for an answer to her quasi-rhetorical question, waiting for an explanation for this invasion of her turf.

"I, uh," I stammered at last, if only to break that deadly silence, "I needed to, uh, find a file to, uh, check out an obscure reference. There wasn't anyone around, so I, uh, tried to find it on my own. Sorry," I added lamely.

"You know the rules, Doctor," she said huskily, pushing past me to reclaim her territory. I hastily withdrew to the "customer" side of the counter. "*No* unauthorized searches. *No* exceptions."

"Yes, ma'am," I responded as light-heartedly as I dared, hoping against hope that a little levity might thaw out the room. The effort only got me another frigid stare. "I've learned my lesson."

"I suppose you would've taken the file without signing it out, either."

"Of course not. That would have been…unprofessional."

"I'm sure it would." She relaxed visibly and adopted her professional attitude. I relaxed as well, glad that my reprimanding had been short-lived. "Now, whose file did you want?"

"Um, Melissa Waterman's. Please."

So much for mollification. At the mention of Melissa's name, the Ice Maiden became glacial again, and I really thought she might throw me out bodily. A neat trick for any *ordinary* person – but I wouldn't have put anything past this woman. I shrank back.

"That file is not available," she murmured through barely moving lips.

"You haven't even looked. Has it been signed out already?"

"That file is not available," she repeated even more icily (if that were possible!). "I'm sorry, Doctor. Is there another file you'd like?"

"Uh, no. Sorry to have troubled you, Nurse."

"Good day, Doctor."

I walked out of the records room like a zombie. What a horrific experience that had been! I felt like retreating to the kitchen and sitting on a hot stove for a few hours just to return my body temperature to normal.

I guess I was lucky to have gotten out of there with a whole skin. And I hadn't advanced my cause any.

If Melissa's file was "not available" (assuming for the moment that Petrie was being truthful with me – and why would she be otherwise?), then it had to be in Dr. Vengtman's office. That possibility posed a larger problem, as I could not simply walk in and ask to see his patient's file for no other reason than to satisfy my own morbid curiosity and, incidentally, to solve the riddle of Mathias Hinkelman's suicide. He would be quite justified in showing me the door and perhaps re-evaluating my employment here. If the situation were reversed, I certainly would have done so. As I walked about in a fog, I ran into Dr. Vengtman the Younger – again.

"Not again!" she yelped. "Really, Dr. Maxwell, we've got to stop meeting like this. It's becoming hazardous to my health."

"Lord, I'm sorry, Nan. I guess I was in another daze."

"Another one, or the same one as before?"

"The same one, I suppose." I related the conversation I'd had with Melissa at breakfast. I did *not* tell her about Hinkelman's journal; until I'd had a chance to read it through and analyze it thoroughly, no one was going to learn about it – and maybe not even then. "I'll give her this: she's very consistent, even though her story gets wilder as it goes along. Which reminds me – do you know why she's here? Nurse Petrie tells me her file is 'unavailable,' and she won't say why."

"Surely Uncle Lowell has asked for your co-operation in this matter."

"He has. And I told him I'd be discreet. But, haven't you – and the rest of the professional staff – been the least little curious? I know I have. I've been here less than a week, and I'm perplexed – as you've pointed out so graciously."

"We've all been curious, Ken, but not to the point of interfering with the doctor-patient relationship."

"Oh, really? We talk about everyone else at the staff meeting. What makes Melissa Waterman so special that she's exempt from the SOP?"

Nan sighed heavily, and the expression on her face made it clear that she had no desire to continue this conversation.

"All I can you is that Uncle Lowell made a request not to discuss Melissa's case and that the rest of us agreed to honor his wishes. Look, Ken, God knows he's no saint, but neither is he the Devil incarnate. You've got to trust him in this. He's hardly an amateur."

"Well, somehow I have to find out more about that girl. She's become an itch I have to scratch."

"Obviously. Do you have any idea why she's telling *you* this story of hers, rather than someone who's been here longer?"

"Apparently, she has a high regard for me. What she bases that regard on, she hasn't said. I hesitate to mention it, but she exhibits all the symptoms of infatuation."

I had expected Nan to laugh at that observation. In the first place, it would have jibed with the human penchant for laughing at the patently ridiculous; and, in the second place, it would have jibed with her personality which was to see a lot of things as patently ridiculous. She had already displayed signs of a quirky sense of humor (a trait I appreciated in women), taking things as they came. Now, however, she regarded me – oddly, I thought – and pursed her lips. Was she attempting to comprehend what a teenaged girl might find so fascinating about me? Or was she worried that I might be taking Melissa too seriously? If she knew what I knew then, she would have had no cause for worry. Oh, I took Melissa seriously, all right, but only because I thought she spelled trouble under the right (wrong?) circumstances.

"What's wrong, Nan?"

"What? Oh, nothing. I was just reminded of something else." The mischievous twinkle returned to her eyes. "Really, Doctor, whatever is causing your distraction must be contagious. Perhaps we ought to keep our distance."

"Oh, no!" I protested. "We still have a date, remember?"

"I remember. And that reminds me of another thing. Any news on your, ah, initiation?"

"Nope. I'm sure I've been a big disappointment to a lot of people."

"Yes, you have. I may as well tell you that tonight is my night in the pool. So, I have *two* reasons to hope you're successful."

"If you want to know the truth, I've also got two reasons – maybe the same two you have – for wanting to get this business over with. I'm getting damned tired of it."

"Me too," she said softly. "Well, if you're out of your daze, I'll be off. Bye-bye."

Later in the afternoon, I received another shock – one more pleasant this time. Since our initial conversation, Fred (the "wolf man") had refused to talk to me on the grounds that I was not a "member of the pack." For three days, I had dropped in on him and, each time, he would hunch up on his bed and eye me menacingly. In his mind, I was an outsider, not to be trusted, not to be admitted to the "territory," and certainly not to be communicated with. I had sat in a chair on the opposite side of his room, throwing out the standard ice-breaking questions and generally waiting him out; when it became clear that he wasn't going to respond, I had left, hoping that eventually I could wear him down and pass through his defenses.

Perhaps I succeeded that day (though I have called that entire two-week period into question since then), for when I entered his room, I found him standing at the window and peering out at the grounds. Since his room faced north, he had a fairly good view of the wooded section at the rear of the property. I had no idea what was fascinating him; but, whatever it was caused him at one point to shudder violently. I was afraid he was having another psychotic episode. Abruptly, he threw back his head and howled – just like a wolf! Animal behaviorists say that each species has its own language. If so, then Fred was probably venting his frustrations in "Wolfian." While I don't pretend to know "Wolfian," the impression I received from the intensity and the inflection of the howl was one of fear and loathing. I wanted to look out the window to see what had set him off but didn't wish to get too close to him, just in case. Instead, I sat down in my "regular" chair and played the waiting game again. Presently, he turned, walked to the center of the room, and took *his* accustomed seat on the floor.

"Hello, Dr. Maxwell."

If nothing else came of this session, then at the very least I could claim a moral victory.

"Hello, Fred. Are you in a talking mood today?"

He gave me a half-smile and rocked back and forth.

"I heard what happened this morning. I wish I could've been there to see you face down those two rogues."

"Um, well, I just did what I thought had to be done."

"Still, it was a brave thing to do. I've discussed the incident with the rest of the pack, and they seem inclined to re-evaluate your status with us. In these troubled times, we need fearless and loyal members."

"I appreciate your confidence. I, uh, would like to join the pack – if I may."

Now, why had I said that? I was supposed to be *curing* Fred of his psychosis, not fueling it. I was beginning to behave like my predecessor and adopting his unorthodox methods. They might have worked for him (however unlikely the probability), but I wasn't Mathias Hinkelman; I had my own methods, and I didn't care to graft someone else's onto them.

The statement had simply popped out of my mouth before I realized what I said.

"We'll see. Mathias was an important member, and his…passing left a great emptiness in the soul of the community. No one can replace him."

"Uh, I wouldn't presume to do that. I'll be content to, uh, fill my own niche."

He nodded, then fell silent. Mentally, I cursed myself for falling into Hinkelman's rut. Yet, I also saw my chance to gain another view on his demise.

"Tell me about…Mathias, Fred. What, uh, role did he play in the, uh, community?"

"Mathias was – there isn't any word in English which conveys an exact meaning – a 'devil's advocate.' Whatever was discussed in the circle, he would automatically take the contrary view for the purpose of examining the validity of the main thesis. In other words, he kept us on our toes."

That sounded like the Hinkelman of old, all right. In his essays and book reviews, I had seen contrariness taken to new heights. He had been hyper-critical in his approach, asking no quarter and giving none; he had had definite opinions and no qualms about sharing them with one and all. Still, what was the purpose of acting as "devil's advocate" in *this* case – unless it was to force Fred to question his own lycanthropy?

"And what were the end results?" I asked, hoping to draw the same conclusion out of Fred.

"Some of us began…to doubt the necessity of our community. They said we should disband and function individually. The rest of us criticized Mathias for provoking dissension, but he replied that he was only doing what was expected of him."

Very good! Doubt is generally recognized as the first step toward wisdom or, in this context, the first step toward rationality. Fred's remarks confirmed Hinkelman's comments in his journal. And, true to form, his removal from the scene restored Fred's psychosis to its original state.

"What happened to Mathias? How was he…removed from the, uh, pack?"

"Hunters!" Fred spat out. "Vicious creatures, seeking not food but pure destruction. They saw him as a very vulnerable specimen and hunted him unmercifully. First, they wounded him most grievously and watched him suffer; only when their unholy appetite for pain and agony had been sated did they put him out of his misery."

That was about as allegorical a view as I was likely to get concerning one man's descent into madness and suicide. In the wolf-pack analogy, Hinkelman had fallen prey to some external agency rather than some natural cause, and whatever or whoever it was had been very ruthless in its/their methods. I asked the next logical question.

"Who were these…hunters?"

Fred went very quiet then and, for a long moment, I thought I had lost him again. Abruptly, he leaped to his feet and began to circle the room. I have seen dogs become disturbed and chase themselves. I was now witnessing a human being behaving in the same fashion. It was both fascinating and upsetting – the one because Fred had expanded his lycanthropy into all phases of existence, the other because it meant he was sinking deeper into his psychosis. And there wasn't a damned thing I could do about it – unless I wanted to embrace Hinkelman's unorthodoxy, working from the inside out. I wasn't prepared to go that far – yet. Presently, Fred calmed down (I had my thumb on the "panic button" just in case) and resumed his seat on the floor.

"Sorry, Doctor. Nervous tension."

"Why is that?"

"The hunters are still in the area, still on the look-out for new prey."

"But, who *are* they? I, uh, need to recognize them for what they are."

"I can't tell you at this time. If you're accepted into the community, then all will be revealed." He looked toward the window. "I've said more than I should already. You'd better leave."

I took that as my cue that he was going to lapse into non-co-operation again and departed. I was still nowhere near a resolution of why Hinkelman had killed himself; yet, I was gathering from the unlikeliest sources a consistent tale of enmity against him and of a conscious and willful effort to destroy him. I just needed to keep probing. My only caveat was, would I then call attention to myself and thus provoke those mysterious Others to act against *me*? No matter – I had to know everything, and the Devil take those Others!

Obviously, I could hardly wait until the evening meal was done with so that I could return to my cottage and get down to business. I intended to read Hinkelman's journal from cover to cover and hopefully find some answers to all the nagging questions which had been buzzing like bees in my head for the past few days. Inasmuch as the following day was a Saturday and I didn't have any monitoring duties until the afternoon, I figured I could stay up late and sleep late. (Silly me, as it turned out.) And, lest I forget and bring more of Nurse Petrie's wrath down upon my already bruised head, I checked my files back in and immediately checked them back out for another seventy-two-hour period. The Ice Maiden received me with all the kindness of a lioness protecting her cubs and curtly thanked me for following the rules. She then returned to her desk – as succinct a dismissal as one is ever likely to get in this world. I idly searched around for a thermometer to see how far the room temperature had dropped in the previous five seconds. Finding none, I exited quickly.

As luck would have it, Bertie collared me as I was heading toward the dining room. Since the staff meeting on Monday when I had nominally supported his argument in the debate with Harry, he had tried to engage me in a protracted discussion on avoidant personality disorders (his specialty); every time he saw me (which I deliberately kept to a minimum), he usually turned the conversation to that topic, and each time I had to invent a new excuse to keep the conversation short. I wasn't indifferent to other branches of psychiatric medicine – that would have been unprofessional of me – and I didn't know everything there was to know about personality disorders. Bluntly speaking, Dr. Lambert MacIntosh had a very annoying habit that just bugged the hell out of me. Perhaps this was not a professional attitude either, but I couldn't help myself. I have already mentioned that Bertie's clothes didn't fit him at all; they were too baggy and hung on his gangly frame like rags on a wire fence. Consequently, he was forever tugging at one piece of clothing or another in a futile effort to straighten everything out in order to become "presentable"; in particular, he seemed especially fond of grabbing the crotch of his trousers and pulling this way and that. This habit did not interfere one bit with his speaking, as he could talk and tug at the same time. Yet, the act and the *area* of the act distracted from the conversation to such a degree that one despaired even to be near him. No one ever notices his/her own idiosyncrasies – they have become ingrained and thus performed unconsciously – yet, they are no less unacceptable, unless one *wishes* to create social tension. One must learn to ignore them (if at all possible).

Therefore, I gritted my teeth, chit-chatted for a few minutes until his damned tugging threatened to drive me up a wall, and thankfully excused myself to confer with the head cook about the evening's menu. Even after the evening meal had concluded, he would not let me go but insisted on accompanying me back to my cottage. And so we walked and tugged and talked some more.

Imagine my chagrin, then, when he halted before cottage number one and prepared to take his leave. Cottage number one, of course, was the source of the wonderful Chopin to which I'd been treated since my arrival and piqued my curiosity as to who my fellow aficionado was. I was dumbfounded! How was it possible that a coarse person like Bertie MacIntosh could be so acculturated? But I quickly reminded myself that I was a fine one to judge, since I had once called the streets of Chicago "home." Anyone who loved Chopin couldn't be all bad. Therefore, I made a mental note to re-evaluate my attitude toward Bertie.

I hurried off, partly out of relief but mostly out of embarrassment. Once inside my own cottage, I kicked off my shoes, tossed aside my smock and tie, and loosened my shirt. I wished I had had a bottle of something so I could really relax, but payday was still two-and-a-half weeks away (the professional staff were paid only once a month, on the first day of the month), and I had to nurse what little money I had left to cover the necessities. While Dr. Vengtman frowned on the presence of alcoholic beverages on the premises for obvious reasons, neither had he laid down any hard and fast rules but permitted each of us to use our own judgment. The one person I knew who had a bottle (and probably more than one) was the Senior, and I was sure he was nipping away that very minute. I put those thoughts aside and reached underneath the sofa-bed to retrieve the journal. No sooner had I pulled it loose than there was a tapping at the door. Muttering under my breath, I shoved the book back in its place and answered the knock.

Speak of the Devil! There stood Harry – with a bottle of cognac and two glasses in hand.

"Hello, Ken. Mind if I come in?"

Yes, Harry, I do mind.

"No. Come on in."

"Thanks. I brought a little something to help pass the time."

"Amazing! I was just thinking I'd like to have a couple of snorts."

"Hah! There you are! Birds of a feather, and all that."

I checked the label on the bottle and mentally whistled. Harry Rauschenburg certainly didn't scrimp when it came to his creature comforts. He was sporting a very expensive brand of cognac. Despite the fact that he was interfering with my own plans, I felt honored that he'd share it with the "new boy." I directed him to the lone chair in the cottage and plopped down on the sofa-bed. He poured a hefty measure in each glass, handed one over to me, and proposed a toast.

"Here's to a long and successful career!"

"I'll certainly drink to that."

I took a long sip. The liquor went down smooth, like cold liquid fire, and radiated warmth and euphoria throughout my body. A *very* good brand of cognac! I noted that Harry had tossed back half his glass in one gulp. That was no way to treat good liquor; good liquor ought to go down slow and easy. I had to laugh at myself then. That was a strange sentiment for a former street kid!

"Well, Ken," Harry said, once the toast had been completed, "I understand you've been rather busy with your inquiry into Mathias Hinkelman's death."

"Yes, I have. And I've learned a couple of things. Nothing you can put your finger on yet, but I think I'm on the right path." I wasn't too keen to discuss my recent findings with anyone just then and hoped he would accept my noncommittal remarks at face value. "I am hampered by the fact that some people are reluctant to talk about it."

"Meaning me, I suppose?" I shrugged. "Well, you should know that Mathias' death came as a huge shock – especially to those who were…close to him. It's been difficult for us to reconcile ourselves to the incident."

"I understand."

He finished off his glass, refilled it, and held out the bottle to me. I took another long sip and passed my glass over to be freshened. We both drank in silence.

"I like you, Ken," Harry said presently. "I believe you have a right to know what happened to Mathias. Therefore, I'm going to tell you what I know. Perhaps it will help you draw a conclusion."

Naturally, I was all ears!

"I suppose it's no secret," he began matter-of-factly, "that I'm gay." I nodded in agreement. "The scuttlebutt is that, before he went mad, Mathias was my lover. Nothing could be further from the truth." He swallowed another half glass. "I wish it had been true. I…loved Mathias, but he never reciprocated. After he broke off his affair with Maddie, he and I had many long talks – mostly about what was happening to him – but that's as far as our relationship went. Unfortunately, rumors have a tendency to have a life of their own."

"I get the impression that it was a rumor that drove him mad."

He peered at me curiously.

"Do you really? *I* hadn't that impression, and I pride myself on keeping my finger on the pulse of activity at the Home. I had no idea of what demons possessed him. I don't think he knew himself. I can tell you, however – based on our conversations – that he believed someone here

– someone high up – had been conspiring against him because he allegedly represented a threat to their position."

More alarm bells! What was it that Ray had told me? He had said (admittedly from a psychotic point of view) that the "town fathers" were all corrupt, that "Preacher Mathias" was the only one bold enough to stand up against them, and that they had killed him to silence him. The web of intrigue was becoming more complex.

"Did he suspect anyone in particular?"

"If he did, he never told me. Fear was part of his mental state – especially in the final weeks." He paused, toyed with his glass, then finished it off. He filled it up again. "There is one thing you ought to know, since your own recent experience seems to be paralleling Mathias'."

"My experience?"

"Yes. It has to do with Melissa Waterman."

Now I was *really* all ears!

"I understand she, uh, attached herself to Hinkelman."

"'Attached'?" He snorted derisively. "Oh, you could put it that way. It was something of a minor scandal around here, and I heard rumors to the effect that they were having sex. Mathias assured me that that was not the case, and I believed him. Melissa is a strange child, but I rather doubt she is a *sexual* creature, even in her own eyes. Yet, when Mathias and Maddie became lovers, Melissa was like a madwoman. Then, his... problems began."

"Do you think she had anything to do with them?"

"I don't see how. It is quite a co-incidence, however."

"I don't believe in co-incidences, man, and I don't think you do either."

"No? Well, then, you'd better believe you'll be in for a spot of trouble if you allow Melissa to attach herself to you. You've already become the 'talk of the town,' and you've only been here less than a week. And, I don't mind telling you, Himself is also worried."

"Dr. Vengtman? I've already told him I'd be discreet."

"Nevertheless, he's taken a dim view of the attention she's been paying you."

"*Humph!* Short of knocking her around a bit, I don't see what I can do to discourage her. She seems to have a mind of her own."

"So she does, so she does."

After that, the conversation fell to other, more mundane matters – exchanging personal histories and exploring mutual likes and dislikes – and we talked far into the night. We also finished off that fine cognac.

DAY SEVEN:
Saturday, 07.12.1997
INITIATION

As I've already stated, we professional staff had to pay our "dues" for the privilege of working at the Home in the form of various monitoring duties. Four of the six major over-sight functions occurred on a daily basis, the fifth one was a weekly one, and the sixth a quarterly one (more on the latter shortly). Since the duty roster rotated amongst only six people, it was not the least uncommon thing that each of us was engaged in monitoring every day. Before I arrived, the Home had been short-handed following the death of Mathias Hinkelman; the staff had then been on a five-day rotation and often found themselves on two rosters in a single day. Not that that had been a terrific burden or a drain on their energies – but time spent tending to the mechanics of the Home was time lost to treating patients. Thus, when I came aboard (amid, I have no doubt, great sighs of relief), the duty rosters resumed their six-day form, and the strain was reduced accordingly. I had not, of course, been thrown into the pool immediately as Monday had been my "orientation day" and Tuesday my "patient-introduction" day." Once that was behind me, however, I was quickly baptized.

I make this summary of the preceding week because it had a great deal to do with how I spent my first Saturday there. Ordinarily, the professional staff had the week-end off – off from patient-treating, that is. Since the patients were in residence twenty-four hours a day, seven days a week, the daily monitoring had to continue as usual; only those not on a roster had the week-end off (and even then perhaps not the entire week-end). Invariably, there was one exception to this "rule," and that was Visitors Day. Visitors Day fell on the second and fourth Saturdays of the month, the only times that relatives and friends of the patients were allowed to see them socially. Consequently, the entire professional staff was required to be in attendance in order to field any questions the visitors might have regarding the progress (or lack thereof) of the treatment regimen. (We were also "advised" to "mingle" and give the appearance that everything was under control. The possibility that it may not have been under control mattered little; those who were paying the bills needed to be assured that they were getting their money's worth.) Visiting hours were from 2 p.m. (right after lunch) to 6 p.m. (right before dinner), not too much time out of one's week-end but enough to hamper any long-range plans. As this was my first Visitors Day, I had been handed a memo from Dr. Vengtman to the effect that I should take care to make a "good impression" – as if I needed to be reminded!

In retrospect, if I had known beforehand what was to occur, I believe

I would have made some very different decisions that day. Hindsight sure is wonderful!

Having spent the previous evening getting soused on some of the best liquor I'd had in a long time and listening to Harry Rauschenburg expound on the current state of psychotherapy and what he'd do if he were in charge (of what, he hadn't been too specific), I didn't get to bed until after midnight. So, I had set my "internal alarm clock" for eight o'clock and slept like a log. Just before I dozed off, it occurred to me (vaguely, in an alcoholic fog) that the evening's festivities might have forestalled my so-called "initiation." I had the distinct impression that something of a *sexual* nature was involved. What if I had been "scheduled" to be "initiated" at the time I was carousing with Harry? Would he have gracefully exited, or would he have been part of it all along? Knowing him as I did, I suspected the latter was more likely. The idea of a *homosexual* seduction was a repugnant thought, and it nearly kept me awake all night.

In any event, I awoke at precisely eight o'clock, tended to my biological obligations, and threw on some old clothes. I had half-expected to have a large head due to all the drinking; but, apparently, my anticipation of the next day's events had served to act as a sobrietant. My morning agenda was to head into nearby Aurora and seclude myself in the local library with Hinkelman's journal. I'm sure I could have found a closer place to hide, but I also wanted to stop along "restaurant row" and grab a late breakfast-to-go. I threw the journal into my briefcase and headed toward the staff parking lot.

The best laid plans, etc., etc.

Just as I emerged from the wooded area, I spotted Melissa off to my right. She was squatting on the ground near the Home's service entrance and "holding court" with two fat raccoons which, presumably, had wandered onto the property on a scavenging foray. Had one (or both) of them been my "visitor" my first night here? And had it (or they) been spying on me rather than looking for a hand-out? It seemed incredible – not to mention paranoid – yet, there they were, "talking" to Melissa. The animals were sitting on their own haunches, raptly intent on the girl as if they were soldiers reporting to their commanding officer. It was an eerie sight, and I vainly tried to suppress a shudder of horror. I picked up my pace and hoped I could get to the parking lot without attracting her attention.

I had no sooner stepped onto the asphalt when I heard the *caw* of a crow high above me. Ordinarily, I would not have paid any heed to it; even a city boy like me, unused to the sounds of wildlife (beyond stray dogs and cats and the hordes of rats), had learned to filter out all but the most essential sounds. I did not live in ordinary times in those days, however. I had seen too many strange sights involving animals in the space of a week to ignore any beastly noises. So, I looked up and saw the crow circling overhead, cawing its head off. It was probably my imagination, but the bird sounded angry. Immediately, I turned in Melissa's direction. She too was observing the crow. Did she understand what it was "saying"? Then she spied me, waved cheerily, but made no move to intercept me. I thanked my lucky stars and kept moving. Even while I was pulling out of the lot, I peered into the rear-view mirror to see if the coast was clear. It wasn't: the damned crow was following me!

The Aurora Public Library seemed unusually crowded for a Saturday morning in July. I could understand the place being packed with teenagers during the school year as they researched for a term paper, but not now. Upon closer inspection, I soon recognized the situation for what it was. These "patrons" wore an all too-familiar vacuous expression, marking them as members of the growing array of homeless people, devoid of hope, looking for a place (however temporarily) to interrupt their aimless wanderings. It had become an everyday occurrence in Chicago, and even hospitals were now a "port of call" in the economic storm. I recalled one of the security guards at R-PSL telling me how, when he arrived for work, he had counted at least two dozen persons – black and white, male and female, young and old – curled up in the doorways, under the overhangs, behind the dumpsters, wherever it was relatively dry and windless. While I waited for the library clerk to serve me, I observed the security guard rouse some of the indigents who had dozed off and ask them to leave. I was shocked to learn that this woeful situation had extended out to the fringes of the metropolitan area. The shock must have been written all over my face, because the clerk followed my gaze and shrugged noncommittally.

As soon as I had introduced myself as an "out-of-towner" and an employee of the Vengtman Home for the Emotionally Disturbed and been given the "house rules," I checked out the reading area on the main level, west of the stacks. It was too crowded for my liking, and I went up to the second floor. Indigents lounged here as well, on the west side of the building; the east side, however, was practically deserted. Only two middle-aged men, engaged in a spirited conversation, occupied that space. I passed by their table (loaded with books and newspapers), settled down in the far corner, and began to read.

It didn't take me long to realize that Hinkelman's journal entries followed the same pattern as his notations in the files of his patients. Generally speaking, they grew less and less lucid as whatever evil tightened its grip upon his mind; the paragraphs devolved into single sentences, the sentences became disjointed, and finally everything was reduced to only phrases and/or single words strung out in quasi-rational fashion. I noted one curiosity: Hinkelman's repeated use of one particular phrase – "whispers in the mind" – or some variation of it. Though he had declined to say who or what was doing the whispering or how it was done (if, indeed, he possessed that information), he apparently realized that he was the object of manipulation and that someone wanted him out of the way. My own inclination was to view this repeated expression as a rationalization for his growing madness; in his confused state, he was transforming vicious rumor into a fantastic mental power and thereby feeding his own psychosis. I didn't know anyone who put credence in the concept of Svengali-like "mind-control," simply because "mind-control" could be achieved by rather ordinary and mundane methods.

In the beginning, Hinkelman wrote an entry every day, relating his woes from the time of discovering Melissa's jealousy of his affair with Maddie until he could no longer think rationally. As he retrogressed, the entries became less frequent until they occurred only every fourth day. If I had been looking for any fresh insights, I was doomed to failure; all I was getting was a compendium of dysfunctional events, compounded one upon another. I quote in its entirety the entry for December 12, 1996 – a week before his break-down and ten weeks before his suicide – as a representative example:

> dr. vengtman called me into his office this morning wanted to know what was going on why the staff was complaining about my BAD temper my LACK of decisiveness my WILD speech i told him i had no idea what he was talking about he wasn't too happy with that response suggested i take some time off even hinted at SEEKING SOME *PROFESSIONAL* HELP
> *FUCK HIS "SUGGESTIONS"!!!*
> i know what is wrong someone is *whispering in my mind!* and i can't make them stop!
> saw madeleine at lunch today she avoids me like the plague now can't blame her oh god how i miss her! if only i could tell her about the hurt in my mind she'd

understand but i can't she wouldn't believe me nobody
would believe me

saw melissa today too *DAMN HER!* it's all her fault!
the way she looks at me the way those *FUCKING* squirrels
look at me!

all of them *WHISPERING IN MY MIND!!!*
why won't they stop?

It was evident that his mind was starting to go even before this date,
before the time that the general consensus had placed it. But here had
been a cry for help, and no one had heard it. If someone had been able
to read these early-warning signs, then, conceivably, Hinkelman might
have been saved, brought back from the brink, and restored to sanity.
And, conceivably, someone might have discovered who or what had been
responsible for his deterioration and moved to counter it.

I was beginning to harbor a dark thought about my co-workers: they
knew but did nothing to help. Why? Had they been impotent in the face of
evil influence? Had they decided not to invite the same fate to themselves?
More than ever, I had to learn the truth of the matter. *I* wasn't powerless
– yet – and I was certainly no stranger to trouble. If someone wanted to
get down and dirty, they'd find more than a match in me!

I discovered one discrepancy as I read. A page toward the end of the
journal was missing – torn out hastily, apparently, as there was still a
fragment remaining in the binding with the word "her" clearly legible.
I could only surmise that this page had been written during a period of
semi-lucidity and, when Hinkelman realized what he had written, ripped
out. Did he then destroy that page? Or did he secrete it in another place
so that, even if his unknown tormentor – the "whisperer in his mind" –
chanced to discover the journal, it would be denied the most damning
"evidence" of all? It seemed to me that this missing page might hold the
key to what had befallen my predecessor and that, if one were to locate it,
this Great Mystery would be solved once and for all. Of course, being the
pragmatic sort, I thought I had the proverbial snowball's chance in Hell
of ever finding the page, although I intended to turn my cottage upside
down if I had to.

I glanced at my watch and was startled to read 12:15. I'd been here
nearly three hours! I had time, however, to photocopy the journal. I
intended to show the book to Dr. Vengtman at my earliest opportunity
and get his opinion, but I also wanted a copy in case the original somehow

got "misplaced." Not that I didn't trust the Director – it was just that, if Mathias Hinkelman believed extreme precautions had been necessary, then so did I.

I left the library half an hour later. Incredibly, the two middle-aged men were still immersed in their conversation. It was a rare sight in this "age of the information highway" with its array of satellite relays and computers to see people still take the time to actually *talk* to each other face to face. Whether these gentlemen realized it or not, they represented a dying breed.

By the time I returned to the Home, it was the middle of the second lunch period. I had enough time to go to my cottage, put Hinkelman's journal back in its hiding place, change into my doctor's "uniform," and grab a sandwich and a cup of coffee before the hordes of visitors descended upon us to disturb our island of tranquility. Or so I thought....

As I approached the cottage, I was unnerved to see Melissa sitting cross-legged on the stoop, watching me intently. And she was not alone. The two raccoons I'd seen with her earlier flanked her. They also watched me intently and showed no fear of humans.

I pulled up in front of her and flashed the best smile I had with me at the time. I doubted I was fooling anybody with my show of sincerity. *I* certainly didn't feel sincere. The proof of that came an instant later (or so I now believe) as a new vision flickered past my inner eye. Until that moment, I hadn't the least idea of what was involved in atom-splitting; nuclear physics had never been my strong suit. I know now. That day, I was afforded a highly graphic demonstration. I saw (in my mind in vivid color) a stray neutron winging its way from God-knew-where and crashing headlong into an atom. The collision was forceful enough to break the atom apart and send the protons and neutrons in its nucleus flying in all directions. Each of those particles in their turn smashed into neighboring atoms, and a chain reaction resulted. With frightening clarity, I observed a brilliant white light as the smashed atoms released all of their energy, followed by the familiar mushroom cloud of radioactive debris. I think I braced myself against an imaginary fireball and shock wave. I *know* I broke out in a cold sweat. My throat became the Sahara Desert, and my legs turned to Jell-o.

All the while, Melissa peered at me in wide-eyed innocence!

"What can I do for you, Melissa?" I rasped as soon as my head cleared.

"You're mad at me, aren't you?" she responded disingenuously.

"Well, let's say that I don't appreciate your saying horrible things about people and not explaining why."

"I told you why I can't."

"Why don't you let me be the judge of what I can or cannot believe?"

She bit her lip and looked away. As if sensing her unease, the raccoons chattered briefly and looked at me in a menacing way. I ignored them and concentrated on Melissa. Despite my reservations concerning her motives, her present anguish seemed genuine; she was wrestling with whatever passed as a conscience for her, trying to decide whether she ought to (or could) confide in me. It could have been an act, of course, in order to gain my sympathy and deflect me from further scrutiny of her motives.

"I don't know," she said at last. "Soon, maybe."

"Melissa, if you have a problem with someone, it helps if you talk about it – preferably with the other party, but definitely with someone you can trust."

"I know, I know," she murmured. "I used to trust Dr. Vengtman. But, as I got older, I realized what he was trying to do to me."

"Did you trust Dr. Hinkelman?"

If I'd wanted to drop a bombshell in order to see what effect it would have, I succeeded – maybe too well. Melissa's amethyst eyes widened, and her jaw almost fell off. The two raccoons chattered even louder and began to turn in circles. Evidently, she hadn't expected me to know anything about my predecessor. The real question was why did she react with such horror. Was it because she harbored guilt feelings over her displays of jealousy and believed I had learned about them? I took some small satisfaction in discovering that, on one point, she was as vulnerable as anyone to fits of emotionalism.

My smugness was short-lived, however. Instantly, another image popped into my head: a man screaming and falling into an abyss. If it was supposed to be a representation of Mathias Hinkelman and his fate, it certainly was apropos. It was also disturbing, and I felt like adding my voice to the "raccoon choir." The image subsided shortly as Melissa recovered from her initial shock and searched my face for understanding.

"How – how do you know about – *him*? she whispered.

"I know a great deal, mostly by having asked a lot of questions. Not everyone here is as distrusting as you are. For instance, I know you had a crush on him, and you followed him around like a puppy." She blanched and began to wring her hands. "I also know," I pressed the point, "that you became jealous when he and Dr. Chantrier became lovers." Now, she buried her face in her hands. "Tell me, Melissa, what did you do to him to drive him mad?"

"*No-o-o-o!*" she wailed. "I wouldn't do anything to him! I wouldn't. I – I *loved* him. I did, I did, *I did!*" She rocked back and forth. The raccoons, having apparently been overwhelmed by the emotional storm that had overtaken her, scampered off in a fright toward the back of the property. "I didn't want to hurt him, even though he wouldn't love me back. But – but, *he* forced me to."

"'He'? Who is 'he'?" A brief pause. "Dr.Vengtman?"

"Oh, God! I've said too much!"

She leaped to her feet and ran off in the direction the raccoons had taken. I had almost had a full confession out of her; she had been on the verge of divulging her part in my predecessor's death and that of some co-conspirator (though I suspected that she might be fabricating the existence of an "evil mastermind" in order to assuage her own guilt). I hoped I hadn't scared her so much that she would never speak to me again or even come near me. The staff and patients could tell me only so much – the latter through the filters of their psychoses, a most unreliable method of fact-finding – and Hinkelman's journal likewise. Melissa was in possession of the whole story, and I had to shift into high gear and go after it without faltering.

Of course, there was always the possibility that she might retaliate against *me* for exposing her sordid acts to the light of day and initiate a whispering campaign to discredit and/or to destroy me. It thus behooved me to anticipate any allegations she might raise and present counter-arguments. My best defense was to go to the Director and lay all the cards on the table; then, whatever Melissa dreamed up would boomerang on her. My only question in that regard was whether I should do so now as soon as the opportunity presented itself or wait until the Monday morning staff meeting. It depended, I supposed, on how soon Melissa acted (if she acted at all).

It is one of the peculiarities of us humans that we never adhere to a strict punctuality. We have a "biological clock" within us all, keeping "time" over all the rhythmic functions of our bodies. Yet, this clock never strikes the same "hour" for any two persons; it is "turned on" at the moment of conception and ticks away within its own parameters until Death turns it off. No human has an "atomic clock" which measures Time on the macro-cosmic scale and helps us keep our everyday appointments at the exact moments they are to be kept. No one in the history of the species, therefore, has ever been "on time." Rather, (s)he has been either early or late, even by a fraction of a second. The former state reflects gross mismanagement of one's affairs, and the latter careless disregard for them. But, if all the billions on Earth were ever "on time," we should be a race of robots instead of flesh-and-blood creatures, trading in our individual idiosyncrasies for the rigid precision of a machine. One must take the bad with the good.

Thus it was that the first of the day's visitors drove up the driveway around one-forty-five, someone so anxious to see his/her loved one that (s)he couldn't wait another fifteen minutes. At times like these (so said Dr. Vengtman), we were supposed to be "flexible" and not begrudge the early arrival. That's all very well and good if you're not trying to stuff something into your belly so that you have the strength to carry out your assigned tasks; that's all very well and good if you're not the "new boy" and the Director doesn't want to introduce you to each and every visitor and particularly to those whose loved ones you are treating.

As my "luck" would have it, that first arrival (tooling up the driveway in a silver Lincoln Continental) was Georgina's banker husband, and he was naturally anxious about his wife's progress in light of the demise of her former doctor and the hiring of a replacement – one who was *untested* and perhaps not the best use of the hefty fees he was paying. Dr. Vengtman had me paged over the PA system, requesting my immediate presence in the parlor. I crammed the sandwich I had just started into my mouth, chewed a couple of times, and swallowed, expediting the process with a large gulp of coffee. I was sure I would need an antacid tablet (or two or three) later on. Then I hot-footed it toward the parlor.

Like everyone else associated with the Home, visitors were required to sign in and out. The rationale for this had a security factor built in, but that was not the prime reason for having the procedure. Another of the Great Man's innovative ideas had been the correlation of a positive social environment to a patient's "cure rate"; part of that PSE was the frequency of visitations whereby the patient (theoretically) progressed (or not) according to the degree of interest his relations had in his well-being. Visitations were always encouraged, and the number of visitors a patient received during his/her stay at the Home figured into the evaluations made by the staff. Upon signing in, visitors consulted with the appropriate staff person before being escorted to the visitor's area – the veranda in clement weather and the parlor at other times. The consultations themselves served a double purpose: (1) to update the visitor, and (2) to allow the counselor to observe his/her attitudes and reactions, all of which also went into the evaluations. Dr. Vengtman believed that no stone should be left unturned in the healing process.

It is not a pleasant task to greet a relative when you have nothing positive to tell him/her. Even if you're the "new boy" and are just feeling your way around, you can't use that as an excuse – not to one who's paying your salary. Instead, you must smile cheerfully, welcome him/her heartily, and say something – anything – by way of encouragement. It sounds deceitful – and probably is – but that was the protocol to follow.

So I did. I told Mr. W. all of the little white lies I'd heard during my days of internship and used during my days of residency at R-PSL and made up a few of my own. I even sounded sincere too. The sad fact of the matter was that Georgina was as psychotic as the day she'd been committed. Mathias Hinkelman had had a modicum of success (however he had accomplished it); but his death had left her without a sustained source of PSE, and she'd suffered a relapse. She might have accepted me as her new counselor – or not (I wasn't too sure on that point) – but I was nowhere near finding a hook upon which to hang a cure – unless, of course, I wanted to imitate Hinkelman's role-playing.

As soon as Mr. W. had been taken to his wife, the Director had another person he wanted to show me off to. After the sixth one to sign in (Arthur's older brother), I was beginning to feel like the prize bull at the county fair. Around four o'clock, there was a welcome lull, and I was given leave to relax a while. And not a moment too soon, for my bladder was signaling for relief!

When I had taken care of business and was returning to the parlor, I spied Nurse Clement quick-stepping toward the kitchen. Since I was behind him, he never spotted me. I wondered what he was doing here; according to the day's work schedule, this was his day off. Did he love the place so much that he felt a need to hang out here on his own time? I might not have given much thought about his motives ordinarily as he might have had a legitimate reason for being here. In any event it wasn't my responsibility to monitor the activities of the non-professional staff. Still, because of the enmity he had shown toward me (with, I might add, the least provocation from me) and Melissa's warnings about "extra-curricular" activities on his part, my suspicions shot up a few notches, and I decided to follow him.

He did not enter the kitchen after all but halted at the door leading to the basement. Alarm bells sounded. Was it true then what Melissa had said about him? Was he on his way to yet another secret tryst? I kept out of sight as Clement waited there for a couple of minutes. Then, I heard the soft padding of crepe-soled shoes on the carpeting behind me, and I pressed further into my hiding place. A female nurse glided by, her head down. I was shocked when I saw who it was – the nervous Nurse Michaels – and from the look on her face, I deduced that she'd rather have been somewhere else than here. When she joined Clement, he flashed her a big garbage-eating grin and opened the door for her. She didn't quite meet his gaze. The two of them quickly entered the basement.

I allowed them a minute's head start in order to give Clement a chance to incriminate himself while not letting him go too far in his actions. I wasn't interested in salvaging (or savaging, for that matter) reputations – it was too late for that – but only in hustling them out of the basement in the shortest time possible. After a count of sixty, I carefully opened the basement door myself, quietly closed it behind me, and slowly descended the squeaky stairs so as to make the minimal amount of noise. Hopefully, the trysting couple would be too absorbed in their activity to hear an errant creak or two. At the bottom of the stairs, I took my bearings again. It was easy to do, since I now heard two voices from the direction of the furnace. As I crept closer, the voices grew more distinct.

Clement: "...me a blow job this time."

Michaels: "God, you're sick!"

Clement: "Maybe, sweet thing, but that's what I want."

By the time I had reached the furnace and was peeking around it, Clement was sitting on the cot, his trousers and underwear bunched down around his ankles. Michaels knelt before him, her head bent low. I didn't need the *Kama Sutra* to tell me what was going on. I stepped around the furnace.

"That's far enough, you two!" I declared in what I hoped was an authoritative voice. Michaels, still on her knees, twisted around, recognized me, and let out a loud scream. Her sudden movement threw her off balance, and she fell sideways against the cot. Clement jerked his head up at the intrusion, his eyes wide with fright; he was on his feet in an instant, clawing at his clothes and pulling them up as fast as he could. When he recognized the intruder, fright turned to pure hatred.

"Son-of-a-*bitch*! Fuckin' Dr. Maxwell!"

"Well, Clement, I finally caught you with your pants down – literally."

"Oh, please, Dr. Maxwell!" Michaels cried out. "He forced me! He said that was the only way I could advance here."

"Shut yer fuckin' mouth, bitch!" Clement roared. "Or I'll shut it for ya!"

"You can claim 'sexual harassment' if you want, Michaels, but you'll do it before the Director."

"You gonna report this?" Clement asked.

"What do you think?" I sneered.

"You motherfucker! I had a good thing goin' here, and I ain't gonna let some fuckin' nigger fuck it up."

I hadn't heard the "N-word" since I left the streets of Chicago. The last person to call me that was a cop who had busted me for possession of drugs (which he had planted on me in the first place). Occasionally, I still visualize his sneering face and the hatred in his eyes. I saw the same in the person before me there at the Home, and it was *déjà vu* all over again. This time, however, I was not the same street punk at the mercy of one of Chicago's "finest"; I held the high moral ground, and I was in charge of the situation.

"You just said the 'magic word,' Clement. Come and get me."

He stepped forward and delivered a round-house right that would have decked anyone with whom it connected. It did not connect with me, however. I was a veteran of more street fights than I cared to remember, and I knew when to swing and when to duck. I ducked by moving backwards, and Clement's punch hit only air. Unfortunately, I had temporarily forgotten about the maze of low-level pipes and ducts down here; when I moved backwards, I cracked my head against one of them, creating a sharp pain throughout my skull. Perhaps it was the combination of the racial slur, the impromptu assault, and the agonizing pain, but I experienced something I thought I had left behind in my former life. All of a sudden, despite the fact that I was now a doctor sworn to preserve life, I wanted to take this joker out in the worst way.

Consequently, I set my feet in an all-too-familiar manner and waited for Clement to come at me again. He did not disappoint me. I had no idea of his background (and cared even less), but I was sure that, as a fighter, he was strictly an amateur. He telegraphed his next move and left himself wide open. I easily blocked it, stepped forward, and gave him a solid blow to the stomach. He groaned loudly and doubled up. I hit him twice more for good measure, and he collapsed to the floor unconscious. A doctor is not supposed to yield to violent impulses, but I must confess that it felt *good* to punch that dude's lights out. I'd take my chances with any criticism, if and when the time came.

Michaels eyed me fearfully. I looked at her with both pity and contempt. Maybe it wasn't her fault that she had gotten mixed up with a creep like Clement; yet, in this day and age of raised consciousness, she should have been more resistant.

"Wh-what are you goin' to do about me?" she stammered.

"I'll report this incident, of course, and you can tell your story to Dr. Vengtman. Maybe you'll catch him in a good mood. Now, get out of here!"

She didn't have to be told twice. Quickly scrambling to her feet, she made a mad dash for the stairs. Too many mad dashes, in fact -- I heard distinct thuds as her head connected with the damned pipes, followed by two yelps of pain. Then, apparently, she lost her footing on the way up, for I heard a sharp crack as of bone against wood, followed this time by a most unladylike curse.

I left Clement lying where he was and exited the basement myself. If he knew what was good for him, he'd leave the Home and never come back. On the way to the stairs, however, I was startled to see a pair of red eyes peering at me from behind the furnace. By the time I had reached the stairs, the eyes' owner had scurried away. I was still being "monitored" by the wildlife here.

When I returned upstairs, I heard the PA system urgently calling me to the parlor. I quick-marched the short distance and confronted a half-perplexed, half-annoyed Dr. Vengtman. Nan was with him.

"Well," he said suavely, "we'd begun to think you had gotten lost."

"Sorry, sir. My...business took a bit longer than I thought. What have I missed?"

"Matthew J.'s daughter arrived – she's with him now – but you can catch her on her way out. In the meantime, I'd like you to submit a written evaluation of today's visitors."

"An...evaluation?"

"First impressions, that sort of thing. Ordinarily, I'd ask Harry to do it; but, as you're a fresh face, I want to get a fresh perspective. Don't look so distraught, my boy. Remember, you're the one who raised the issue of 'social environment' at our last staff meeting. Well, this is part of the fact-gathering process."

"Yes, sir. If I'd known about this earlier, I'd have paid closer attention to the visitors."

"Do your best. Um, before I forget, I want to commend you for the way you handled that incident in the dining room. It showed great restraint on the one hand and great resolve on the other. You realize, of course, that you've acquired a certain reputation for taking charge."

"Thank you, sir. I'd like to think I've been inspired by my own 'social environment.'"

"Heh-heh. Flattery may get you everywhere, or it may not. But, tell me, weren't you afraid of compounding the combatants' delusions by offering yourself as a target?"

Out of the corner of my eye, I saw Nan smirking at me. Obviously, she enjoyed watching people squirm under the scrutiny of her uncle. Any personal feelings I had for her aside, I was not going to give her any satisfaction!

"On the contrary, Dr. Vengtman. Since the prime function of the counselor is to sound out the patient and lead him to confront his problem squarely, I was merely following established techniques." I gestured placatingly. "Well, my own variation of established techniques."

"And admirably too. I've received nothing but good words from professional and non-professional staff alike. You've been an immense help to the Home – so far."

A word of praise and a word of caution in the same breath – so typical of Lowell Vengtman. For the second time since my arrival, I blushed like a schoolboy. He started to take his leave. I was then reminded of the one non-professional staff person who probably *didn't* have a kind word for me.

"Excuse me, sir. There's another matter I need to report."

"Yes?"

"Um, I think I'd better put it in writing and make it official."

"Very well," he said, somewhat miffed. "Turn in your report along with your evaluations."

Characteristically, he walked off without another word. I glanced at Nan. She was still smirking.

"And what, may I ask, is so damned funny?"

"You," she replied candidly. "You seem to be so in awe of Uncle Lowell."

"I guess I am. After all, he's a giant in the field."

"So he is, so he is. Sorry, Ken. I'm being very unfair about this. I grew up with the man, and so I have a slightly different perspective. 'Awe' was not part of it."

"What *is* your perspective then?"

She looked off in the direction her uncle had taken, a pensive expression on her face.

"Once upon a time, he was as care-free as they come, if you can believe that. Oh, he was serious about his work – dedicated as well, in fact – but he never let work interfere with his private life. He never married – don't ask me why – and never had a family of his own. So, he sort of 'adopted' his nephews and nieces and doted on us all. He was my personal inspiration to pick psychotherapy as a career, and I'd like to think I've succeeded by my own ability. Yet, I sometimes wonder how much difference having the Vengtman name made.

"Anyway, Uncle Lowell changed – almost overnight. This was in 1984, a couple of years after he established the first Home in Harrisburg, Pennsylvania. What happened, I have no idea – he's never talked about it – but, suddenly, he was no longer the Dutch-uncle type he used to be. He'd have mood swings, and sometimes he went around for days on end as if the weight of the world was on his shoulders. Oh, he was still nice to the family, but he…just put more distance between himself and us."

"That's definitely the Lowell Vengtman I know. One minute, he sees you; the next, you're invisible."

"Exactly. I've tried to get him to open up, but he always changes the subject."

"So, the Great Man has a dark side after all. That would make for a super case study."

"Don't expect any co-operation from me," she said sharply, "if you're planning such a project. I've told you all this in strictest confidence; I won't be a party to public dissection."

"Not to worry, Nan. I was just thinking out loud."

"I'm glad to hear it. Uh, before I forget, how rich am I today?"

"Excuse me?"

"Did I win the pool, you ninny?"

"Oh. Sorry, no, you didn't."

She grimaced in frustration, and I had the distinct impression that she wasn't too terribly concerned about the money. Was she then as anxious as I was to go out on a date? I certainly hoped so!

"Damn!" she whispered. "No initiation yet?"

"Not unless drinking and shooting the bull with Harry all night constitutes an 'initiation.'"

"You were with *Harry* all night?" she asked suspiciously.

"Yeah. He came over with a bottle of cognac, and we sorta unwound." Then I noticed a trace of worry slide across her face. "Hey! It's not what you're thinking! I don't play *those* games." Instant relief washed over her.

"It was just a couple of guys getting drunk – except I think Harry got drunker. He seems to have a problem in that department."

"Uh-huh. The rest of us try to drop subtle hints now and – "

She was cut off by the squealing of tires in the front drive. We went to the window adjacent to the main entrance and peeked out, just in time to observe a blue-and-white pick-up truck disappear behind the lilac bushes on its way off the property. The tire-squealing repeated itself at each curve; whoever was driving was in a big hurry.

"What the hell?" I muttered.

"That looked like Clement's truck. I wonder what he was doing here."

I didn't have to wonder. I knew why. Yet, I kept silent. This was still between me and the Director and not for public discussion.

I assumed, by Dr. Vengtman's abrupt departure, that there were no more visitors for me to greet. I couldn't dismiss myself just yet, however, in case one in my group had a question. So, I took a seat on the veranda and mentally composed the reports I was going to submit. Nan excused herself to the powder room, promising to see me at the evening meal.

The visitor evaluation was the more difficult to write than the whistle-blowing. Try describing another's emotional state simply by observing his physical gestures. Further, describe them and not allow your own emotions to color your opinions. A rational view of emotion sounds like an oxymoron; but, though it requires a great deal of self-discipline, it can be accomplished. I didn't know if I had as much as I needed. The incident with Clement was still on my mind and kept getting in the way. I must have struggled for a good half hour before I dared to put anything on paper.

While I was cogitating, I spotted Melissa again, returning from the woods in the company of some of her squirrels. She looked in my direction briefly, then quickly turned away. Apparently, she was still laboring under our earlier conversation. If she wanted to avoid me for a while, that was her business; there was plenty of time to confront her and get her to open up to me.

Eventually, Visitors Day came to a close, and I set my reports aside long enough to see the last visitor off. I noted with no small amount of wryness that all of them to a man and woman seemed even grimmer than when they had first arrived. That was not entirely unexpected. If I had been in their shoes, showing up twice a month and seeing no improvement in their loved ones, I'd have been gloomy too. I was glad I didn't have to look at those forlorn faces more often; I didn't think I could have looked at them on a steady basis. On the other hand, their relatives were probably in the best place they could be; the Vengtman Homes were, to use an electronics-industry term, "state-of-the-art." It may have been sheer braggadocio to say so, but if the patients could not be cured at a Home, they could not be cured anywhere. When the last vehicle pulled out of the gate, I was able to call it a day.

After supper, I retrieved Hinkelman's journal again in order to scrutinize it even more closely. Specifically, I wanted to correlate precisely the dates of each entry with similar (if any) dates in his notations in his patients' files; by cross-referencing, I hoped to establish (if at all possible) a day-by-day, week-by-week timetable of his decline into madness. I had observed previously that troubled people tended to use identical language in different contexts. If Hinkelman had run true to form, then he should have written much the same thing in both the journal and the files. The key lay in certain words and phrases not ordinarily used in one's general writings. I already had one such phrase – "whispers in the mind" – and, if it occurred at the same frequency in both formats, I'd have a rudimentary timetable.

Because this had to be done methodically, I began by plopping down on the floor and setting the five files in a row in front of me. Then, with the journal opened to the first entry, I took up my notepad and wrote at the top of the page "August 10, 1996." One by one, I searched the files for that date (or one very close to it) and wrote down a synopsis of what Hinkelman had written. Had anyone peeped in the window and seen what I was doing, he might have feared for *my* sanity. When I had completed the "first round," the first page of my notepad appeared as follows:

> MH (journal) – states that MW is jealous of his affair with MC. Says the way she looks at him is "nothing short of eerie." Specifically mentions MJ and GW being on the "road to recovery," using treatment that is "bizarre."

> RW (file) – no notations.

> MJ (file) – tells "invisible man" he is acting "bizarrely," and the old man agrees for the first time.

> FK (file)– no notation on this date, but two days later, the

"wolf man" asks why M W looks so "eerie." Non-committal reply given. (The "grapevine " in any organization being what it is, news of changing relationships between people travels fast – even among emotionally-disturbed persons.)

TM (file) – "Poe" quotes "The Raven." Places emphasis on the line "take thy beak from out my heart." Wonders if this is related to others' reactions.

GW (file) – no notation on this date, but the day before, "Lewis" is alleged to have said that something "bizarre" is going on but will not elaborate. (There seems to be a mutual feed-back at work here, whereby Hinkelman was picking up vocabulary from his patients and *vice versa*. Discovering an increase in this sort of activity will signify a deepening psychosis.)

Upon re-reading the page, I found that I was off to a good start, as long as I remained alert to the fact that I was dealing with *blocks* of time and not just individual dates. This suggested to me that Hinkelman's descent into insanity may not have been gradual, but incremental. How and why this should be, I wasn't prepared to say – it was only a proto-theory – yet the answers, I was sure, lay somewhere in these records. Doggedly then, I proceeded to the next entry.

About halfway through the second page of my notepad, I heard a tapping at my door. At first, I was startled because of my absorption in my task, and I jerked upright and twisted around toward the door. Who could have been calling at that hour? Harry again with more booze? I had been counting on having the evening to myself, and instantly astonishment turned to annoyance at the unwelcome intrusion. If it was Harry again, seeking relief for his loneliness, I would have to let him know that he couldn't just barge in on me any time he damned please and that I needed my space once in a while.

I requested the caller to wait a minute and scrambled to gather up the piles of papers on the floor. The files were tossed hastily on the chair, and the journal went back to its accustomed place. I made a quick glance around to make sure all was in order, then answered the door. As I swung it open, I prepared to give the intruder a large piece of my mind. I got the shock of my young life when I saw who it was.

Nurse Petrie!

And she was *smiling*!

I don't know what surprised me more, her being here or her smiling. Both were out of character. Perhaps it was a snap judgment on my part – I didn't know anything about her background – but I had little to go on beyond her previous behavior toward me. In any event, I scrutinized her face on the sly just to see if it were cracking. The smile she wore was a coy one, the kind a fox would make (if a fox could smile) after being questioned about the loss of some chickens from the coop, the kind a human being would make when he is up to something not quite kosher. Was that why she was here? Was she going to raise more hell about yesterday's contretemps? Couldn't she wait until Monday morning?

She was wearing a pair of faded jeans, a rumpled gray sweatshirt with the logo of Aurora University (I presumed it was where she had taken her nursing degree), and a pair of beach sandals. She almost looked human, but I knew that was an illusion. I stayed on my guard.

"Good evening, Dr. Maxwell," she greeted me (and I could have sworn she *purred*!).

"Good evening, Nurse Petrie," I replied stiffly. "To what do I owe the pleasure of this visit?"

"There's no need to be so sarcastic, Doctor. I'm paying a social call."

"A social call?" I almost laughed out loud but restrained myself. "You mean you're not here to rag me about yesterday?"

"Of course not. I would have come last night, but I was still upset. Tonight, that incident is ancient history. May I come in?"

Actually, no. I'm right in the middle of a big research project, and I don't care to be disturbed. Especially by a frigid bitch like you.

"Sure. Why not?"

She eased by me slowly, brushing up against me. I reeled slightly – not from the contact, but from the heady perfume she was wearing. Once inside, she circled the room nonchalantly, examining each object minutely. When she spied the files piled carelessly on the chair, I steeled myself; I was sure she'd have a cow over how I was treating them. She said not a word, however, but continued her inspection – which even included the bathroom. When she returned to the main room, she stood in the middle of the floor, arms folded across her chest, and eyed me wolfishly. She was acting damned strange, and I wished I knew what she was up to. I didn't believe for a minute that she was paying a "social call."

"Are you aware, Doctor," she said breathily, "that a murder took place here?"

In my present frame of mind, at first I thought she was talking about Mathias Hinkelman, and a spark of interest began to ignite in me. Then I realized she was referring to the *prior* history of the mansion-cum-Home and became annoyed again at this attempt at small talk.

"Uh, yes. I heard the story when I first applied for the, uh, vacant position. A local scandal, wasn't it?"

"Right. But, do you know *exactly* where the murder occurred?"

"No, but I'm sure you're going to tell me."

"Here, right where I'm standing. One of the guests didn't think his 'date' was friendly enough. They argued, and she gutted him." She looked at me coyly. "Don't you find that...exciting?"

"Not really. Where I grew up, that sort of thing was an everyday occurrence. One tended to shrug it off."

"Ah, poor Dr. Maxwell." She stared off into the distance. "Such a stunted childhood. May I sit down?"

What in the world was she doing? She sounded almost...sympathetic. Perhaps she was under the influence of some new designer drug, like "lace," and was riding a "high." Why else would she have paid a "social call" on someone whom she barely tolerated on the job if she were not in her right mind? If so, it would have been a startling development, and I could just picture the Director having a cow himself when he learned that members of his staff were drug abusers.

"Please. I'm forgetting my manners."

She sat down on the edge of the sofa-bed, crossed her legs, and leaned forward. And still she held onto that guess-what's-on-my-mind smile. Awkwardly, I set the files on the floor and plopped into the chair. What now? As far as I knew, we had nothing in common, and any conversation was going to be limited. I supposed I could have asked her about her work, tedious as that sounded. If only she stopped looking at me like I was a T-bone steak!

"So, Nurse," I mumbled, "how long have you been working at the Home?"

"Since it opened," she replied smoothly. "You might say I was one of the first inmates."

"*Humph*! I would hardly classify you as an 'inmate.'"

"And how *would* you classify me?"

"Don't ask."

"'Ice maiden'? 'Petrie the Popsicle'? 'The Iceberg.'? 'Deep-freeze Donna'? Take your pick, Doctor."

"Um, well, I –"

"Don't be embarrassed on my account. I'm quite used to it by now."

"Well, uh, if maybe you, uh, *smiled* more…"

"I'm smiling now."

Was it getting warmer in the room?

"Yes, I can see that."

"And my face hasn't cracked, has it?"

I grinned in spite of myself. Perhaps there was a hidden side to Nurse Petrie, one that only needed encouragement. Now, there would have been a challenge-and-a-half!

"No, it hasn't."

Abruptly, she stood up and sauntered across the room. I started to rise as well, but she placed a hand on my chest and gently pushed me back down. Before I realized what was happening, she settled in my lap, facing me and straddling my legs. She placed both hands on my shoulders, leaned forward, and gave me the juiciest French kiss I'd ever had. Even if my mouth had been free, I still would've been at a loss for words. Her action had been so unexpected that I responded instinctively (as any normal male would) and forgot momentarily who I was kissing. It was not unpleasant, and I suddenly became aware of how long it had been since I was with a woman. However she had done it, Petrie had pushed all the right buttons. Presently, she came up for air.

"Now, Doctor, if I'm such an 'iceberg,' would I have been capable of that?"

"Ah, n-o-o-o."

"Or this?"

She slid one hand down my arm, clasped my hand, and pushed it under her sweatshirt. Guiding my hand up the warm, soft flesh of her belly and lower rib cage, she brought it to rest over a medium-sized breast. On my own initiative, I ran my other hand under the sweatshirt and massaged both breasts with slow, kneading motions. Petrie "Frenched" me again. By now, I knew what was coming next; and, despite the unusual circumstances and the unlikely partner, I wanted it to happen. It *had* been too long since the last woman. She seemed to sense my need as well; casually, she slid a hand down to my crotch and massaged me there, though it was hardly necessary. I was fully erect, and my manhood was ready to rip a hole in my pants. Deftly, she unzipped me, reached in, and pulled it out. With one forefinger, she lightly stroked the shaft, and I began to ache all over.

Petrie "Frenched" me a third time, clambered off my lap, and knelt before me. She gripped my penis and licked the head with long, languorous strokes of her tongue. A huge wave of desire coursed through my body, and the aching intensified. Instantly, she swallowed me whole, sucking the shaft from top to bottom and playing her tongue around and around it. I hoped I could hold out for as long as possible as the pressure in my groin increased; Petrie certainly knew what she was doing, and I didn't want her to stop on account of a lack of endurance. Soon -- all too soon -- I exploded in a tremendous climax and leaned back in the chair, totally spent. She reached into a pocket of her jeans, pulled out a handkerchief, and spat into it. Then she rose, sat down on my lap again, and grinned hugely.

"Was that the right prescription, Doctor?" she murmured.

"Absolutely!" I rasped. "Thank you for your expert assistance, Nurse."

"You're entirely welcome."

She leaned forward and "Frenched" me yet again. Then she stood up and turned to leave. I was thunderstruck. I thought she was here for the night and said as much.

"You've had your quota, dear Dr. Maxwell. Just enjoy what you've gotten."

"But – but –"

"No buts." She sauntered toward the door, turned back, and smiled again. "Welcome to the Home, Doctor."

Then she was gone. I sat there stupefied. I'd had the most colossal "blow job" from the last person on earth I would have suspected of such an act, and now I was being cut off before I had a chance to show my new partner what *I* was capable of. I could not hope that Nurse Petrie would be more amenable in the future; she seemed to have hinted that this had been strictly a one-night stand.

And, while I was pondering that thought, her last words finally sank in, and the realization hit me like a sledgehammer. Despite my exhausted state, I laughed like a madman. After all the waiting, after all the anxious questioning by my co-workers, after all my puzzling over the anticipated event, The Moment had arrived – without warning and in a most pleasant fashion.

I had just been "initiated"!

DAY EIGHT:
Sunday, 07.13.1997
INVESTIGATION

This day, the chickens came home to roost.

I woke up feeling greatly refreshed and ready to tackle the world. They say that sex is an excellent soporific; if one has trouble falling asleep, a roll in the hay is highly recommended. Maybe, and maybe not. I have never had any trouble sleeping. My problem was finding the time. In any event, I didn't look at sex as an aid to *insomnia*. Nurse Petrie had stimulated every fiber of my being and pushed my pleasure threshold to new heights, but I doubted that she contributed to a good night's sleep.

To my great annoyance, however, my co-workers had waited eagerly for me to be "initiated," the nature and details of which they had kept highly secret, and they had wagered money on the event as if it were a horse race or a lottery. My feelings on the matter had not concerned them one bit; I had been expected to carry on the "tradition." Enjoyable as my time with the "Ice Maiden" had been, that's all it had been to her – a tradition she had long ago agreed to participate in for her own reasons – and I would probably be wasting my time in attempting to pursue her.

And if Petrie reverted to her former self, there was always Nancy Vengtman, whom I still lusted after. I suspected she was as anxious to be with me as I was to be with her; she had practically guaranteed me a date once I had been "initiated." Well, the waiting was over, and there was nothing to prevent me from exploring Nan's charms – nothing, that is, except my own ineptness (and I had never had any problems in that department either!).

The Sunday meal schedule was a bit different than the week-day schedule: two meals instead of three – brunch from 9 a.m. to 11 a.m. and supper from 5 p.m. to 7 p.m. I had a couple of hours to kill before the first shift, and I spent them in continuing to record the similarities in phraseology between Hinkelman's journal and his notations in the medical files. It was nothing short of astonishing to note how more parallel Hinkelman's vocabulary became the further one moved along the time line of the journal. Certain words and phrases popped up with increasing regularity as if the deeper he plunged into insanity, the less he could distinguish between his private and professional musings and the more apt he was to use whatever medium was closest to hand.

The most frequent expression – "whispers in the mind" – first saw the light of day in the journal entry for September 1, 1996; and, curiously, it had cropped up in Fred's file the day after that, as Hinkelman had been talking to the "wolf-man" about a new danger to the "pack" and used the phrase to provide emphasis. According to the file, Fred had replied that he too sensed a "disturbing influence." Strange that I hadn't noticed this the first time I'd read his file. On the other hand, I had been attempting to get a handle on Hinkelman's "methodology," not solving the mystery of his untimely death. Now that I had a different mission, I was more thorough than ever; and, by the time I had analyzed three-fourths of the journal, I had written nearly thirty pages in my notepad. I was now making more detailed observations with each succeeding entry, and I found myself backtracking continually in order not to overlook even the most innocuous word or phrase. I was not going to leave anything to chance!

It was time for a break, and I was very hungry. And I was getting very stiff, sitting on the floor in an awkward position, craning my neck to check out one file or another, and trying to write while the notepad was also on the floor. I stood up, stretched hugely, and went off to Sunday brunch.

In one of those rare instances, all but one of my colleagues were seated in the staff dining room. (The exception was Bertie, who was meal monitor for the day.) They were in various stages of feeding their faces, but they halted the instant I walked in. Harry and Nan regarded me with bemusement, while Maddie and Dante showed expectation. I halted in the middle of the room and declared in a loud voice:

"You can all stop wondering now. It happened last night. I hope you're happy. I know I am."

This announcement produced a hearty round of applause from the group. Harry put on his widest, toothiest grin yet.

"So, you're initiated, eh? And how did you like your 'ordeal'?"

"You want me to tell you in front of the ladies?"

"These 'ladies'" Nan retorted, "have heard a lot more than anything you might tell us. Give us the juicy details, Ken."

I could swear she was licking her chops!

"Sorry, folks. I'm not the 'kiss-and-tell' type. I will say, however, that I got my socks knocked off – in more ways than one. So, who's the big winner?"

"You'll never guess in a million years," Harry replied with a smirk.

He pulled a sheet of paper out his jacket pocket, glanced briefly at it, and handed it over to me. I took one look at it and goggled.

"You have got to be kidding!" I exclaimed. Harry shook his head. I looked at the name again and murmured: "I'll be damned!"

Actually, "I'll be damned" was entirely too mild a response to express what I felt at that moment. Who would have believed that the eminent Dr. Lowell Vengtman would participate in a lottery based on someone's sexual encounters? Not I, I can tell you! It seemed quite beneath the Great Man's dignity – or that of any of this distinguished company. I could well imagine a bunch of adolescent males engaging in such antics (and, in my younger days, I had seen – and done – plenty of that), but not a group of psychotherapists. What was it the Director had told me when I'd questioned him about the prurient limericks he allowed at staff meetings? In an atmosphere of high tensions and high expectations, one needed an outlet to relieve oneself – even if the outlet appeared to be gross and/or obscene to the outsider. Obviously, Dr. Vengtman also needed his outlets as well and had chosen this bit of voyeurism as his relief valve. Shocking though it had been at first, I soon realized the rationale for his participation.

Once the shock had subsided, I turned my attention to the matter of having brunch. Just as I did my first morning here, I took a little of everything – maybe a little extra on the eggs Benedict – and had to pile it up in order to fit it all on the plate. Sunday brunch was considered a special meal, and the head cook had expanded the menu with a few extra items not ordinarily seen during the week. For a brief moment, I considered using *two* plates (I noticed Harry had done so); but, on second thought, I decided that, if I was still hungry, I could always go back for seconds. I sat down opposite Nan and dug in. She eyed first the mound of food, then me. Propping her elbows on the table, she rested her chin on clasped hands and regarded me with her all-knowing smile. Between mouthfuls, I gave her a quizzical expression.

"My, my," she murmured, "we've got a healthy appetite this morning, haven't we?"

"Indeed, Dr. Vengtman." If she was going to be coy, I damned well could be coy too. "When one labors mightily in the area of maintaining good working relationships with one's colleagues, one must keep up the energy reserves. One never knows when one will be called upon to perform one's duty."

"Bullshit!"

I nearly choked on a bite of toast at the sudden profanity.

"How unladylike and unprofessional!" I chided mockingly.

"Just telling it like it is, Ken dear."

"Speaking of which, were you and Maddie 'initiated' in the same fashion as well?" She gave me a sharp look, and I held up a hand in a conciliatory gesture. "I know I asked you about that before I knew what was going to happen, but now that I do know, I'm just curious."

She paused for the longest time, a mannerism she obviously had picked up from her uncle. Then:

"Is it important that you know?" I shrugged. "I'm not a 'kiss-and-tell' person either."

"I see a double standard here," I said with feigned wounded innocence. "Everyone knows about *my* sexual partner of last night, but I'm denied knowledge of others' partners."

"Put a sock in it, Doctor!" Now she assumed a more serious attitude. "Someday I'll tell you, when we're – Well, I'll tell you. Right now, I'd rather not think about it."

"OK, I give up." I smirked at this point and elicited a quizzical expression from her. "You may be upset to learn that Petrie robbed you of the pot. She told me she had intended to stop by Friday night, but she was upset with me that day and so postponed our 'date.'"

"And how did you manage to upset the 'Iceberg'?" I told her about my little unannounced foray, and she grimaced. "I'm surprised she bothered to see you at all. That was certainly a stupid thing to do."

"Yeah. Next time, I'll wait until after dark, then break into the place." That got a shocked look out of her. "Just kidding, Nan." I began to pick at my eggs Benedict. "Um, now that I have been through the hoops, are we still on for dinner?"

"Unless you're lusting after Nurse Petrie, we are."

"I don't think she's interested in a return engagement. She's done her part for The Cause. Look, tonight is out; I'm scheduled for my first over-nighter. How's tomorrow sound?"

"No can do. I've switched with Maddie on *her* overnighter. Day after tomorrow?"

"You're on. I can't wait."

"Neither can I."

I walked Nan back to her cottage, making small talk and big plans. When she asked me in, I was very tempted. But, I remembered that I still had two pieces of unfinished business – the two reports I owed her uncle and an analysis of the last segment of Hinkelman's journal – and I said so without going into specifics. She gave me an odd look, a what-could-be-more-important-than-time-spent-with-me type of look, but did not attempt to dissuade me. Reluctantly, I took my leave.

An hour later, I sauntered into the office and was gratified to see Mrs. Oliphant back in her accustomed place. However, she was not her usual cheery self. Did I dare ask what was troubling her? Yes, I did.

"Good afternoon, Mrs. O.," I said pleasantly enough.

"Good afternoon, Dr. Maxwell," she responded dully.

"You'll excuse me for saying so, but I've seen happier people on death row."

"I'm sorry, Doctor. I'm just not myself today."

"Obviously."

"Have you heard the news about Nurse Clement yet?"

"Uh, no, I haven't. What happened to him?"

She bit her lip to hold back the emotion that was threatening to overwhelm her.

"He – he was *killed* in an auto accident early last night. It was on the radio this morning."

I was of two minds over this bit of news. As a doctor, I was professionally disturbed at the violent loss of life. Yet, as someone who had recently tangled with Clement and had no use for him (professionally or personally), I didn't feel any particular loss here. Of course, I wasn't about to tell Mrs. Oliphant that! Instead, I pursed my lips as if in deep thought.

"Any details?"

"Well, there are conflicting reports. He lives – *lived* in Geneva and was traveling south on Rte. 31 when he crashed into a telephone pole. The sheriff's police found open liquor – and a handgun -- on the front seat and think he was under the influence and lost control. But an eye witness claimed she saw a deer leap out into the road in front of him, and he swerved to avoid hitting it."

Alarm bells!

"A...*deer*?"

"Yes. There are still some in this area, especially in the Red Oaks Nature Preserve across the river."

"Oh, I don't doubt that, Mrs. O. I guess because I'm from Chicago, I can't quite picture it."

That was a half-truth. The full truth was I couldn't quite picture this incident as an *accident*. On the surface, it was a logical explanation: another highway death due to drunken driving for the statistically minded. Yet, I had already seen too many strange things in the past week to take anything at face value any more; and, especially where there was an *animal* involved, an incident tended to take on a surrealistic quality. It didn't take a rocket scientist to figure out why Clement was on the road in the first place. After having roared away from the Home like a madman, he returned home, got himself liquored up, and decided he'd get even with me – permanently.

That's where reality ended and unreality began. If I had been a betting man, I would have given even odds that I was going crazy for thinking the thoughts I was thinking at that moment.

Consider this scenario: the unseen creature in the basement sees the tussle between Clement and me and "reports" it to Melissa. Because of the enmity she feels toward Clement, or because of her infatuation with me – perhaps a little of both as long as we're letting our imagination run wild, Dr. Maxwell – the girl decides to take matters into her own hands (sparing me further agony?) and has Clement watched. When he starts to return to the Home hell-bent on destruction, the "monitor" alerts Melissa, and she sends a deer to intercept him. End of Clement. I could picture the entire scenario, from start to finish, just as if it had been a film adaptation of a Stephen King novel. I never had much of an imagination before, but I could imagine this pretty well. Given the topsy-turvy nature of the past week, anything was possible.

"What's wrong, Doctor?"

"Um, I guess this news is just now sinking in." Another half-truth. "What time did the, uh, accident occur?"

"Let's see. I think they said around 7 p.m. Why?"

"I'm thinking how fragile human existence is. I saw Clement here yesterday afternoon; he left the grounds around five o'clock. Who can figure it?"

"'We must needs die, and are as water spilt upon the ground, which cannot be gathered up again.'"

"Excuse me?"

"I Samuel 11:14. The prophet was commenting on the fragile nature of life as well. I remember the passage because Rabbi Goldstein used it in his sermon Friday evening."

I left the office more determined than ever to learn the truth about Melissa Waterman. While I could scarcely credit the possibility that she had caused Clement's death by powers of "witchcraft," still she *was* linked to all of the other odd goings-on at the Home in the past year. After our confrontation of the day before, I had thought she would avoid me altogether. I realized then that I couldn't let that happen; instead, I had to put more pressure on her to confess all that she knew by however means I could. But first, I needed her file in order to understand why she was a patient here, why she had been given free run of the place (a privilege not accorded to any other patient, past or present), and especially why the mere mention of her name sent shivers up and down people's spines. I had promised Dr. Vengtman (the Elder) that I'd be discreet – respecting the doctor-patient relationship as I must – but I had *not* promised I'd stop being curious. Therefore, I was forced to adopt stealth, to creep about like a spy in some popular novel. It wasn't a role I relished, and I didn't have any particular talent for espionage; yet, speedy action was called for before any further tragedies occurred. Luckily, I had the perfect opportunity later on, which would transform my humorous remark to Nan into grim reality. In the meantime, I had that second project to finish.

And I would have, if I hadn't heard shouting coming from the south wing of the building – angry shouting by three or four individuals, one of whom I recognized immediately. I trotted off in that direction.

Originally, the southeastern corner of the old mansion had been a private conservatory. Having a great deal of money to throw around, the first occupant had indulged in many whims, and one of these was to hold cultural events in his home rather than troubling himself with driving hither and yon in all sorts of weather. Thus, for the further entertainment of his guests (and their "dates"), he contracted with local groups to come and perform solo and chamber-music recitals, poetry and dramatic readings, one-act plays, arts and crafts demonstrations, and even portrait-painting. It was rumored that a well-known comic – before he had become well-known – had performed here once a month, testing his material (as it were) on a quasi-captive audience. So reputed had these events been that an ever larger crowd curried the wealthy man's favor in the hopes of garnering an invitation to see, and be seen by, the "right people." In the course of the changing of hands since the original owner's death, the conservatory had been many things, and not all of them were consistent with a *cultural* purpose.

When Lowell Vengtman took title to the property, he restored the room to its (somewhat) original plan and turned it into a recreation room for patients and staff. The Great Man believed in recreation and exercise as yet additional tools of psychotherapy. If a patient were allowed to sit about and mope, his mental re-orientation would require a longer time than necessary. If, on the other hand, he were kept occupied at activities which required some degree of creativity and/or group interaction, he would have more belief in himself, a necessary component in mental equilibrium.

That was the theory. If the Director's track record were any indicator, the theory had translated very well into practice. The week-day routine consisted of an hour of exercise and/or physical therapy (outside, weather permitting) and two hours of arts and crafts in the morning; in the afternoon, it was two hours of group recreation and one hour of quasi-cultural appreciation. All of this was supervised, of course, but the patients were encouraged to make suggestions and/or criticize the procedures. (One immediately realizes that such a schedule required the counselors to be "creative" in our own schedules.) On the week-ends, this schedule was not as rigidly controlled, and the patients were allowed to decide what they wanted to do when they wanted to do it. This small bit of "free will" also was part of the self-esteem approach.

Obviously, in the context of the Home, there was bound to be conflicts as one psychosis collided with another – as the contretemps to be described shortly demonstrated – and all recreational activities had to be closely monitored. Of all the monitoring duties we counselors had to perform, this one was the most demanding (even more so than meal-monitoring, if one could believe it!). I knew who was on duty that day, and I knew he was capable of handling the situation. Still, as long as I was in the "neighborhood," I was sure he wouldn't mind a helping hand.

One "recreational" fixture that was conspicuously absent from the Home was television. The Great Man had forbade its presence anywhere on the premises, calling it – and I quote – "a damned bloody nuisance without any redeeming qualities." I couldn't agree entirely with that assessment, despite the fact that I had never had much time to watch TV while at R-PSL; but I did agree that it was a distraction and that it helped the emotionally disturbed not in the least. If anything, it put them in a state of limbo. During my last year in medical school, after I had decided to go into psychiatric medicine, I enrolled in an elective course called, officially, "Insanity in the Mass Media" and, unofficially, "Hollywood Goes Nuts." The course dealt with popular conceptions of mental illness; we watched, then evaluated, any film or TV series which featured insane people and/or mental-health facilities. At the end of the term, we were expected to arrive at some means to counter these popular conceptions – "*mis*conceptions," the professor had said in a no-nonsense manner – and to educate the general public in the correct conceptions.

One film which stood out was 1991's *Rain Man* with Dustin Hoffman in an Oscar-winning role. After viewing it, the professor asked us to comment specifically on the impact television had played in the treatment – or non-treatment – of Hoffman's character. The class was nearly evenly divided in its assessment. One faction claimed that TV had acted as an anchor in the lives of the patients, a hook upon which they could hang their fragile existences, the one constant in self-perceived shifting mental currents; the other faction argued that the patients had become addicted to TV, that they based their lives around its programming, and that, in its absence, they displayed withdrawal symptoms and caused untold damage to themselves and others. Both sides provided convincing proofs, and nothing was resolved in that particular instance. Not until I had become an intern at R-PSL and heard Lowell Vengtman lecture on various topics that my mind was made up.

The Director was of the firm opinion – and he argued most convincingly – that television was a "pernicious drug to those whose powers of rationality and discernment were greatly diminished," doing more harm than good. Television, he said, was too often used in mental-health facilities as a convenient method to "sedate" the patients and get them out of the way; by plopping them in front of a TV set for hours at a time or at specific times, the staff did not have to make any effort to actually and effectively *treat* them. Dr. Vengtman stated further that he would never substitute TV-viewing for hands-on psychotherapy. And he had put this view into practice; at the several Homes he had established, the patients were offered various other forms of recreation, forms which would give them the opportunity to take an active role in their own recovery, rather than becoming passive lumps – passive *money-making* lumps. (I must point out, as a footnote, that even the staff was not permitted to possess TV sets. Instead, we were supposed to fill our "free" time with reading or *cultural* pursuits or anything else which amused us.)

I half-expected to walk in on a riot. To my great surprise, I observed, not bedlam, but the patients lined up in two rows opposite each other. Dante was pacing up and down between them and pointing in rapid succession at first one individual, then another; whomever he selected shouted out loudly some word or phrase. Most of the patients seemed to be enjoying this activity; the rest wore expressions of exasperation or boredom. Among the former group was the one whose voice I had recognized out in the hallway – Terry. I was both amazed and delighted – amazed because I had considered him so haughty and disdainful in his Poe persona that I'd never expect him to be a willing – much less an *enthusiastic* – participant in whatever Dante was up to, and delighted because it appeared he was enjoying this word game (as, perhaps, a "writer" might) and doing his best to create the biggest words he could think of in order to trip up the others. He who finds fun in psychotherapy is halfway towards a cure.

Dante was enjoying himself immensely as well, behaving as if he were a symphony orchestra leader directing his performers. His gestures were large and grandiose, and he would fling his head back and his arms up periodically in a theatrical manner. I thought perhaps he had missed his true calling. Upon spotting me with my bemused expression, he called a temporary halt in the byplay in order – as he explained – "to re-enehjerze da creative juices."

"What *are* you doing, Dante?" I asked.

"An exehcize of me own devising, Kenny. An experiment, really. It's a mass free- association where da *patients* t'row out da woids instead o' da doctor."

"And your part?"

"As soon as one poisson has said a woid suggested to him by da previous speaker, I choose anot'er at random to free-associate – at random because den it forces everyone to listen to all o' da woids and be prepared to come up wit' one o' deir own."

"Interesting. I assume you want to achieve the same goals as you might in a one-on-one session."

"Exactly. Da interacting wit' ot'ers is an extra aspect."

"Have you tried psycho-drama? I hear it's all the rage on the West Coast."

"Huh! What would yez expect from a place where everyt'ing is play-acting? But, seriously, Kenny, our fearless leader has looked down his nose at group t'erapy in general. I meself see some value in it, and dat's why I'm conducting dese experiments – in da hopes dat dey will break down da Director's resehvations."

I chuckled to myself over Dante's optimism but kept my silence. My mind was already rushing ahead to other matters as soon as I spied Nurse Michaels enter the room. I made some perfunctory remarks and took my leave. As I walked away, I heard Dante gather his charges again and ask one of them where they had left off. Michaels realized that I was heading straight for her, and her expression changed immediately from blandness to apprehension.

"Good afternoon, Nurse Michaels," I said as disarmingly as I could.

"Good afternoon, Dr. Maxwell," she replied passively, not in the least disarmed.

"Have you heard about Clement?"

"Yes. Mrs. Oliphant is the unofficial town crier here."

"Well, unless Dr. Vengtman has other ideas, Clement's death will make you the new Senior Nurse."

"I ain't holdin' my breath, Doctor. Once you make your report to the Old Man, I might as well look for another job."

"Maybe, and maybe not. There's still one thing on my mind besides yesterday's incident that I need to resolve. Otherwise, I won't get along with the new Senior Nurse any better than I did with the old one."

"What's that?"

"Why have you been so damned nervous every time I show up? Is it my horns or my forked tail?"

She looked me straight in the eye for a change.

"Are you sure you wanna know?"

"I didn't survive the streets of Chicago by wimping out. Lay it on me, mama."

"All right, Doctor, you asked for it. Frankly, I ain't the only one who's edgy; I reckon I'm just good at coverin' my feelings up. It's not so much *you* as it is who you hang out with."

"Excuse me?"

"I'm talkin' about your relationship with – with that white girl, Melissa Waterman."

"I don't have a 'relationship' with Melissa," I growled, scowling. "Who says I do?"

"I don't mean in a *romantic* way. Hell, no! I guess what I mean to say is people are concerned by the way she always hangin' around you. They think you'll end up like – like –"

"Like Mathias Hinkelman?"

She gasped sharply, and the color drained from her face. She looked away, flustered and confused. Then, in a whisper:

"You know about Dr. Mathias?"

"I'm beginning to. I know that Melissa developed a crush on him, that she became jealous when he and Dr. Maddie started their affair, and that, soon afterwards, he began to have his...troubles. So, what can you add?"

"If you know all that, then there ain't much I can add." She gazed around the conservatory where Dante was still free-associating. "Look, Dr. Maxwell, can we go somewhere else? I don't want nobody to hear what I got to say next."

We walked out of the conservatory and onto the veranda and took a seat at a table. Michaels traced an imaginary doodle on the vinyl surface several times, then made eye contact again. Her face was like stone.

"Strange as it may sound, Dr. Mathias was a lady-killer. He wasn't all that good-looking, but he was such a shy guy and women found it refreshing. A lot of the female nurses here would've liked to jump into the sack with him, but he chose Dr. Maddie instead. Or maybe I should say *she* chose *him*. They were both lonely and seemed to hit it off." She sighed deeply. "It didn't last, of course. That little bitch, Melissa – excuse my French, Doctor, but I'm just tellin' it like it is – that little bitch took it in her head that Dr. Mathias was *her* personal property. And, if she couldn't have him, well, nobody could. I dunno what she did, but I could tell Dr. Mathias was miserable as hell. Even after he broke off with Dr. Maddie, his problems continued until he – until he –"

Michaels' voice choked up, and she buried her face in her hands. I heard muffled sobbing but was helpless to do anything. After a minute or so, she straightened up and wiped the tears away. Her stoniness returned.

"So you see, Dr. Maxwell, when we see Melissa hangin' around you, talkin' to you, we see a re-run of what happened before."

"If it's any comfort to you, Nurse, I don't intend to go crazy. Now that I'm aware of the situation, I can deal with whatever happens. Of course, Melissa's got no reason to be jealous on my account."

"Don't be too sure of that. The rumors about you and Dr. Nan are makin' the rounds. If anything develops between you two, Melissa's jealousy could return. And, even if it don't" – here, she half-smirked, half-grimaced – "well, some of the girls wouldn't mind takin' a trip to the basement with you themselves."

"The basement, eh? That seems to be a popular hang-out."

A dark cloud passed over her face. I thought she was going to spit then and there.

"That bastard Clement hoped to get us all down there and start up his own little harem. I ain't sorry at all to hear he's dead, if you wanna know the truth. A lot of us will sleep easy from now on." She checked her watch. "I got to go now. Thanks for listenin' to me."

She rose and quickly walked away. Despite my wanting to be elsewhere, I remained on the veranda a while longer, mulling over Michaels' remarks. Here another opinion had been garnered, and it corresponded somewhat with others I had received; slowly but surely, a consensus was building concerning the last days of Mathias Hinkelman, and it encouraged me in the task ahead. I didn't relish the idea of being a "cat burglar" or a "secret agent," but all I had learned so far was compelling me toward that role.

One other point to consider: for the first time since I had arrived at the Home, someone was solicitous of my well-being, even if it had only been implicit in nature. I was sure all of my co-workers had my best interests at heart – with the exception of the late, unlamented Clement – yet no one had actually come to me and asked me to be careful. That Michaels had hinted at such precautions suggested an element of danger lurking about the grounds. On the face of it, it sounded like so much paranoia, given recent events. In any event, I thought any warnings were unnecessary; I had already weighed the pros and cons of my investigation, and I felt that the risks involved were minor compared to the benefits to be gained in solving the Great Mystery of Hinkelman's death.

I have already mentioned that all of the professional staff's monitoring duties were tedious. One of them, however, was both tedious *and* tiring: the "over-nighter." Illness—physical or mental – does not keep a clock; it does not stop when the "official" day is done or when the time for "lights out" arrives. It is a twenty-four-hour-a-day phenomenon, and a given patient may experience a psychotic episode at any time. Should one occur, common decency and professional ethics require that (s)he be treated immediately. At the Vengtman Homes, it had become a point of honor that only two or three minor episodes per day and one major one a week took place. Thanks to the field-tested methodologies of Lowell Vengtman, few patients ever had to be sedated and/or physically restrained. Yet, since there were episodes, there also had to be monitors.

As far as the non-professional staff was concerned, the day consisted of three eight-hour shifts. A nurse put in his/her time and went home. For the professionals, the day never ended; we had our "official" day of counseling our patients and our "unofficial" one of fulfilling other obligations. And, for one of us each day, the "unofficial" day stretched far into the night. We were on call for any emergencies which might occur, to provide medical treatment where needed, and to supervise the nurses in restoring order. We weren't required to stay awake all night; we were only required to sleep with one eye and both ears open. Since most of the incidents were minimal, there tended to be a lot of dead space during the night, and it behooved the monitor to keep him/herself occupied and thus alert.

Ordinarily, I would have whiled away the hours working crossword puzzles. I have been an inveterate word-puzzle freak since high school (when I wasn't avoiding being killed!); the puzzles tended to keep my mind sharp, and I could have spent hours (if I had had hours, and I didn't most of the time) working one after another. I had no need for puzzles that night, however. Being on-call gave me the perfect excuse for being in the main building at night, and I intended to practice my "burgling" skills by ransacking the medical-records room at my leisure, without fear of being discovered by the redoubtable Nurse Petrie (though I hoped she would be mellower now that we had spent some time together). To play it safe, I waited until all the lights in the other cottages had been turned on, then stealthily walked down the path – not an easy task, as I had discovered my first night there.

Call it heightened senses due to an increased flow of adrenalin. Call it a sixth sense. Whatever you want to call it, I had the eerie feeling I was being followed despite my precautions. I halted and whirled around, not knowing what to expect. I should have expected, however, what I did see, for I'd seen it several times already. A pair of gleaming yellow eyes stared back at me about five yards away. My "old friend," Melissa's "spy," was still on the job. And I still had no idea what sort of creature it was. But, I wasn't going to let it deter me from my self-appointed rounds. Once I was inside the main building, the creature couldn't follow me anymore. I pushed on, the prickly feeling at the back of my neck keeping me informed of the other's continued presence.

Quietly slipping through the front door, I peered out the side window. My "tail" seemed to have disappeared. I smiled in self-congratulation, then made straight for my target. Even though the hallways at the Home were carpeted, the nature of my business negated (in my mind anyway) the lack of sound; consequently, my every footstep seemed like a drum beat, announcing to the whole world what I was up to. I had to force myself to walk slowly and deliberately and to avoid seeing things in the shadows and hearing whispering at my back. We humans still had a long way to go before we finally shed our primitive fear of the Unknown; even well-educated professionals were not absolutely immune to the "monsters of the Id" (to quote a phrase from the sci-fi classic, *Forbidden Planet*). The main hallway appeared to lengthen into infinity, and I walked it for eons before arriving at the scene of future crime. At one point, I was startled by the appearance of a nurse emerging from a linen-supply closet; she merely nodded to me and continued on her way. I nearly lost my resolve then and there!

I stood at the door to the medical-records room for the longest time, attempting to slow down my rapidly beating heart and contemplating the enormity of my actions. If I'd been in Chicago that night, I'd probably be in the back seat of a squad car by now, on my way to the Cook County jail. Out here, in the "boonies," the worst that could have happened to me (I supposed) was a sharp reprimand from the Director and the eternal suspicions of my colleagues (including lovely, luscious Nan, who would never again give me the time of day) – all because of the curious remarks of a teen-aged girl with amethyst eyes who "talked" to animals.

Well, it was too late to turn back. I was committed. I took a deep breath, pulled out my one credit card (issued by the Home for use in Home-related transactions) out of my wallet, and slid it into the gap between the door and jamb. I'd seen this stunt done in any number of spy movies, and it looked easy enough. Yet, I had to remind myself that this was real life, not a film plot. Overall, I felt foolish even as I shoved the card against the latch. So, imagine my surprise when the damned trick worked!

Scarcely believing my good fortune, I slowly pushed the door open. But, before I stepped inside, I experienced the prickly feeling again. I jerked my head around to the right, toward the end of the hallway. Nothing. I swung back to the left, toward the direction from which I had come – and gasped in shock! Creeping along the baseboard on the opposite side was an ebony lump that held a pair of yellow eyes. Somehow, my "tail" had found a way in. Did it know where I was and sought me out? I shook my head vigorously. I was letting my imagination run away with me. There was no way in hell *that* was possible, despite the strange things that had already occurred so far; there simply had to be a more rational explanation. I *hoped* there was a more rational explanation.

In any event, the identity of the creature was no longer in question. In the dim light of the hallway, it was now revealed as one of Melissa's raccoons, one of her "lieutenants" whom she trusted to carry out important "missions." When it came opposite me, it halted and peered at me without a trace of fear. I stared back incredulously. It gave all the appearance of knowing what I was up to, watching my every move so that it could report accurately back to its "commander."

Refusing to impute any intelligent motive to the raccoon, I entered the records room and closed the door behind me. Let the damned animal sit outside and stare at the bare walls; I had business (albeit *illegal* business) to attend to. I pulled out the flashlight I'd thought to bring along, clicked it on, and located the filing cabinets. Methodically, I searched in the drawers, beginning at the point where I had been the other day when Petrie had caught me *in flagrante delicto*; the task took just over an hour, thanks to Dr. Vengtman's insistence upon efficiency. Unfortunately, I came up empty. Melissa's file was nowhere to be found here. If it existed at all, it had to be in the Director's office. (I wondered sarcastically if he had signed it out *officially*.)

Which meant that my new "career" in burgling was not yet at an end, that I had another "job" to do before I could "retire." Perhaps the professional criminal derives as much thrill out of the risk-taking involved in his work as of obtaining the actual loot. Criminal psychology is a wide field, but I'd had no interest in it. If I had known that burgling was ahead of me, I might have read up on it before venturing into the business, because I was experiencing then – not "thrills," but a massive gut-wrenching brought on (no doubt) by a "guilty conscience."

I did make one interesting discovery while poking about. One filing cabinet was marked "Personnel Records" and, on a hunch, I searched it for Mathias Hinkelman's file. I should say "files," for there were *two* of them. (Everyone else had only one, but some of those were rather thick. Mine was necessarily thin, but I wondered how soon that would change.) One of the files was marked "Hinkelman AM," and the other "Hinkelman PM"; both were equal in thickness. As far as I knew, "AM" and "PM" stood for "ante-meridian" and "post-meridian" time-keeping designations. Why then these terms in a personnel file? I soon learned why when I began scanning the folders' contents. Most of the contents were job-evaluation forms, and they came in sets; once a month, each of the professional staff (including the Director) and the Senior Nurse submitted his/her reasoned opinion of an individual's performance. From these reports, the Director judged the fitness of each in the continuance of his/her employment.

The last set of evaluations in the first file was dated August 1, 1996, nine days before the first date in Hinkelman's journal, *before he started to lose his grip on reality*. The first set of reports in the second folder was dated, naturally, September 1, 1996. Thus, "AM" and "PM" had to stand for "ante-mentalis" and "post-mentalis" – before and after the madness. I read these two sets very carefully. *Ante-mentalis*, the staff had seen very little in Hinkelman's behavior to suggest he was on the verge of a mental break-down; they did, however, continue to comment – sometimes praisingly, sometimes not – on his unorthodox methods of treatment. *Post-mentalis*, the staff began to make note of what I had already gleaned from other sources – the paranoia, the erratic behavior, the disjointed speech patterns – all in precise, clinical terms.

The very last set of evaluations was dated April 1, 1997, the day before Hinkelman committed suicide. By this time, he had become a patient himself (under the personal care of Dr. Vengtman), and the reports read more like medical records than opinions on job performance. On an impulse, I decided to take those files back to my cottage for more systematic study. I doubted anyone would miss them – at least until the beginning of

August. I could replace them during my next over-nighter. After all, I was now a "professional burglar," wasn't I?

I extinguished the flashlight, stuck it in back into my pocket, and turned to go. Just as I was about to grab the doorknob, I heard a feminine shriek outside in the hallway. I cracked the door open and peeped out. Nurse Michaels was flapping her arms frantically and shouting "Shoo! Get outa here!" at something. It did not take a rocket scientist to deduce what was upsetting her; she had obviously stumbled across my "tail" where she least expected it to be. While her attention was focused on the raccoon, I slipped out of the records room. She would never suspect where I had been.

"What's the problem, Nurse?" I asked innocently.

My sudden appearance provoked as much fright in her as the raccoon had. She gasped and whirled around, clutching at her breast. When she recognized me, she swallowed nervously.

"Oh, God! You scared the hell outa me!" I gestured in placation. "I'm sorry, Doctor, but I found *that* in here."

She pointed at the furry creature, now creeping backwards in response to her violent motions and tone of voice, seemingly reluctant to desert its "post" before its "mission" was complete. Whyever it was here in the first place, its tenacity was nothing short of amazing.

"I'll take care of the raccoon, Michaels. Go back to what you were doing."

"Thank you, Doctor," she murmured, very relieved, and started to leave.

"Just a moment."

She turned back, her usual air of apprehension once more in place.

"Why are you still on duty?"

"This was supposed to be Clement's shift," she replied, her face twisting in disgust. "Since he ain't here to take it, I guess it's up to me to fill in until the Director hires someone else."

"Very admirable."

"Is there anything else, Doctor?"

"Yes. I did turn in an incident report this morning." She hung her head in defeat. "But, Monday morning, I'm going to repudiate it. Now that Clement's dead, I don't see any reason to create unnecessary problems. As far as I'm concerned, the incident never happened. OK?"

She now gazed at me in a new light, one suffused with gratitude. She even managed a tiny smile.

"Oh, Lord, you don't know how relieved I am. Thank you, Dr. Maxwell, thank you. I owe you one."

She rushed off, leaving me to cope with the raccoon. I regarded the animal again. It was crouching against the wall, having halted its retreat during the exchange between Michaels and me. How I would get it out of the building when it clearly was not in a mood to leave was a problem. Perhaps, if it were really following me, it would leave when I did, presumably the same way it had got in. In any event, I had no time to worry about its welfare; I had my own "mission" to complete. I walked to the end of the main hallway; but before I turned into the side hallway that led to the Director's office, I looked back. The raccoon was still hot on my trail, scurrying along the baseboard at a steady clip yet always careful not to get too close to me. I shook my head in astonishment and hurried on.

The trick with the credit card did not work a second time, for the simple reason that Dr. Vengtman had installed a dead-bolt lock on his door. I would've needed either a key or a drill to access his office. The presence of a dead-bolt raised an interesting question: what was in his office that Lowell Vengtman had deemed so sensitive that he had to take extra security precautions? The patients' medical files were, of course, confidential, and one would need a court order to obtain them. But dead-bolts smacked of classified information and espionage – hardly the sort of thing one would associate with a health-care facility. Had the Great Man something to hide after all? What in God's name could it have been?

I stood there longer than I should have. Behind me, the raccoon studied me closely. I had to find another way to examine the Director's personal files – how easy it was to consider seriously illegal actions once one started along that path! – but I didn't have the criminal know-how or experience to take the next step. Dejectedly, I headed back toward the main door. Once, I looked over my shoulder; the raccoon was now dogging my heels. Apparently, familiarity with my person had emboldened it to the point where it now behaved as if it were a "companion."

At the entrance, I pulled open the door and gestured to the animal that it had a clear path to the outside. It just sat there, alternately eyeing me and peering into the darkened landscape as if weighing its options. Finally, it scooted through the door and out onto the portico; but, instead of dashing across the lawn and losing itself in the woods, *it waited there for me to exit!* Grinning wryly, I strolled out and headed for my cottage. The raccoon fell into line and accompanied me the whole way. After I had gone inside, I peeked through the window, only to find that it had departed now that its business for the night had been concluded.

My business, however, was still unfinished. With the evaluation reports in hand, I intended to correlate them (if possible) with the information from the medical files and the journal, specifically looking for echoes of Hinkelman's oft-repeated words and phrases. If they appeared in his colleagues' opinions of him, it meant that, on an unconscious level, he had been crying out for help and despairing that none was forthcoming.

I hunkered down on the floor as before and waded in.

DAY NINE:
Monday, 07.14.1997
INCULCATION

The best laid plans…

The phone jangled incessantly. Even though it was on the other side of the room, in my sleep-befuddled state, it sounded as if it were perched on my ear. I had been attempting to stay awake by going through my "time-line" of the demise of Dr. Mathias Hinkelman for the umpteenth time and fine-tuning it where needed; alternately, I had been doing crossword puzzles to break the monotony. I hadn't done an "over-nighter" since my intern days at R-PSL, and I had gotten out of "practice." I found myself dozing off repeatedly, forcing me to re-double my efforts to stay awake. The ringing phone caught me during a "doze" period.

I got to my feet and tramped over to the side table. My watch read 3:50 AM. Shaking some of the cobwebs out of my head, I grabbed the phone as I would my worst enemy (which, at that particular moment, it certainly was!).

"Yes, what is it?"

"Sorry to disturb you, Doctor," came a deep male voice at the other end. "We got an incident."

"Who?"

"One of your group, in fact –Ray W."

"Symptoms?"

"He's tossin' the furniture around and shoutin' 'they're after me!' repeatedly."

"Have you made any efforts to restrain him?"

"Yes, sir. When we first heard the noise, we tried to go into his room. I nearly got cold cocked by a flying lamp. That's when I decided to call you. We'll charge 'im all at once, if you want us to."

"Wait until I get there. Give me five minutes."

"Right."

A doctor's worst fear is to have his patient suffer a relapse. His worst *nightmare* is to have his *violent* patient suffer a relapse; not only is there danger to the patient but also to anyone within his range of outburst. Ray, the ex-gang member whose life had been marred by frequent episodes of brutality (the life I might have led if not for the timely counsel of a high school football coach) and who now in his psychotic delusions believed himself to be the re-incarnation of a Wild West gunslinger, had somehow been triggered into another bout of vicious paranoia. From our previous talks (and a thorough reading of his medical file), I had judged him to be reacting to authority in general -- which he fantasized as frontier-town figures – but specifically to the father who had never given him any support or encouragement in more constructive enterprises. Perhaps Ray never knew who his father was, having been raised by an unwed mother; if so, his psychosis might have reached deeper into his unconscious than hitherto reported. In any event, it was up to me to talk him back from where he had hidden his ego. Failing that, I'd have to sedate him.

I put on my smock and grabbed the Black Bag. The Black Bag was just that: a black, nineteenth-century-style doctor's valise in which my professional forebears had carried the tools of their trade. This bag also carried tools, but they were much more sophisticated than the primitive instruments of a century or more ago. (Whenever I watched TV shows like "Doctor Quinn, Medicine Woman," I had to force myself to believe that, for that era, those museum pieces were "state-of-the-art.") It also contained potentially addictive and/or lethal drugs and so was locked up when not in use. It was the emergency "first-aid kit" for both group activities and over-nighters; one signed for it at the administration office at the beginning of the activity and returned it at the end of it. Dr. Vengtman left nothing to chance.

I trotted from my cottage (stumbling in all the wrong places) to the main building and arrived in less than five minutes. Even before I reached Ray's room, I could hear him yelling, though his voice was considerably muffled by the sound-proofing. If not for that, he might have awakened the entire Home and set off some of the other patients, and we'd have had a real brouhaha on our hands. I was greeted by the senior floor nurse – now elevated to that position by the demise of Clement – a tall, thin fellow named Jones who sported a shock of red hair and dull, lifeless eyes and walked with a slight limp. He nodded perfunctorily at me, and I did likewise.

"Any change in behavior, Nurse?"

"Nope. He's gonna yell hisself hoarse, I guess."

"No doubt." I looked behind him at the four other male nurses he had quickly recruited. "Are you gentlemen ready?" They all murmured an assent. "Very well. I'll try to calm him down, if I can. Otherwise, I'll divert his attention while you jump him."

Bold words, Dr. Maxwell, I thought. *You're just as frightened as they are about what could happen.*

I stepped over to the door and rapped sharply three times. The yelling did not abate. Now, I could hear distinct words and phrases:

"...*fuckers!* You won't...get you all hung!...real law 'n' order in this... me, you *bastards!*"

Ray's ranting consisted of only four or five phrases that he repeated over and over. It was like listening to a broken record. In retrospect, that is an apt analogy. In a psychotic's world, one aspect of "reality" is concentrated on to the exclusion of all others; whatever existence he creates for himself, it is always in terms of that narrow focus. In Ray's case, he was concerned with "corruption" in high places and with his fate if the "town officials" discovered he was aware of their corruption. It was a classical case of paranoid delusion; and, like a broken record, he could not get out of his chosen "groove."

I knocked again, this time with more force.

"Billy!" I shouted, forcing myself to address his assumed persona. I was reluctant to role-play but, under the present circumstances, I had to go by Ray's rules if I ever hoped to get through to him. "Billy, listen to me! It's me – Preacher Ken!"

The yelling abated, but I could still faintly hear furniture being roughly pushed aside. Then all was quiet. I don't know which side of the door was the more soundless. I realized I had been holding my breath lest I miss anything Ray might say to me. Behind me, no one moved a muscle.

"Billy," I said in a normal tone, "did you hear me? It's Preacher Ken."

Through the door came a voice filled with subdued anger.

"Preacher? That really you? You alone?"

"No. Some of the, uh, town folk are with me. May I come in?"

More silence. Then:

"Send the others away. Ah don't want no one else around."

"All right. Whatever you say." I turned to Nurse Jones. "Stay out of sight until I'm inside, then stand by."

"You sure you wanna go in there alone, Doctor? That bozo already put one nurse in the hospital. That was before your time."

"That's 'patient,' Jones," I bristled, "*not* 'bozo.' And, yes, I'm sure. Ray trusts me – I think. If I signal, you come in like gang busters, OK?"

"Right."

The squad of nurses moved down the hallway out of line of sight of Ray's door. I rapped again.

"I've sent everyone away, Billy. Open the door, please."

A crack appeared in the doorway, and inside the crack was a single green-gray eye. It too was filled subdued anger. The crack widened, and the other eye appeared. When the crack permitted, Ray stuck his head out and peered down the hallway in both directions; satisfied that I was indeed alone, he stepped aside to let me in.

I entered a shambles. Not one object in the room was where it had been on my last visit; some giant hand had picked up the place and shaken its contents vigorously. The bed was overturned, and the sheets and blanket were draped over other objects. The table was upside-down in a corner; one of its legs was broken off, and another was splintered. The chair to the table squatted in the middle of the room, its back missing entirely. The table lamp – a thing of metal in order to prevent the possibility of using shards of ceramic as weapons – was dented in a dozen places, and its shade crushed flat. The drapes to the window were torn off and lying in a heap near the door. I surveyed the chaos with a shiver up my spine. Adrenaline flow in the psychotic individual was a wonder to behold – and best beheld at a distance!

"What happened, Billy? Why are you so angry?"

He did not reply right away but stared at me defiantly. Yet, even as I met his gaze calmly and steadily, I noted that he was desperately trying to relax. Facial and jaw muscles twitched in a St. Vitus dance, and fists clenched and unclenched in rapid succession. By increments, he worked through his anger, then looked about with a small amount of regret.

"Sorry 'bout this, preacher," he muttered. "Things sorta got outa hand."

"What happened?" I repeated.

"Ah saw 'em, preacher. They wuz comin' fer me."

"Saw who?"

"The mayor, the sheriff, the whole fuckin' town council. They had a rope. They wuz gonna fuckin' string me up."

"Where were they?"

"On the lawn. They wuz comin' from the fuckin' woods."

The woods! That set off the alarm bells again.

"Why were they in the woods?"

"Damfino, preacher. Maybe they wuz pickin' out a tree fer me." He scowled at me. "You believe me, doncha?"

"I believe you saw something. But, it's dark out there. It could've been anybody." Cautiously, I edged toward the window and peered out at the lawn. It was an amalgam of dark and darker shapes beyond the security lights. "Describe them for me, Billy, each and every one."

The descriptions he gave me were sketchy, to say the least. In some instances, he began to list physical characteristics, only to change his mind and construct a different sort of list; in others, he seemed to be describing two separate individuals while speaking about one. He was exhibiting the confusion that embodies a quasi-hallucinatory state, when the subject barely perceives images and cannot recall them upon returning to lucidity. In Ray's mind, a "lynch mob" walked the grounds of the Home, seeking "frontier justice." Now that I had calmed him down (comparatively speaking), I needed to discover the root cause of these disturbing images.

"Now, tell me what you were doing when you first saw them."

"What's that got to do with anything?"

"Humor me, please."

"Well, if ya think it's important…"

"I do."

"Well, Ah couldn't sleep. All's Ah did was stare at the ceiling. So Ah got up 'n' paced the floor some, hopin' to wear mahself out. After a while, Ah heered a ruckus outside 'n' looked out the window." He leaned forward, nearly pressing his nose against the plexiglas. At first, I thought he was re-enacting his experience. Abruptly, he gasped sharply. "Look, preacher! There they are agin!"

I squinted in order to focus my vision and gazed in the general direction Ray was pointing to. Something *was* out there – several somethings, in fact. I strained harder to penetrate the darkness; finally, I made out distinct shapes, one humanoid strolling casually across the lawn away from the building and half a dozen or so small quadrupeds scurrying beside and behind the larger creature. I didn't need to be drawn a picture to tell me who they were – not a "lynch mob," but Melissa and her horde of squirrels. What was she doing outside at this time of the night? I glanced at Ray. He was keenly eyeing the group and breathing heavily. After a long pause, he spoke.

"Do ya see 'em, preacher?"

"I see something, Billy, but it doesn't look like a 'necktie party' to me."

"No? What the fuck *does* it look like then?"

I was now at a crossroads, and I wondered how Hinkelman would have dealt with this situation – if he had had to deal with it at all. Given his unorthodox methods, it seemed more than problematical. One of the dangers of inserting oneself into the fantasies of a delusional individual (as Hinkelman had done in order to "work from the inside and burrow out") is the very real possibility of re-enforcing what one wishes to resolve. Sharing the unreal world of the psychotic means accepting his imagery and his rules; therefore, *ipso facto*, one has to create new fantasies to explain one's own presence so that the patient does not experience violent

193

disorientation. It is a paradox of the first magnitude: acting as a "cancer" in an organism while at the same time assimilating it. I had to humor Ray in his Wild West delusion because Hinkelman had created a thorny problem and I didn't know where to start. I certainly didn't want to play Ray's game; unfortunately, he had posed a question which forced me to do just that. I had to think fast to come up with a response that would at once seem plausible (in his current frame of mind) and wean him away from his paranoia. Not an easy task, believe me. My predecessor and his odd approach to psychotherapy had been both problem *and* solution!

To this day, I can't explain how I arrived at the stratagem I chose. The unofficial explanation is still too fantastic to completely accept. All I know is that it worked. I decided to tell Ray the truth – *part* of the truth, anyway.

"You know, Billy, it looks like Melissa to me."

"*Melissa!*" he exploded. "Damnation! What's that fuckin' whore up to now? She been a burr under mah saddle fer a year."

"How so?"

"It all has to do with Preacher Mathias. She wuz sweet on 'im at one time, but he di'n't have no time fer whores. He wanted to save 'lost souls' but sure as hell di'n't wanna *sleep* with 'em. Somehow, she got the notion that me 'n' some o' the boys wuz the reason he di'n't court her, and she begun bad-mouthin' the lot of us – and him too. She found ready ears in the corrupt town fathers."

Another corroboration in yet another convoluted fashion.

"Interesting. But, tell me, who did you really see out on the lawn – the town council, or Melissa?"

Ray fell silent again. The twitching of facial muscles told me that his mental gears were shifting rapidly as he tried to sort out conflicting ideas.

"Ah dunno, preacher," he replied finally. "Sometimes, Ah get confused. Maybe it *wuz* her, and Ah just assumed the council wuz with her. They're all in cahoots, y' know."

"Possibly." I surveyed the room. "You made quite a mess here. You'll have to help clean it up."

"Yeah." He regarded me curiously. "Damn, preacher! You took a mighty big chance comin' in here. Ah mighta hurt you."

"In my business, I have to take chances once in a while. Nothing ventured, nothing gained, they say. Besides, I don't think you would've hurt me. You know I'm here to help you – just like Preacher Mathias."

"Yeah."

I departed then. Ray had turned back to resume his vigil at the window, searching for God-knew-what. Outside, I drew Nurse Jones aside.

"He's calmed down for the moment. Check on him every half hour. Call me immediately if there's a change in his behavior. I'll look in on him personally before breakfast."

"Right."

Wearily, I trudged back downstairs and thanked my lucky stars that I had succeeded in averting a potentially more serious incident. Ray was correct about the risk I had taken; walking into a veritable lion's den without a second thought for my personal safety is not a guarantee for long life. Actually, it had been a *calculated* risk, since I had the advantage of foreknowledge. Ray's files suggested that he had been a lot more violent in the beginning; and once Hinkelman had begun to work on him, his episodes became less frequent. There was, of course, always the chance variable, such as my psychological clumsiness in handling the matter. Still, I knew where my patient stood, mentally speaking, and I had calculated that he would transfer his trust in Hinkelman to me for the simple reason that he needed to trust someone in a sea of alleged enemies. I had no guarantee that I would be as successful the next time (if there was a next time), though the odds against success were sure to decrease now that I had ingratiated myself into Ray's world.

All that aside, I had gotten Ray in touch – briefly – with reality. He had expressed doubts about his delusions. Doubt leads not only to wisdom, but also to mental health. I believed I had regained some lost ground due to my predecessor's death and could build on that, guiding Ray the rest of the way out of his psychosis. And, since he was the Home's most difficult patient, I had perhaps accomplished a great deal that morning.

I wasn't ready to slap myself on the back just yet, for there was still the matter of Melissa Waterman, who had now figured in yet another facet of this institution. I was beginning to believe that there was no facet which she had *not* affected, that her background was sufficient to instill unholy fear in all those with whom she came into contact and in those who had merely heard about her through the grapevine – a most chilling thought!

I, of course, did not count myself in that number. The girl did not frighten me in the least; she merely puzzled and annoyed me. Little did I realize that that was about to change soon.

I returned to my cottage. The encounter with Ray had drained what little energy reserves I possessed after trying to stay awake during the over-nighter. I was even too tired to notice if my "traveling companion" was with me – not that it would've made much difference to me if it had – and hit the sack fully clothed.

Despite the extra activity, my internal "alarm clock" did not allow me any extra sleep. I was awake at the regular time. I took a quick shower, changed clothes, and departed. As promised, I went straight to Ray's floor and conferred with Nurse Jones before he went off shift; he informed me in his taciturn manner that all had been quiet after I left and Ray's room had been (somewhat) straightened out. I thanked him and went to breakfast.

When I arrived at the staff dining room, I was surprised to discover that a place at a table had been "reserved" just for me. A place-card with my name inscribed on it in a floral script occupied the head position of a very proper table setting – a dinner plate in the center upon which a linen napkin had been tented; to the right, a dessert knife, a dinner knife, a butter knife, a dessert spoon, a dinner spoon, and a soup spoon; to the left, a dessert fork, a dinner fork, and a salad fork; at the "one o'clock" position, a cup and saucer; at the "eleven o'clock" position, a wine glass. The one incongruous note in this little tableau was that, under the napkin, the table setter had placed a small, flat package wrapped gaily with silvery paper. Since I knew it wasn't my birthday, I deduced that someone – a *fat* someone – was pulling another practical joke. As I walked in, my colleagues politely applauded me. I smiled back magnanimously.

"Dare I ask what the occasion is?" I asked.

"It's the final phase of your initiation, dear boy," Harry spoke for the group. "Even though none of us profited by it – thanks to persons best left unnamed – we are not so miffed as to deny you the full treatment. Go ahead, Ken, open your present."

I picked up the small package as if it were a vicious rat and slowly unwrapped it. I guffawed when I saw what was inside: a box of condoms in a variety of colors.

"My, my, just what the doctor ordered – and my favorite brand too. How did you know?"

"A lucky guess, no doubt. Now, if you'll be seated, we'll serve you breakfast."

"Really? I can't wait."

I sat down, dreading what was to come. Given the Senior's fondness for juvenile humor, I imagined that "breakfast" would consist of a cream pie in my face and a bucket of water down my pants. One by one, my colleagues served a heaping portion of something from the serving line

— Harry, scrambled eggs; Maddie, a bowl of oatmeal; Bertie, a stack of pancakes; Dante, a rasher of bacon; and lastly, Nan (who had taken a short break from meal-monitor duty), a saucerful of toast and a large glass of orange juice.

I stared at this array in frank astonishment. It was too good to be true. Where was the gag? Then it occurred to me that they had doctored the food. They must have set these portions under the serving counter and pretended to dish them out from the line. Now, they expected me to eat all of it. I grimaced in agony.

"Go ahead, Ken," Harry coaxed. "Eat up."

"You bastards!" I mumbled and took a forkful of scrambled eggs, half expecting them to be loaded with cayenne pepper and salsa.

I was wrong. The eggs tasted just like scrambled eggs ought to taste, with diced ham folded in to give them added flavor. I moved to the bacon. *They picked out the rancid part*, I thought as I picked up the first strip. Wrong again: it was the sweetest honey-cured bacon I had ever eaten. Next, the pancakes. *OK, they put sawdust in the batter*, I reasoned, *or glue in the syrup*. No so: buckwheat pancakes with real maple syrup, just like Mama whipped up on Sunday mornings. I went to the oatmeal. *Soap shavings here?* I guessed first. *Or, how about salt instead of sugar?* Another miss: steel-ground oats with a hint of brown sugar and cinnamon. Lastly, the toast. *The bread was dipped in vinegar.* Nope: toasted whole wheat, with creamy rich butter.

I glared at everyone in turn, but all I received back were five deadpan expressions.

"OK, I give up. What kind of trick are you playing?"

A pained look came over Harry's face, and he placed his hand on his heart.

"You wound us to the quick, dear boy. We only wished to welcome you officially into our ranks. And we have done so."

"Uh-huh," I muttered and took a long swig of orange juice.

Big mistake!

They had suckered me after all. Five seconds after I set the glass down, my vision began to blur. Five human beings morphed into five multi-colored blobs. My last conscious thought was, *oh, man, they slipped a "mickey" in the OJ!*

When I regained consciousness, I found myself in a most unlikely place, the parlor-*cum*-staff-meeting room. I was seated in the same stuffed chair I had occupied the Monday before, my notepad and pencil resting primly on my lap. As soon as my vision cleared, I glanced about. Six multi-colored blobs morphed into six human beings. Five of them exhibited great concern, though two of them – Harry and Nan -- could barely keep a straight face, while the sixth regarded me sternly (and wasn't *he* trying not to smile either?). I rose to my feet, prepared to shower them with some choice South Side expressions dealing with family ties and social customs, and just as quickly slumped back into the chair. Whatever drug I had been given was exerting residual effects in the form of a thundering headache and general weakness. I looked at the Director helplessly.

"If you're quite through with your nap, Dr. Maxwell," he intoned in his best officious tone of voice, "I'd like to conduct a staff meeting."

"Yes, sir," was all I could say.

In retrospect, I have to admit that it had been a first-class prank. Obviously, this bunch had honed their skills to a fine point. The last time I'd been involved in such a well-thought-out gag, I and some of my fellow last-year interns had removed six corpses from R-PSL's morgue, propped them up in the Administrator's office, and placed signs on them reading "ON STRIKE – UNSAFE WORKING CONDITIONS." Harry and the others had carefully allowed me to believe that the *food* was doctored; and, when I ate with no ill effects, I had let my guard down – which was what they had been counting on. Of all the things I thought might have been done, spiked orange juice had been at the bottom of my list. All in all, the perfect practical joke. My only regret was that I had been on the receiving end; I might have enjoyed it more.

The usual routine of the staff meeting was temporarily disrupted when Dr. Vengtman, before proceeding with the regular business, announced for the benefit of those who hadn't yet heard about it the "tragic automobile accident that has claimed the life of Nurse Clement." I scanned the faces in the room; they were all hard and emotionless. Clement certainly had no friends among the professional staff either – which surprised me not in the least. He had been an unpleasant sort, not concerned with building strong social and professional relationships but with amassing power over his co-workers through extortion and blackmail. The Director's intention to send flowers to the funeral home was probably his own idea, a token conforming to established norms of behavior rather than expressing genuine remorse. I idly wondered how many people would show up at the memorial service. Unless I was ordered to be there, I wouldn't go.

As before, I won't attempt to record the entire session, only a representative portion in order to demonstrate the caliber of thinking encouraged by the Great Man. It had been Maddie's turn to begin the reports on caseloads; at some length she spoke of her interaction of one Myra P., a middle-aged woman who had been diagnosed with schizotypal personality disorder. While hanging ornaments on a Christmas tree, Myra had fallen off the chair she was using and knocked herself out. When she recovered, she insisted that she was seeing "spirit beings" in the room who were apparently roaming the Earth because they were "not at peace." Thereafter, wherever she went, she claimed to see these apparitions, clamoring to be "set free." Her exasperated husband, a well-to-do stock broker, brought her straight to the Home for treatment; and, Maddie stated, in the four months Myra had been there, she had been a difficult case.

> MC: She 'as not been difficult in ze sense zat she will not communicate wis me. *Au contraire.* She…babbles – is zat ze correct English word? – babbles on and on about one sing or anozair. But, it all comes back to zese 'spirit beings' she claims to see all around her. She is obsessive on zat point.

> VY: I'd like to take a page from Ken's book and ask if there's a 'social-environment' factor involved. That is, has Myra been in a specific, recurring situation or near a certain individual when she's had these…'visions'?

> MC: Not zat I am aware of, Nan. I must confess, zough, zat I 'ad not been looking at ze social factors in quite zat fashion. Oh, wait! Now, I remembair! Myra was 'anging pictures on ze wall on two occasions. Is zat what you mean?

> RB: I think Nan's onto something here, Maddie. 'Decorating' may be the key. After all, that's what she was doing when this all started; perhaps seeing these 'spirit beings' is an unconscious reaction to her accident, and anything that reminds her of it triggers the episodes.

> MN: I realize we've been through this before, but this

'social-environment' factor is further proof of an *avoidant* personality disorder, rather than a schizotypal one.

VY: Oh, really now, Bertie!

MN: Consider the possibility that certain environmental factors trigger these episodes. Isn't that just another way of saying that Myra had been uncomfortable with her former surroundings and that she is attempting to create *new* ones with which she can be more comfortable? If that's not avoidance, then I don't know what is.

MS: Excuse me again for throwing another monkey wrench into the works.

VE: Another brilliant thought, Dr. Maxwell?

MS: Ah, well, not so much an insight as a puzzle. What I would like to know is *when* Myra sees these 'spirit beings.' I don't think that's been discussed yet.

RB: Good point, Ken. Maddie?

MC: I cannot say, 'arry. *Mon Dieu*, Ken! Where do you get zese ideas?

MS: From a certain genius in the field who always admonished his audiences never to overlook any factor, no matter how trivial.

VE: Ahem, well, it seems as if you have new avenues to explore, Madeleine. Do you have anything else for us? No? Then, I think I'll put our newest acquisition in the hot seat. That is, if he's got all of his wits back yet.

Whoever had retrieved my notepad and pencil had failed to bring along my notes from the files, and I was forced to report my progress (such as it was) from memory. Not that I had much to say -- the sessions I'd had with my patients were mostly get-acquainted talks and reviews of Dr.

Hinkelman's relationships with them. Nevertheless, my colleagues grilled me as if I were an old hand. (If I ever have occasion to study for a Ph.D. in anything, I'll be well prepared for the oral examination!) They were particularly interested in how I had handled Ray W. earlier.

> MN: Weren't you the least bit frightened, Kenny? I was a boxing champion in college three years in a row, and I'd think twice before confronting anyone with sociopathic tendencies.

> MS: I was frightened as hell, Bertie, if you really want to know the truth. But, just in the case of animals, you shouldn't show fear. The violently-minded feed on it. In the face of firm resolve, they become indecisive and thus easier to deal with. By the way, I didn't learn that out of a textbook – or from our esteemed Director. Them's street smarts, folks.

> VY: Can you really equate a violent human being with a wild animal, Ken? That sounds rather uncharitable.

> MS: Strip away our veneer of civilization, and any of us would revert to the law of the jungle. And, believe me, Nan, I've been in the jungle! That's what happened to Ray, except he never had a veneer of civilization to begin with. He has always acted on instinct. I used to myself. Fortunately, I had a sympathetic shoulder to fall back on. Ray didn't.

> VE: Well said, Doctor. I think an empathetic relationship in this case will prove a plus in the patient's recovery.

> MS: Yes, sir, my sentiments exactly.

> VE: I would like to add here that this is not the first time our 'boy wonder' has faced down Ray. [He describes the incident in the dining room between Ray and Arthur. A couple of eyebrows shoot up in reaction; apparently, this is the first time the owners of the eyebrows have

heard of that incident. I receive fresh looks of respect and admiration. I blush furiously.] I'd hazard to guess that he has become something of an expert on the subject of violent confrontations.

RB: Hear, hear! P'r'aps we ought to put him in charge of the 'violent ward' as a matter of institutional safety.

VE [chuckles]: Perhaps. Tell us, Dr. Maxwell, how much does Ray trust you?

MS: I'd have to say a little less than he trusted Dr. Hinkelman. Of course, I haven't been here as long as my predecessor. Given more time, I'm confident Ray will come to regard me in the same light.

I wound up my presentation, happy to have put it behind me. One's "maiden voyage" is always the trickiest, because one never knows what to expect. But I felt I had weathered it well enough – considering that I had begun it in a drugged state! The remainder of the staff meeting droned on to its inevitable conclusion. Dr. Vengtman had only three announcements to make: first, the head cook had begun his annual vacation (I sent up silent thanks for small favors inasmuch as the head cook generally conducted himself like a royal pain in the ass); second, the promotion of Nurse Michaels to the post of Senior Nurse (with the usual increase in pay, perks, and responsibilities); and, third, a short leave of absence by Bertie due to a death in the family (which elicited the usual heartfelt condolences from the group).

Then, it was "Blue Limerick" time. I gritted my teeth. I still had reservations about this form of "therapy"; but, since I was in no position to criticize, I was obliged to go along with the crowd.

"Dante!" Harry boomed. "You're on!"

The nattily dressed little man sprang to his feet eagerly, a sheet of paper held loosely in his hand. He cleared his throat in a melodramatic fashion.

"Dere once was a hunk named Massey,
Whose auto was considered quite classy.
Da women all said,

As by dem he sped,
'I wish he'd check out *my* chassis!'"

A stony silence followed his recitation, and he looked about with anguish. His pride deeply wounded, he sat down dejectedly.

"Hell's bells!" Harry grumbled. "Another 'vehicular' limerick? The first one might have been unique, but now you're repeating yourself, Dante."

"Now, now, Harry," the Director admonished. "Don't you think establishing a continuing motif demonstrates a certain skill?"

"Yeah, Harry," Dante sniffed, "don't yez?"

"No, sir, I do not!" the Senior roared back, unmindful of matters of status. "I think Dante has – you'll pardon the expression – *slipped his gears* by not showing originality."

"Oh, pooh, Harry," Nan tossed in her two cents' worth. "This was your idea to begin with, but you never set down any guidelines. So, don't go all huffy if we don't show brilliance every time."

"She's got you there, Harry," the Director chortled.

"*Humph!*" was all our Senior Counselor could say.

After we had been summarily dismissed and I started to leave (wobbly!) in order to return the Black Bag – since my co-workers' little prank had sidetracked me – Dr. Vengtman called me back.

"Two matters, Ken," he said casually. "First, I read your report concerning the, uh, incident with our late colleague. I think, under the circumstances, that it is best forgotten so as not to distract us from our mission here. That's why I decided to promote Michaels. She has seniority and the requisite experience and know-how to handle the position. Do you concur?"

"Yes, sir. I had planned to suggest that very thing the first chance I got. In fact, I had already promised Michaels I wouldn't hinder any promotion."

"Excellent. Some day, you'll make a fine administrator. Which brings me to the second matter." He paused dramatically as he was wont to do. "I didn't want to say anything during the staff meeting for fear of swelling your head more than necessary, but you ought to know that, in the short time you've been here, you've made a favorable impression on several of the patients. I realize that their opinions may be tainted by the circumstances of their being here; yet, the trust a counselor elicits from any of them counts for much in the long run." He looked at me curiously as if debating with himself over continuing. Then: "Even Melissa has had kind words to say about you. During our counseling sessions, she often goes on and on about what a thoughtful and caring person you are. If I didn't know better, I'd swear she had a crush on you. Are you all right, Doctor? You seem… disturbed all of a sudden."

"Disturbed" was hardly adequate to describe my state of mind at that moment. I could scarcely believe my ears to hear that the Home's greatest enigma was singing my praises to others when I knew for a certainty that she was weaving a web of intrigue to snare me into her paranoid delusions. She was displaying all the symptoms of an amoral person who does not know the difference between right and wrong and thus has no idea of the effects his/her words/actions have on those around him/her. The business with the late Mathias Hinkelman was old stuff; there was nothing to be done about it beyond setting the record straight. But, now, Melissa had gone on to whisper rumors about the Director himself. I couldn't permit her to get away with it if it were in my power to stop her.

"I'm fine, Dr. Vengtman," I replied in a strained voice, "up to a point. You see, I've found Melissa to be something of a…contradiction." I updated him on my experiences with the teenager, being careful, however, not to mention her implied accusations against him. There was no sense in complicating things until I could satisfactorily debunk her. "I'm of the opinion that she suffers from paranoid delusions. Excuse me, sir. I know you requested discretion where Melissa is concerned; but, in light of your previous remarks, I feel obliged to offer my personal observations."

"And I'll certainly accept them in the spirit they deserve," he said simply (and a bit huffily, I thought). "Thank you, Dr. Maxwell. Carry on."

Once I had returned the Black Bag, I decided to take a short nap before lunch. I was still woozy from the "mickey" and didn't feel much like doing anything that required moving or thinking. I was halfway to the main entrance when a familiar sensation came over me, the sensation that I was not alone. I halted and swiveled on the balls of my feet. Gazing concernedly at me with her piercing amethyst eyes was Melissa. Her ability to creep up on me was beginning to unnerve me.

"Hello, Melissa," I said noncommittally. "How are you?"

"Are you still mad at me?"

"Of course not. I've never been mad at you. I *am* upset, however, by your behavior. I don't appreciate what you've been doing lately."

She stared at me in disbelief.

"You can't possibly mean that. I've tried to help you in your work, and this is the thanks I get."

"Really, Melissa, there's no need to be melodramatic. I know how you 'helped' Dr. Hinkelman. Now he's dead. I don't want to be 'helped' in the same way."

Either she was a very good actress, or she was genuinely horrified. Her amethyst eyes widened with shock, and her face blanched several degrees. Instantly, there came into my mind an image of a meteor shower, an unusually heavy one. The night sky was literally raining rocks by the dozens; bright flashes lit up the darkness in a brilliant display of natural fireworks. Some of the meteors survived to reach the ground, sending huge gouts of earth flying upward and outward, creating a pock-marked landscape from horizon to horizon. I staggered backward a couple of steps and shook my head vigorously in order to rid myself of the image. Whether that did the trick or the image-maker simply turned off the light-show, I couldn't say; as quickly as the vision had come, it departed, leaving my already drugged brain reeling.

"Why are you doing this to me, Melissa?" I whispered.

She bowed her head in contrition.

"I – I'm sorry, Ken. I…overreacted. You've got it all wrong, though. I *am* trying to help you. I can't tell you how; you wouldn't believe me."

"I'm really tired of this air of mystery you've created. If you're not ready to be straight with me, I don't see any need to talk to you any more."

I started to walk away, secretly hoping that my anger – mostly genuine – would shake her up and induce co-operation in her. It was another calculated risk on my part, I freely admit; had it backfired, I might have precipitated the very behavior I wanted to derail.

"Wait!" she cried out. "Why were you trying to break into Dr. Vengtman's office last night?"

That wasn't exactly the response I was looking for. I halted dead in my tracks (though, in retrospect, I probably shouldn't have) and faced her with false bravado.

"You know about that, eh? Your little friend 'reported' the incident, did he? Girl, why the hell are you spying on me?"

"I told you. I want to help you. What you're doing could be dangerous. I – I don't want what happened to Mathias to happen to you."

"And what did happen to Mathias?"

She bit her lip and stared off into the distance.

"Oh, God! I want so much to tell you, but I'm afraid Dr. Vengtman will destroy you if you learn the whole story."

"There you go again with the damned mystery. What could he possibly do to 'destroy' me?"

"Don't press me, Ken! I shouldn't have said anything at all. It may be too late already."

She pushed past me and trotted down the hallway. I called out to her to come back – in vain, for she turned a corner and was gone.

The conundrum was growing more complex by the day. Not only had Melissa continued to stick to her wild story concerning alleged evil machinations at the hands of Lowell Vengtman, she had now included a potential death threat by him to me as well. And still, she professed nothing but kindness and respect toward me. Without being too specific, I had told the Director that she suffered from paranoid delusions. With each encounter with me, she added fuel to that fire. In her fantasy world, she imagined all manner of secret activities at work, and any public disclosure of them would lead to instant destruction of all investigators. Had she, I wondered, played the same game with Hinkelman? So far, I had no evidence to support the theory that he had been aware of her drawing him into her delusional world. On the other hand, there was plenty of evidence for his isolation from the real world by her own evil machinations; nowhere had Lowell Vengtman's name been mentioned – only Melissa's.

Whatever her psychological state, it was driving me to acts of petty espionage. There were two possible explanations for her knowledge of my nocturnal investigations, both of which had no basis in fact. One, *she* had followed me into the building (and the raccoon had been following her) and lurked in the shadows to watch my every move. It might not have been difficult for her to do this; as the Home's first resident, she would have had enough opportunity to explore all the nooks and crannies of the former mansion and therefore been able to slip past any watchful eyes. Two, the raccoon *did* "report" back to her. Which meant she really could talk to animals and wield influence over them. That notion sent a chill up my spine. Believing that was enough to make *anyone* paranoid!

Physician, heal thyself!

How long I stood there lost in thought, I couldn't say. The next thing I was aware of was a familiar, gently mocking female voice.

"Still in a fog, Doctor? The least you could do is to move to one side and not block traffic." I reddened and slowly turned to confront Nan. She was grinning from ear to ear, her eyes twinkling mischievously. "Honestly,

Ken, we only gave you five cc's of sodium pentathol. You should be fully recovered by now."

"That's not what's bothering me. I just had another run-in with Melissa."

"Again? This is getting serious."

"Tell me about it." I recounted the recent conversation, hastily editing in order to cover up my own illicit movements. I couldn't take anyone into my confidence just yet – especially the Director's niece! "Tell me, Nan, has she ever made such remarks to you?"

"No, never."

"How about the others?"

"Not to my knowledge."

"Damn! Why is she singling me out then?"

"Perhaps it's your boyish good looks." That got her a sharp glance from me. "Sorry, Ken. Bad joke. But, seriously, I'd hate to see you go off the deep end." (Did I detect a note of more than simple professional concern? That was encouraging.) "Have you talked to Uncle Lowell about this?"

"Oh, yeah, I can see it now. 'By the way, Dr. Vengtman, Melissa Waterman says you're performing illegal experiments in the basement. Are you picking up where Dr. Frankenstein left off?' I'd be out the door in no time."

"You may be anyway, if you can't resolve your little dilemma. You'd be very poor company otherwise."

"Not like now, huh?"

She smiled sweetly, brushed my cheek lightly with her fingers, and sauntered away.

I must have been more fatigued than I thought. My "short nap before lunch" turned into a long snooze *through* lunch and into the middle of the afternoon. I awoke somewhat disoriented, and I spent a good ten minutes bringing myself up to date. Some of the memories I dredged up I wished I had left alone. Soon, my stomach was informing me that I hadn't eaten a decent meal since the prior evening. I debated going down the road for some take-out food, decided that I could wait a few more hours until supper, and busied myself in order not to think of my empty, growling stomach.

I should have been on recreation-monitor duty that afternoon. Thanks to Dante's flu and the swap I had made on Friday – his meal monitor for my recreation monitor – I was free for the day (a rare instance!). Consequently, I turned to the evaluation reports on Mathias Hinkelman

I had pilfered. Hunkering down on the floor once more with the stack of notes I had already made correlating the journal with the medical files, I spread out the evaluations in chronological order and took up the set dated September 1, 1996, the first instance the staff had observed signs of abnormal behavior on the part of their colleague.

At first, they were not unanimous in their opinion of him – not very surprising given seven uniquely talented individuals – and merely hinted that he was becoming self-absorbed, occasionally non-communicative, and frequently irritable. They did not notice (probably because they were not looking for) repeated words and phrases, vocal or written. Not until he had broken off his affair with Maddie, when he was full of angst and dread, and began to confide (in a limited way) with Harry was there a significant change in the tone of the evaluations; now the staff was (more or less) of one mind, though they were writing independently of each other. In the journal entry for October 26, 1996, for instance, Hinkelman had written:

> "Madeleine is hurt by my not seeing her any more. She refuses to speak to me any more than she has to. Can't blame her. It was a terrible thing to do to her. Oh, God, how I wish I could go back to her! But the voices won't stop. Those damned *whispers in my mind*! *They just won't stop!*"

In his evaluation dated November 1, Harry had written:

> "...[Hinkelman] has reduced the number of his counseling sessions below the accepted minimum. If this practice continues, it may be necessary to reprimand him formally.... I should point out -- though it is hardly a professional thing to say -- that he seems to be a troubled soul when he complains that unknown entities are persecuting him. I have heard him use the phrase 'whispering in my mind,' but he has not elaborated upon it...."

In a more anguished voice (admittedly, I was reading between the lines), Maddie had written for November:

> "...He has strained his relationship with the rest of

the staff almost to the breaking point, having become increasingly moody and temperamental. What has pushed him into this mode of behavior is a mystery.... I fear for his sanity."

Until the time Hinkelman was formally admitted as a patient at the beginning of February 1997, the evaluations took on an ever more strident and alarmist tone as his behavior and speech patterns – as evidenced by both the journal and his notations in the files – affected one and all. Nowhere in any of these reports, however, did anyone have a clue as to a *cause* of his break-down. He would not – or could not – tell his co-workers what was happening to him, and they were at a loss to understand his behavior since it seemingly had no demonstrable origin. In essence, they were stumbling about in the dark, not recognizing the parts of the elephant for what they were.

I, on the other hand, had no such handicap. Through careful research and a desire to solve a Great Mystery, I *knew* what had destroyed Mathias Hinkelman. And I was determined to expose the destroyer. Where my colleagues had failed, I would succeed in rehabilitating my predecessor.

What bravado I possessed in those days! If I had known then what my curiosity would provoke, I might have walked away from the Great Mystery altogether. Perhaps I might have walked away from the Home itself. Yet, since hindsight is 20/20, I stumbled about blithely!

By the time I had re-read nearly six months of evaluations, my stomach was really in an uproar. I couldn't hold it at bay any longer. Even if it meant elbowing Harry Rauschenburg out of the serving line, even if it meant looking over the shoulders of the kitchen staff as they pulled the food out of the ovens, I had to eat something ASAP. Fortunately, I had to do neither, but it was a near thing.

While I was gorging myself, I made an interesting deduction – and an equally momentous decision. In the course of piecing together the mystery of Mathias Hinkelman – as seen through the eyes of various (and varied) persons, not the least of whom had been the victim himself – I had come to realize that there had been a *second* victim in this tragedy. The first had lost his life, but the second had lost something just as valuable – love. This second person was none other than Dr. Madeleine Chantrier, Hinkelman's ex-lover, who, through no fault of her own, had been deprived of whatever happiness she and he had had during their brief affair.

Obviously, I could not restore their relationship. I could, however, ease

Maddie's pain by showing her proof that Mathias still loved her, even after he had broken off the affair, and had been as anguished over the break-up as he had over his inability to cope with the "whispers in his mind." Despite my reluctance to make public what I had learned so far, I decided that she had a right to know some of the truth in advance of my publication. I did not have to show her *all* of my findings – they were as yet incomplete, pending an examination of Melissa's file – only a photocopy of relevant entries in the journal. That in itself would go a long way toward assuaging any guilt feelings she might have been harboring. Later, when this bizarre affair was concluded, I would give her the entire journal as a memento.

As it happened, I had to wait for another day to fulfill that little quest. Maddie was not in the dining room at any time I was there; in fact, no one recalled having seen her since the staff meeting. On my return to my cottage, I made a side-trip to hers. There was no response to my knock, which meant she must have been off the grounds altogether.

Having nothing else to do that night – as long as Nancy Vengtman was still unavailable – I decided to take in a movie. "Silence of the Lambs II" was playing locally; that would be as entertaining as anything else. I really needed to take my mind off Mathias Hinkelman and Melissa Waterman, or else I might have gone bonkers myself!

DAY TEN:
Tuesday, 07.15.1997
ASSIGNATION

The next day, I was scheduled for morning-recreation-monitor duty. Recreation monitor was the only required task that was split into two parts – a morning session and an afternoon session. Since each session lasted two hours, the logic went, a counselor would have been too neglectful of his patients if (s)he oversaw both sessions; therefore, there was a separate duty roster for each – and yet another opportunity for conflicts of scheduling. (I had no desire to ever become a Senior Counselor; having to juggle all those rosters would have driven me to drink. And, come to think of it, that may have been the reason for Harry's excessive imbibing.) The morning session – a half hour of calisthenics and an hour-and-a-half of arts and crafts – was considered the easier of the two to oversee from a psychological point of view; because the patients were, more or less, involved in individual projects, there were fewer chances for personality conflict. Conflict was never entirely avoidable. The best we could ever hope for was to minimize it.

After a leisurely breakfast, I ambled into the erstwhile conservatory to keep an eye on things. Weather permitting, the calisthenics were usually held outdoors on the lawn. Storm clouds had rolled into the area during the night, creating a very threatening sky, and the Director had cancelled any outdoor activity. Monitors were not required to participate in the patients' activities – that was left to their own discretion – but they were encouraged to do more than just stand around like statues. Dante's little word exercise on Sunday had not been exactly kosher since it hadn't involved *physical* activity; yet, from the enthusiastic response from the patients, I gathered that it had been a welcome diversion from the usual routine, and therefore had the Director's blessing.

Most of the patients were waiting impatiently for someone to begin. Subconsciously, I noted that two of my patients were in this group: Matt and Fred. Matt actually had clothes on but not by choice; this was a mixed group, and some of the women had complained vehemently when he showed up "invisibly." Fred was as withdrawn as usual, and I half-expected him to crouch down and howl plaintively.

I signaled to the senior nurse present—a stocky fellow named Martinez, who tended to swagger when he walked—that he should get his butt in gear, a gesture which netted me a scowl from him. The man must've been a drill sergeant in a previous life because he actually called the group to attention, lined everyone up in two rows, and announced the first exercise in a monotone. Then, in a crisp military fashion, he began to count out the cadence. Some of the patients fell into the routine readily enough (those whose psychoses produced withdrawal symptoms), but the rest muttered and grumbled all the way through and made little effort to follow the cadence.

While it is important to keep the body in shape, it is also important that one's program of physical exercise fit one's needs. Fitting one's needs, then, presupposes a choice in constructing the program. Calisthenics imposed from an external source becomes a bore and soon loses whatever value it might have had. Military personnel endure such routine due to the consequences of "mutinous" behavior. Emotionally disturbed persons, on the other hand, cannot be punished for "mutiny" since (1) they are prone to continue their "mutiny" despite any consequences and (2) they are unable to distinguish between acceptable and unacceptable behavior in the first place. In the Home, it was clear that the patients resented either the calisthenics themselves or the manner in which they were presented (or both), and they protested in the only manner open to them, short of simply walking away – which was always a possibility. Having been here only a week, I didn't know if this scene was a daily occurrence; yet I saw a potential problem in the making unless I defused it somehow. In a moment of "inspiration," I decided to intervene with a Bold New Idea.

One of my deep dark secrets that I hoped never got back to my old South Side neighborhood was my participation in an aerobic-dancing class. You've seen the videos produced by one celebrity or another and perhaps dismissed the activity as just for women – or sissies. I used to feel that way myself and wouldn't have touched aerobics with the proverbial ten-foot pole. But, I'm a convert now! As I have mentioned, sports had been a crucial element in my life; it got me off the streets and onto the road toward a more constructive existence. I played both football and basketball in high school and college (the latter via an athletic scholarship). During my college days, our basketball team was not quite championship caliber; in fact, we usually finished with a losing record. In my senior year, the team acquired a new coach, the sort who dissected problems with an analytical eye and came up with innovative solutions. He had decided, after watching videos from previous seasons, that we had lacked "synchronization" and therefore needed to "get back into sync" with both ourselves and with each other.

To that end, he enrolled all of us in aerobic-dancing classes at the local YMCA. Howls of protest greeted this idea, and we were told it was either aerobics or dismissal from the team. (One fellow did quit and transfer to another school. I have never heard anything about him since.) So we danced – from the beginner's class through the intermediate and on to the advanced group. And, while no one admitted it in public, we *loved* it! (If nothing else, it was a great way to meet women!) We even created new routines based on basketball plays and performed them before the class in special presentations; they were well received and later incorporated into the "Y's" classes. More importantly, however, the dancing put us "back in sync"; and, though we never made it into any post-season tournaments, we finished with a winning record for the first time in ten years. (As far as I know, aerobics is still required for the BB team there.) After entrance into medical school, I tried to keep up with the latest routines as much as possible, but my schedule militated against anything on a regular basis. (I still go through some of the old routines now and then.)

So, it was with a great deal of bravado that I interrupted the calisthenics. Inasmuch as Nurse Martinez was getting nowhere fast with his approach, he was all too happy to hand the inmates over to me. I suspected he wanted to see the great Dr. Maxwell, whose "reputation" was growing by leaps and bounds, fall flat on his face. I wondered briefly if I might succeed in doing just that.

"OK, people, listen up," I announced. "I guess this PE stuff is pretty boring, right?" Much mumbling issued from the crowd. "Well, let's try something different, huh?"

"How about nude leap-frog, Doc?" Matt called out. "Get a *real* work-out there."

Hoots and cat-calls to that suggestion came instantaneously, plus indignant protests from the two women present.

"I want *all* of us to enjoy this, Matt. What you do on your own time is your business."

"Spoilsport!" the old man joked.

"I'm going to demonstrate a few simple aerobic steps. Then I want you to try them."

"Aerobics?" exclaimed a patient in the back row. "That's *sissy* stuff!"

"Not so," countered Fred, to my great surprise. "A cultural ritual, as old as the species, eh, Doctor? Teach us then."

"All right. To begin, take three steps to the left, like so." I shuffled off in the proper direction, placing the left foot at comfortable distance from the right one and shifting my body so that the right foot ended up where the left one had been. "After the third step, kick your left foot out, like so." I imitated the action of a football punter. "Now, your turn."

There was hesitation for all of five seconds as the group debated whether to comply with my directions. Seeing that no one else was willing to take the first step, my "wolf-man" at the end of the front row stepped off and completed the maneuver. The person next to him, perhaps encouraged by his example, followed after him. The rest of the line awkwardly followed suit, and then the second line joined in. The kicks at the end of the move were as uncoordinated as one might have expected and more resembled flailing than choreography. Still, it was a beginning.

"All *right*!" I hooted by way of positive feed-back. "Now, back to the right, like so" – I demonstrated – "and kick!"

This time, everyone started (more or less) at once, though they still looked like a rag-tag bunch. With practice, I knew, they'd get the hang of it. The important thing was to provide a type of exercise they would view as fun as well as healthful, a type they could change as the spirit moved them and not be bogged down in some boring routine. Physical therapy as much as psychotherapy is self-defeating if it does not stimulate the organism holistically.

"Better, better. Now, we'll do it all at once. Left, left, left, and *kick*!" I moved out, and the group was three seconds behind me. "Right, right, right, and *kick*!" Only a two-second delay on that repetition; they were catching on. We did three more repetitions, and the group was right with me all the way. "Now, we'll add something. Along with the kick, clap your hands, like so." I raised my arms so that my hands were before my face and clapped sharply. "Let's do it! Left, left, left, kick and clap! Right, right, right, kick and clap!" Then, I dropped a bombshell: "OK, you nurses, form your own line! No one stands around with their finger up their nose!"

One might have thought I had asked them to drop their pants for all the shocked reaction I received from the entire contingent of nurses, especially the male ones. Their jaws dropped almost in unison, and they gaped at me in disbelief. Obviously, they were not of a mind to be placed on the same level as the patients. On the other hand, they were expected to follow the directives of the professional staff so long as those directives were not life-threatening. Thus, a state of profound confusion gripped them all.

"Damn straight!" Matt yelled out. "No one with his finger up his nose!"

"Absolutely!" Fred added. "We must be unified."

Almost as one, the patients turned toward the nurses and began to chant: "No fingers up the nose!" Some of the more demonstrative – like Matt – actually put fingers up *their* noses and pointed at the nurses with mock contempt (although, in some cases, I think the contempt was real). It was a ludicrous sight, but it accomplished the purpose. With a mixture of chagrin, exasperation, bemusement, and resignation, the non-professionals joined my "chorus line" and formed their own row, for which they received a sarcastic round of applause. I grinned hugely. Perhaps I had missed my true calling!

"OK, people, you know the drill. Let's do it!"

I had them perform several more repetitions just to make sure the nurses were familiar with the routine (and did I see a smile on some of their faces?), then added a few new moves. I still kept it simple so as not to overtax or confuse anybody; but, by the time the half hour was up, I had introduced them to three variations of the original exercise. If I do say so myself, I was well pleased with what I'd accomplished.

As the group broke up to go to the arts-and-crafts rooms, Fred came up to me, smiled a Mona-Lisa smile, and said:

"The new pack member does well."

And he quick-marched out of the conservatory without another word.

To say that I was dumbfounded is an understatement. There had been no prelude to the fact that Fred had accepted me as much as he had Mathias Hinkelman and was willing to trust me with "pack lore." Just a simple statement, and then he was gone. When the import of his words had sunk in, I experienced both relief and satisfaction at having finally won him over. Now, the real work could begin.

As I turned to leave for the arts-and-crafts rooms myself, I spotted Nan leaning against the lintel of the entryway, her arms folded across her stomach. She pursed her lips when I approached.

"My, my," she murmured, "you're just full of surprises."

"How long have you been here?"

"Long enough to witness history in the making."

"Excuse me?"

"Aerobics as psychotherapy, silly. Wait until I tell Uncle Lowell. He'll love this."

"He'll probably fall down laughing," I attempted self-effacement. "After which, I'll get another stern lecture."

"I don't think so. Uncle Lowell is an innovator, you know, and he'll seriously consider incorporating a program of aerobics into the daily routine. Perhaps he'll ask you to conduct it."

"Yeah, right. As if I haven't enough to do."

"Well, you've got no one to blame but yourself, Ken dear. You started it."

"I guess so. Are we still on for tonight?"

"I'm counting the hours," she replied mischievously. "I just hope you can pick me up without getting lost."

"Very funny. I'll be there – and on time too!"

"All art is a kind of confession, more or less oblique," wrote James Baldwin in *Nobody Knows My Name*. "All artists, if they are to survive, are forced, at last, to tell the whole story, to vomit the anguish up."

Lowell Vengtman would not have put it quite that way, but he certainly would have agreed with Baldwin's sentiments. Art, as a form of self-expression, reflects not only the artist's hopes and desires and aspirations, but also his/her fears and terrors and nightmares; in its many forms, it gives shape and substance and dimension to the inner life of the individual and reveals that which (s)he must bear each day of his/her existence. Some humans follow their muse along flower-strewn paths through golden meadows and dance with the angels. Others must pick their way through rocky passes, fleeing from demons. Save for a difference in circumstances, Renoir would have been van Gogh, George Sands Steinbeck, or Saint Saens Tchaikovsky. Art echoes the inner experience and turns it inside out.

For as long as psychology has been an accepted science, it has utilized art to reach into the human psyche and pull that experience into the light of day so that the emotionally disturbed can be better understood. Rorschach ink blots have been a basic tool in unraveling the twisted mind. Children who undergo trauma are always encouraged to draw pictures of the events and/or persons they believe are at the root of their traumas. By extension, the Great Man sought to draw out the same information from traumatized adults through arts and crafts. And whatever the patients created through whatever medium became as much a part of their medical files as any counselor's interview, to be analyzed by the staff in much the same manner as the verbal responses. If the patients enjoyed themselves in the process, so much the better. Therapy takes many forms.

Ordinarily, arts-and-crafts sessions were performed outside during clement weather. With a potential storm brewing, a back-up system was used, consisting of two adjacent rooms at the back of the former mansion. Once, these rooms had been servants' quarters – in size, smaller than the cottages but still comfortable – one for the butler/chauffeur, the other for the maid/cook. Cleared of furniture, the one resembled a miniature art gallery, while the other was a bric-a-brac shop. The patients were divided into two groups (still at random). For the first forty-five minutes, one group went to the "art" room and the other to the "crafts" room; they then switched rooms during the second forty-five-minute period. We monitors were left to our own discretion as to how to oversee these varied activities. I had decided on fifteen-minute "shifts," shuttling from one room to the other and back again; it was the only thing I could think of to combat the boredom of it all.

Except that that day proved to be far from boring!

It was toward the end of the first period, and the nurses were urging the patients to put away their materials for the switch in rooms. I was in the "crafts" room, strolling between the tables and casually examining for the second time the works-in-progress. Some of the patients, more skilled with their hands, had applied themselves diligently; the rest struggled furiously, exhibiting varying degrees of exasperation, frustration, and outright anger. These latter I kept a close eye on. The projects themselves reflected a wide range of interests, from crocheting to – yes – basket-weaving. I noted with some amusement that Georgina was whipping out yet more samplers adorned with the letter "L" in remembrance of her dead son; apparently, she had no desire to attempt any other sort of project, a fixation which demonstrated the depth of her psychosis. As I began a new circuit of the room, one of the nurses from the "arts" room appeared at the door and signaled for my attention.

"What is it?" I asked in a low voice, so as not to alarm anyone else.

"You better come quick, Doctor," the middle-aged, graying brunette woman whispered. "Melissa Waterman just walked into our room, and she's inspecting everybody's projects."

By now, I had become sensitized to the reactions of both staff and patients to the unannounced comings and goings of this strange girl. Their fear and loathing of her was almost palpable, and it was anybody's guess how Melissa felt about *them*. She behaved so aloofly and distantly that a read of her was next to impossible, and it was not altogether unreasonable to suppose that she did not care for – or about – others in any way. She was one of that rare breed who were *in* this world but not *of* it; her body was here, but her mind was elsewhere. If the two parts interacted, it usually presaged trouble for someone. Only her animal "friends" rated special attention from her.

Be that as it may, it was also "common knowledge" that Melissa had a certain respect – if she was capable of respect at all – for me and that she behaved almost human in my presence. "Respect" was a debatable concept as far as I was concerned, given her previous dealings with me; still, I had to admit that she was more subdued whenever I was around. I followed the nurse with more of a sense of annoyance than of urgency.

Melissa was peering intently at a lump of clay when I arrived. The lump was supposed to be a human head with eyes, nose, ears, and mouth; the sculptor, Arthur the food-fighter, was having a difficult time visualizing a human head. As a consequence, the nose was bent in one direction, one ear was larger than the other, the mouth was too far to one side, and the general shape of the skull resembled a mushroom. In his twisted psyche, perhaps that was how Arthur perceived a human head, but it clearly did not jibe with Melissa's ideas. She frowned and shook her head in disgust. Meanwhile, Arthur stared at her, fear and hate warring with each other for the dominant position; he dared not move, lest his movement provoke some unpleasant reaction from her. Everyone else in the room seemed equally apprehensive and paralyzed and watched her like chickens in a fox house. The nurses, in particular, unsure of how to handle her (apparently never having encountered this situation before), held themselves in abeyance, effectively dumping the problem squarely into my lap. But, then, that was why I was being paid the big bucks, wasn't it?

"Good morning, Melissa," I greeted her as casually as I could. "Have you decided to join us? I can get you any materials you need."

She turned toward me and pierced me with those damned amethyst eyes. I tensed because, for a fraction of a second, I saw the coldness and blackness of outer space in them. As soon as she recognized me, however, the eyes softened, and she gave me her usual little-lost-girl look.

"Hello, Ken. Maybe I will. I certainly could do better than 'Mr. Potato Head' here."

Arthur's eyes bugged at the insult, and his fear briefly yielded to hate. I moved quickly to mediate.

"We're not here to create perfect art, Melissa. We're here to express our inner feelings. As Arthur's sense of self strengthens, so will his outward expressions."

For some reason, she had an itch she couldn't scratch, and it was bothering the hell out of her. She wouldn't let go of the train of thought she was on.

"All *I* see" – she gestured at the lump of clay – "is a piece of...*shit*!" She faced Arthur squarely. "I want you to change it, Arthur!"

Arthur gaped at her in confusion. Then, his face blanched, and his eyes glazed over. Slowly, he twisted to one side and uttered a low, drawn-out moan. For a couple of seconds, he simply stared at the lump of clay as if he could will it to re-form itself. Abruptly, he raised a hand, made a fist, and brought it crashing down upon the malformed head, flattening it beyond recognition. "Stunned beyond belief" was probably the operable phrase to describe that moment. All motion in the room ceased with that brief act of destruction. I forced myself to look at Melissa and instantly wished I hadn't. Her amethyst eyes were actually glowing like twin fires! I was thunderstruck. Had she caused Arthur to destroy his work of art? If so, how had she done it? More germane, what could I do to dissuade her from doing it again? Arthur continued to gaze stuporously at the ruined clay, drool running down his chin. Melissa grinned with delight.

"There!" she announced triumphantly. "That's much better!"

Before I could check myself, I instinctively stepped up to her, seized her by the shoulder, and yanked her around. She regarded me with shock; obviously, my reaction was the last thing she expected from anyone, especially me. And, truth to tell, it was the last thing *I* expected from me. My desire to break the spell (if that was the proper term) she had cast over Arthur by any means available was paramount to any professionalism I had ever learned. I tensed again, not knowing if she would now lose her "respect" for me and work her "magic" on me. I breathed a mental sigh when she did not but lapsed into a what-have-I-done mode and cast a chastened look at the floor.

"What did you do to him?" I demanded. "Tell me!"

By way of response, she pressed herself against me, wrapped her arms around my neck, and laid her head on my chest. She was as soft and warm as any woman I'd known until then, and I was filled with a most pleasant sensation.

"You mustn't be angry with me, Ken. I – I sometimes lose control. I try so hard not to. I care for you, Ken, and I'd never do anything to upset you. You must believe me."

"I do believe you, Melissa," I responded as the pleasant feeling built up inside me, saturating every fiber of my being with peace and serenity. "You'll try hard to maintain your control in the future."

"I know you care for me too." She gazed into my face, and I fell into those amethyst eyes surrounded by an all-encompassing love. "Don't you?"

"Of course, I care for you," I murmured, even as the warmth and the peace and the love crescendoed and made me giddy. "I –"

Released from the grip of Melissa's "spell," Arthur had come to his (comparatively good) senses and seen what had become of his sculpture. He howled in protest and beat his fists on the table. The racket was sufficient to interrupt what I was about to say, and I came back to reality as if from a dream. I stared at Melissa in disbelief, then in righteous anger. She *had* attempted to work "magic" on me, had attempted to *seduce* me so that I'd be all peaches and cream toward her. I must confess that, at that moment, I reverted to my street persona which I had so carefully cloaked over in the recent past.

"Don't you *ever* do that to me again, bitch!" I shook her roughly for good measure. "You got that straight?"

Either she was genuinely horrified by the enormity of her actions, or she was genuinely crushed by the immensity of my words and actions. Whichever it was made no difference to me (then) as long as it stopped her in her tracks. Her eyes actually became moist, and her lips quivered minutely. I scowled fiercely at her. Most of my anger centered on her unconscionable acts; the rest rebounded against me for my stupidity at being suckered in like that. All around us, the staff and patients imitated statues; no one dared to (or could?) move or speak, lest (s)he draw attention to him/herself. Melissa pushed away from me and covered her face.

"Oh, God! I've done it again! Please forgive me, Ken! *Please!*"

The immensity of my words and actions finally reached into my own consciousness, and I mentally cursed myself for behaving as if I were back on the streets, yielding to a fit of anger and lashing out at the nearest handy target. What would the staff, both professional and non-professional, think of the wonderful Dr. Maxwell, now that he had acted like a normal human being? I forced myself to relax. I could salvage my tarnished reputation later (if possible); right now, I had my job to do and mediate the situation I had unwittingly participated in.

"If you're truly sorry, Melissa, I will. But you have to apologize to Arthur as well."

She glanced at the would-be sculptor who sat there with a snarl on his lips. She clenched her fists and pressed them against her head.

"No-o-o-o!" she whined. "I can't – I can't – *I can't!*"

And she fled out of the room. Anyone who stood in her way had to leap aside to avoid being run over. I watched her go but made no move to halt her; and, when she had vanished from sight, I shook my head in regret. I hadn't accomplished much – beyond losing my temper – had I? If Melissa's remorse had been genuine (and, knowing her, who could say?), it was probably temporary. The next time she gave into her passions, she would behave as she had minutes before; and, if there was no one able or willing to check her as I had, she would work her will unimpeded. I was as certain of that as I was of the sun's rising in the east. No one, apparently, had the intestinal fortitude to stand up to her. Only fools like Kenneth Maxwell rushed in, because he was abysmally ignorant of Melissa's background. Which realization strengthened my resolve to locate her file, by hook or by crook, and learn the truth about her.

I was not aware of the presence at my side of Nurse Martinez until he cleared his throat. I turned and regarded him with a vacant look. He pursed his lips and blinked rapidly.

"You OK, Doctor? Boy, that was one helluva show-down. I woulda shit my pants if I'd been in your shoes."

I grimaced at his uncouthness, but I could appreciate his sentiments. It *had* been a near thing.

"Any time you want to be in my shoes, friend, just say the word."

"Huh? Oh, hell, no! Not even for Old Man Vengtman's bank account."

My face hardened.

"That's *Dr.* Vengtman, Nurse. You need a lesson in civility." And, before he had a chance to speak again, I turned my back on him and said to all present: "All right, everyone, back to what you were doing. The show's over."

After lunch, I paid a call on Matt. The old man was at the window, gazing intently at the scenery outside. His room faced south and, from there, one could just barely see the fence that marked the southern boundary of the Home's property. Beyond was a smaller estate, privately owned. The woodland thinned out at that point, though whether it was by natural causes or human design was difficult to say. This view was not as scenic as the eastern or western ones – the latter with the main body of the woods and the former with the magnificent, multi-colored flower gardens -- but only slightly more so than the northern one which was mostly empty lawn (beyond which was yet another privately-owned estate). I wondered what attracted Matt's attention so – until I joined him at the window.

Melissa, seemingly unshaken by the morning's incident, was cavorting with her coterie of squirrels like a child with a litter of puppies. It was nothing short of astounding to watch her relate to wildlife. To her, animals were not "wildlife" at all; rather, they were her "pets." Yet, there was no sense of domestication evident in their behavior; they frolicked and gamboled as squirrels ordinarily do, but now they did so with a participating human being.

And participate this human being did. She rolled on the ground or crawled on hands and knees while her "pets" leaped and scrambled over and around her. At this distance, none of the creatures – non-human as well as human – could be heard, but I imagined that they all emitted sounds of unbounded glee. The tableau had such an aura of innocence to it that one might be excused if he lost sight of the nature of the actors. That nature was wholly incongruous to the action and stretched the limits of credulity.

After a while, Matt sighed heavily, turned away, and looked at me with distress. I could almost *hear* his consternation. I didn't initiate any conversation, however, but gave him time to work things out in his own mind. Presently, he rubbed his jaw and began pacing the floor. Still, I kept my silence. Then, he halted and regarded me sadly.

"You can see me, can't you, Doc?"

There was a question-and-a-half! How did one answer it? On the one hand, it would have been the simplest thing in the world to say "yes" and end the charade. I certainly hadn't felt comfortable pretending not to see him. Suppose, though, that he was testing me and that he was seeking a confirmation of his psychotic construct? A "yes" on my part conceivably might provoke an adverse reaction and drive him deeper into his psychosis. On the other hand, a "no" would go counter to the goal toward which I was striving; I'd merely confirm his belief in his invisibility and not provide the guidance I was committed to giving. Ideally, the true course was to have the patient himself realize the unreality of his internal world and walk out of it under his own strength. How could I accomplish that in a positive manner? I decided to take the middle ground and see what happened.

"Well, Matt, I hadn't planned on saying anything just yet, in case I was wrong. But, yes, sometimes, out of the corner of my eye, I do."

He scratched his head.

"Yeah, I figured as much. I seem to have become visible to a lot of people lately. Hell, I'm beginning to wonder if I ever was invisible in the first place."

I had to smile to myself. At last, I was getting somewhere with him. In one unexpected admission, Matt had taken his first step. The next move was mine: to coax him into taking a second step, and a third, and so on. First, though, I had to calm myself down! This break-through had created all sorts of wild thoughts, and they were racing through my mind like an out-of-control forest fire. I scarcely knew where to begin to push the old man down the right path, because there were so many options from which to choose. So, I picked one at random.

"It's not just Melissa any more then?"

"Uh-uh. She did something to me – neutralized my power little by little."

"Does it upset you, knowing that?"

"Yes and no." He started pacing again. "I *liked* being invisible, Doc; I could make observations no one else could."

"Don't you think you could've made them without being invisible? I mean, couldn't it have been just your reporter's instinct?"

"Could be, could be. I have been making observations long before I became invisible."

"Or, long before you *thought* you were invisible?"

"Hmmm. I see where you're going with this. I dunno. I'll have to think some more on it."

"Fine. Now, tell me why *not* being invisible wouldn't upset you."
He chuckled.

"Well, besides making my kids happy at not having to shell out any more money to you people, I guess I'd make all my pals happy if they could see me again."

"That's a good thought, Matt. Hold on to it."

"Sure thing, Doc. Say, speaking of Melissa, I heard about that little fracas in art-and-crafts this morning."

I kept my face a mask of neutrality.

"And?"

"And, it's only fair to warn you. If you aren't careful, you'll end up fucking her. And she ain't that good of a fuck."

I had to laugh in spite of myself.

"How would you know what kind of a fuck she is, my friend?"

"Reporter's instinct?" he replied, laying an index finger along side of his nose. "Seriously, son, you're a nice fella – for a shrink, that is – and I don't want you to wind up like Hinkelman."

My ears perked up at that remark.

"What do you know about that?"

"Hell, it's common knowledge around here. He was a nice fella too – for a shrink – before he had his little tete-a-tete with Melissa. She tried to seduce him too, but he wouldn't go for it. So, she put the evil eye on him."

"'Evil eye'? Really, Matt!"

"You know what I mean. You've seen what she can do. I can't explain it, but she's got some kind of weird power."

"I think you're worrying needlessly. I have a pretty good idea what happened to Hinkelman, and it doesn't involve 'witchcraft.'"

"Maybe, and maybe not. Just watch your step."

"Do you think I need to?"

"Look at it this way. I can stop being invisible, but you won't be able to stop being dead."

"We'll see. I appreciate your concern, though. I'll see you tomorrow."

"Common knowledge around here" Matt had said. Despite his psychosis, the old man could be as lucid as anyone, and his former occupation had trained him to be a keen observer. If he said "common knowledge," that's exactly what he meant. But, "common" to whom? To the patients? To the staff? Or to everyone except the skeptical Dr. Maxwell? So far, I had received any number of views concerning Hinkelman's demise; yet, since many of them had come from normally unreliable sources, one could dismiss them as the run-of-the-mill rumors one always hears in any organization of whatever nature. A sanitarium was not immune to "grape-vine talk." The evidence (such as it was) was still wholly circumstantial. I needed something solid I could sink my teeth into.

The rest of the day passed without incident (with the possible exception of a couple of the female nurses giving me some rather *meaningful* looks!), and I shifted my thoughts to my long awaited dinner date with Nancy Vengtman – lovely, luscious Nan. On the surface, I might have been accused of "brown-nosing"; after all, she *was* the Director's niece and I *was* an up-and-coming young Turk. And I'd be less than honest if I said the idea had never crossed my mind. There were, however, two counter-arguments to that criticism. One, Lowell Vengtman had singled me out for employment based on my past performance before I ever laid eyes on his niece; from his sparse comments of the past week, he expected great things of me and was willing to give me my head in accomplishing them. Two, Nan herself was not the sort of woman who dated everything in pants; she was smart and savvy and – beyond possessing a sarcastic streak – knew what she wanted in a man. If there is such a thing as Fate, it had acted to bring us together. She was everything *I* wanted in a woman, and I was going to take advantage of all my opportunities.

On my way to Nan's cottage, I spied Melissa again at a spot further north. She had just entered the woods with her full "honor guard" with her: the flock of squirrels at her heels, the two raccoons acting as "flankers," and the terrier I'd seen my first day here at the head of the pack as a "point man." A cold chill swept over me as I watched that impossible menagerie disappear into the trees, and the image stayed with me until I reached cottage #1 ("Venus's Bower," another of those lurid captions dreamed up by the original owner to put his guests in the proper mood).

Happily, the Director's niece had a cure for "Melissa-itis." She answered my knock with the sweetest smile I'd seen in a long time and a promise of things to come in her eyes. She was dressed in the same stunning outfit she'd worn the day we first met – the blue-white-lavender combo, right down to the carnation in her lapel. Had she chosen this outfit deliberately for the occasion? It didn't make much difference to me what she wore; she'd look good in a potato sack. I was instantly filled with desire, and my mind reviewed one scenario after another as I planned my conquest of this delectable creature. A quiet dinner, some wine, some small talk, more wine, the return to someone's cottage, and finally – *logistics*!

As I have stated before, I had never had much opportunity to sample the restaurants this far from Chicago, and I was looking forward to checking out the recommendations I'd been given by my former colleagues at R-PSL. One of the advantages of urban life, of course, is the wide spectrum of eateries to choose from. Though I had never "gone the cycle" – that is to say, eaten at a different place until I had been to them all – I was curious about the restaurants in the "boonies." Fast-food joints were all right for a change of pace, but there was nothing like a leisurely meal in a pleasant ambience to instill in one a sense of the "good life." And, if one has a beautiful woman on one's arm, so much the better. While I had first told Nan that I knew of a great place for ribs, I was looking to make a really lasting impression on her on the first date; therefore, I took her to a restaurant outside of Downers Grove on Ogden Avenue that, according to my informant from this area, served beef bourguignon which "makes your mouth envy your stomach."

The dinner date went swimmingly for a while. Nan and I exchanged biographies – she had been born on the Gold Coast and had spent her youth cavorting along Lake Shore Drive, as far removed economically and culturally from my South Side origins as one could get – and discussed our goals and hopes and aspirations in life. Then, somewhere between the main course and dessert, my mind took a detour. Nan had asked me if I still carried mental baggage from my poverty-stricken background and I had started to reply that it mostly showed up in my speech patterns when I wasn't careful. Without any warning, the image of Melissa Waterman and her menagerie came swarming into my consciousness. It was rather disconcerting, to say the least, to have my end of the conversation degenerate to the point of meaningless. After a long pause, during which I was fixated by a pair of amethyst eyes, I was jolted out of my trance by Nan's soft voice and her piquant sense of humor.

"I should tell you, Ken dear, that the rest of the staff has taken bets on how fast you can get me into bed."

My head snapped up in shock.

"*What did you say?*"

"Excuse me, Dr. Maxwell, if I'm boring the hell out of you. I had hoped to get a little more mileage."

"God! I'm sorry, Nan, really, *really* sorry. You're the least boring person I've ever met. It's just that I – well, for some unknown reason, Melissa Waterman popped into my head."

She eyed me both curiously and warily and, frankly, I didn't blame her one bit. If our roles had been reversed, I'd've done the same. It can't be too thrilling to be speaking to a person, only to have him take a hike (mentally speaking) in the middle of the conversation. I have known people who have simply "phased out" when those around them became too boring; they listen on one level, but their minds are on a different level altogether. If one is discerning enough, he will spot the signals. Further, if one is discerning enough, he will have the good sense to shut up – or not be boring in the first place. I had "phased out" in the presence of the one person I had wanted to make a good impression on, and the impression I *was* making was disastrous. Kenneth Maxwell strikes again!

"You've become obsessed with her, haven't you?" Nan was asking. "I really think you should talk to Uncle Lowell."

"Not until I have something solid to give him," I replied stubbornly. "You know your uncle's reputation as well as anyone. He'll expect me to have incontrovertible proof of my allegations – especially since Melissa is his patient."

"Even at the cost of your peace of mind? You can be good for a laugh or two, Ken. I'd hate to see you deteriorate" – she paused briefly, mulling over her next thought – "like Mathias Hinkelman."

Was she speaking strictly professionally? I looked into her eyes deeply and saw, not pity or fear but genuine concern for my well-being. And some of it was, I suspected (or rather, I *hoped*), of a personal nature.

"Look, let me tell you what happened this morning, and then you can decide whether I should go to your uncle or hold off. Regardless of your decision, I've got to get this off my chest, or I'll go nuts!"

"My, my, a confession – and I forgot to bring my couch."

"Actually," I leered in spite of myself, "I had another piece of furniture in mind."

She smiled coyly.

"Tell me your story first."

So I did, every single detail I could remember, including the sensations I had experienced while Melissa was attempting to seduce me, Svengali-style. Nan did not comment until I had finished; neither did she betray any emotion but gave me her full attention like the professional she was. When I had run down, she remained silent a moment longer, fingering her wine glass. Then:

"What do you want to do about her?"

"I want – no, I *need* to find out why she's a patient here. The answer to this riddle is in her medical file. I'm as sure of that as anything in this world." I looked her straight in the eye and came to a quick decision. I had drawn her into this little conspiracy part of the way; I might as well complete her "recruitment." I just hoped she wouldn't hate me too much later on. "Will you help me?"

She lapsed into another, longer silence, and I could just picture the wheels in her mind turning over and over. Thick suspicion oozed between the cracks of her trust in me. I was taking a tremendous risk by asking her to be a sneak thief for me. I hoped she would keep a confidence, but I could not count on it. She would have been well within her rights (and responsibilities) to report this conversation to the Director – who would be well within *his* rights (and responsibilities) to either reprimand me or fire me on the spot. She might not believe the risk I was asking her to take was worth her career – or her uncle's devotion. Silently, I cursed the necessity that had driven me to involve her in my schemes, but it was too late in the day for niceties. I was overcome by a sense of urgency, a sense that something horrible lurked on the grounds of the Vengtman Home for the Emotionally Disturbed (Illinois branch). I now realized that what had happened to Mathias Hinkelman was merely the tip of the iceberg; a greater evil was present, and I was compelled to act quickly to thwart it. No sacrifice at that moment in time seemed too great....

Presently, Nan spoke, and she spoke in such a low voice that I had to strain to hear her.

"If you're suggesting what I think you're suggesting, you're asking me to betray a trust, to interfere in a doctor-patient relationship, to risk everything I've worked for, all for the sake of – what? A hunch? A gut instinct? Ken dear, if it weren't for certain...feelings I'm developing for you, I'd call Uncle Lowell this instant and hand you over to him. Instead, I'm willing to give you the benefit of the doubt."

"Then you'll try to get Melissa's file?"

"I'm not promising anything. I have to think over what you've told me."

"Fair enough. Thanks for listening to me."

"Huh! What else have I got to do with my free time? I listen to my patients bitch all day long. Why not listen to doctors with a pre-occupation with impending doom?"

"I'm so glad you're so understanding. Shall we order dessert now?"

The remainder of the dinner passed quietly. We fell back into small talk; I discussed the possibility of introducing flower gardening into the "curriculum" on the grounds that color and aroma might have a therapeutic effect on the patients, and Nan needled me further about my aerobic-dancing abilities. By the time we had gone through our third glass of wine, I was feeling an urgency of a different sort, and I proposed that we take our leave. She was readily agreeable, and soon we were back at the Home again. From the parking lot to her cottage, we ambled hand in hand. At her door, she faced me, and I took her other hand and drew her close to me. I bent down and kissed her passionately; she responded eagerly, opening her mouth and pressing her tongue against mine. I released her hands, slipped my arms around her supple waist, and embraced her tightly. She wrapped her arms around my neck and continued her tongue-and-lip massage. The sense of urgency I had experienced earlier now intensified, and I searched her eyes for what I hoped was clear intent. Her eyes seemed to relay the same message (or so I wanted to believe).

"I suppose," she whispered huskily, "that you're waiting for me to invite you in."

"Yes, I am."

"Well, then, would you like to come in?"

"Yes, thank you."

She disengaged herself from me, fumbled in her purse, and extracted her key. The fact that she actually had difficulty inserting the key in the lock suggested that she was as anxious as I was to get inside and expedite our business. On the fourth try, she succeeded and pushed the door open roughly. Grabbing me by the wrist, she practically dragged me in – though, truth to tell, I pushed her inside a little bit as well. I observed at once that she had planned ahead; the sofa-bed had been pulled out and the covers neatly turned back, ready for immediate use.

As soon as she had casually tossed her purse aside, she came into my arms again, and I covered her face and neck with wet, lingering kisses. The scent of her perfume and of her body combined to create a most effective aphrodisiac, and I felt my cock straining furiously to be set free from its confines. Our fingers found buttons and zippers, and we tore at each other's clothing. It seemed like ages before the last garment had been carelessly dropped on the floor, but at last we stood face to face in our nakedness. In the back of my mind, I had to hand it to old Matt; he'd described Nan's attributes to a "T" when he said she had "great knockers." They were two firm but yielding mounds of cream-colored flesh the size of softballs, topped by fully erect, pink nipples.

I set my attention on them, kissing each one in turn several times and tickling the nipples with my tongue. Nan moaned softly and pulled my head closer so that my head nestled between her breasts. From there, I traveled downward, kissing first her belly, then her abdomen. Kneeling before her, I caressed her buttocks with my hands while kissing her public mound. I moved further down and kissed both nether lips one by one, then parted them ever so slightly to taste the sweetness inside. Once more, Nan moaned and pressed my head closer; she also thrust her hips forward and parted her legs so that I could push my tongue further inside her.

"Dearest Dr. Maxwell," she rasped, "if you don't make love to me this instant, I'll scream!"

I needed no second invitation. My own desire threatened to overwhelm me, and I needed to release the tension that was building up in my groin. Somehow, I found my own voice.

"I *hate* screaming women, sweet Dr. Vengtman. Prepare to be made love to!"

We did not so much as lay down on the bed as we threw ourselves on it (or perhaps fell on it). We both laughed madly as we scrambled around to get into the proper position. I made a last round of kissing breasts and vagina, then rolled over on top of her. She spread her legs unhesitatingly, and I thrust myself inside her with one quick movement. She gasped in surprise as my manhood went in up to the hilt but moaned with pleasure as I began a rhythmic stroking inside her. She draped her legs across my hips and squeezed me which served to increase the length of my strokes. My own pleasure intensified as she moved her hips in counterpoint to mine. All too soon (as far as I was concerned), I climaxed tremendously and lay in her grasp, panting heavily.

Presently, I rolled free and snuggled up to her. Nan swung a leg over

231

DAY ELEVEN:
Wednesday, 07.16.1997
INSINUATION

It had been some time since I awoke in someone else's bed. And, so, when I did awake, I was momentarily disoriented. Then I gazed upon the supple body next to me, and pleasant memories rushed to the fore. I leaned over, kissed Nan on the cheek, and inadvertently stirred her into wakefulness. She looked up at me dreamily, gripped my arms, and pulled me down on top of her. We kissed repeatedly until passion overcame us, then made love again (with Nan on top, a position she seemed to especially enjoy).

I would have liked to stay and explore more of Nan's charms (and, believe me, she had plenty of them), but duty called and its siren song was not to be denied. Invalid excuses for not reporting for monitor duty merited reprimands the first two times and dismissal the third time. Now that I and Nan had finally gotten together, I didn't want to do anything that jeopardized my position at the Home and thus my relationship with her.

Duty in this instance was yet another stint as meal monitor – a regularly scheduled one this time. If I could have gotten out of it, I would have; since the rosters were carefully crafted by our punctilious Senior Counselor, however, only the direst emergency would have moved him to alter it. Duty for Nan that day was less exacting (in my opinion anyway) – the infirmary. (In a manner of speaking, she had already started, having increased my adrenaline level considerably!) It was with great reluctance that I dragged myself out of her bed, hastily threw on my clothes (scattered all over, it seemed), and returned to my own cottage to take a quick shower and put on fresh clothes. Before I left, we embraced and massaged each other's tongues again.

"Thank you for a wonderful evening," I murmured when we came up for air. "It was just what the doctor ordered."

"If you need a refill of your 'prescription,'" she responded coyly, "just give me a call."

"In a New York minute! See you later?"

"I'll scream if you don't."

With encouragement like that, how could I miss?

I might have touched the ground on my way to the main building, but I don't remember having done so. A new chapter in my life had just opened, and I looked forward to many more days – and especially nights – at the Home. Not alone did I have my work to keep me occupied and challenged; now, I had an additional reason to believe I was on the fast track to the Good Life, professionally and personally.

I have already mentioned that, in a relatively short time, I had acquired a reputation as a "trouble-shooter." Even the Great Man himself had alluded to it. The incident in the art-and-crafts room had enhanced it considerably. Whether that boded good or ill for me remained to be seen; I didn't mind lending a helping hand when called upon (I would have been very remiss in my job otherwise), but neither did I care to be depended upon to handle every little flare-up that occurred. Sooner or later – sooner, if I had my choice in the matter – someone else had to learn to run with the ball. I say all this because, as soon as the first shift arrived for breakfast, all eyes were on me. And I do mean *all* eyes. Even the non-professional staff gave me smiles or nods of approval or mumbled words of encouragement. While I enjoyed being complimented as much as the next fellow, I was well aware of why I was receiving so many accolades. No one else in the Home had had the intestinal fortitude to do what (I thought) was necessary, and everyone was relieved and/or pleased that I had assumed the burden.

One supposes that having a reputation like I had then might have been advantageous. For instance, if a flare-up did occur, a sharp glance or a forceful remark or even a certain posture on the part of "The Enforcer" would suffice to quell the disturbance. Personally, I thought it was a most unenviable position to be in, because it raised everyone's expectations for future conduct, which I may or may not have been able to fulfill. And there is nothing like a hero with clay feet – what has come to be known as the "O.J. Simpson Syndrome" – to destroy one's cherished ideals, not to mention his credibility!

It was a very eerie feeling to sit at my usual post for an hour and a half and listen to – *nothing*. No one argued, no one complained, no one said one harsh word against or about another. All of the patients ate their breakfasts in complete serenity. One might have believed one were in a public restaurant instead of a sanitarium full of psychoses. I fully expected someone to bitch about the oatmeal being cold (a common complaint) or about their neighbor's bad breath or about the "sucking" quality of life in general – maybe I *hoped* someone would, just to break the monotony – but it never happened. No one wanted to call attention to himself and risk my "wrath." One of the most boring tasks imaginable had just become even more so. If I had not been the type who reads while he eats, I think I might have started licking the walls!

To my mild surprise, Melissa entered near the end of the second shift, took an apple and a glass of milk (was that all she ever ate?), and secluded herself in the corner. Naturally, she elicited the same reactions she always did, but now they were only temporary. I suspected they believed themselves to be secure in their persons simply because I was there to protect them from her "evil eye." Had I not been there, they'd undoubtedly be quaking in their shoes until she left. I suppressed the very wicked idea of getting up and walking out in order to "prove" the truth of my supposition. However, I didn't care to be the cause – indirect or otherwise – of loosing chaos upon this insecure crowd.

Melissa did not look my way, although I was sure she was aware of my presence, but merely stared out the window. Was she too embarrassed by the events of the day before to make eye contact? I didn't care if she was or not. She had tried to manipulate me, and I was not so professional that I could shrug off a personal attack stoically. She owed me an apology and, as far as I was concerned, that was the basis of future communications between us. She remained detached until the last of the patients shuffled out, then zipped over to my table and plunked herself down with her typical brazenness. As if to compensate for her earlier disregard, she now stared at me with those devastating amethyst eyes. I grimaced in response to her sudden attention.

"You probably think I'm a horrible person, don't you, Ken?" she began without preamble.

"No," I fibbed. "But I do think you're greatly disturbed." She scowled at the remark but refrained from comment. "I only wish I knew what your background was. Perhaps I could understand you better."

"If you knew my background, you *would* think I was horrible. Dr. Vengtman thinks I am."

"Oh? And has he said so?"

"He doesn't have to. I can...sense these things."

"Really?"

"Really. I know you don't believe me. If you did, you wouldn't be so – What *do* you think I am?"

"I already told you. Also, you're willful and amoral. You treat others with utter contempt. If anyone looks at you cross-eyed, you throw a temper tantrum. I'd say you haven't had much parental guidance."

"If you only knew," she muttered.

"Part of your problem, Melissa – as long as you've asked me for my opinion – is these damned cryptic remarks you keep making. You surround yourself with an air of mystery, then wonder why no one likes you. Are you ashamed of what you are? Or, are you trying to compensate for a possible inferiority complex?"

"No, to both questions." She bit her lip and balled up her fists. Inner turmoil was writ large across her face, and I idly wondered how *she* liked being toyed with. "I – I…just…can't…tell…you…about…myself," she said through clenched teeth. "*He* won't let me."

"'He'? Dr. Vengtman, you mean?" She nodded. "That's another part of your problem: blaming others for your troubles. Dr. Vengtman could help you, if you'd just get past your paranoia. He's a good and wise man and he –"

"No, he isn't!" she exploded. "He isn't – he isn't – he *isn't!*" With each "isn't," she beat her fists on the table. Tears began to dribble down her cheeks. Frankly, I half-expected her to fly into a real rage and overturn the table – and me with it! "Oh, *God*! If you only knew what horrors there are here!"

"Give it a rest, Melissa," I said in exasperation. "If you're not going to confide in me, then I think we have nothing more to say to each other."

"But – but – *I love you!*"

A rose by any other name is still a rose. And so is a thorn bush.

Had anyone except Melissa Waterman blurted out that startling admission, I would have immediately chalked it up to the typical teenaged infatuation for an authority/father figure – a common symptom since the race began which our modern technological era has done nothing to assuage. Yet, this *was* Melissa Waterman, a total enigma, and, out of her mouth, the admission rang false. Quite possibly, in her own mind (as in the minds of all teenagers), she believed she was in love with me. Other teenagers, however, did not make nuisances of themselves unless they were emotionally disturbed as well. Melissa was definitely in this category.

For the emotionally disturbed, admissions of affection were as much a weapon as a gun. They used their beliefs as a means to intimidate and/or extort and/or blackmail and place the object of their "love" in extreme jeopardy. Melissa's track record had already demonstrated that she was not above using alleged affection to get her way; the sad fate of my predecessor was proof enough. Had she transferred her "love" for Hinkleman to me now? And did she plan a similar fate for me if I had the bad taste to "spurn" her (as it might seem to her if she became aware of my budding relationship with Nan)? Fortunately, I had the advantage of foreknowledge over my predecessor, and I intended to use it to go on the offense.

"After all you've said and done," I said softly, "do you really expect me to believe that?"

She bowed her head and wrung her hands.

"No, but it's true anyway."

"I'm sure you think so, just as you once believed you were in love with Mathias Hinkleman – until he began his affair with Dr. Chantrier. Then your jealousy drove you to ruin him. Only you went too far; he went mad and killed himself."

Her head snapped up, and I saw such an expression of horror that I was momentarily startled. The color drained out of her face. Was she remembering the events earlier that year and the enormity of her behavior? In psychological circles, my actions came under the category of "shock therapy," and not to be used lightly. I had judged the circumstances to warrant this approach, because Melissa had proven herself immune to normal methods. I had apparently hit a nerve. Of course, there was always a risk involved – which fact I was ever mindful of – but jolting the girl back to reality would be worth it.

"Yes," she said distantly, "I *was* jealous, and I *did* think evil thoughts." Now the fire had returned to her. "But I never intended to hurt Mathias. I was young and naïve then, and –"

"'Young and naïve'?" I barked. "It's been less than a year. Are you really more 'mature' now?"

"I think so. That's why I don't want what happened to Mathias to happen to you."

"And why should anything happen to me, Melissa?" As soon as I had asked the question, I knew the answer. "Do you know about Nancy Vengtman and me?"

She blushed. I *think* she blushed.

"Yes. You were with her last night – all night."

"That's *another* part of your problem, girl – constantly spying on people. But, never mind about that. Are you going to let your jealousy get the better of you again?"

"No! I won't make that mistake again. I've learned my lesson, Ken. Really, I have. I'll do whatever I can to keep you safe."

"And how do you propose to do that, seeing that you were responsible for Hinkelman's death in the first place?"

"I keep telling you: I *wasn't* responsible! Yes, I did…things to him, but I was…*forced* to."

"Oh, no, it wasn't *your* fault," I mocked, "was it, Melissa? It's the 'evil' Dr. Lowell Vengtman who's responsible. He pulls your strings, and you dance. Svengali and Trilby, the two of you. This is getting old, girl. When are you going to stop rationalizing?"

"It's not rationalizing! If he thinks you're too close to exposing him, Dr. Vengtman will do to you what he did to Mathias."

"All right. Just for the sake of argument, let's say that you're speaking truthfully. What threat was Hinkelman to the Director that he needed to be squashed?"

She didn't speak for a couple of minutes. Rather, she stared out the window and wrung her hands. A nervous tic appeared under her left eye. I continued to stare at her.

"Dr. Vengtman didn't want my attention diverted to anyone else," she finally responded in a quiet voice. "He wanted…exclusive rights."

Talk about bombshells! My jaw unhinged, and my senses reeled. When I found my tongue, my voice was hoarse.

"You're saying Lowell Vengtman had…*designs* on you and he saw Hinkelman as a…*rival*?"

"No, it wasn't anything like that at all. You wouldn't believe what it was all about."

"You're damned right I wouldn't. All I see is fantasizing." I looked at my watch. "You'll excuse me now. I have other matters to attend to." An expression of anguish passed across her face. "If you want to be more honest with me, I'll be glad to listen. Otherwise, don't bother me."

I rose to my feet and exited the dining room, my mind awhirl with conflicting thoughts. Which – if any – of Melissa's remarks could I accept? None of them had any basis in reality; she was still being the "mystery woman" she'd been from the beginning, always tantalizing with a word here and a phrase there, always putting the proper emotional spin on her speech to simulate sincerity. It had to be utter nonsense. If one believed anything she'd said so far, then one had to believe that the Vengtman Home for the Emotionally Disturbed was a veritable chamber of horrors, overseen by a sinister Dr. Lowell Vengtman, who manipulated people according to a secret agenda. And what was that agenda? Personal pleasure? Callous, immoral experiments to test the limits of emotional frailty? Sadism, for the sake of sadism? Easier to believe the sun rose in the west!

Melissa was displaying the classical symptoms of guilt-avoidance common to paranoid personality disorder. Though she had implicated herself in the death of Mathias Hinkelman (but, here too, she had chosen to wrap herself in enigma concerning her methods), she rejected the notion of direct responsibility and shifted the blame onto another in order to be exonerated. Moreover, she had transferred her own feelings of jealousy onto this other person and presented *him* as the one full of envy and hate, further rationalizing away her own guilt. Given that my conclusions were based upon a few observations without recourse to studying her past medical history, I risked making a misstep in dealing with her. On the other hand, those few observations had suggested that it made no difference what steps were taken, that Melissa was so deep into her psychosis that only radical methods would work.

And, yet, I thought I had finally gotten somewhere with her by forcing her to make statements she had been reluctant to make before. These new "admissions" might have been as nonsensical as the old ones, but at least they provided extra pieces to the puzzle. My problem was where in the puzzle did the pieces fit. Her admitting to a part in the destruction of Mathias Hinkelman was one thing; the *means* by which she had accomplished it was quite another. The secret to tearing down the barriers she had erected lay in discovering the *how*. And the *how* – it always came back to this – was located in her file. Which meant I would have to be more persuasive in getting Nan to access it for me.

While I pondered my dilemma, I decided to have my first chat of the day with Terry, who had had his own problems in the art of persuasion. The instant I walked through the door, he leaped to his feet and began to recite:

> "At midnight, in the month of June,
> I stand beneath the mystic moon.
> An opiate vapor, dewy, dim,
> Exhales from out her golden rim.
> And, softly dropping, drop by drop,
> Upon the quiet mountain top,
> Steals drowsily and musically
> Into the universal valley.
> The rosemary nods upon the grave;
> The lily lolls upon the wave;
> Wrapping the fog about its breast,
> The ruin moulders into rest;
> Looking like Lethe, see! the lake
> A conscious slumber seems to take,
> And would not, for the world, awake.
> All beauty sleeps! – and lo! where lies
> Irene, with her destinies!"

He looked at me expectantly. I supposed he was waiting for a "review" of his latest "work." I had to assume he was quoting another of Poe's poems – though I hadn't a clue as to which one it was, never having been a great fan of horror fiction – and I also had to assume he was looking for some sort of approval on my part. Well, I didn't intend to make it easy for him; he'd just have to suffer some disappointment. It was the only way to bring him back to reality.

"It needs a little work, Terry," I stated. "The rhythm is a bit shaky, and some of your allusions are obscure."

I wondered then if I would have made a good literary critic. It seemed easy enough; all you had to do was to throw in some jargon about style, and you were halfway there. Look at what Hinkelman had done. If his hatchet jobs were able to be published, then I shouldn't have any problem.

If I had hoped to throw Terry for a loop, I was the one to suffer disappointment. Rather than standing there crest-fallen and frustrated over yet another "rejection," he grew very pensive; re-reading the piece again, he frowned and shook his head. Then he crumpled the paper up and tossed it aside. Perhaps I would hate myself in the morning, but the sooner he shed his delusions, the better.

"You're right, Dr. Maxwell. It's *crap* – nothing but *crap!*"

"I wouldn't go *that* far, Terry. I suggest you try something different as a change of pace. There must be other forms to work with."

"Yes, there are. I should have listened to Dr. Hinkelman when he made the same suggestion. Maybe I wouldn't have wasted all this time."

"And what exactly did he suggest?"

My mind was racing furiously in an effort to recall my predecessor's commentary in Terry's file. I had been so put off by the fact that he had assumed the persona of the raven from Poe's poem – nagging at his patient, as it were, in order to snap him back to reality – that whatever conclusions and recommendations he had arrived at hadn't sunk in very deeply. Now, I remembered (vaguely) the notation he had made two days before the first entry in his journal, a sort of reminder to himself to set Terry down a new path. It was a reminder half-forgotten, for I had come across only one other reference to it thereafter. Apparently, subconsciously, I had picked up the ball and was running with it.

"Let me see," Terry was saying, "it's been nearly a year. Ah, now I remember! He thought I should get away from all the somberness and moodiness and try some light verse, or perhaps something along the line of the Romanticists."

"That sounds promising."

"The trouble is I don't know much about romanticism. I've had this obsession with Edgar and ignored everything else."

Aha! A break-through! I had to seize upon this remark and use it as a prod.

"I can get you some books on the subject, I think. But, it seems to me that you should be writing what *you* want to write instead of imitating someone else."

He stared at me for the longest time, mulling over my insistence upon individuality. Then, he turned toward the desk, still covered with sheets of paper, and began gathering them up; when he had accumulated a sizeable handful, he gave the sheets a baleful glance and pitched them into the wastepaper basket. Facing me again, he brushed his hands off and displayed an expression of determination.

"As of now, Doctor, I'm going to show those bastards in the publishing world just what I'm capable of!"

"Excellent, Terry. And, if you want me to critique your stuff, I'll be glad to." I peered at him in mock-conspiratorial fashion. "Just don't tell anyone else about my offer, or they'll *all* want me to read their stuff. I haven't got the time."

"Ha-ha! Right!"

We chatted some more about several tentative projects he had secretly wanted to do. I nodded in approval at some and frowned at others. My reactions, however, were purely arbitrary, for I still did not have a clue as to what constituted suitable literary material. Yet, I had to give the *appearance* of knowing what I was talking about in order to keep Terry firmly on this new path. Somehow, the conversation strayed back to the realm of madness (Poe's stock-in-trade), and Terry became pensive again.

"Do you know," he said abruptly, "that I was the last person to see Dr. Hinkelman alive?"

I looked at him with mild surprise. What had brought that on? It couldn't have been an associative train of thought, for suicide had never been a factor in any of Poe's writing. Self-destruction of the mind, perhaps, but not of the body – in which case madness leads to torture and homicide. That is not suicide, *per se*, because no one *chooses* to go mad. In any event, it was an odd admission, yet not so odd that it did not pique my curiosity. Anything about Hinkelman I could get my hands on – no matter the source – was valuable.

"No, I didn't," I replied evenly. "Most people here are reluctant to talk about him. I've had to get my information by bits and pieces."

"Well, here's another piece, for what it's worth." He leaned back in his chair and gazed at the ceiling. "It was the night before he, uh, did away with himself. He had the room two doors down the hall. Damned ironic, huh? A shrink ending up in his own loony bin. Anyway, by this time, he was all gibberish and crying. Wouldn't talk to anybody, wouldn't come out of his room. They had to bring his meals to him – not that he ate much. I was having my own problems with all the rejection slips I'd been getting from fools who couldn't put two words together coherently but thought they knew what 'good literature' was, so I didn't pay much attention to Hinkelman.

"That last night, he must've slipped out of his room when no one was looking, because he pounded on my door and woke me up. When I answered, he pushed his way in and went straight to the window. What he was looking for, I still don't know; but the idea of him barging in like that sat in my craw, and I had half a mind to call for a nurse. Then he looked at me much like Roderick Usher must have when he realized he had buried his sister alive. Frankly, Doctor, I got real scared. I didn't know what he was going to do.

"'Terry,' he says, 'I've got to talk to you because you're the only one who will understand what I've done. I've been keeping a journal since my...problems began, trying to make sense of what's happening to me. Sometimes I can, sometimes – it's been *hell*! I've figured out who's behind the attack against me, and the name is in the journal. I want you to do me a favor – one writer to another – in case anything...terrible happens to me. I want you to tell someone you can trust about the journal.'

"Just to get him out of my room, I promised him I would. I guess that satisfied him, because he dashed out as fast as he came in. The next morning, they found him with his wrists slashed."

Now it was my turn to be pensive. Here was a new twist. How much of Terry's story was believable was open to question, of course. Emotionally disturbed people often see things – and report on them – in relation to their psychoses; what they will accept is given a personal spin, and the rest is rejected. In the present instance, one was supposed to believe that Mathias Hinkelman had been lucid long enough to devise a plan of action and confide in a fellow patient. Given his circumstances, the odds against lucidity were very high, and no one could have been blamed for taking this story with a grain of salt.

Still, there was one incontrovertible fact: the journal existed, and I had read it. It tended to lend a touch of credibility to Terry's account. The question then was did I want to acknowledge that I already knew about it. I still wasn't ready to reveal its existence, especially to one who might or might not keep a confidence, until I had all the facts at hand. A premature disclosure could have had unpleasant repercussions.

"He was clear-headed at that time?" was all I asked.

"Well, sort of. His words came out a few at a time, as if he had to search for them first."

"Undoubtedly he did. Um, this journal he mentioned – did he say where he hid it?"

"Not a word. I assume it was in his cottage. To tell you the truth, Doctor, I forgot about it as soon as he was out the door. For some reason, it just popped back into my head again."

"And you trust me enough to tell me about it?"

"You're a decent sort – a lousy critic, though – and, as long as you've inherited Hinkelman's spot, you may as well have all of it."

"I appreciate that, Terry. First chance I get, I'll look for that journal."

Ah, little white lies! What would we humans do without them?

I decided to end our session on that "upbeat" note and returned to the main floor. As I approached the front entrance, I spotted Madeleine Chantrier, whom I hadn't seen in two days, on her way out of the building.

"Maddie!" I called out. "Wait up!"

She turned and gave me her best Gallic smile. But, as I drew near, I saw it was a forced smile. Her face was haggard and drawn, and there was a weariness in her eyes that shattered the elfin quality of her usual demeanor. Moreover, her posture was slumped, and she appeared on the verge of collapse at any moment.

"'Allo, Ken. 'Ow are you?"

"I'm fine, but you look terrible. Haven't you been getting enough sleep?"

"No, not much. I 'ave learned of a serious illness in ze family – a close relative – and I am still feeling ze effects."

"I'm sorry to hear that. I've gone down that road myself – the hazards of living in a concrete jungle. I have something for you, though, which might cheer you up."

"Sank you, *mon ami*. I could use some cheer."

I opened my clipboard and pulled out the photocopy of the first two pages of Hinkelman's journal which I'd been carrying around on the off-chance that I'd run into Maddie. She deserved to have it and, with the news of her relative, needed a boost in spirits.

"Mathias kept a journal during his last months." Her eyes widened in wonder, and there was a slight tremor on her lower lip. "I found it quite by accident. You can see his descent into madness with each succeeding page. These are the first two pages. He didn't desert you after all, Maddie."

She seized the pages anxiously and read them slowly. By the time she had finished, tears were streaming down her cheeks and dripping onto the paper. Impulsively, she kissed each of the sheets and murmured something in French. It sounded like a prayer. Wiping away the tears with the back of her hand, she regarded me with something more than friendship but less than reverence.

"My poor, poor Mat'ias," she breathed. "Such a lost little boy 'e was when – when we were togezair. 'Ow 'e tried to please me! I sink zat time was ze 'appiest of 'is life." She gazed at the photocopy again. "Much too brief a time. We 'ad made plans to marry, 'e and I."

Maddie began to cry again, and I wrapped my arms around her. She pressed against me and sobbed quietly, while I stroked her hair in sympathy. Presently, she looked up at me pleadingly.

"You say zere is more of ze zhournal?"

"Yes. There's maybe a couple of blank pages at the end. Most of it is hard to follow, as you might imagine."

"Please, Ken, may I see it?"

"Considering your present state, I don't think that's a good idea. But, I promise you, I'll give it to you when I'm through analyzing it."

"What do you 'ope to learn?"

"The exact circumstances of his death. He had a lot going for him – a promising career, supporting co-workers, a good woman. Something – or someone – took it all away from him. I mean to find out what – or who – it was."

"Zat wicked, wicked child!" she muttered.

"Excuse me?"

"Melissa." She spoke the name like a curse. "I warned Mat'ias about 'er. I told 'im not to encourazhe 'er attentions. But, 'e sought zat Melissa was a 'lost soul' in great need of 'elp. *Mon Dieu!* but 'e could be so naïve at times."

"Melissa needs help all right, but I think Mathias was out of his league as far as she was concerned."

"I agree. And now I read zat her all-consuming zhealousy destroyed

246

our love. Zat wicked, *wicked* child!" Her hard face softened abruptly. She stood on tiptoes and kissed me on the cheek. "*Merci beaucoup,* my dear friend Ken, for zis precious gift. I shall treasure it always."

After Maddie had departed, I stood there for a long time, mulling over what she had told me. I never knew Hinkelman but by the bits and pieces I'd gleaned over the past week and a half; from what little I did know, I had to conclude that he had been one lucky SOB. I had told Maddie the truth when I said he had had everything going for him. Who knew what heights – both professionally and personally – he could have reached? I hoped that I might be as lucky. I already had the promising career and supportive co-workers; what happened between Nan and me would determine if I got the third part of that equation.

"I swear! Here you are again, blocking traffic! I'll have to put a warning sign on you."

I turned toward the speaker with a huge grin on my face.

"Hello, Nan. You can hang anything you want on me. I'll take it as a token of your devotion."

"Such an ego you have, Doctor! One roll in the hay, and you think you're Superman."

"As far as you're concerned, I am."

"Good grief!" She rolled her eyes heavenward. "Someone get a straitjacket! The man's gone berserk!"

At that point, we both broke out in laughter.

"Will I see you tonight?" I asked in a more sober tone.

"I don't know. Uncle Lowell has asked me to help him after dinner with an address he's giving Saturday evening. I have no idea how long that'll take. If I get away at all, it'll be late."

"Whenever. I have something to show you."

An expression of mock surprise diffused over her face.

"But, Ken dear, I've already seen it, haven't I?"

I grimaced at her suggestive remark.

"I'm not talking about *that,* dingbat. I have something else in mind."

"Oh, my, a *treat* for little ol' me? In that case" – she leaned forward and kissed me lightly on the lips – "I'll make it a point to be there."

As I have said, finding Mathias Hinkelman's journal was an act of serendipity. Thus far, it had been the linchpin in my investigation into his death. After lunch, serendipity struck again.

I had gone back to my cottage to update the file on Terry when – as they say – Nature called. Another damned delay! Unfortunately, I couldn't ignore this one, could I? Uttering a few choice phrases, I relieved myself. But, when I attempted to flush the toilet afterwards, I encountered some resistance to the valve's action. I tried twice more without success. It was obvious that something was jamming the arm. Grumbling mightily, I removed the cover to the tank and peered inside. There was the usual amount of rust and corrosion on the interior walls and the metal parts. Then I saw at the bottom of the tank, lodged against the valve, an object which had no business being there. Why hadn't it jammed the valve before now? I could only speculate that, over the weeks and months, each successive flushing had moved the object around until it had fallen into its present location. I rolled up my sleeve and, cursing loudly, immersed my arm into the cold water nearly up to my elbow. I grabbed the foreign object, pulled it out, and shook off the excess water.

The thing was one of those resealable plastic bags used for refrigerating left-over food. Except, there was no food in this one – only a folded piece of paper. What was so confidential that someone had had to secrete it in a toilet tank? Instantly, I had a nagging suspicion about it. I undid the seal, extracted the paper, and carefully unfolded it. My suspicion was confirmed at once.

It was the missing page from Hinkelman's journal!

So monumental had been his paranoia in those last days before he became a patient in his own sanitarium that he had seen fit to create a secret within a secret within a secret. First, he had told no one about his journal while he wrote in it, perhaps out of fear of reprisal from whomever he had believed was acting against him. Second, he had hidden the damned thing underneath the sofa-bed so that only a very determined search would have discovered it. Third, he had torn out the most damning "revelation" of all and placed it in a separate hidey-hole where no one would find it except by pure chance. And fourth, when he had told someone about the journal, it was one of his former patients whose own delusions would have caused an investigator to discount any and all statements made on the subject.

I doubted that Hinkelman had foreseen my arrival at the Home, my subsequent interest in his demise, or my quick discovery of his journal. Perhaps he did believe that someone in the distant future might stumble across it and have his/her interest mildly piqued; perhaps he also believed that future individual would have no reason to fear the machinations of his persecutor and publish the full story of the "horrors" which had been perpetrated there in the past. I wasn't certain – yet – about the "horrors," but I did intend to publish Hinkelman's story – as soon as I had all the facts, that is.

I held the page with trembling hands, and the trembling was not entirely due to the cold water in which I had been forced to dunk my arm. The words written on it were sufficient by themselves. Dated January 28, 1997 (a week before Hinkelman was admitted as a patient), the entry read:

> I know now who whispers in my mind. Should have known from the start.
>
> Who but Melissa could be so cruel?
>
> Didn't think – God! *couldn't* think! – her jealousy was that – what's the word I want? – was so *obsessive*.
>
> Don't know how she does it, how she *reaches into my mind and squeezes it like a sponge!* All the vital juices gone. Only a shell of a man left. Don't know how long I can hold out.
>
> One other thing: Melissa *not* alone. She can't get away with her whispering unless – *SHE HAS HELP!* Who helps? Who is is the son-of-a-bitch?
>
> Only one can control her. *THE DIRECTOR! He* controls [missing word].
>
> WHY?
>
> WHY?

One questioned answered, several others raised. That's how that business had been going all along. I was happy to learn that my predecessor had finally stumbled across the identity of his tormentor. While his "leap of faith" had taken longer to unfold than mine had (I had had the advantage of accumulated knowledge), he had made it. He might not have been able to do anything about his predicament (another difference between us); yet, perhaps he had achieved some small moral victory before the end.

And it was a *small* moral victory, for the last part of the entry raised some profoundly disturbing, profoundly far-reaching questions. Frankly, I wished I hadn't read it all. In the first place, there had been no prior discussion of the allegation which might lead logically to the conclusion, no body of evidence to support the argument. In the second place, the presentation was incoherent and lacked structure. In this light, one might reasonably dismiss the allegation out of hand. Hinkelman had shown himself here as the Hinkelman of the inflammatory book reviews, full of spite and pettiness and ill temper, speaking off the top of his head in order to puff up his own ego.

And yet – and yet, I could not put that damnable sheet of paper down. I stared a hole through it, re-reading it over and over as if, by will power alone, I could change the words into something more acceptable. That entry had touched a nerve, all right, and I was powerless to resist its pressure.

It was a monstrous thing to do: to accuse Lowell Vengtman -- a man I had admired since the day I first heard him lecture during my internship and in whose footsteps I hoped to walk – of gross, illegal, and immoral behavior, of manipulating and inducing madness in people for some mysterious purpose (if not outright malevolence), of setting himself up as a god to re-order Life and Death as he saw fit. It was a monstrous thing to do: to even suggest that Lowell Vengtman was less than an honorable man, a Brutus before the Roman Senate, and that he harbored evil thoughts beneath a smiling exterior – in short, to speak of him as the Devil incarnate. I could not believe he was capable of the acts Mathias Hinkelman had implied. I *would* not believe.

And yet – and yet, this was *not* the old Hinkelman, was it? This was a man at his wits' end, on the brink of the abyss. The name of the game had changed, hadn't it?

Now, all of those cryptic remarks Melissa had made came crashing into my consciousness. She had told me repeatedly that she was not a free agent, that she was being controlled and forced to do what she done. And I had refused to heed her because her charges were absurd on the face of them. The charges were still absurd; I had only the word of a very disturbed teenaged girl and a certified psychotic. Before I could fully accept the charges, I had to see the gross, illegal, immoral behavior for myself.

The irony of this matter was that both perpetrator and victim had corroborated each other – inadvertently, to be sure, but positively nevertheless. I couldn't ignore that fact even if I had wanted to. So, for the sake of argument, I had to suppose the Great Man was the "mastermind" behind some hideous scheme. "Why?" Hinkelman had asked. "Why?" I also had to ask. What purpose would have been served in driving another human being mad? Melissa had implied that the Director was envious of Hinkelman's attention toward her and that he ordered her to reject him. This supposition – that Lowell Vengtman was a vindictive, self-centered, heartless beast (hardly the Lowell Vengtman I knew) – necessarily failed for lack of evidence; in fact, all the evidence was stacked against it. The only plausible explanation was that Melissa had lied in order to shift blame away from herself and somehow had convinced Hinkelman that someone else was to blame.

And yet – and yet, why was I even bothering to argue the point in the first place? Was I now so unsure of the Director's character that I must convince myself anew of his professionalism? This mystery was beginning to take its toll on me; I had immersed myself into it so deeply that I saw conspiracies everywhere. The sooner I concluded my investigation, the better. Otherwise, I would also become a permanent "guest" at the Home!

I replaced the journal page in the plastic bag. But, instead of returning it to the toilet tank, I slipped it under the sofa-bed next to the journal itself. After I had had time to settle my thoughts and look at the problem in a saner frame of mind, I hoped to put that curious page in its proper context. Perhaps then, it would make more sense. At least, I *hoped* it would. Needless to say, my subsequent activities suffered from a subconscious distraction and, at one point, I wondered if I should bother going through the motions.

At the beginning of the first supper period, subconscious conjecturing yielded to that of the conscious level when Dr. Vengtman unexpectedly strolled into the dining room. He cast a glance around, and the benignity on his face elicited the same variety of reactions I had observed on a previous visit. I had to set it down then to the awe the Great Man struck in all with whom he came into contact; no one with his expertise and reputation could have failed to do otherwise. Now, however, I had my lunatic conjecturing to color my observations (not to mention my own reaction to his appearance), and I wondered how the staff and patients *really* regarded him. Did they fear him because he had experimented on them too? Did they fear him because he had the power of Life and Death over them? It was a futile line of thought, and I willed it out of my head.

After scanning the dining area, he turned his attention toward me and gave me his usual patronizing smile. What was behind that smile? Was he –

Stop it, Maxwell! I ordered myself. *Just be cool!*

"Good evening, sir," I greeted him calmly.

"Good evening, Dr. Maxwell. The very person I was seeking."

"I am?"

"Yes. It seems you created quite a stir yesterday."

"I did?"

"Your innovative exercise program made a huge impression on staff and patients alike. So much so that they – at least, the patients – were clamoring for more *this* morning. Naturally, the staff hadn't your, ah, expertise and were left floundering. The patients subsequently gave them a rough time of it, though, as I understand it, one of your own patients – Matthew, I think – was willing to fill the vacuum."

"That sounds like old Matt," I murmured. "I regret having disrupted the routine, sir. At the time, I felt the patients would like a change of pace. I should have cleared it with you first."

"No need to apologize, my boy. Perhaps we do need a change of pace once in a while. On the other hand, you've left us in a quandary."

"Sir?"

"If the patients demand more aerobic exercises, we'll have to find someone who can lead them every day. To date, you're our only 'expert.' But, it wouldn't be fair to either you or your patients to consume so much of your time. What to do?"

"I'd be willing to volunteer on a *quid pro quo* basis. That is, if I relieve some of the other staff of this particular duty, then perhaps they could substitute for me elsewhere."

"An excellent idea, Doctor. I'll make a note to bring it up at the next staff meeting." He flashed me another smile. "Carry on, Ken."

As soon as he had departed, I relaxed visibly. His visit seemed harmless enough, but now I was assigning double meanings to every statement he made. In most instances, the second meaning was ludicrous in the extreme; in some others, it was contradictory. The plain fact of the matter was that I was letting my imagination run away with me; I was fast losing my professionalism and my sense of perspective – all because of some insane accusation. I realized all too well where this sort of thinking would lead me – doubting everything I'd been taught about psychiatric medicine. Coloring Lowell Vengtman with evil intent was only the tip of the iceberg; once I had derogated the Great Man and all his works, it was a mere trifle to cast dispersion on "lesser lights" in the field. I'd end up like Hinkelman had begun – a complete cynic, seeing no good, only evil, in the whole world. I shuddered at the notion and quickly glanced around to see if anyone had noticed my distress.

Now there would have been a grand irony! The oh-so smooth Kenneth Maxwell, who could mediate conflicts with a simple wave of the hand, who could bail troubled people out with a single word, who could cause men and women alike to swoon when he entered a room and to fall all over themselves to please him – the mighty Kenneth Maxwell, sitting in a corner and shaking like a leaf because of some nameless dread. My "reputation" would evaporate like dew before the sun, and no one would ever trust me again.

Well, it wasn't going to happen, if I had anything to say about it (and I thought I did). I just needed to buckle down, bring the "Hinkelman mystery" to a speedy close, and put the whole sorry business behind me. My "reputation" would take care of itself!

Around 11 PM, I heard a soft rapping at my door. I had been re-reading all of my notes on the journal and the files (including Hinkelman's personnel file which I still hadn't returned), attempting to integrate the missing page into the Big Picture (if possible). Actually, I was killing time until Nan showed up, and I think I dozed off a couple of times. I bounded to the door, eager to usher her in. As soon as I saw her, however, I realized at once she was not in a mood for fun and games – or much else, for that matter. She appeared bleary-eyed, and her shoulders slumped as if she were carrying a one-ton rock.

"I didn't think you were coming at all," I said artlessly. "I was about to turn in."

"I almost didn't come," she replied wearily, easing past me. "I helped Uncle Lowell write and re-write that damned speech half a dozen times. I think I've got it memorized."

I took her in my arms and kissed her passionately. She responded only half-way; after the kiss, she slumped into the only available chair and sighed heavily.

"I hope you don't mind if I don't stay. I am just dead!" She managed a slightly coy smile. "I'll make it up to you tomorrow."

"Hmmm. With a promise like that, how can I object?"

"So, what's so special that you wanted me to see?"

I went to the sofa-bed, reached underneath, and extracted the journal and the missing page. Nan watched me incredulously, undoubtedly thinking I was acting a bit odd. How right she was! Never in my wildest dreams two weeks ago would I have been behaving as I did then; playing "detective" and "cat burglar" and "spy" had come to me almost unconsciously. I held up the journal first.

"I found this quite by accident, exactly where you saw me get it. It'll blow your mind."

She came over to the sofa-bed and sat down. I sat down beside her and slipped an arm around her shoulder. She opened the journal and began reading the first page, her eyes widening as she went. Abruptly, she set the book in her lap and looked at me in amazement.

"Was this written by who I think wrote it?"

"Uh-huh. Hinkelman's own record of his insanity, so to speak. The last entry was made shortly before he was admitted as a patient."

Now Nan read with more enthusiasm, her former weariness dissipating before the discovery of a new document. Fully alert now, she scanned the pages quickly; professional interest fairly radiated from her. I could just picture the wheels turning in her head as she absorbed each sentence or phrase. And, in that moment, I saw Lowell Vengtman in her: keen-eyed, sharp-minded, mentally wide-ranging, intuitive, and conceptual. The genetic roulette wheel had produced two winners in the same family as far as intelligence levels were concerned; Nan was truly the female counterpart to the Great Man and perhaps one day would eclipse his already tremendous contributions to the field. My feelings for her at that moment were of great admiration, beyond simple lust; whether we were "made for each other" was a matter for the future. For now, I was willing to enjoy her for what she was.

The last page read, she laid the journal carefully on the sofa-bed and stared at the wall. Like a highly efficient computer, she was busily correlating data and forming hypotheses. Shortly, she turned to me again, a strange look in her eyes, and searched my face for God-knew-what. In a whispery voice, she said:

"I've never read anything so incredible. I could almost *feel* his mind disintegrating. And yet, he still had the strength to keep recording his thoughts."

"My sentiments exactly, babe. This journal is the main reason I've become so absorbed lately."

"And I thought it was Melissa."

"Oh, she's a big part of it, all right – as you can see from Hinkelman's own words – but she's not *all* of it. There's something else – something *weird* – going on here at the Home, and old Mathias got caught in the middle of it."

"A new 'conspiracy'?"

"Yeah. Look, you may have noticed there's a page missing toward the end of the journal." She double-checked, then nodded in agreement. "Well, I just found it – hidden in the toilet tank, of all places." I went back under the sofa-bed, retrieved the sheet, and held it up for her inspection. "If you thought what you just read was unreal, wait'll you eyeball this."

As quickly as she had scanned the main body of the journal, she perused the astonishing "revelation." At the crucial point, she gasped audibly and jumped to her feet, the page held out before her like a poisonous snake. She peered at me accusingly, as if she thought *I* had written the damned thing.

"I don't believe it!" she muttered, shaking the page at me. "This is some sort of sick joke!"

I reached out, took her free hand, and gently pulled her back on the sofa-bed. She resisted only slightly and sat down facing me. I lifted the hand I was holding and pressed it to my lips by way of mollification. The gesture soothed her only minutely.

"Nan, honey, this is sick for sure, but it ain't no joke. Hinkelman was completely out of it when he wrote those words, and I think Melissa convinced him somehow that she was not acting alone."

"Yes, yes, that makes sense. Not because Uncle Lowell is guilty of... gross impropriety, but because Mathias became confused in the end. It follows from his previous statements."

"Right. I've been piecing this thing together for the past week, and it's still a mystery to me." I paused ever so briefly, then plunged ahead. "That's why I've got to get my hands on Melissa's file. All the answers are in it. I just know it!"

Now, she pulled her hand free of my grip and stared off into space. The gears were turning again as she mulled over my previous request to pilfer medical files from her uncle's office and the implications – professionally and personally – that it entailed. Abruptly, she shuddered. Rising to her feet, she regarded me sadly and brushed my cheek with her fingertips. Despite my eagerness to have her comply with my request, I wasn't about to press the issue just then; in her place, I too would have had difficulty resolving such a conflict of interest. I gazed at her with as much sympathy as I could muster.

"I have to sleep on this, Ken," she said finally. "My head isn't very clear right now."

"Of course." I got to my own feet and took her in my arms again. "I understand – really I do." I kissed her lightly. "Think it over, honey, but don't take too long about it. Time is getting short; I have a feeling that Melissa is about to explode. And God only knows what'll happen when she does."

DAY TWELVE:
Thursday, 07.17.97
INFLAMMATION

The telephone rang insistently and scared the hell out of me.

I had had a terrible time getting to sleep in the first place. The previous day's revelations were still on my mind when I retired (shortly after Nan left), and I had mulled them over and over into what seemed the wee hours. Not that I slept well when I finally did nod off; sleep came in fits and starts, and I think I stared at the ceiling more often than not.

So, who the hell was calling at that ungodly hour? And why?

It hadn't been my time for another "overnighter." That was still a day away. Therefore, I should not have been called out on an emergency. It was not quite 6 AM, close enough to my usual waking hour for me to seriously consider getting up but not so close that some *rude* person should insist on giving me a wake-up call. Cursing under my breath, I fumbled for the phone.

"Yes?" I rasped.

"Fire drill, Doctor," were the only words spoken, to be replaced by a dial tone.

Any organization or business which deals with the public is obliged to observe local and state fire codes. Those in which people reside, either temporarily or permanently, are particularly under the gun. The Vengtman Home for the Emotionally Disturbed clearly fell into this category and so was regularly inspected. While not required, periodic fire drills were "highly recommended" in order that the patients' safety was maintained in cases of emergency. Dr. Vengtman, as a matter of routine, held one once a month, and only he knew the day and the time of the drill (I suspected he held his own private "lottery" to determine the *when*). He communicated this information to the senior nurse on duty fifteen minutes before the event; this gave the latter enough time to rouse the professional staff. The Director reasoned that, since a real fire would not give any advanced warning, neither would he. Both professional and non-professional staff were obligated to know the drill procedures and the locations of the designated emergency exits, and they were expected to do what they had to do automatically.

Because the Home was a unique institution, unique fire drills had been designed to conduct orderly and effective evacuations. The chief difficulty lay in the fact that one had to deal with a wide range of psychoses; whereas, in a "normal" situation, one tended to herd people out of doors as quickly as possible, here one had to avoid aggravating the residents due to careless handling. To a certain extent, the patients *were* "herded" but in a manner that seemed as if they were merely on their way to another activity. Once the SNOD received the "go" signal from the Director, the first thing he did was to ring up the fire-drill monitor; the second thing he did was to pull the master alarm switch that activated a sound-and-light show to alert other staff and patients. One by one, the patients were guided to the appropriate exits and thence to "holding areas" (the nurses were kept hopping). Any deviation from established procedure was likely to end in disaster. Hence, the presence of the monitor – yet one more god-awful duty roster to check whose sole consolation was that it rotated only monthly. (S)he had to oversee all the procedures and deal with any exigencies as they arose. (In case of a real fire, the monitor acted as a liaison between the Home and the respondent fire units.) When everyone had been gathered (and nose-counted), the monitor sounded the "all clear," and the patients were sent back inside.

Fire drills were much more crucial to the well-being of the institution and much more complex in their observances than the routine activities; thus, greater involvement than one's mere presence was required. The monitor had to personally check all areas (in conjunction with the SNOD) before (s)he could issue the "all clear"; (s)he had to secure those areas in which there was a potential danger of flash fires and/or toxic smoke; (s)he had to assure that staff and patients went to their designated areas and take roll call. In short, the monitor had to be on the double-quick for the space of half an hour. If (s)he hadn't the slightest idea of what to do or tried to cut corners, it meant (potentially) instant tragedy – not to mention endless lawsuits down the line.

I should not have been fire-drill monitor for this month and when (*not if*) the Director learned of my "tour of duty," he was sure to have some sharp words for all parties concerned. As the "new boy" at the Home, I was expected to have at least one drill under my belt strictly as a participant so that I understood the procedures. I and the one who was supposed to have been the monitor for that month (Bertie) were very aware of all this, but we still agreed to swap places because of the death in his family. So, in exchange for a dreaded meal-monitor turn, I figured I couldn't be any worse off, and it would have been good on-the-job training.

How wrong I was!

So, when the words "Fire drill, Doctor" rang in my ear, I was instantly alert and jumped out of bed. As I hastily dressed, I mentally reviewed the drill procedures as set down in the resident-staff's manual, going so far as to enumerate them aloud by the numbers. By the time I had reached the main building, the phrases were dancing madly through my head like the latest advertising jingle. I heard the bleating of the alarm system and saw the flashing blue lights from twenty-five yards away. (Blue, not red, because the latter is more common in cases of color-blindness.) I visualized the nurses scrambling to their assigned stations, methodically hammering on doors to roust the patients, backtracking and re-working the floors to see that all of the residents were up and about, dressed, and ready to evacuate, directing them to the exits, assisting those whose psychoses inhibited free movement, and gathering them into the "safe" areas.

Out of the corner of my eye, I spied a tall lithe shape quickly moving away from the building. I didn't need to be a rocket scientist to determine who she was. Apparently, Melissa was conducting her own private fire drill. I watched as she made a bee-line for her favorite haunt, the far reaches of the woods; I didn't attempt to call her back, since I knew the effort would have been wasted. Melissa, I knew all too well, did what she wanted to do, regardless of the established rules. In any event, I had other concerns.

I located the SNOD (as it happened, the taciturn Nurse Jones), and together we semi-trotted up to the third floor. In our own methodical fashion, we examined each room to insure that it was empty and even checked the hall closets in case a patient might be hiding there out of fear (or spite!). Each area was marked off on a list that was part of a monitor's report; we did not leave the floor until all areas were certified as "clear." In this manner, we worked our way back downstairs. I checked the locks on the doors to the infirmary, the medical-records room, the library, and the administration office, while my cohort saw to the kitchen, the arts-and-crafts rooms, the parlor, the conservatory, and the basement. When we were both satisfied that all was in order, we joined the others outside.

It was a rag-tag bunch that greeted my eyes. The patients – most of whom had been roused from a sound sleep – stood around bleary-eyed and clearly unhappy about the situation. Clad only in pajamas or robes hastily thrown on (even old Matt had succumbed to a state of modesty – a sure sign that he was returning to rationality), they all looked ready to curse the responsible party up one side and down the other for inconveniencing them. (This might sound strange to the average person, since the majority of them had gone through this routine many times; on the other hand, routine fire drills tend to get old, even for us "normals.") Had I been in their place, I might have been just as P.O.'ed. Yet, my "reputation" was sufficient to hold their tongues. Said reputation, however, did not prevent them from glaring balefully at me. I just smiled cheerfully. I had a good reason for smiling too; my very first fire drill had gone smoothly. Self-congratulations floated freely in my head.

Little did I know!

I had my check-list at hand and proceeded to call the roll. Some of the patients answered civilly, some did not, and some refused to answer at all. Staff assisted me by pointing at the recalcitrant ones. When I came to the end of the list, I hit a snag.

"Ray W.?"

"Billy the Kid" did not respond.

"*Billy*, speak up!"

"He's not here, Doctor," Jones called out, panic rising in his voice.

"Not here? What the hell?" I paced down the line and scanned each face myself. "Does anyone remember seeing him?"

One of the junior nurses, a freckled-faced young man who reminded me of Howdy Doody, stepped forward.

"I think I saw him in the hallway, Doctor, just as I was doubling back. It looked to me like he was headed for the exit."

"You *think* you saw him? That's not very reassuring, Nurse." I took a deep breath to calm myself down. All of those glowing self-congratulations were rapidly going down the toilet! "All right, people, listen up. When the patients have been returned to their rooms, I want all but two of the nurses – Jones, you select the two – to report back here. We're going to have to search the grounds."

Now, it was not only the patients who grumbled. This crew was near the end of its shift; having to search for a missing patient meant a delay in going home and tending to their own affairs. It couldn't be helped, of course; Ray had to be found – and soon – since he posed a potential danger to himself and to anyone he might encounter in his wanderings. Just like the outlaws of the Wild West, "Billy the Kid" had just broken out of "jail," and he would do anything to avoid being returned to "custody."

Before Jones departed, I halted him.

"Is this sort of thing common?" I asked him.

"No, Doctor." Did he have a sneer in his tone of voice? "Once in a while, someone starts to wander off, but we've always been able to round 'im up. This is the first time, though, we've lost track of a patient."

"Great!" I muttered. "Just *fucking great!*"

There were two ways to look at that turn of events, and I didn't care much for either of them. One: it being my first time out as fire-drill monitor, my total lack of experience had caused me to overlook some areas of the building whereby I had "misplaced" a patient. In the eyes of the Director, when he learned of the incident, I'd be the first-year medical student again who has just asked an obvious question; he'd shake his head in disbelief and cluck his tongue, and I'd melt away under his withering gaze and be reduced to a slag heap. Two: it being my first time out as fire-drill monitor, despite my total lack of experience, I had reacted to an emergency situation by fact-finding and plan-implementing whereby the Director would commend me for my quick thinking and decisive action and I'd gawk like a school boy and accept his praise with all due modesty.

It made no difference which scenario would be the right one, however. The fact of the matter was *I had lost a patient!* Never mind that some of the nurses had not been as attentive as they should have been. Never mind that Ray might have been able to outsmart us even on our best days. Never mind that it had been the very first time such a thing had happened. It had happened on *my* watch; I alone was responsible. As I waited for the return of the "volunteer" search party, I luxuriated in kicking myself repeatedly (and figuratively) as hard as I could.

When the nurses re-appeared, I saw surliness writ large. Did they also blame me for the loss of a patient? Or were they cursing Ray for his impulsive behavior? Either way, only a speedy (and successful) search would mollify them.

"Thank you for your forbearance, everybody," I announced. "We'll split up into two groups. Nurse Jones, you'll take one group and search the southern half of the grounds; I'll take the other group and search the northern half. One word of advice: Ray may think he's an escaped prisoner, and he may behave like one. Therefore, he may be dangerous. Bear that in mind, and watch each other's back."

For the purposes of dividing up the search party, I had decided on the simple formula of equal numbers of male and female nurses in each group. I was able to do this, thanks to Dr. Vengtman's policy, laid down years ago, of hiring equal numbers of each gender for the non-professional staff. The women in the search party might have regretted this bit of "political correctness," but the Director had insisted on equalization. There weren't too many places on the main grounds for a person to hide; therefore, I assumed that Ray would head for the woods (a decidedly rugged terrain for a city boy!) If anybody complained, it would have been due to "unequal" treatment.

I regarded my "volunteers" briefly and arbitrarily selected five of the nine for my group. I took the larger number because the cottages were in the northern sector; if Ray had gone in that direction and threatened the residents, I wanted superior manpower behind me. On the way there, we were met by Harry, Dante, Maddie, and Nan. All seemed fairly safe. I quickly brought them up to speed.

"Hmmm," the Senior reacted, rubbing his jowls, "I can't say I'm too surprised. I expected Ray to try to disappear on us long ago. God knows he's had opportunities enough. Well, I'm afraid I can't help you, Ken. I'm the meal monitor today. And Maddie was the over-nighter; she needs to get some sleep." He grinned hugely. "I *can* volunteer Dante and Nan, however."

"T'anks, Harry," the dapper little man responded with no little sarcasm in his voice. "I always enjer a walk in da woods befoh breakfast."

"You join Jones's group, Dante," Nan jumped in. "I'll go with Ken's group."

"Sure t'ing, Nan. I just –"

What his next thought was was lost for all eternity, for it was canceled out by a blood-curdling scream, the likes of which I had heard only once before in my short life. In fact, the extreme distressful nature of that outcry was so similar to the earlier experience that, momentarily, my mind slipped into the past to unveil a partially buried memory of a woman who had lived two doors down from my old South Side apartment building and who had been slashed to death by her live-in boyfriend. The wailing had begun on a high note and increased in pitch until one might well believe that the tearing of vocal cords was imminent. The duration of the scream had been pushed beyond the limits of human capacity to sustain it, only to be choked off in mid-note and replaced by an unholy silence. To my mind, past memory and present occurrence commingled briefly, and I nearly succumbed to a fainting spell.

My distress must have been obvious, for Nan stared at me, wide-eyed and pale, in a state of shock. Instinctively, she reached out and laid a hand gently on my arm. The contact was sufficient to bring me back to the present if not to completely mitigate my sense of helplessness, and I began to breathe normally again. With the return of equipoise, I attempted to analyze the scream.

That it had been a human scream I had no doubt. Once a person has heard the agony of another, he will never mistake it for any other sound (nor forget it). That it had been a deathly scream I also had no doubt (and for the same reason). Ominously, it had issued from the very direction

I was about to lead my search group, from the northwest corner of the property. I say "ominously" because I knew from past observations that, during her inexplicable meanderings, Melissa Waterman always headed in that direction. I stared that way, trying to pierce the early-dawn gloom of the forest and learn what might be taking place in its stygian depths.

"Good God!" Harry whispered.

"*Mon Dieu!*" Maddie cried out and crossed herself.

"Jesus, Mary, and Joseph!" Dante rasped and crossed himself.

Nan remained silent. But, if she could have become any paler, I think she would have done so.

"Harry," I advised, "you'd better call 9-1-1. I have a nasty feeling about this."

"Right you are, Ken. Dante, you round up Jones's lot and then join up with Ken's group. Maddie, you're with me."

"You don't have to come along if you don't want to," I told Nan.

"Don't be absurd, Doctor," she replied with a great deal of bravado. "I volunteered for this mission, and I'm not going to back out now."

"Suit yourself. All right, people, let's move out. And stay alert!"

Fortunately for us, we did not have to search the entire woods. Geographically, they covered twenty acres; but since the original estate had been only five acres, that portion from the main grounds to the rear of the property was no more than a hundred yards. To the urban eye, they just *looked* deep! Still, because of the high density of the trees, vision and mobility were necessarily hampered. To cover the maximum amount of territory and yet maintain minimum contact with each other, I spread the group out no more than five yards between each person. We moved out from the path that linked the cottages and advanced with a slow, steady pace. Always, we glanced periodically from side to side to keep our "flankers" in sight.

Even though the sun was now well above the horizon, the woods were still a twilight world, possessing an eeriness that chilled the soul. In ancient times, this unearthly atmosphere would have conjured up visions of demons and evil spirits, all prepared to wreak havoc upon mortal beings; our ancestors, a superstitious lot, imagined forests to be places of enchantment and/or horror to be appeased before they could pass safely through. Such is the fear of the Unknown, simply because it is difficult to see very far and prepare oneself for sudden events. The woods do present dangers, of course, and the cautious person is wise to take note of them. These dangers are, however, purely *physical* in nature – wild animals, fire, extreme cold, and the like – rather than metaphysical. Whatever danger lurked in these woods, I couldn't have said, but whoever had voiced that horrendous scream had encountered it to his everlasting peril. Thus, we moved no faster than we had to.

I glanced at Nan. She appeared grim and resolute, taking the eerie atmosphere in stride. I liked that in a woman – no nervous Nellies for me! Maybe Nan was faking it for my sake, but I admired her nevertheless.

We had covered nearly two-thirds of the search area when I heard a second scream off to my left. This scream – a female scream -- was radically different from the first one; it was short-lived and full of terror, but not of mortal terror. Apparently, one of the nurses had discovered something disagreeable. Nan and I shifted directions and headed toward the scream's source. We soon encountered said source bounding toward us as fast as the terrain would let her. Nurse Blakely had horror painted across her face, and she was as white as the proverbial sheet. I intercepted her, but it was like holding on to a wild animal. Whatever she had seen had put her in an absolute panic that nothing could break. I shook her roughly, and she ceased her mewling.

"What is it, Nurse? What did you see?"

She stared at me blankly. There was not a hint of intelligence in her eyes. Then, the dam burst, and she yielded to great, convulsive sobbing. Nan stepped forward and embraced the woman gently. I let her cry for a few moments, then pressed the issue.

"What happened, Blakely? What's out there?"

"Oh, my Lord!" she said in a muffled voice. "It's – it's...*horrible!*"

"What is?"

"Back there." She gestured in the general direction from which she had come. "It looks like – Oh, God! I don't know what it looks like. It's *horrible!*"

At that point, a male nurse – the freckle-faced fellow – put in an appearance. He too seemed to be shaken to the core; though he had not given in to panic, he was ashen and nauseated. He looked at me helplessly.

"Well?" I demanded.

"You better see this for yourself, Doctor. I can't put it into words."

"Very well. Nan, take Blakely back to the main building. Then wait for the EMT and escort them back here."

"Check. Be careful, Ken."

"I always am." I gave her a reassuring smile, then turned to the male nurse. "Lead the way."

Two minutes later, I gazed upon what had horrified the nurses – gazed upon it and shuddered. It *was* horrible, the more so because it had clearly been a human being once, a human being who had suffered a hideous fate. It was covered in blood, and blood was still oozing out of dozens of tiny lacerations. On closer inspection, the lacerations appeared to have been made by the teeth and claws of a small animal – or, rather, a large number of small animals. Flesh, ripped away in tiny shreds, hung loosely from the wounds. There was hardly a place on the body which had not been touched.

Despite his many wounds, the victim was still recognizable.

It was Ray.

I squatted to check for a pulse. Astonishingly, he was still alive – barely. His respiration was shallow, and his pulse was weak. If we could staunch the bleeding, perhaps he could hang on until the paramedics arrived. My touch must have stirred him into consciousness, for he opened his eyes halfway and looked up at me, first in confusion, then in recognition. It was difficult to keep my attention fixed on his torn and bleeding body, but somehow I managed. I even eked out a comforting smile. Ray smiled back.

"Never...thought," he murmured, "the last...face Ah'd...see...would be...a preacher's."

"Just take it easy, Billy," I soothed. "The...doc will be here soon. He'll fix you up good as new."

"Too late...fer the...sawbones. Ah got...a date...with...Old Scratch."

"What happened here, Billy?"

"Got...bushwhacked...preacher. Whole rotten...bunch...of 'em...wuz waitin'...fer me. She...shot me...up...good."

"*Who*...bushwhacked you?"

He was no longer listening to me, as he had slipped back into unconsciousness. He had said "she." Had he been referring to Melissa? Then it dawned on me: all those tiny lacerations must have been the work of Melissa's menagerie, although it seemed ludicrous on the face of it. Squirrels and raccoons don't ordinarily attack humans unless – like all creatures of the wild – they have been cornered or their young have been threatened. As far as I could determine, Ray had done neither. There was

267

another possibility, but I refused to countenance it; it was too monstrous to contemplate and, in any event, I had no proof.

None of this deduction was helping Ray. He needed first-aid immediately. I stood up, stripped off my smock, and began tearing it into long strips.

"Yours too," I commanded the young male nurse. "We'll need lots of make-shift bandages."

Soon, both of our smocks were reduced to a pile of shreds, and we wrapped them around the most serious wounds. For some odd reason, once we were finished with our handiwork, I recalled an elderly man in my old neighborhood who had been a medical corpsman in Vietnam during the war there. He had regaled me with all sorts of war stories, particularly the types of wounds he had had to treat with what medical supplies he had at hand. Would he, after checking out Ray, have approved of my own "field dressings"? I suddenly entertained a sincere hope that I would never have to ply my trade in a similar situation.

It seemed like hours before the paramedics arrived (it was really only fifteen minutes, counting the time they had to traverse the woods), along with two Kane County deputy sheriffs. The former were of the less-than-professional opinion that the attack was "pretty gruesome" and that Ray looked like "hamburger." I wanted to knock them down where they stood and tell them to stop wasting time on inane comments. The latter were slightly less sanguine about the incident, asking all the usual police-style questions and taking statements from everyone in the search party. In retrospect, I should never have mentioned that the victim was one of my personal patients – it had seemed like an innocent remark at the time – for it prompted the deputies to ask several pointed questions which reflected on (or so I thought) my competence to practice medicine. I wanted to knock *them* down too. But Nan – bless her! – sensing my mood, gave me a nudge in the ribs as a signal to "chill out." When the formalities were finally completed, I accompanied the gurney bearing Ray back to the EMT vehicle. To the paramedics' annoyance, I insisted on returning with them to the hospital on the grounds that the victim was still my patient.

Sadly, my emergency first-aid had been too little and too late. Ray had lost too much blood by the time we had found him, and he never regained consciousness. He drew his last breathe, ironically, just as the EMT pulled into the drive of Mercy Center in Aurora. There was nothing to do then but to let the senior ER doctor pronounce Ray as a "DOA" and send the body to the Center's morgue pending notification of the next-of-kin. I recognized the ER doctor from my days at R-PSL, and I asked him, both as a personal favor and as a professional courtesy, to do the autopsy himself. Afterwards, when the sheriff's office had been notified of the DOA, there were yet more questions to be answered, and I did not return to the Home until nearly ten o'clock.

I went straight to the Director's office in order to make a full report on the incident. Mrs. Oliphant, all bleary-eyed herself, informed me that he was on the telephone, and would I please have a seat. I spent the time mulling over and over the horrific scene until I was sure I could describe it to the last detail. Presently, Mrs. Oliphant declared that I could see the Director.

Dr. Vengtman appeared to have shrunk since I last saw him. And now that I thought about it, at that time he had not seemed as robust (comparatively speaking) as the time before that. Had he contracted some debilitating disease, such as Parkinson's or Alzheimer's, and was wasting away? Only in his eyes were there still the alertness and keenness and intelligence I had always associated with him. When I entered his office, he put on a pleasant smile and waved me to a chair. The smile was forced (I thought), and the gesture weak. He leaned forward, his forearms resting on the desk and his hands folded, and peered steadily at me for a few seconds. If he were trying to read my mind, he'd probably have had an easy time of it; just then, I was wearing my feelings on my sleeve.

"Well, Dr. Maxwell," he said at last, "you've had quite a morning so far."

"Yes, sir," I responded desultorily. "I only hope the rest of my career isn't this exciting."

"I daresay that you comported yourself admirably, from the accounts of the others at the scene. It's unfortunate, of course, that you didn't arrive sooner, but you can't be faulted for that."

"You'll excuse me for saying so, Dr. Vengtman," I said with sudden passion, "but that's a matter of opinion."

"Nonsense. Look, Ken, we all do what we can, here or elsewhere. No one is guaranteed success each and every time an incident occurs. I won't have you blaming yourself for events beyond your control. You're no good to me if you do. I selected you because I saw something in you I believed should be developed. Don't disappoint me. Don't disappoint *yourself.*"

"I'll try to remember that, sir."

"Fine. Now, I've heard from the other witnesses, and I've just got off the phone with the sheriff's office. I need to have your account. Ray's family will want to know everything about his death."

Though my heart wasn't in it, I told him everything that I had witnessed. Almost everything, that is – I withheld from my account the cryptic remarks Ray had made before he lapsed into unconsciousness. I withheld them because I wished to discuss them with Dr. Vengtman "off the record." Since Melissa might be involved, I believed he should be given the option of deciding if those remarks ought to be a permanent part of the record.

"Excellent, Ken. This corroborates the other reports."

"There is something else, sir, something I didn't even tell the deputy sheriffs."

"Really?" he said suspiciously. "I wouldn't have thought you capable of deceit."

"Well, it's not so much deceit as it's, um, *caution*." I then related the remarks Ray had made. "So, you see, I felt that, if I had told the deputies what he had said, it might have, uh, muddied things up. If you think I should make an additional statement, I will."

Once more, he regarded me in his typical analytic fashion. I ought to have been used to such scrutiny by then, but I still felt squeamish – not to mention very tired from my ordeal.

"I'm pleased you did come to me first, Ken. I think, in light of what's happened, we can ascribe Ray's comments to simple delirium brought on by the trauma of his attack. As such, it won't add much to the official report. We can't know for certain that he actually referred to Melissa, can we?"

"No, sir. It *was* pretty vague."

"Of course. Well, I'd hazard to guess you'd like to get some rest. Why don't you cancel whatever appointments you have today and relax? If you have any monitor duty, I'll get Harry to shuffle the rosters."

"Thank you, sir. I'd like some time off, but it's not necessary to take me off the rosters. I'll be fine, once I get some rest."

"That's the spirit, my boy! I'll talk to you later."

Now that I had time on my hands with nothing to do, my stomach reminded me that I had had nothing to eat all morning except a doughnut and a cup of coffee at Mercy Center while waiting for the bus to take me back to the Home. It was now close to eleven o'clock, and the first serving period was still more than half an hour away. If I didn't put something in my belly, I'd have been tempted to graze the lawn! I ambled down the hallway to the dining room and stuck my head in. The kitchen staff was just beginning to set up the serving line. The aroma of the food issuing from the kitchen raised the issue of hunger to new heights, and I half-seriously entertained the idea of pirating something when no one was looking. Just then, I spied Harry emerging from the kitchen and remembered that he was meal monitor that day. He spotted me at almost at the same time and rushed over.

"Ken, dear boy, how long have you been back?"

"Not long. I've just been with Himself to bring him up to speed. Um, he gave me the rest of the day off."

"Hmmm. Damned decent of him." He peered at me worriedly. "You don't look at all well. You probably do need some time off, after what you've been through."

"Yeah, and I need to chow down too. Think you could help me jump the line?"

"Not a problem. Follow me!"

Since the head cook was now on vacation, we had to seek out his assistant. That individual – a pudgy little fellow who behaved as if he were permanently on steroids – was just the opposite of his superior; he was obsequious to a fault and couldn't do enough to make us happy. I don't know which I preferred – surliness or obsequiousness – but, in any event, I had never endeared myself to any of the other kitchen staff. When Harry and I marched into the kitchen and the Senior "requested" that I be served immediately due to an "emergency," my stock with them took another nose-dive. Amid mumbling and grumbling, I was allowed to help myself out the cooking pots directly. I was of two minds here. On the one hand, my stomach was telling me to "speed it up"; on the other hand, I felt quite sheepish at bending the rules for strictly personal reasons. As soon as I had heaped my plate, I retreated quickly to the staff dining room. All the way out, I sensed the kitchen crew (minus the assistant head cook) staring daggers in my back.

While I was wolfing down my lunch, Nan came in and took the seat opposite me. Tired as I was, I still managed a semi-cheery smile.

"Anything exciting happen while I was gone?" I joked.

"Oh, just the usual. Lying, cheating, theft, adultery, and mayhem. And that was just the doctors. The nurses were something else." She became sober at once. "I heard about Ray. I'm sorry."

"I'm not the first doctor to lose a patient, and I won't be the last. It's still cold comfort."

"Have you any idea why he was in the woods in the first place?"

"Yes, he had just broken out of jail, and he was looking for a hide-out. Unfortunately, he went off in the wrong direction and got himself murdered."

"'Murdered'?" she exclaimed wide-eyed. "You're saying Ray was the victim of foul play? Ken, he was attacked by wild animals, as improbable as that seems. How can you say he was *murdered*?" She looked at me suspiciously. "Does Melissa have anything to do with this?"

"I don't want to put anything into words just yet, because it's so crazy. That's all I'm going to say until I investigate further."

"What are you planning to do?"

"After I've eaten, I'm going back into the woods and poke around. If I find proof of foul play, then I'll take my charge to the authorities. If I don't, well, my crazy idea will die quietly."

"If I didn't have delivery-day duty today, I'd go with you. I'm afraid I've caught whatever has infected you."

"Sorry about that, babe. Sometimes I think I'm in over my head – like now, for instance. I sure don't want to expose you to any danger that might be out there."

"In case you haven't noticed, Ken dear, I'm a big girl, and I'm quite capable of taking care of myself. But, thank you for your concern. If it isn't too much trouble, I'd appreciate it if you took care of yourself. Breaking in new staff members is a troublesome task."

"I'll keep that in mind while I'm battling the monsters."

Despite our levity, both of us knew that what I was about to do entailed no small risk. Perhaps, in a few short hours, I'd be joining Ray, a bloodied, mangled corpse rotting beneath a tree. I didn't want Dr. Vengtman the Younger to share that fate; at that point, I think I was beginning to fall in love with her. If Melissa *was* involved in Ray's death – and I hadn't yet conceded that point – I thought I stood a better chance in confronting her than Nan did. Assuming, of course, that the girl was still infatuated with me, I might try to wheedle a confession out of her. In any event, this was my show – and had been from the beginning – and I was going to take any risks alone.

For the first time in my short career, I had doubts about Lowell Vengtman's views on anything. After I had related to him the curious remarks made by the deceased (his final words, as it turned out), the Director had complimented me on keeping mum on the matter. I had the distinct impression that he was all too happy to sweep that aspect of the incident under the proverbial rug (along with Ray!). Why he would do such a thing puzzled me; it was so unlike the Great Man that my hackles had been instantly raised. I hadn't questioned him then but kept my mouth shut, but I intended to get to the bottom of that matter as well. How Dr. Vengtman the Elder might react if he learned I was conducting a clandestine investigation of his patient was a giant unknown. Reprimand and/or firing were certainly potent weapons against meddling fools; yet, he couldn't be sure that I would not inform others about the strange goings-on at the Home. Would he then resort to more drastic, more *physical* methods? I couldn't quite picture him as the mad scientist of the 1930's horror films.

Nevertheless, the Director's feelings were not going to deter me – not now. It was all too apparent that Ray's death was another part of the Great Mystery that was Mathias Hinkelman's demise; where exactly it fit in was as yet undetermined, but time would tell where that place was. Once I had all the facts at hand, and assuming I survived the ordeal, I'd confront the Director and let the chips fall where they may. Melissa had made several remarks concerning his "true" character (which I was also not conceding yet); and, until I could prove or disprove them, I didn't want him mistrusting *me*. It was a gross decision to make – deceiving the one person in this world whose respect I cherished above all else – but, lately, I had been making a lot of hard-and-fast decisions (not all of them too legitimate in nature) because they were expedient if I ever hoped to solve the Great Mystery.

With much trepidation, I took my leave of Nan, obtained a fresh smock, and sauntered across the lawn as Melissa had done many times before. My outward calm belied inner turmoil, and doubts assailed me from all sides. What would I find out there in the woods? If I found anything at all, would all my suspicions be confirmed? Did I *really* want all my suspicions confirmed? What course should I take if they were? In the field of psychology, fear is the greatest enemy. One might have the courage of ten men, facing a material foe with high resolve – wars are often fought and won by such individuals – yet put that same person up against a foe he cannot see or touch or barely imagine, and he dissolves into a quivering lump of flesh. He who knows fear will do anything rather than face this sort of enemy head on, thus compounding the problem.

Fear takes many forms, and any given object or situation will trigger it. Whatever the catalyst is, however, fear is invariably debilitating, robbing one of his vitality. All of us without exemption fear something. I've always had a fear of snakes, though, as a city boy, I saw very few snakes. To this day, I won't go near a zoo, for fear of seeing them. In this light, it may puzzle the reader why I was so willing to enter a woods where, traditionally, snakes live. I can only say that, if I had any fear that day, it wasn't of snakes; rather, it was of discovering unpleasant and disturbing truths about people I thought I knew. An unprofessional attitude to take, I'm sure, but there it was.

Upon entering the woods, I made straight for the spot where we had found Ray. It was not all that difficult to do since at least a dozen people had been tramping through there. A clear trail was visible from the forest edge to the (in my opinion) murder site. Because the idea of homicide was growing in my mind, I half-expected to see the familiar yellow-and-black ribbons with the wording "Police Line – Do Not Cross." There wasn't any, of course, because the sheriff's department was treating the death as an accident. I now glanced around to get a lay of the land. Perhaps it was just my imagination, but the trees seemed denser in this section, making visibility even more problematic. I couldn't take more than three steps in a straight line before I had to detour around a tree. In the city, I had been too used to seeing trees in ordered rows along the curbs or singly in yards; here, the damned things grew haphazardly and formed a colossal obstacle course. My ecologically-minded colleagues would have said this was Nature's way of preserving Life, but the concept did nothing for my ingrained sense of orderliness. For all I knew, I was going around in circles!

I pressed on valiantly, wondering how close to the northern perimeter of the property I was. A fence might be within arm's reach, and I'd never know it because of the thickness of the trees until I walked into it. Meanwhile, I noted how unnaturally quiet it was. Weren't forests supposed to be filled with all sorts of wild creatures? I knew for a fact that there were at least a dozen squirrels and two raccoons here, and I assumed there were birds too. Yet, I had heard nothing – no scurrying in the brush, no flapping of wings, no cries or barks or squeals or chirps of protest at my intrusion. It was too much to believe that all the wildlife had suddenly and unaccountably taken off for parts unknown. So, where was everybody?

In retrospect, I sometimes regret my having been so curious. Terrible visions come into my mind without warning these days, and it takes considerable effort to shake them off. For, no sooner had I put the question to myself than I discovered – to my everlasting horror – the answer.

A few yards ahead of me, I finally caught a glimpse of the fence that separated the estate from the rest of the world. At the same time, I detected a slight movement off to my right. I turned in that direction, but whatever had caused the movement was too fast for me. Nevertheless, I decided to investigate. I quickly stumbled across a natural clearing about two hundred square feet in area (the size of a small front yard). It was grassier than the rest of the woods because the grass did not have to compete with the trees for growing space, sunlight, and rainfall. Furthermore, the grass was of the wild prairie variety indigenous to northern Illinois, not the hybridized, domestic varieties that covered urban and suburban lawns (e.g. the front lawn of the Home itself); it was lush and green and grew in clumps. Encompassing nearly nine-tenths of the clearing was the fence, now plainly visible; in point of fact, the clearing lay at the juncture of the north and west boundaries of the property, forming a natural amphitheater.

I do not use the word "amphitheater" lightly. Since ancient times, man-made structures had been designed and built for the purpose of entertaining or educating large masses of people. While this clearing was miniscule in comparison, still it was serving the same purpose. In this natural amphitheater, however, no people sat. Instead, there were *animals* – more animals than I had ever seen outside of a zoo.

I saw squirrels and raccoons and foxes and opossums and rabbits and chipmunks and weasels. I saw crows and robins and sparrows and cardinals and blue jays and owls and pigeons. I saw (with a shudder) snakes and frogs and lizards. The sight was all the more astonishing because many of those creatures existed in a predator-prey relationship in the natural world; and, yet, there they were, side by side, and none seemed concerned by the presence of a predator/prey. All of them sat in concentric circles around the center of the clearing, each species more or less bunched together. Still more amazing, they all were *silent*! Not a sound did they make, not a muscle did they move. They merely sat in rapt attention, a captive audience to the main attraction.

And, in the center of the circles:

Melissa!

I am not ashamed to admit that I nearly fainted at this tableau. It was so senses-shattering that I believed I was dreaming – or hallucinating. Melissa stood in the middle of that clearing, surrounded by a host of woodland creatures, as a teacher before his students or – perhaps more appropriately – a religious leader before his disciples. And she was stark naked. In another time and in another place, she might have represented erotica – a slender, willowy, buxom Aphrodite in her element. I did not find her as such in that time and that place; rather, she represented terror.

Undoubtedly, she *was* in her element, gathering those creatures unto herself with God-knew-what magical power and commanding them to do – what? -- listen to a sermon about the evils of humanity? learn how to protect themselves against predatory humans? receive marching orders to fight back against predation? all of the above? – all the while bonding with them as no other human in any circumstance in the history of the world had ever done.

She too was silent, pivoting slowly about the circles, addressing each group of her "disciples" in turn, and gesticulating with languorous, graceful motions now and then. Was she then whispering in their minds as she had done to Hinkelman? Was she filling their tiny brains with stunning visions as she had done to me? (This scene was enough to finally convince me of that fact.) And, if she were, what was the nature of those whisperings and visions? What common language did she and they have that kept them in thrall to her?

And still I stood rooted to a spot behind a tree at the edge of the clearing, not daring to move, not daring to breathe, not even daring to blink. Sweat drizzled down my face and neck, not all of it due to the growing heat of the day. I was at once utterly fascinated and utterly horrified – perhaps as much by the menagerie before me as by a naked teenaged girl. As soon as Melissa turned to face my direction (I prayed she wouldn't see me), my heart almost stopped. Her eyes – her compelling, hypnotic amethyst eyes – were *aflame*, like a bonfire! In that instance, I believed that, if she looked at anyone with those awful eyes, she would burn and sear and shrivel his soul in a flash.

Eventually, I decided that I had seen enough, seen enough to haunt me for several lifetimes. With a great effort, I willed my body to swivel around, willed my feet to take first one step, then another. I felt as if I were wading in molasses; at the rate I was moving, I'd need a week to reach my cottage. In my eagerness to quit that evil site, I grew careless and stepped on a twig, snapping it in two. In the silence and the gloom of the woods, the sudden sound took on the dimensions of cannon fire. My heart rose up to lodge in my throat, and a cold chill slid down my spine.

Reaction to the snapping of the twig was instantaneous – and predictable. Held in check for God-knew-how long by what unknown force, keeping their peace until their mistress had finished her "discourse," the animals in the circles responded all at once, each in its own fashion; and there arose such a cacophony of squeaks, growls, chirps, hisses, cries, barks and calls that it seemed that the whole of Nature was in an uproar.

And, in the midst of the animal sounds, I heard one human voice:
"Ken? Is that you? Why are you here?"

I answered with my feet. Somehow, somewhere, I found the strength
to move faster, and I began to run – not an easy task since I had to twist
around a tree every few steps. I thought I was back on a football field,
dodging enemy tacklers on my way to the goal line.

And Melissa whispered in my mind:

Ken, Ken darling! Don't be afraid of me! I won't hurt you! I love you!

I didn't even stop when I reached the path to the cottages but continued
to gallop toward the parking lot. If anyone had seen me loping across the
lawn, they might have believed I had gone mad. And they wouldn't have
been too far from the truth. At the moment, however, I didn't much care
what anyone thought of my behavior; I only wanted to get away from the
Home, to go where it was quiet and restful (even if I had to run all the
way back to Chicago!), to blot out the wretched images that were burning
in my brain.

In the parking lot, I did slow to a fast walk and caught my breath. Only
then did I dare to peer back over my shoulder to see what was behind me.
Happily, I did not witness a horde of furred, feathered, and scaly things
in hot pursuit -- nor a naked girl at their head, pressing them on toward
the consummation of their task – whatever *that* was. Thanking all of the
gods of creation, I jumped into my battered old Nissan and tore out of the
parking lot.

When I was on the streets of Chicago, I drank as much as anyone
else in those circumstances. It had been a mark of "manhood" to try to
outdrink one's buddies. When I traded my "colors" for a football jersey and
a basketball shirt, I necessarily had to cut out the booze. But, after I entered
medical school, I resumed the drinking in order to cope with the grind.
That sounds like a cop-out; but, sad to say, it is endemic in the medical
profession and will continue to be until such time as the powers-that-be
relax the training regimen to a more tolerable level. I cut back considerably,
however, when I decided to go into psychiatric medicine after having
seen first-hand what drugs – any drugs – can do to the human body and
mind. That was all ancient history as far as I was concerned. As I roared
off the property and headed for Aurora, I had but one goal in mind: to
get stupid drunk in the hopes of drowning out those searing images from
the woods.

I recalled there being a tavern in the shopping center on the north end
of town – "Bob's" or "Jim's" or something like that – and that was where I

went. Since it was still the middle of the afternoon, the place was not filled – only a couple of business types at the bar and a young couple at one of the tables. That suited me fine; I wanted to be alone. I drew any number of stares, and I wondered why until I realized I was still wearing my smock and name tag. Apparently, none of the patrons were used to seeing a doctor in his uniform here. (In retrospect, I did not do my profession or myself a great service that day.) I plopped down at an empty table in the far corner and pulled out a twenty-dollar bill. I planned to drink up as many twenties as I could. When the barmaid came over, I instructed her to bring me a Cuba libre every quarter of an hour. I was going to get drunk quickly!

I don't remember anything after that.

DAY THIRTEEN:
Friday, 07.18.1997
REVELATION

I woke up to the sounds of the "Anvil Chorus" playing in my head. Somehow, I had been lucid enough to find my way back to the Home and drag myself into bed.

Wrong!

My vision was still a bit fuzzy, and the details of my surroundings kept wavering like a desert mirage. But, my sense of touch told me I was *not* in my own bed. I had been sleeping on that sofa-bed long enough to distinguish between it and a *real* bed. If you sleep on a sofa-bed the wrong way – with the bar of the folding section underneath the small of your back – you wake up in the morning with a colossal backache. That had happened to me my first night in the cottage, and I had to experiment a while until I found the right position (a tip: don't sleep with your head toward the back of the sofa). I didn't feel any bar where I was; and, with a sweep of my hand, I realized I was lying on a firm mattress. Moreover, the sheets were smoother and silkier than the Home's more functional linen.

So, where the hell was I? What had happened the night before that I wound up in someone else's bed? And who was that "someone else"?

I sat up and tried to focus my eyes by blinking rapidly several times. Slowly, the fuzziness eased, and I could make out a few details. The bed was a queen-sized one; and it, and the room in which it sat, was done up in pastels – pinks, roses, and creams mostly – extending from the walls to the drapes to the carpeting to the sheets and coverlet. Also, there was a faint scent of perfume around the bed, mingled with body odor. *My* body odor, I discovered, as a result of dried sweat produced by vigorous exercise.

I grimaced. There was only one sort of "vigorous exercise" one gets in bed. Had I, in my drunkenness, picked up some woman? Who was she? I glanced about. I was alone in this room at the moment, but the coverlet had been thrown back on the opposite side of the bed, the side where the scent of perfume was the heaviest. My…partner was elsewhere in that – house? apartment?

Now, I spied an alarm clock on the bedside table. It read a little after eight o'clock. Would my co-workers be worried about my absence – especially if anyone had reported seeing me running across the lawn like a madman, jumping in my car, and tearing down the driveway? Would they be tempted to contact the local authorities to learn if I had been involved in an accident? I had to get out of there – wherever the hell "there" was – and report back to the Home. Easier said than done – my head felt like a bale of cotton. I had to force myself to move. Gingerly, I eased off the bed, staggered over to the only window in the room, and pushed aside the filmy drapes.

Big mistake!

The bright morning sun poured into the room like a river of molten lava, smarting my eyes -- and my brain. I staggered back to the bed and flopped down. In my head, the "Anvil Chorus" changed to a Souza march, high-stepping through my skull from one side to the other, back and forth. I willed myself to stand up again until the clamor subsided to a dull roar, then carefully peeked out the window again.

Ground level was three stories below, so I had to be in an apartment building. Unfortunately, I had a rear view rather than a street view, and I couldn't determine where I was. On the other hand, since I was unfamiliar with the Fox River Valley, it wouldn't have helped me at all to know the street name. All I saw was another building, perhaps identical to the one I was in. I stared blankly at it, pondering my next move.

"Ah, you're awake," a soft, feminine – and very familiar – voice cooed behind me. "That's good."

I whirled around – too quickly, however. The band struck up the music again, and I closed my eyes to shut out as much of the pain as possible. I took two deep breaths to pump oxygen into my brain, then opened my eyes again. I wished I hadn't. I did know the woman.

"Nurse Michaels? Is it really you?"

She was wearing only a crimson robe, tied loosely at the waist, and matching slippers. She was not bothering to conceal too much of herself; when she ambled toward me with a coy smile on her lips (incongruous with the hungry look in her eyes), the robe slid aside at intervals to reveal partially her femininity. In another time and another place, I might have found her quite attractive, a quality she had not projected while on duty at the Home. In that time and place, however, she represented a hole in my memory, and all thoughts of physical attraction were temporarily pushed to the back of my consciousness (this, despite the fact that I was still as naked as a jaybird!).

"Yes, Doctor," she replied sweetly, "it really is." She stood on her tiptoes and kissed me on the cheek. "And, last night, you called me 'Flo,' remember?"

I felt my head pounding again, and this time my hang-over had nothing to do with it. I started to sweat again (but not from "vigorous exercise").

"Uh, sorry, uh, *Flo*. I, uh, I'm afraid I don't remember much of anything. What happened last night?"

"Well, because I had been workin' so much lately as Acting Senior Nurse, I needed to unwind, so I stopped at my favorite waterin' hole. And who should I see but little ol' you all by your lonesome. I jus' couldn't let y'all drink alone, could I? We talked, had a few drinks together – more'n a few, in your case – talked a bit more, then came back here to my place."

"We...talked? What about?"

"Oh, the usual. Our childhoods. Ambitions. Likes an' dislikes. That sorta thing."

At least, I hadn't blurted out my experience in the woods! Thank God for small favors!

"Uh, did we, uh...?"

She reached down, untied her robe, and let it fall open completely. Her breasts stood out and were slightly upraised; though not as big as Nan's, they were yet a pleasant handful, and their nipples were large and almost black. She slipped her arms around my waist and pressed her body against mine. It was getting uncomfortably warm in the room; and, despite my need to leave and return to the Home, I sensed another urge stirring within me. Michaels sensed it too, for she began to rub her body across mine, hastening an erection.

"Honey, we sure did. Y'all don't remember *that* either? I feel hurt."

"Sorry, Nur – uh, Flo. I really did have too much to drink last night."

"Well, even if y'all don't remember, y'all were still fun. I enjoyed every minute of it. Besides, I owed you for savin' my career."

"Well, don't get your hopes up. I'm interested in someone else."

"Yeah, I know. Nancy Vengtman. You two are the hottest item on the grapevine. Well, I've had my fun – while it lasted. And, Doctor, if it don't work out between you two, y'all know where I am."

"Thank you, Nurse. I'll keep it in mind. Now, I really must be going. Duty calls."

"Can't leave without havin' some breakfast, not after I went to the trouble of fixin' it."

"Very well. Plenty of coffee!"

Michaels lived on the far west side of Aurora, two blocks north of yet another major shopping center. She had to drive me back to the other one because I had been too drunk to drive, and my car was still there. One supposes that was embarrassing enough; yet, I had to compound my embarrassment by blanking out all memory of what should have been an enjoyable evening.

What was worse, I feared to face Nan. We weren't engaged or anything like that, and we hadn't made any promises or commitments. It had just been a mutual understanding that we were right for each other and that we should build on our relationship. I didn't want to lose her on a technicality now that we were in the groove. Should I then confess my "infidelity" and blame it on "Demon Rum," hoping that she would accept the explanation and forgive me my "waywardness"? Or, should I simply keep quiet about the whole thing and pray that she never found out? Further, could I trust Michaels to keep a secret? Or would her own lust push her toward some rash action? Lord, the decisions a man must make! Best to play it by ear for the time being and keep my fingers crossed.

In any event, I had a larger problem than the future of my love life. I had to arrive at some resolution concerning Melissa Waterman. It was becoming painfully clear that she could no longer be classified as a normal human being with an emotional disorder; in fact, I was toying with the idea that she had *never* had an emotional disorder in the first place, that she was at the Home so she couldn't harm anyone. Lowell Vengtman must have realized some time ago what she was capable of and "admitted" her as a permanent resident. She was, for all practical purposes, a prisoner, shut away for the good of the world. The irony was that, despite the Great Man's good intentions, he had not been able to prevent her from working her will on the *Home's* population. Melissa had destroyed Mathias Hinkelman with her jealousy-driven whispering campaign, and (I was sure) she had had a part in the demise of Ray W. (though how she had achieved it was yet unclear). And, while I was on that train of thought, did she also have a part in Nurse Clement's accident? She hadn't liked him at all, and he had died only a few hours after he had duked it out with me and was returning to the Home with a gun. Melissa claimed to be keeping me from harm. Was the fatal eliminating of my "enemies" part of the "game plan"? It was horrific to think in those terms, but putting anything past that girl could have been a colossal mistake.

When I pulled into the driveway of the Home, I debated what I should do first and decided that a shower and a change of clothes ought to have the highest priority. Sometime during my drunken orgy, I had spilled liquor on myself, and my shirt and pants still held a faint odor of rum. There was also the lingering aroma of Nurse Michaels' perfume! My arrival might have gone unnoticed except for the fact that the patients had their exercise period outside that morning and were now filing back inside. Some of them (and a couple of the nurses) spied me and waved vigorously. I waved back, pleased to know that some people appreciated my being here, and walked briskly to my cottage.

There was a note taped to the door, written in Nan's florid handwriting. It read simply:

"Must talk ASAP. Love you."

On my mental list of priorities, getting in contact with her had been number three. Number two was reporting to her uncle and letting him know that I was still among the living (just in case he was concerned by my absence). Which meeting would have been the more wrenching was difficult to say; both of the Vengtmans were strong-willed people, and neither would tolerate any flimsy excuses I might dream up. I had to tell them the truth about my experiences – perhaps not *all* of the truth right away, but just enough to satisfy their curiosity – regardless of the harm to my character – and reputation. Otherwise, I would have lost the trust and respectability of the one and the trust and love of the other.

Walking into the administration office was like walking into a dark room. One might encounter anything, even something nasty. I knew what was *supposed* to be there, but I had no guarantee that it *was* there. And I was not put at ease by Mrs. Oliphant promptly waving me into the Director's office; it meant that he had become aware of my undignified departure, puzzled over it, and expected an explanation when I returned. I braced myself for a stern lecture on professional behavior. I was disappointed on that score, however. He looked up at me, not sternly but expectantly, and quietly invited me to take a seat. In some respects, I wished he had chewed me out and pounded the desk for emphasis, because sitting there and enduring that microscopic examination was a worse punishment for whatever transgressions I had committed than anything I could have imagined.

"There's a rumor going about, Dr. Maxwell," he began casually, "that you were observed leaving the premises in an undignified manner. Would you care to comment?"

"It's more than a rumor, sir. I, uh, I'm afraid that I behaved – well, rather unprofessionally. I, uh, saw something in the woods that put the fear of God in me."

"It must have been quite incomprehensible to put the fear of God into a big, strapping fellow like you."

"Yes, sir."

"Whyever were you in the woods in the first place?"

"I was looking for some clues as to why Ray was there and what happened to him."

"It's patently clear that Ray was acting out his 'Wild West' fantasies. As for the manner of his death, I believe we've already agreed that he was attacked by wild animals. What else did you expect to find?"

"I'm not sure. Certainly not what I did find."

"And that was?"

I hesitated for a long moment. Did I really want to tell the Director a fantastic story about his personal patient? Now that I had time to reflect on the matter, it seemed so surrealistic, and Dr. Vengtman might well believe I had imagined it all. And, since it did involve Melissa, over whom I had detected a note of protectionism, he might also believe I was being impertinent. Sooner or later, however, I had to tell him everything I knew. I decided then and there it was going to be later.

"With all due respect, sir, I'm not prepared at this time to answer that question. I'm still trying to sort it out in my own mind. I assure you, however, that I will submit a full, written report for your evaluation."

"I see. Well, I'll eagerly await that report." He gave me one of his patented what-am-I-to-do-with-you glares. Then: "I must tell you, Doctor, that unprofessional behavior will not be tolerated in this institution and that, under other circumstances, a reprimand would be in order." I swallowed a large lump in my throat. "However, I did give you the day off, and so you were not bound to remain on the premises if you did not wish to. And, because you had been under considerable strain at the time, I'm willing to allow you a little leeway. Therefore, no *official* reprimand will go into your personnel file. I will caution you, though, against future demonstrations."

"Thank you for your forbearance, sir. I promise it won't happen again."

"*Humph!* Forbearance has nothing to do with it, my boy. Consider it 'enlightened self-interest.' You're a valuable member of this team, and I would hate to lose you due to some…misinterpretations on your part."

"Yes, sir. I appreciate your support."

"Think nothing of it." He smiled grandly. "That'll be all, Doctor. Thank you for coming by. Oh, and on your way out, would you send Mrs. Oliphant in?"

I was extremely happy to get out of there in relatively one piece. It wouldn't have done my career any good to have an official reprimand in my personnel file the second week on the job (or any week, for that matter) – particularly one from the likes of Lowell Vengtman. The Great Man had a formidable reputation for selecting his employees; if *he* didn't want you, you had to settle for some considerably lesser position. (I shudder to think I might have had to return to R-PSL!) It took a bold person to apply to him in the first place; but once in, people began to take notice of you and to give greater weight to your views. Screw up, and you were *persona non grata* in the profession, for all practical purposes.

One thing about our conversation puzzled me. No, more than puzzled – it *disturbed* me. Dr. Vengtman had said that he would hate to lose me because of my "misinterpretations." Misinterpretations of what? That choice of words implied he knew what I had seen in the woods and was attempting to persuade me that either I had not seen it but had imagined it or I had seen something entirely different than what I did see. How could he have possibly known what was in the woods? He hadn't been there; he hadn't witnessed that incongruous menagerie gathered together to... *worship* Melissa Waterman; he hadn't observed her "communing" with her "disciples" and "preaching" her "gospel" to them.

Or had he?

A sudden chill crept up my spine. Did I really want to think thoughts like that? I was as much as accusing the Great Man of participating in a sinister conspiracy and cover-up of torture and murder. And yet, Melissa's damning words came rushing back to me: "*He* forced me...." And the damning words of Mathias Hinkelman also sprang back into life: "Only one...the Director." Having started down that booby-trapped path, I now recalled Dr. Vengtman's own seemingly casual commentary during my orientation: "Melissa has a rapport with animals." I had forgotten that remark in the intervening period, but it suddenly acquired new meaning. The question I should be asking then was not *whether* he knew of Melissa's eerie abilities, but *how much* he knew. More to the point: was he encouraging them?

I reckoned I knew the answer to that question even as I formed it. If he had knowledge of Melissa, it followed that he was allowing her to work her will. The girl had free run of the property, and patients and staff were scared witless of her but did not formally complain. All discussion of her case was forbidden, and no file on her was available. If the Director permitted those things to occur, it meant he had some ulterior motive. What exactly did he and Melissa talk about during her counseling sessions?

287

Did she report to him even as her pets "reported" to her? My stomach lurched towards queasiness.

There arose yet another disturbing notion. Suppose I had all of my questions answered and learned that Dr. Vengtman was involved in some secretive enterprise. What should I do about it? Confront him with the evidence and force him to confess? Threaten him with public exposure if he refused? Assuming I'd be believed – it would be my word against his – what purpose would I serve by going public? Would I be placing myself in jeopardy – physically, mentally, or professionally (or all three!) – if I did? I now regretted the curiosity which had sent me down that troublesome path; had I kept my nose out of other people's business, I might not have had that moment of crisis. Sometimes, ignorance really is bliss!

With some effort, I pushed the unsettled (and unsettling) questions onto the back burners. I still had another Vengtman to deal with, and I needed a clear head. Before leaving the administration office, I made a quick check of the duty rosters and discovered that Nan was monitoring arts-and-crafts that day. That suited me fine, for it made talking with her easier.

If Nan were at all concerned with her public image and with wagging tongues, she did not evidence it when she spotted me at the door to the crafts room. She had been engaged at the moment in offering encouragement to Georgina to create some design other than the letter "L." A female nurse gained her attention and nodded in my direction. Instantly, she was at my side, clutching my arm and searching my face with fear-laden eyes.

"My God!" she whispered. "Are you all right? I was worried sick when I heard you'd disappeared."

"I'm fine, Nan. Thanks for your concern. I'm ashamed to admit that I went out and got drunk. After that, everything is hazy." True enough, as far as it went. No need to tell her I had awakened in another woman's bed. Maybe later – *much later* – maybe never. "I've already spoken to your uncle about my behavior, and we've reached an equitable understanding."

"But what happened? What made you go berserk?"

"'Berserk.' That's probably as good a way to describe my experience. You won't believe what I've been through." I took her arm. "Let's take a short walk, and I'll tell you the whole ghastly story."

And I did, in as much detail as I could through an alcohol-deadened memory. Nan's face registered the same gamut of emotions she'd run through upon reading the page that Hinkelman had torn out of his journal; her grip on my arm now tightened to the point where I had to forcibly remove the hand before she cut off my circulation. The silence that followed the end of my account was thick enough to slice, and I could swear I heard insects tramping across the floor. Nan looked at me, ashen-faced, and shook her head in disbelief.

"You're right, Ken. I don't believe it. It's just too – too *fantastic!*" Now she leaned against me wearily. "But, I guess I'd better believe you. Why would you want to make up a story like that?"

"I wouldn't. No way! Not even as an April fool's gag – and I've pulled plenty of those in my day."

"You know, it's just occurred to me that maybe Mathias saw the same thing, and that's why he went mad."

"A reasonable hypothesis, seeing that he had been semi-involved with Melissa." Personally, I didn't think that was the real reason; I was coming to a different but no less sinister conclusion. I didn't want to voice that opinion, however, until I had proof. "I nearly went bananas myself."

"But you survived," she cooed and smiled sweetly. "And I'm going to see to it that you stay sane."

"I'm looking forward to your, *ahem*, bedside manner, honey. Starting with dinner tonight?"

"I thought you'd never ask. The usual time?"

"Absolutely. I'm a creature of habit. Um, time for you to get back to work." I wrapped myself around her and gave her a long, passionate kiss. "I'll see you at lunch."

I marked time in the library while waiting for the arts-and-crafts periods to conclude. Despite having lost one of my patients, I still had four others who required counseling; despite the fact that my head and heart weren't really too enthused about looking them in the face and knowing that they might know what had happened (and having them blame me for the loss), I needed to keep myself occupied and avoid excessive brooding over recent events. On a whim, I checked the files for the writings of Emil Razumov which Hinkelman had raked over the coals; I found one monograph in English (apparently the only one he did write in that language) and called it up on my assigned monitor. I felt that what was occurring at the Home bordered on the occult and that it behooved me to learn what I could about the subject.

Parapsychology was not one of more demanding disciplines at any university. One had to be very dedicated in order to endure the sometimes-subtle, sometimes not-so-subtle derision showered upon the field by mainstream psychologists. Though I was not a psychologist *per se* – having only sufficient training to relate to my career in psychiatric medicine – I had shared some of those attitudes myself. One of them was that parapsychology was pure bunk, that those who claimed to have experienced psychic/occult phenomena were all delusional, and that anyone who studied the topic was wasting his time. Based upon what I had witnessed in such a short period of time, I was now not so sure of those attitudes. I had seen things I couldn't explain through the conventional theories. Either the phenomena had been real, or I was going crazy. And I didn't *feel* crazy. (Of course, how could anyone be sure of his sanity? The truly insane always think that *everyone else* is crazy!) So, I had to look at *psi* with new eyes.

I had read about Dr. Razumov fleeing the Soviet Union because of his controversial theories and especially because of his insistence on being heard. In America, he was hailed as a "hero"; then the publicity died away, and he fell into relative obscurity. Still, he had created as big a stir in this country as he had in his own, and his name kept cropping up from time to time. Since I didn't travel strictly in psychological circles, I wasn't privy to all the details. The brouhaha centered around what Razumov called "radiopsychology," as nutty an idea as one was likely to hear (or so I thought at the time). He claimed to have discovered a scientific basis for astrology and ghosts and mental telepathy and dowsing and a lot of other *outré* stuff; that basis was the interaction of radio energy with the human brain and, depending on the frequency of the carrier wave, the interaction produced different effects. I'm paraphrasing here, because I don't pretend to understand any of it.

The monograph on my monitor's screen was titled "Birth, Behavioral Patterns, and Planetary Alignments," published in the *Journal of the American Psychological Association*, which one of the staff thought should have been included in the library's offerings. It discussed astrology, pure and simple, wearing a coat of scientific jargon, the sort of thing one might hear on a late-night TV talk-show. It all *sounded* logical, of course – Razumov was, if nothing else, quite clever in presenting his "evidence" – and one might be tricked into swallowing the notion of radiopsychology.

Unfortunately, the monograph didn't help me in the least. I wasn't interested in mood changes; I wanted to learn something about rapport between humans and animals. I'd have to make a special trip to the Chicago Public Library and check its card catalog (though I suspected I'd be better off doing my research at the University of Chicago's library). A task for another day, however, as the second of the arts-and-crafts periods had just concluded and I had at least half an hour before visiting one of my patients. Utilizing my random system, I "selected" Georgina for the first session of the day.

As I was crossing the foyer on my way to the staircase, I ran into (quite literally) Harry. The Senior may have *looked* blubbery, but I felt as if I'd hit a brick wall; Harry was more muscle than anyone gave him credit for. He peered at me in disbelief, then broke out in an enormous grin.

"Ken, dear boy!" he boomed. "They said you were back." He seized my shoulders and gently jostled me. I found it quite annoying. "How the hell are you? You had us all worried."

"For which I apologize profusely, Senior Counselor," I replied grandiosely. "You're probably as curious as everyone else about yesterday. I've already told Himself that I'll be writing up a complete report which I'll present at Monday's staff meeting."

"Splendid, splendid. Do come by tonight, and we'll toast your safe return to the land of the living."

"Sorry, Harry. Nan and I have a dinner date."

"I see." He didn't bother to disguise his disappointment. And did I detect a note of disgust in his voice? No matter – I had no desire to drink another night away. "Well, another time perhaps. Um, before I forget it, you were on yesterday's group-activities roster. Maddie had to fill in when you, ah, left the premises. If you wouldn't mind taking her spot this afternoon, dear boy, I would greatly appreciate it."

I could scarcely refuse the request, since my recent behavior had forced one of my co-workers to take on an extra work-load. It was only fair that I return the favor. Of course, that favor would have taken away time for counseling; I would have to squeeze three sessions in somewhere, either that day or the following day (Saturday) – except that I wanted to go into Chicago on Saturday. Priorities dictated that I put off personal pursuits. What was another day or two? I was soon to find out – the hard way.

"Not a problem, Harry," I responded as magnanimously as I could. "It's the least I could do."

"Excellent. I'll see you at lunch then."

I suspected Harry Rauschenburg was a very lonely man – a gay man only partly out of the closet – and that was why he drank so much. If he couldn't find a lover, then he hoped at least to have a drinking companion and/or a verbal sparring partner. In another time, I might have provided him with the latter; but, since I had involved myself with Nan, my interests lay elsewhere. I was afraid Harry was on the path to self-destruction, and it was only a matter of time before his alcoholism overtook him. Because he apparently eschewed any professional help – even from his closest colleagues whom we thought he could trust the most – he was fighting a no-win battle, drinking when alone, drinking when with someone else. I wanted to help, but he had to ask for it first. In the meantime, I was not going to hasten his downfall by participating in his habits.

I discovered Georgina sitting on the floor, surrounded by all of her well-crafted (albeit obsession-oriented) needlepoint. The individual pieces, I saw with a shock, had not been placed randomly but in concentric circles by color. For a hot minute, I was projected back to the circles in the woods of the day before. I think I broke out in a cold sweat then and had to take a few moments to re-compose myself. One by one, Georgina traced the monogrammed "L" on the nearest piece absentmindedly with an index finger and hummed artlessly.

I had had the least success in breaking down the barriers of psychosis with Fred and Georgina. And, had I been more successful with Ray, he might still be alive. I decided, on a subconscious level at least, to redouble my efforts with Georgina. Hers was an iffy case; grief-stricken by the untimely death of her son, she moved in and out of the shadows of unreality as the mood took her. I never knew, from one day to the next, how she would react to any given line of questioning. Which is why the first words out of her mouth took me completely by surprise.

"Lewis is dead."

How to proceed? Be cautious and ask her to explain that statement? Or be bold and not let her retreat from it? I chose the latter, for no other reason than I felt like it. Such was *my* frame of mind that day!

"You've known that all along, Georgina, haven't you?"

"Yes, but I didn't want to believe it. It's hard to lose a child, especially so senselessly. You lose all hope."

"And the drugs didn't help?"

"Oh, Lord, no! They just made things worse! They made me – they made me hear…voices in my head. Lewis's voice."

"Are you still hearing his voice?"

"Not since yesterday afternoon. Once or twice, I thought I heard him. But, when I spoke to him, he never answered me. I'm a bit confused right now."

"But you know it wasn't *Lewis* talking to you."

"I – I don't know for sure. Sometimes – I just don't know."

I felt I had gone far enough with that line of thought. Georgina had made a remarkable admission, and she expressed doubts about her psychotic delusions. That was more progress than I had expected, and I didn't want to jeopardize my gains by being pushy. Let her ponder on her doubts for a while; in time, she would be ready for the next step. At least, I hoped she would. Given her track record, there was no guarantee. Having got that much out of her, I switched to another tactic.

"That's an interesting lay-out you have there," I said casually, gesturing at the needlepoint. "I've, ah, seen a similar display only recently."

She inspected the array again, touching each one lightly with her fingertips. Now that I had a chance to take a closer look myself, I noticed that not only were the pieces segregated by color, but they were also arranged by the increasing size of the "L" in each grouping. Since many of the monograms seemed to be the same size, it must have taken a great deal of concentration to measure each one mentally and set it in its "proper" place. What was more amazing (apart from the feat itself) was that one who suffers from schizophrenia (Georgina's sub-type was a perception disorder) cannot focus at all on real things but are locked into his/her delusions which subsume all brain activity. How then had she been able to be so extraordinarily precise? Was it indeed a sure sign that she was returning to sanity?

"It's funny you should mention it, Dr. Maxwell. The idea came to me yesterday afternoon too, about the same time that…Lewis left me. First, it was all a jumble in my mind; then, in slow motion, all of the pieces moved around like a kaleidoscope until they ended up like you see them. All I had to do was to remember what went where. It was the *eeriest* feeling – like watching a movie, only in your mind."

Yesterday afternoon? Alarm bells sounded again. It was tempting to ascribe Georgina's mental "movie" and my own experience in the woods as sheer co-incidence. Yet, as I have stated before, there had been too many strange occurrences at the Home to shrug off as "co-incidence." I could have speculated that Georgina's own experience had been a direct result of mine – the *why* of it eluded me at the moment – but, since I had no proof, the idea would remain speculation. There was one way, however, to test the "hypothesis"; I'd check on my other patients and correlate any unusual visions they might have had recently with Georgina's. If a correlation existed, it still didn't prove anything; it only ruled out co-incidence as an explanation.

"I take it you've never had a vision like that before."

"No, never. I have no idea where it came from. And, when I moved the pieces around, it was like watching someone else do it." She peered at me anxiously. "Does this mean I'm still…sick?"

"No, it doesn't. I can assure you that, if you recognize what you experienced as unreal, then you're on the path to recovery."

"When will I be able to go home? I miss my husband."

"Um, well, that's hard to say. We're not on a timetable here, you know. Perhaps in another week or so, depending on your progress."

"Thank you, Doctor." She gazed at her needlepoint array again. "Do you think I should throw these away?"

"That would be advisable. They'll only remind you of what you need to put behind you."

In my present frame of mind, I was in no mood to hunt for my other patients. I'd let them come to me, so to speak. To that end, I went straight to the dining room and parked myself in my accustomed place, much to the surprise and consternation of Dante, who was the monitor for the day. I mollified him by explaining (partially) why I was there; thereafter, he left me alone – which suited me fine. Nor was he the only one who was nonplussed; the sight of two of the professional staff in the same area gave rise to wagging tongues, even amongst the non-professional staff. And, because one of those professionals was one with The Reputation, the level of gossip was necessarily higher. I paid little heed to their anxiety because, frankly, why I was there was none of their business.

As luck would have it, two of my "targets," Matt and Fred, were present in the first lunch period, and I invited myself to their tables in turn (provoking even more nervousness on the part of their tablemates). Both were astonished that I would ask, out of the blue, about "visions" but admitted that, yes, they had seen them and, no, they didn't know why. Like Georgina, they had witnessed order out of chaos, although objects more familiar to their individual cases were involved. Matt saw circles of newspapers arranged in chronological order and ascending cover price, while Fred saw circles of wolf prey grouped by size and speed. I returned to my table shaking my head in wonder. Terry came in during the second shift. (While waiting for him, I took a light lunch and behaved as if *I* were the monitor.) He told me – in rather florid terms – that he had seen all of Poe's fiction arranged in alphabetical order and by genre. Once I had his input, I took my leave. The level of the intensity of the buzzing by perplexed patients and staff increased even before I hit the door.

The implication of these varied but oh-so-similar accounts was obvious. Melissa was sending *me* a message in her own inimical fashion. What sort of message? A reminder of my experience of the day before? A warning against interfering in her affairs? An invitation to join her in her arcane activity (possibly permanently)? Or something else equally unwholesome? The closer I seemed to come to solving one of the Great Mysteries at the Home, the more elusive it became. And all because I could not access one damned medical file!

I was so frustrated that I seriously considered taking an axe to Dr. Vengtman's office door and forcing an entrance. I would have satisfied my curiosity all right. I would also have been out of a job – and possibly jailed! I supposed I could have run away again and found solace in a bottle; yet, the previous bout hadn't solved anything (and perhaps had made things worse), and I doubted a repetition would change my luck. In any event, I had other commitments after lunch.

Afternoons at the Home were reserved for group activities. Lowell Vengtman had decreed two periods, one for sports and the other for games. As a general rule, psychotic people are paranoid; regardless of their particular disorders, the fear of being alone in the world and of being assailed on all sides by unseen "enemies" is a common thread throughout the spectrum of mental illness. Overcoming this paranoia is the counselor's chief – and most difficult – task, and (s)he expends much effort in breaching the walls that the mentally ill build up around themselves. As part of the psychotherapy at the Home, participation in recreational activities on a daily basis required a patient to interact and to co-operate with others; by doing so, he might observe (hopefully) that he had nothing to fear from those about him, thus eroding those walls of paranoia. A case in point had been my little class in aerobics. The group had become a single unit, and they seemed to have enjoyed the change in an otherwise boring routine. The trick was getting them to *think* they were enjoying themselves, for personal enjoyment led – in theory anyway – to an upward shift in one's sense of self-worth and thence to the dispersion of one's demons.

Monday through Friday, the patients were exposed during the first period to group sports, such as volleyball, croquet, and flag football when the weather was clement and to ping pong, shuffleboard, and basketball when it was not. During the second period, the patients were permitted to choose their own activity, ranging from card games to board games and everything in between. The idea was to encourage everyone to interact on his/her own as well as being coerced. The Director had decided that (as in the song from *Mary Poppins* had stated) "a spoonful of sugar helps the medicine go down." So far, he had been proved correct.

Naturally, the program meant another damned duty roster. And, because I had missed my turn in the rotation the day before due to my impromptu "day off," I had to make up for it that Friday. The Director hadn't really lost anything by my absence, but that shouldn't have come as any big surprise, given his reputation for exacting the maximum effort out of his employees. I first made a side trip to the administration office to check out the key to the equipment-storage room and then rendezvoused with the SNOD.

That day was volleyball day (outdoors), and we obtained enough equipment for four teams. While the squad of nurses set up the nets on the lawn, I took a head count. It really wasn't required, but I wasn't going to risk losing another patient to the wilds of Illinois on account of a blasé attitude. All were present, except for one of Harry's patients who had suffered an epileptic seizure just before lunch and was resting in her room. For once, the volleyball teams would consist of equal numbers of players (seven). The patients themselves were allowed to choose who would play on whose team and which teams would play each other; after the usual squabbling and petulance, they began their matches. Personally, I thought volleyball was a bore – very little movement was involved – and I quickly tired of watching the ball occasionally cross the net. On a more positive note, I spied the elderly gardener, Ben – and he me – and I excused myself (to no one in particular) to talk to him.

"Hey, Chicago boy!" he greeted me enthusiastically, then clapped his hand over his mouth. "Oops, Ah mean *Doctor* Chicago boy."

"Ha-ha," I chuckled as I shook his hand. "Just what I need: someone to put me in my place. And how are you, sir?"

"'Sir,' hell! It's 'Ben,' 'member?"

"Ah, yes, right – Ben. You can call me 'Ken.'"

"OK, Ken. Ah see it's yore turn to guahd de inmates."

"*Humph!* I do that every day. I'm not usually so obvious about it." I gestured at the flower patch where he had been weeding daffodils. "How're the flowers coming along?"

"Good, good. Got a lotta bulbs dis year, 'cause o' de heavy rains dis spring. Dunno what Ah'm gonna do wif 'em all. Can't plant 'em here – not enough room."

"Aren't there other places you can plant them?"

"Mebbe," he replied, shrugging. "Never had to worry 'bout it afore."

"Um, I've got an idea, Ben. You know about the cottages behind the main building? Well, I think it might spruce things up a bit if you planted some flowers around them – whatever extra you have on hand. I could speak to Dr. Vengtman and get his approval."

"Hey, dat's a good ideer, son. Wou'n't be no extra work fer me. Ah gots to be here free days a week anyways, an' a lotta days Ah ends up havin' to fahnd sumpin to do to fill up de tahme."

"Consider it done then."

"Bah de way, Ah heered dey wuz a ruckus here yesterday. Some'un bein' kilt?"

"Uh-huh. One of the…inmates wandered off into the woods and was attacked by wild animals."

"Man, oh, man! Had to be a lotta wahld animals. Ah ain't seen nuffin' in dem woods big enough to 'tack a man bah itself."

"Could be." I didn't feel like discussing this subject any more than I had to, and so I steered the conversation back to Ben's gardening. "Speaking of animals, are they still staying clear of the flowers?"

"Yep. Dat strange whahte girl Ah tol' y'all about – she axed me de same fing couple o' days ago. Lahk she wuz checkin' to see if'n de animals wuz doin' what she tol' 'em to do. Heh-heh-heh."

"Uh-huh. I wonder what *really* keeps them away."

"Dunno. Ah'm jus' glad dey do." A look of wonder spread over his sweaty face as he looked past me. "Be damned! Speakin' o' de Debbil, dere she be."

I whirled and spotted Melissa on the portico, half-standing, half-leaning against the column that held up the northeast corner of the overhang. She was staring straight at me as if willing me to notice her. At that instant, I could very well have agreed with Ben's idiomatic expression: she *was* a devil, weaving spells and wreaking havoc upon all who crossed her path for the sheer pleasure of it – all in the guise of an attractive but shy eighteen-year-old girl. It was amazing how her appearance could be so deceiving.

How long she had been standing there was anybody's guess. But, as soon as she had been spotted, she slowly crossed the lawn in my direction. All activity came to a screeching halt. The game of volleyball quickly lost whatever appeal it might have had as the patients and nurses alike stared nervously at her, milled about like leaderless sheep (which was an apt analogy), and muttered to each other (or to themselves). The SNOD – Jones again – predictably turned toward me and gestured helplessly. I grimaced. This was a job for "Superdoctor," who must battle the forces of evil and protect all mankind.

I excused myself to Ben and strode slowly but purposely toward Melissa. And still she never took her eyes off me. The closer I came, the more I thought about the incidents in the woods. If I appeared outwardly calm, it was strictly a front; inside, it was an entirely different story. My stomach was tied up in knots, and my breathing was erratic. I kept telling myself not to panic or to show fear; if I showed fear, the battle would be lost before it had begun.

I halted three paces in front of her. She gazed at me serenely – deceptively serenely, I thought – and her awesome amethyst eyes searched mine for any sign of reciprocal feelings. God only knew what thoughts she was thinking; I certainly didn't want to imagine what they were. We stared each other down for a few seconds, and each second seemed like a century. I half-expected my mind to be filled with yet another boggling "vision," knowing that there was no way I could prevent it. I may or may not have been disappointed when no "daymare" entered my head – I don't remember – but Melissa apparently was restraining herself for reasons known only to herself. Presently, she broke the unnatural silence.

"Ken, we have to talk."

That was the understatement of the century!

"And what," I forced the words out with great effort, "shall we talk about, Melissa?"

"You know what. Don't play games with me."

"Huh! You're a fine one to talk about playing games. But, yes, I do know what we have to talk about, though I doubt very much it's what *you* had in mind." She regarded me puzzlingly. "If you're prepared to be completely honest with me and tell me everything I want to know, then we'll talk. If not, then you'd better leave."

Play-acting or not, tears started trickling down her cheeks. Under other circumstances, it might have been easy to sympathize with her; she looked for all the world like a lost, confused, emotion-wracked teenager, and one would have wanted to console her and drive the hurt away, restoring her faith in humanity. But, this was Melissa Waterman, and she was *not* a normal teenager – not even a normal human being – and I was not about to treat her as such, not after all I had been through. Perhaps that was an unprofessional attitude to take, but I found it easy to steel myself against her lost-little-girl mask.

"Please don't do this to me, Ken. I – I will be honest with you, but" – she glanced over her shoulder – "not now, not here."

"Well, don't expect me to hold my breath waiting. You'd better go now. You're disturbing everyone here."

She surveyed the assembly on the lawn with a barely disguised sneer. Her amethyst eyes appeared brighter then, and I feared the worst. Since I had my back to everyone else, I could not see the expressions on their faces, though I could imagine they were all filled with horror by her unholy scrutiny. I did hear several gasps or short cries of terror here and there. Her eyes softened when they returned to me. Still, I remained impassive (or as impassive as I could be under the circumstances). Melissa stretched out her hand to touch me. I regarded it with disdain, and she pulled it back. More tears streamed down her face. At last, she turned and fled across the lawn toward the woods. I released the breath I had been holding and, behind me, sighs of relief sounded audibly.

"Thank God!" one female nurse murmured. "I thought she'd never leave."

"Yeah," muttered Jones next to her. "I wanted to break her neck."

I turned on the pair and glared at them. Both flinched as if I had taken a swing at them (and I did entertain such a thought).

"If I hear any more remarks like that from either of you – or from any other nurse – I'll do my damnedest to get you fired. I won't tolerate petty behavior. Do I make myself clear?"

Jones swallowed compulsively and nodded nervously. The woman blanched and added her own acquiescence. One of the "positive" aspects of my "reputation" was an instant respect. Thoroughly cowed, the pair shuffled off to be somewhere else. I waved to the group with an air of dismissal.

"OK, everybody, back to your volleyball. The show's over."

Both patients and nurses were happy to comply with my request and to put the incident behind them. As soon as the matches resumed, I rejoined Ben. The old man had been watching the tableau intently all this time; and, when I approached, he shook his head in wonder.

"Boy, Ah don' know what dat wuz all about, an' Ah don' *want* to know. But, Ah reckon dey wuz some pow'ful feelin's at work."

"Right on, my man. If you only knew *how* powerful."

"No, sah! Ah fink Ah'd lahk to stay ignorant, if y'all don' mahnd."

"I can dig it, Ben. I wish *I* could forget everything I know about Melissa."

I did not see Melissa again until late in the evening, but she was hardly out of my mind (as Nan had so thoughtfully pointed out). After the incident at the volleyball match, the rest of the day proceeded quietly, and I looked forward to my date with the lovely Dr. Vengtman the Younger.

A few hours in her company (and in her bed), I believed, was just the right prescription to chase away the doldrums that had swallowed me up lately.

I picked her up shortly after six o'clock, and we drove around for a while discussing our day's business and generally unwinding. Eventually, we ended up at the Fox Valley Center on the far east side of Aurora, the premier shopping mall in the far western suburbs (actually the largest component of a much more extensive network). I remembered that my colleague at R-PSL who was familiar with the area had recommended an eatery in the mall that featured broasted chicken, and I suggested to Nan that we check it out.

The mall – and the eatery – was crowded (not unusual for a Friday evening), and we had to wait half an hour for a table. In the meantime, we had a cocktail and continued our conversation. Naturally, I appreciated Nan as a sex partner. But, any woman who can hold her own in the dialogue department also appeals to me. Other men might not care, but I do. No bimbos for me! And Nan was as good a conversationalist as she was a sex partner; she could talk shop or politics or the weather as easily as breathing. I could have talked with her for hours. That night, however, I found my mind wandering again, and Nan's voice seemed to be a million miles away. Even after we had been seated, I felt as if I was watching someone else go through the motions of ordering.

"Ken, dear," she said at one point in an exasperated tone, "you're doing it again."

"Eh? What's that?"

"I see your body, but I don't see *you. You* are somewhere else." She placed her hand on mine. "It's Melissa, isn't it?"

"Oh, God, I'm sorry, Nan. I'm becoming a real jerk. Yeah, who else? I'm afraid yesterday's business has gotten under my skin, and it's just eating me up. I won't have any peace until I get the answers to all the questions in my mind." I looked her square in the eye. "And it all boils down to Melissa's file in your uncle's office."

She regarded me steadily for a moment or two. Her face remained impassive, but I could well believe that her mind was in turmoil. We'd had this conversation before, and she knew where I was going with it. She didn't like the idea one bit since it involved betraying the doctor-patient relationship and her uncle's trust in her. I didn't like the idea either, for that matter, and I wished there was another way than burglary. Yet, I was overcome by a sense of urgency, a sense that something horrible lurked inside the Home and that I had to act quickly to thwart it. I was entangled in a giant web of intrigue and deception, and survival depended upon my disentangling it, i.e. "enlightened self-interest." Call it delusions of grandeur – Dr. Kenneth Maxwell, Savior of the Earth! – but there it was. I hated to involve Nan in this affair, but she held the key – quite literally – to the puzzle. Presently, a long, breathy sigh issued from her mouth, and she bowed her head.

"You're determined to get into Uncle Lowell's office?"

"Yes. I'll break down the freakin' door if I have to, but I'd rather not. I just have to have that freakin' file!"

"I must admit to a certain curiosity myself in light of what I've seen and heard about. I'll probably hate myself in the morning for what I'm about to do, but – for the sake of your peace of mind and…certain feelings I've developed toward you – I'll go along with this scheme of yours." Her head snapped up, and she pierced me with a cold-steel glare. "You'd better be right about this, Doctor Maxwell; otherwise, I'll see that you never work here again."

"Fair enough. Can you get into the office tonight?"

She checked her watch.

"Uncle Lowell should be gone by now. He was scheduled for an evening flight to Houston. He'll be attending an all-day conference on behavior modification and giving the keynote address tomorrow evening."

"All right. Let's get out of here."

As luck would have it, the traffic was unusually heavy, and I found myself on the brink of exasperation. I drove like a madman, weaving back and forth from one lane to another in order to have a few yards' clear space in front of me at all times; and I passed other vehicles in rapid succession, taking risks I never would have ordinarily, even during my wild days on the South Side. Beside me, Nan gritted her teeth and gripped the car seat in desperation. It seemed to take forever to reach the Home, but at last we pulled into the drive.

For some unfathomable reason, my mind flashed back to the morning I had first made this trip up the driveway. How many centuries ago had it been? Surely, it couldn't have been a mere two weeks! The innocent-looking lilac bushes, so neatly trimmed, had once represented horticultural art. Now, they formed a formidable barrier, a great divide beyond which I courted destruction. The lawn, so immaculately manicured, had once been a finely-woven carpet, inviting one to sink one's bare feet in it. Now, it was a tar pit, ready to swallow me up if I came too close to it. The buildings had once offered a new opportunity to advance my career and a new chapter in my personal life. Now, I saw them as monuments to youthful folly and a dead-end on the road of Life, a crushing end to naiveté and innocence. Never had I dreamed that such a day as that day would have come to pass and that I would have shunned the Vengtman Home for the Emotionally Disturbed forever. And now, here I was, rushing into that snare and trap like History's greatest fool!

I pulled up before the front entrance and tried to calm my suddenly jangled nerves. I glanced at Nan, who continued to stare straight ahead. God only knew what *she* was thinking just then. Undoubtedly, she was regretting having volunteered to be the "assistant fool"!

"Are you OK?" I whispered.

"I think I lost my wits in the restaurant. I *know* I lost my stomach on the road. Why shouldn't I be OK?"

I grinned in spite of myself.

"At least, you haven't lost your sense of humor."

"That, my darling, may be next on the list. Let's get this over with."

We piled out of the car and hurried inside. Two nurses passed us by as we walked toward the Director's office. Their appearance gave us a fright, and I might have lost my resolve then and there, except that I didn't want to show weakness in front of Nan, especially after I had practically drafted her into that venture. Call it "male vanity," if you like; it was the least thing I was guilty of that evening. The nurses were pleasantly surprised to see us but, happily, did not see fit to challenge us. I was not in a mood for interrogation or small talk.

As before, during my initiation as a "cat burglar," the hallways were transformed into long, dark tunnels with no end in sight. They stretched into infinity and drained our energies as we traversed them. We quick-marched the entire distance; yet, the target seemed no closer than when we had entered the building. The sounds of our footsteps reverberated throughout the Home like kettledrums, and our heartbeats underscored the sense of impending doom. I kept looking over my shoulder in an irrational attempt to spot lurkers in the shadows spying on us. We were both breathless by the time we reached our goal. I looked at Nan expectantly. She fumbled in her purse, withdrew a single key on a red plastic tag, and wordlessly handed it to me.

"Just out of curiosity," I murmured in order to break the tension, "how come you have a key to this office?"

"Uncle Lowell keeps all of his personal papers in here. It isn't well-known, but he has cancer as a result of – he believes – the Three-Mile Island incident in 1979 when he was established in Harrisburg, Pennsylvania. I'm his nearest living relative, and he's given me power-of-attorney in case he can't function anymore. I'm also executrix of his estate upon his death."

Cancer: the twentieth century's biological time-bomb which ticks away benignly for years and then explodes and breaks down all of an organism's bodily functions. That had to explain the Great Man's gaunt appearance. Whatever toxic agent he had been exposed to had finally made its mark on him; once visible, the disease would progress rapidly until he expired. Yet, why had he kept it a secret? Pride? A sense of denial? Disregard for self-preservation? Eventually, he would have become so debilitated that he could no longer conceal his condition or function in his profession, and the shock wave of realization would have shaken the psychological community to its foundations. There was no shame in admitting illness, and he could certainly seek help without question.

Still, that was a matter for the future. At that time, I had other fish to fry.

"Lucky for me that you do."

"Yes, isn't it?" Nan replied flatly.

As I inserted the key into the lock, the creepy-crawly feeling I'd experienced before suddenly came over me, and I quickly turned around. I couldn't believe my eyes! Crouched against the baseboard on the opposite side of the hallway, peering intently at us, was the damned raccoon that had followed me in previously (I was pretty sure it was the same one). Apparently, its monitoring duties were not at an end. Alarmed by the expression on my face, Nan followed my gaze, spotted the animal, and clutched at my arm.

"My God!" she breathed. "How did that get in here?"

"I don't know. I can tell you that it's been trailing me for days. Melissa… sent it to spy on me."

"Ken, you can't be serious!"

"I wish I weren't, babe. It's been like a giant nightmare for me." I brushed her cheek with my fingers. "Now you know why I've been so anxious to get in here."

We entered the office and risked turning on the lights. Quite possibly, should one of the duty nurses wander by and make an inquiry, Nan could invent a plausible excuse. Who was going to question the Director's niece? The only danger was that the Director himself might learn of this intrusion through the grapevine. Nan might be excused because of family ties. But, I had no *legitimate* reason to be there, and his suspicions would surely – and justifiably –be raised. I couldn't count on Nan lying for me and jeopardizing her own career. She had already warned me of that. And I certainly didn't want her hating me for the rest of either of our lives.

To my great relief, I did not have to search very hard for Melissa's file. It was lying – open – on the middle of Dr. Vengtman's desk. Obviously, he had been consulting it and forgotten about it in his rush to get to the airport. I smiled tightly. Finally, something was going right for me. Curiously, the file had no color coding whatsoever, neither in the matter of illness or in case-disposition; one would have to conclude that Melissa either had no illness or had not yet been admitted as a patient (whether as an "original" or a "transfer"). If that was the case, then why was she here? And why make up a file on her? The queasiness in my stomach was beginning to return, and I dreaded learning the answers to those (and many other) questions.

Paper-clipped to the cover of the folder was a note the Director had written to himself. It read simply:

"Ask M about remarks made to KM."

Was that the "spirit" in which Dr. Vengtman intended to take my views on Melissa's strange behavior? By grilling her on whatever had passed between her and me? The reference to me was obvious, for there was only one "KM" on the premises. So, what did he hope to gain? Did he believe I had been interfering in his practice even after he had "requested" me not to? Or – I recalled Melissa's allusions to such an emotional state in regards to Mathias Hinkelman – was he envious of her attachment to me? Surely, this was not the Lowell Vengtman I knew. Something was rotten in the State of Illinois!

Despite the lack of coding, there was an admissions form inside, on top where it should be. It was well-worn from a great deal of handling, and a couple of the corners were dog-eared. Moreover, some of the handwritten wording had begun to fade. Enough was legible, however, to fill me in on some of Melissa's background, and what I learned floored me.

"Nan, listen to this. Melissa was born in Goldsboro, Pennsylvania, in September of 1979 and admitted to your uncle's facility in Harrisburg in 1984. She's been his patient *since she was five years old!*"

"And he took her wherever he went?" she responded with amazement. "Even *I* didn't know that. But why? What sort of disorder does she have that requires such long and close supervision?"

I flipped through the next several pages. Melissa had been orphaned at the age of four when her parents died in an auto accident. She was placed in a state orphanage; I read a copy of a request filed by a court-appointed guardian to transfer her to a foster home. This was accompanied by several affidavits by staff members of the orphanage concerning "odd" behavior; according to the reports, her moods shifted from willfulness to near-autism – typical of bi-polar personality disorder – and she complained of hearing "voices" in her head. After a year of failing to cope with her problems, the orphanage called in the region's foremost psychologist, Lowell Vengtman. He confirmed the original diagnosis; and, on his own hook, he made arrangements to have her transferred to his facility in Harrisburg. To anyone's knowledge, she was the youngest person on record to be admitted to a sanitarium, but there had been little notice taken by the news media.

Something nagged at the back of my mind – *two* somethings actually – and I leafed back to the initial report. There it was, bold as brass, and a chill ran up my spine. Melissa's parents had died while avoiding a dog which had suddenly appeared on the road. Nurse Clement had died while avoiding a deer. Another person might have called these two events a "co-incidence"; yet, where Melissa Waterman was concerned, "co-incidence" was the *last* word I would have used to describe the parallel. I said as much to Nan, and she stared at me in disbelief.

"Really, Ken! You don't mean to imply that Melissa is guilty of... *murder?*"

"I'm just making an observation, honey. I'd rather not think about the implications. Too scary. Yet, her rapport with animals – your uncle's words, you should know – is beyond question – as far as I'm concerned, anyway. Just how well do any of us know her? You uncle probably knows her best, but he hasn't been willing to discuss her case publicly."

"Come to think of it, do you remember my telling you that he had become moody at one point and none of the family ever knew why? Well, it just occurs to me that his mood changed shortly after the time Melissa was admitted to the Harrisburg Home. Do you think there's a connection?"

"Right now, I'm ready to believe the moon is made of green cheese. The second something that's bothering me is Harrisburg, 1979. Didn't you say that was the time of the Three-Mile Island incident, when your uncle thinks he might have developed his cancer?"

"Right. Everyone in the metropolitan area had a radiation scare." Sudden realization lit up her face like a hundred-watt bulb. *"And Goldsboro is a suburb of Harrisburg!* My God! Was Melissa's disorder radiation-induced?

There are medical studies in the literature to support the hypothesis. See if Uncle Lowell mentions it."

Now I sat down at the desk in order to be more comfortable. Nan perched herself on the arm of the chair and put her arms around my shoulders.

The remainder of the file consisted of one transcript after another of Dr. Vengtman's counseling sessions with his "patient" over the years. The first was dated October 22, 1984, two days after Melissa had been admitted to the Home in Harrisburg. A quick glance at the last transcript revealed yesterday's date. The counseling sessions occurred as often as four times a week. At first, they were short in length out of respect for Melissa's tender age; as she grew older, however, the interviews lengthened. Often, the interviewer had hand-written in the margin comments and questions as afterthoughts, a typical psychoanalytical technique; I had indulged in it myself during my stint at R-PSL and continued it at the Home. At first, the commentary was of a general nature as the interviewer carefully probed his subject's psyche in order to ascertain her disorder. But, abruptly, the marginal notes took a bizarre turn, and I found myself reading about Melissa's "developing mental powers."

I must confess that, at that juncture, I wasn't a bit surprised. I had already been introduced – rather rudely, if truth be told – to Melissa's "developing mental powers." I didn't need to read about them in a twelve-year-old medical file. Nevertheless, learning that Lowell Vengtman had discovered them long ago filled me with unease. Melissa's cryptic remarks began to flit around in my consciousness and screech for my attention. The Great Man's comments suggested that, not only was he cognizant of the girl's true nature but he was also utterly fascinated by it. A case in point was a short marginal note:

> I am convinced that M.'s interaction with non-human organisms is not feigned behavior. Incredible as it may sound, she actually does communicate with animals, and they with her. I have witnessed this phenomenon many times myself.

And, further on:

> M. continues to amaze me with her mental feats. The
> mechanism by which she achieves this, however, continues
> to elude me.

At no time did he hint that he planned to divulge whatever he had
learned to anyone, not even trusted colleagues. Rather, he intended to
keep Melissa all to himself as if he were conducting some far-reaching
experiment for his personal edification. What had he hoped to gain by
concealing what Melissa Waterman was? If her abilities were genuine
– and I for one no longer doubted them – then she must be examined
by the scientific community and her abilities put to good use. She was
too valuable a resource to be hoarded by one individual – even the likes
of the eminent Lowell Vengtman. The truth of this was borne out by
Melissa's behavior. She was almost an animal herself, acting purely on
instinct, amoral in nature; she required guidance, not just the sort of
control that Dr. Vengtman had apparently rendered over her. Without
it, she was capable of all sorts of mischief. Perhaps it was already too late;
perhaps she had reached the point of irredeemability. That remained to
be seen, however. What was imperative was that she be turned over to the
authorities – with or without Lowell Vengtman's co-operation.

All this while, Nan had not said a word. If, in the beginning, she was
as alarmed as I was over those revelations, she was now keeping her feelings
in check. And who could blame her? We were, after all, speaking of a close
relative, a man whom she had known, loved, and admired most of her life.
It would have been difficult for her to believe that he had a darker side
to his character. Not until I read aloud the word "telepath" did she react
audibly.

"Ken!" she exclaimed. "Do you realize what that means? It means that
Uncle Lowell thinks Melissa is a genetic freak, some sort of – of –"

"Mutant," came a gravelly voice from the doorway.

"Dr. Vengtman!"

"Uncle Lowell!"

The Director stepped into his office, slowly, deliberately. Gaunt he may
have been, but he was still capable of fury; a dark rage covered his thin face,
and his rheumy eyes blazed with righteous indignation. It was a side of the
Great Man I (or anyone else, I'm sure) had never seen before – and never
hoped to again. He halted in the middle of the room, his fists clenching
and unclenching. As he glared at each of us in turn, it was anyone's guess
which he deemed the guiltier of this invasion of his privacy. Instinctively, I

307

rose to my feet and braced myself for whatever might come. I didn't think he would be so reckless as to attack me physically; on the other hand, I was beginning to realize I did not know him as well as I had thought. Nan moved closer to me (if that was possible) and gripped my arm. It didn't require an expert in psychology to understand the significance of the gesture. *Our* expert recognized it at once, and it served to fuel his rage.

"I returned," he stated finally in a low but even tone, "to get some notes I'd forgotten. But not in time, it appears, to prevent burglars from ransacking my office. I doubt either of you has a legitimate reason for being here, so I'll just ask you what you hoped to accomplish."

I held up Melissa's file.

"Possibly the key to a few mysteries, Doctor. I've been attempting to understand what happened to Mathias Hinkelman, and I believed that learning more about Melissa would shed some light on the subject. What I have learned, however, is even more interesting. Would you care to explain what this is all about?"

It was sheer bravado on my part, a colossal bluff in order to divert attention away from my own unethical behavior. The Director called my bluff by stepping forward and ripping the file out of my hand. Then he smiled wickedly.

"So, you've discovered that Melissa is a...special case. Her parents lived half a mile from Three-Mile Island at the time of the nuclear melt-down. Her mother was three months pregnant, and I'm certain the fetus received a large dose of radiation. A genetic mutation was created." I could not, nor did I want to, contain an expression of incredulity; but, in order to forestall any protest on my part, he held up a hand for forbearance. "I know what you're thinking, Doctor. Most mutagenic agents produce only deleterious birth defects. Most, but not all. Melissa is that rare exception."

"Really, Dr. Vengtman!" I fumed, unable to hold back my doubts. "Atomic mutation? That's 1950's sci-fi stuff, and bad sci-fi at that. We're closing in on the twenty-first century."

Now, he held up the file.

"You've read this, young man. And you've observed Melissa's behavior. Can you really deny the evidence?"

He had me there. The "evidence" – while it wouldn't have stood up in a court of law – or a board of inquiry, for that matter – was undeniable. The Director believed in her abilities, and I was 99% convinced myself. Proving it to outsiders might be a problem, but the "evidence" was there for anyone to see. Given the rapport Melissa had with animals, it was only a short step toward accepting the possibility she could do the same with human beings. And hadn't I already had a demonstration of that little feat? The visions I'd seen when she became overcome with emotion, the blank looks on the patients when she became angry, her "voice" echoing in my head as I fled incontinently from the "ritual" in the woods – all these had been a result of a force of will alone – *her* will. The notion of atomic mutation might seem impossible only to those who hadn't experienced what I had; if they had, they would never doubt again.

"Whispering in my mind," Mathias Hinkelman had said over and over again. He had provoked jealousy in a telepath, and she reacted in typical teenaged fashion by tormenting her "faithless lover" in the only manner she knew how. And, because he had not been able to understand – except, at the last, on an instinctual basis – what was happening to him, he went over the edge and killed himself. His could easily have been my fate as well, since I hadn't been as responsive to Melissa's "overtures" as she might have wished. Yet, she hadn't desired to destroy me but had gone out of her way to avoid a nasty confrontation. Why had she restrained herself on my account? Perhaps I shouldn't have looked a gift horse in the mouth but counted myself lucky to still be in one piece (comparatively speaking).

"Assuming this is all true, Uncle Lowell," Nan jumped into the conversation, "why haven't you made this public? Think of the valuable research into brain processes that could be achieved. What have you been doing for the past twelve years?"

"I should think that was fairly obvious," the Director snorted. "I'm doing the work I was trained for – understanding the human mind. And I'm using a most remarkable tool – Melissa's gift (and it *is* a gift) – to cure my patients. Why do you think I've been so successful in my practice?"

It didn't take a rocket scientist to imagine the benefits of having a telepath doing psychoanalysis. A mind-reader could see past the lies we all tell ourselves to whitewash our inner worlds, see past the fantasies we create to puff up our fragile egos, see past the rationalizations we invent to justify wholly irrational behavior, see past the thousand and one defenses on the conscious and subconscious levels we erect to protect ourselves from Reality. The mind-reader could penetrate the barriers with ease and expose the fears and the horrors and the secret desires that lay buried in the primeval ooze – expose them *gradually*, of course, so that the patient might see them for the impotent things they really were. Reporting these findings to a sympathetic profession would advance the science of psychology a thousand-fold; in the right hands, a climate of mental health could be achieved in a matter of months instead of the plodding years it usually required.

And there was the kicker: *was* Melissa Waterman in the "right hands"? Lowell Vengtman's reputation was secure; he had the respect and admiration of the entire profession. His lectures were widely attended, and his books – if not actually required reading in college curricula – were highly recommended reading in medical schools. He wasn't a fabulously wealthy man, because he had chosen not to be one. His dedication to his work was unparalleled, and no one had grounds to challenge his authority.

Until now.

To learn that his reputation was a house of cards based not upon the techniques he had pioneered but upon unproven "shortcuts" involving an unstable teenaged girl would be difficult to accept. Worse, he had covered himself with subterfuge and deceit and taken credit where none should have been given. I felt...devastated. I had practically *worshipped* the ground he walked on. Now, his feet of clay were revealed to me. Melissa had labeled him an "evil man." Once, that allegation might have been dismissed as hyperbole and teenage rebelliousness; now, the facts of the matter painted, if not an *evil* personage, then a *devious* one which could lash out at its critics in unthinkable ways. From that point, I had to be careful about what I said and how I said it.

"Dr. Vengtman, Melissa told me, more than once, that you forced her to do...certain acts against her will. What exactly is your relationship with her?"

"I'm her doctor. Also her guardian, court-appointed under the laws of Pennsylvania."

"Are you also her jailor?"

That must have touched a nerve, for a fierce scowl raced across his face like a mad bull.

"I believe we've discussed this subject sufficiently," he growled. "The question now arises of what to do about your discovery."

I'm sure I had read too many mystery novels, because my skin started to crawl at that moment. Nan must have caught the creeps from me, for she huddled against me. I envisioned us both lying in a pool of our own blood, the latest victims of a "mad scientist" whose trail of corpses stretched across the nation – the corpses of persons overly inquisitive about his affairs. A ridiculous notion, to be sure – would the eminent Lowell Vengtman kill his own niece? – yet, he had kept a dark secret over the years. What else might he have been capable of?

"Short of cold-blooded murder," I responded with much trepidation, "there's not much you can do."

"You're quite right, Dr. Maxwell. I'm not prepared to go that far. But, neither can I afford any ugly publicity. Thus, I must do what I've had to do before in these circumstances."

"What's that, Uncle Lowell?"

"Re-locate in another part of the country. Melissa and I will simply set up shop in a new Home and start our work anew."

"No, we won't," came a second, younger voice from the doorway.

Melissa stood there stiff as a statue, a pale form silhouetted by the darkness of the hallway. Her face was full of grim determination, and her amethyst eyes were bright and burning. I caught a glimpse of erupting volcanoes. Beside me, Nan stiffened and gasped; she too now understood the true nature of Melissa's awesome power. The girl was focused on the Director, however, and it was anyone's guess what *he* was seeing in his mind. The hard expression on his face hadn't altered one iota; yet, his eyes darted back and forth as if he were under a great strain.

Melissa was not alone either. Flanking her were her two "lieutenants," those damned raccoons who were her chief spies. The one which had followed Nan and me into the building must have "reported" back to her. Had the other one been trailing Dr. Vengtman the Elder? One of the animals kept a steady eye on him, while the other monitored Nan and me. They sat on their haunches in imitation of a military posture.

The Director worked up a half-smile and asked in a tone designed to calm Melissa and to take control of the situation:

"I beg your pardon?"

"I said I'm not going with you this time."

"And why not, my dear?"

She turned her attention to me. Her face softened ever so slightly, and her eyes dimmed somewhat. I did not feel one bit re-assured, since she had already proven herself to be very unpredictable. I swallowed a large lump in my throat.

"I'm going to stay here and work with Ken – Dr. Maxwell. He's a good and kind man. He wants to help people." (I had to wonder if she was being sincere or sarcastic and if I was being set up for something nasty.) "He won't force me to do...*evil* things."

"'Evil things'? Is that how you see it, Melissa? I simply conducted a few experiments, utilizing your gift. It wasn't any different from what you had been doing on your own initiative."

"Excuse me," I interjected. "I seem to have walked into the middle of this movie. Do you mind explaining what the hell you're talking about?"

"He used me, Ken. He's used me for years. He hasn't cured anybody, except when I was helping him. *I* did all the work, and *he* took all the credit."

"Nonsense," the Director retorted. "It was a completely collaborative effort. Melissa is being overly melodramatic, Dr. Maxwell, perhaps because of this schoolgirl crush she has on you. I think she needs a change of scenery."

"I told you," the girl fumed, "I'm not going with you." She closed her eyes briefly and took a deep breath. "Ken, you wanted to know the truth. All right, I'll tell you everything you should know about Lowell Vengtman – even if it means…incriminating myself."

"Melissa," the old man muttered, "I will caution you to hold your tongue." The same rage he had shown Nan and me upon his entrance into the office now returned. The tension in the air was thick enough to walk on. "Remember who and what you are, and what will happen to you if you're discovered."

"I don't care any more. I can't live with the fact that you made me – *you made me kill Mathias!*"

At last! Admission of culpability! It then remained to discover how she had accomplished the act – though I suspected I already knew how from having read her file.

"I've suspected as much, Melissa," I acknowledged. "I'm pleased you've decided to be candid."

"I didn't want to hurt him, because – well, yes, I did have a crush on him, and, yes, I was jealous of Dr. Maddie – but not enough to cause harm to him. It was all because of *his*" – she gestured at the Director – "so-called 'experiments.'"

"Surely, Doctor," Dr. Vengtman huffed, "you aren't going to give credence to these wild accusations? I tell you she's been under considerable strain lately."

"No doubt," I shot back. "But I'm willing to hear what she has to say. I've seen and heard too much these past few days to discount any explanation. I demand to know exactly what was done to Mathias Hinkelman."

"*You demand?* You break into my office – like a common criminal – and rifle through my private papers. Worse, you corrupt my own flesh-

and-blood and persuade her to assist you in your dirty work. You attempt to destroy everything I've worked toward, and you make *demands*? I think you've overstepped the bounds, young man. Frankly, I'm disappointed with you, and I may have to re-evaluate your employment here."

"Spare us the histrionics, Uncle Lowell," Nan interjected. "Something is going on here that needs to be aired." She chewed her lip for a second or two, then: "And, since you've given me power-of-attorney in case of your incapacitation, I have a right to know."

Whether or not she had ever stood up to him on any matter was a moot point. Quite possibly, she was the one person who admired him more than I did, and she had perhaps always deferred to his judgment. It was a tremendous psychological shift for her to take my side; feelings for me might have had something to do with it, but I believed then (and still do) that, like me, the truth was more important than familial ties and loyalties. Lowell Vengtman knew it as well as Nan and I did, and we all sensed that the "balance of power" was tilting away from him. Nan's defiance seemed to have taken the wind out of his sails, and he literally sagged before my eyes and aged years in the space of milliseconds.

"Very well," he responded in a tired voice. "I'll tell you exactly what happened. If you attempt to repeat what I say, I'll deny it. You have no *tangible* proof; it'll be my word against yours. And my word still carries considerable weight.

"As you've already surmised, Melissa is a telepath. She communicates in the form of mental images; that is why she can 'talk' to animals which are non-verbal creatures. *How* she accomplishes this form of communication I have yet to determine, though I have some theories; perhaps her genetic code mutated while she was still in the womb, and hitherto fore unknown neural pathways were opened up. An autopsy might provide some answers in that respect." Here, he smiled most wickedly. I shuddered involuntarily, and I felt Nan reacting similarly. "In any event, I've also discovered that she can delve into the subconscious – which likewise deals in imagery – and read emotional states as easily as you or I read a printed page. Over the years, I've used her gift to reach into a patient's psyche, observe what was amiss there, and introduce 'suggestions' I knew would counteract his/her disorder."

"You actually *manipulated* a person's thoughts?" I marveled. "That – that's...*immoral!*"

"Come now, Doctor. Our thoughts are manipulated every day, through laws and moral codes, peer pressure, the educational process, and especially advertising. All I did was to bypass the externalities and go directly to the core of the matter. In any event, 'morality' is a subjective quality, as you should know. As long as I was able to achieve my goals, questions of morality didn't concern me."

"The ends justify the means?"

"Quite so. In due time, having seen the positive side of Melissa's talent, I naturally desired to learn about the *negative* side; I sought to know what would happen when she planted purely destructive imagery in a person's mind. At first, she balked at the idea, and I had to remind her that, without my protection, the authorities would lock her up and/or experiment on *her*. It remained then to find a suitable test subject, one who wouldn't be missed if he self-destructed."

"You used Mathias as a *guinea pig*?" Nan exclaimed. "You thought so little of him that he became 'fair game'?"

"Hinkelman was a cipher," the Director retorted with an undertone of cruelty in his voice. "You've read his writings. Are they the product of intellect? The man was capable only of attacking his betters."

"That may be, Uncle Lowell, but he was still a human being."

"More 'morality,' my dear? Wasted on the likes of Mathias Hinkelman. He was strictly cannon fodder. As you know, I have a reputation for hand-picking my staff based upon their potential for intellectual growth. Hinkelman was the exception. I hired him for one purpose only.

"Unfortunately, I couldn't begin my experiment on him immediately. Melissa had the bad taste to develop an infatuation for the man, to the point where she was assisting him – without his knowledge, of course – in the same manner as she had assisted me. I had the Devil's own time trying to persuade her to co-operate. As it happened, Hinkelman himself inadvertently provided the convincing argument when he took up with Madeleine; Melissa became insanely jealous and wanted to get back at him. I had no problems after that."

I stole a glance at the girl. Her head was bowed, and her body trembled all over. For a brief moment, I thought to reach out to her in sympathy for the agonizing memories she must have been experiencing. I instantly had second thoughts, realizing that she was not deserving of any sympathy whatsoever. In the first place, if she had been probing the psyches of Hinkelman's patients, then it explained the "success" he had reported in guiding them toward mental health. Melissa had replaced the negative imagery in their subconsciouses with a positive set – not out of altruism but out of a schoolgirl infatuation. Had she then "assisted" me as well due to her infatuation with me? Was that the reason I had seen some "progress" in my patients' recovery? The fact that those efforts might have been the result of telepathic manipulation and not of my own abilities as a doctor did nothing for my sense of self-worth, a good reason to withdraw sympathy.

And that was not the half of it, as I pondered further. In the matter of my predecessor's wholly unorthodox methodologies, what had been the impetus? I was afraid – very afraid – that I knew the answer. Melissa not only manipulated the minds of the patients, she also worked her "magic" on the *counselor* by planting "suggestions" in *his* mind. It was a gross and disgusting idea: someone walking about in your mind without so much as a by-your-leave. I felt sick and unclean at the same time. It would have been very easy to work up an intense hatred of Melissa Waterman.

"And so we commenced," the Director continued. "What thoughts Melissa put in Hinkelman's mind, I can't say. She refused to tell me. Still, I observed that he was being affected by her mind-games. Over the course of eight months, he slowly fell apart psychologically until he reached the point of total despair and committed suicide."

"Oh, Uncle Lowell!" Nan wailed. I saw the tears streaming down her cheeks, and I had to strain to keep my own emotions in check. "How could you? I used to look up to you. Now, I learn that you're a – a *monster!*"

"A 'monster,' eh? Not guilty, my dear. I'm a scientist, using all available tools." He sighed heavily. "Now that you've heard the whole story, you may make of it what you will." He turned to Melissa. "If you're through wallowing in self-pity, go to your room and start packing."

"You're leaving *tonight?*" Nan yelped. "What about the Home? Or the staff?"

"You'll find an envelope in the top drawer of my desk, addressed to Harry. It contains instructions in the event of my leaving. I took this precaution soon after I opened this facility, in case this eventuality arose."

"Excuse me, Dr. Vengtman," I said as boldly as I could, "but this is highly...unprofessional."

"You're a fine one to talk, Dr. Maxwell, considering your current actions." He looked at Melissa. "Are you still here? Go to your room!"

"No, I won't!" she screeched. "I'm staying here!"

"I'm your guardian, young lady," he barked, ignoring us, "and you'll do as I say." He stepped over to the girl and grabbed her by the wrist. "Now, move!"

What happened next I'll never forget as long as I live. Melissa's body stiffened, and her face morphed into a grotesquery, a mask of feral rage. Worse, her amethyst eyes blazed like a furnace. In my head, there came an image of a four-alarm fire. I staggered backwards and to one side; Nan also reeled backwards and toward me, and we nearly knocked each other to the floor. At the last second, we held on to one another and remained upright. Out of the corner of my eye, I saw the Director similarly affected; he released his grip on Melissa's wrist, went pallid, and stared at her in shock and confusion. Apparently, this was the first time she had assaulted him mentally. In the back of my mind, I wondered if he had ever believed she would.

Melissa was not finished venting her anger, however. She made a fist but, rather than striking her tormentor, she raised it and held it upright. At once, I heard a tremendous racket in the hallway, the squealing and yipping and growling of a horde of creatures. Had she then brought her entire menagerie with her? As if in answer to the unspoken question, dozens of animals – much of the same bunch I had seen in the clearing the day before – streamed through the door. The majority was squirrels, but I singled out several more raccoons, a couple of foxes, and even a gopher. They all gathered around Melissa's feet and stood poised for action. Dr. Vengtman blanched in horror. I may have myself, for I was beginning to understand what must have happened to Ray in the woods. He had been wandering about, looking for an escape route, and come upon Melissa's merry little band; and, in order to protect her secret, she had sent the horde after him. And a bloody mess they had made of him too! I had a sick feeling that a "repeat performance" was in the making.

Even so, I was still unprepared for the eventuality. In the blink of an eye, Melissa unclenched her fist and waved her hand at the Director. As one entity, the horde attacked. He cried out hoarsely and, beside me, Nan screamed hysterically. The animals leaped upon him and covered him like a blanket, biting and clawing in murderous fury. He tried to knock them away, but they were too numerous; they pressed the attack again and again. Melissa remained impassive, and her amethyst eyes glowed even brighter and focused on a point beyond her target. Under the force of dozens of biting and clawing animals, Lowell Vengtman dropped to the floor, wailing in anguish. And still they came at him.

Once I had collected my wits, I thought to go to the Director's rescue. I took only two steps. The two raccoons which had originally accompanied Melissa into the office and which had stood apart from the fray now swung into action and came at me, apparently at another silent command from their mistress. They did not attack me, however; their job was to keep me at bay until their comrades had completed their "mission." Melissa was still "protecting" me! So, I was powerless to assist Dr. Vengtman. I fell to my knees and beat the floor with my fists in utter impotence.

"Melissa!" I croaked. "Chill out, girl! *Please!*"

The girl now looked at me, and her mask of vengeance melted away ever so slightly, to be replaced by adolescent confusion over my plight. On an impulse, I played what I hoped was a trump card.

"Melissa! I – I – *I hate you!*"

Confusion gave way to childish fright as the import of my words sunk into her consciousness.

"No-o-o-o!" she whimpered. "You mustn't!"

"If you love me, as you claim, you got to stop fucking around!"

She gazed upon the huddled, bloodied form of Lowell Vengtman and moaned softly. Her amethyst eyes ceased their glowing, and she assumed her lost-little-girl look again. She waved her hand back and forth with quick motions; immediately, her menagerie halted its attack and, as one unit, turned and scampered out of the office. I heard their squeaks and yips and growls fade into the distance and heaved a huge sigh of relief. Melissa regarded me fearfully, and her lip trembled.

"Ken – darling," she whispered. "I – I'm *sorry.*"

Then she too was gone.

Nan and I hurried to Dr. Vengtman's side. His clothing was in shreds, but he was still alive. He bled profusely from scores of tiny wounds; hardly a spot on his body had been spared. This was how Ray must have died: his life's blood oozing away, and no one around to help him. The Director continued to wail mindlessly. Nan was still in hysterics and, both to get her away from that scene of carnage and to occupy her mind, I directed her to go to the infirmary for the first-aid kit and to round up however many nurses she could find. She was reluctant to leave her uncle, and I practically had to push her out the door. As soon as she staggered off, I dialed 9-1-1.

When the paramedics arrived, they were as shocked by the sight as I had expected them to be. No human being who has even the least bit of compassion could have gazed upon the victim of a vicious attack and not experience a twinge of nausea. Nevertheless, they went straight to work. I had staunched the bleeding as best I could, but there was still much to do that only trained professionals could handle. Ironically, the sheriff's deputies who investigated the incident were the same pair who had answered the previous call at Ray's demise. To say that they were skeptical of my explanation that the Director had been attacked by wild animals which had somehow found their way into the building was an understatement.

"I understand," the deputy-in-charge had said in an attempt to sort things out, "how someone might be attacked in the *woods*, Dr. Maxwell. But, how is it possible that these same wild animals can get into a *building* and attack just one person and no one else? Don't you think that's a bit *odd*?"

I had shrugged my shoulders then. If I had told him the real story, he would have measured me up for a straitjacket!

"And speaking of odd things," the deputy had continued, "how is it that *you* were on the scene in both incidents?"

I had replied that it was sheer co-incidence and, if he was quite finished taking statements, I would like to get some rest. He hadn't been too pleased by my gruff manner, but there wasn't a damned thing he could have done about it.

After the EMT had taken Dr. Vengtman to the hospital (Nan insisted on accompanying them), I pondered my next course of action. Under other circumstances, I might have organized a search party to look for Melissa (it would have been by conscription, given the non-professional staff's attitude toward her); in her then frame of mind, she was capable of anything – almost literally. Yet, I had no desire to wander about the grounds – and especially the woods – in the dark, nor to subject any other person to that ordeal, so long as the girl was surrounded by creatures which were ready and willing to obey her every command, up to and including protecting her from all danger. From personal experience, encountering that menagerie in the daylight had been ghastly enough. *If* a search was to be conducted, it would have had to wait until morning.

Naturally, the commotion had aroused the rest of the professional staff, and they all pressed me for explanations. I was still in a state of semi-shock and begged off until I could collect my thoughts. I did take the opportunity, however, to push into Harry's hand the envelope Dr. Vengtman had prepared for him. Whether or not the Director survived this bizarre attack, I doubted he would ever be in a position to handle his administrative duties again; as far as I was concerned, our Senior Counselor was now in charge until further notice. (And I was still debating if I should call for a formal inquiry by the American Psychological Association.) Harry stared at the envelope as if it were a live hand grenade but said nothing. I excused myself and returned to my cottage.

As I approached the cottage, I thought I saw two pairs of eyes piercing the darkness opposite my door – one pair yellow, the other amethyst. When I attempted to make them out more clearly, they winked out of existence, and I wrote them off as delusions created by my boggled mind. I went inside, fell on the sofa-bed without undressing, and tried to sleep. Sleep was slow in coming. The attack on Lowell Vengtman kept playing over and over in my mind like a video tape on an endless loop, and I tossed and turned as a man undergoing torture (which I was, so to speak).

Abruptly, that scene was blotted out, and in its place a vista of drifting clouds in a summer sky took shape. It was pleasant and relaxing, and I felt as if the whole world was at peace. I soon lost consciousness and slept like a log.

DAY FOURTEEN:
Saturday, 07.19.1997
CONFLAGRATION

Why I slept the sleep of the innocent, why I dreamt only pleasant dreams, why I awoke feeling refreshed and energetic, I shall probably never know for certain. I can, however, make a shrewd – if wholly impossible – guess.

By then, I had come to realize that I possessed a "guardian angel" – quite unwanted, of course – who watched over me and had only my well-being at heart. This "angel" was, in reality, a devil, but I could not prevent her from working on my behalf. Melissa's infatuation was such that nothing I could have said or done would have merited her displeasure. I had spoken roughly to her on several occasions, and she remained demure and contrite; I had disbelieved every word she had ever uttered, and she continued to press her case; I had "jilted" her by taking up with another woman, and still she refused to fall into a jealous rage; I had brought her to tears twice, and she refrained from sending her menagerie to "punish" me. More significantly, she had acted whenever she perceived an outside threat to my person, e.g. the food fight in the dining room the first time I had served as meal monitor. And I was fairly convinced that, foreseeing a murderous act against me by Nurse Clement, she had pre-empted him by involving him in a fatal "accident." I also realized that, as she had done for Mathias Hinkelman, she had manipulated my patients' thoughts – and mine as well, for all I knew – in order to cure them. It may have been an unethical approach; yet, she believed she had been helping me. Given all this, it was only a small step to realize that, having sensed my distress over her rebellion against Lowell Vengtman, she had insinuated soothing thoughts into my subconscious mind while I slumbered and let me sleep like a baby.

How did one counter-act such a creature who could work her will with impunity? There was only one way, of course, one sure method used time and time again against such threats – real and perceived – to the "natural order." But, I was a doctor; I had sworn an oath to preserve life, not to take it.

As I replayed the events of the previous two days, I found myself both dismayed and heartened. On the one hand, I had learned that thought processes were no longer inviolate, that they could be re-shaped by means outside the realm of mere persuasion. All thoughts, all ideas, all suggestions which had been given form by anyone at the Home were now suspect; they could not be truly claimed to have belonged to the person forming them. Status meant nothing to the re-shaper; all were fair game. My predecessor had realized that – but too late to save himself from destruction. I too had been "guided." What would happen to my patients once Melissa's telepathic influence over their minds was no longer a factor? Would they then revert to their former psychotic states, as they had after the demise of Hinkelman? (In retrospect, it has occurred to me that even the above analysis, singularly crystal clear at the time, may also have been implanted in my brain.)

Dismaying thoughts indeed. Yet, I was determined not to succumb to despair. Rather, I could take heart by the fact that the whole sad tale had been finally revealed and that all of my questions had been answered (however bizarrely). I was no longer troubled by puzzles and mysteries and enigmas. What I could do with this new-found knowledge remained to be seen; a valuable lesson lay here if I just pondered the matter sufficiently. More important, the horror that had gripped the Vengtman Home for the Emotionally Disturbed was now a thing of the past, and the survivors of it could get on with their lives.

How wrong I was! There was yet one more chapter to be written in this terror tale, and it threatened to dwarf all that had preceded it in terms of enormity.

In addition to awaking refreshed, I was ravenously hungry and ready to eat everything in sight. I showered and dressed hastily and strolled briskly to the main building. I was soon overtaken by Maddie, who fell in beside me and matched me step for step (not an easy task for a short woman). She mumbled a "good morning" but said nothing further. From the curious looks she was giving me, I had a fairly good idea of what was going through her head; she had a hundred questions to ask and no polite way to ask them. For my part, I wasn't going to volunteer any information until the proper moment.

We were not the first staff to arrive for breakfast. Dante was already there, as he was meal monitor for the day. Harry lumbered in and eyed me with no small suspicion bordering on apprehension. I took no notice of his scrutiny. Let him stare, I thought; I had enough on my mind as it was, and I didn't need to burden myself with the problems of my colleagues. To satisfy my hunger, I had taken double portions of everything on the line and was in the process of shoveling it in when the Senior approached my table. He stood there until he had my attention. I regarded him as one might a nuisance (as he surely was at that moment). He held up the envelope I had given him the night before.

"This made for rather interesting reading," he stated in a strained voice. "So much so that I'm calling an emergency staff meeting for nine o'clock this morning."

"I thought you might," I responded evenly between large mouthfuls. "I would have."

"And, if I were you, Dr. Maxwell, I'd be prepared to tell us everything I knew concerning recent events."

"Of course, Dr. Rauschenburg. I had planned to make a full report to the Director – or his assigns."

"Splendid."

He walked off to serve himself. I shook my head in disgust. As far as I was concerned, that conversation had been pointless. Yet, it had had its particular effects, for normally, there was the usual hub-bub of small talk among the staff at meal times. That day, there was none; a hush hung over the dining room like a dark cloud, and all that could be heard was the scrape and clash of silverware against crockery. I finished my breakfast in relative peace, a peace which would soon be short-lived.

An emergency staff meeting represented a huge shift in mental gears for all concerned, employee and patient alike. Those professional staff not on monitor duty would have had the time to pursue their own interests; now, they had to delay their plans by however long it took to resolve the question of what to do in the face of the possible permanent incapacitation of Lowell Vengtman. For my own part, I had been scheduled for "Cultural Appreciation" (more on that later.) Our free time, being limited, was precious to us; loss of any part of it in order to conduct official business naturally provoked a certain amount of resentment and/or exasperation and eroded professional relationships. While no one might object *verbally*, one could see the reaction in an inflection of the voice or a shift in facial expression and/or body posture. The general populace supposed that trained psychologists are above such petty behavior; yet we are human too and subject to all the human foibles that beset the race as a whole.

We could sublimate our resentment and find suitable ways to vent our spleen. Not so the patients whose psychoses had taken them into realms where human emotions were magnified out of all proportion and loomed like monsters in a Grimm Brothers fairy tale. As much providing cures for their illnesses, the Home also sought to occupy their minds with a variety of activities in order to keep emotional outbursts in check; and, though the practice was not always successful, it had worked well enough to be reflected in the demands by the patients themselves for ever more variety.

In addition to the free-form activities built into the daily routine, there were the "special projects," a.k.a. "Cultural Appreciation," scheduled for week-ends. The second and fourth Saturdays of the month were Visitors Days (as already described). The first and third Saturdays were devoted to field trips – half the patients one day, the other half the other day, so as to create more manageable groups – either of a scientific or educational nature. The day was spent in a museum or an historical site or an art gallery or the like, followed in the evening by a musical concert. There was no lack of places to visit in the Chicago metropolitan area, and Lowell Vengtman had intended to expose his wards to all of them, if it were humanly possible. He had viewed appreciation of the cultural side of Life as a form of psychotherapy in that it stimulated those areas of the brain which tended toward atrophy under the onslaught of emotional trauma; by re-invigorating those areas and counter-acting the trauma, the patient ought to be more amenable to positive re-enforcement (the second step in the recovery of mental health).

There were the usual dangers, of course, in allowing a group of potential emotional time bombs to roam about in the outside world. I am reminded of the cult-classic film, *David and Lisa*, which concerned the sort of patients treated at the Home; in one memorable scene, a group on a field trip encounters some unthinking civilian who makes an ill-advised remark about a "bunch of screwballs, spoiling the town." One sees the anguish and pain in the patients' faces as they realize just how "different" they are from the rest of humanity. Hence, another monitoring duty for the professional staff (assisted by half a dozen nurses) to ride roughshod over a disparate bunch and to mediate the inevitable emergency situations. (Since these field trips occurred on the week-ends, the Director had sweetened the pot with an extra stipend; but, in my humble opinion, the money scarcely compensated for the loss of "free" time – especially if one were not particularly culturally inclined!).

That day, I was supposed to have taken my group to the Field Museum in Chicago, followed by a rock concert in Grant Park. With the emergency staff meeting, the trip was canceled. Whether the patients were looking forward to the outing was a moot point; yet, they were bound to pick up on a sudden disruption in the schedule and become anxious. Because Ray's death had already put many of them on edge, this newest disturbance was sure to increase their level of anxiety and possibly undo whatever progress the staff had made in the psychotherapeutic process. To allay any fears, the Senior Counselor declared the day to be "free time" in which the patients could indulge in whatever they chose for amusement (within the law, of course!).

Having stuffed myself to the eyeballs, I departed the dining room as unconcernedly as I had entered and returned to my cottage. If Harry wanted a *full* report on what I knew, then, by damn! that was what he was going to get, and he could puzzle it out for himself. I'd talk until I was blue in the face or he fell asleep. But, the incredible story I was about to tell required the most extensive documentation, and that meant gathering together Hinkelman's journal (the *complete* version), his patients' (now *my* patients') files, his personnel file, all of the notes I had made, and Melissa's file (which I had picked up off the floor where Dr. Vengtman had dropped it when he was attacked and which I had slipped underneath my jacket while waiting for the EMT to arrive). I was preparing a grand lecture, and Harry might have cause to regret having requested it.

I strolled into the parlor at five minutes to nine and took my usual chair. Nearly everyone was there; only Nan was absent as she was still at the hospital. I was mildly surprised to see two persons I had not expected to see. The first was Bertie, who was supposed to be on bereavement leave; apparently, Harry had called him back for the emergency meeting. From his bleary-eyed and hang-dog appearance, I guessed he had taken an early morning flight in order to get back here on time; his clothes looked even more "slept in" than usual. He regarded me noncommittally, and I merely nodded at him. The other was our new Senior Nurse, Michaels. It may seem odd that Lowell Vengtman had never thought to include the Senior Nurse in his staff meetings; one might have believed that, due to the experience (s)he brought to the position, (s)he would have had something worthwhile to contribute. It was a minor oversight on the Director's part, proving that perhaps even geniuses couldn't think of everything. Harry, on the other hand, was not going to make that mistake during his "regime" (however long it lasted); experience would count for something, even if the individual did not have a bunch of letters after his/her name. I winked boldly at her and received a wry smile in return.

At nine o'clock, the Senior cleared his throat and announced he was still waiting for Nan. "Hurry up and wait," I recalled an Army veteran in my old neighborhood describing military life. Harry had been all hot and bothered to have that meeting, to the point of making veiled threats if I failed to co-operate, and now he was forcing us to cool our heels. I decided to use the time to review mentally what I wanted to say (and in what order) and to check that my documentation corresponded to the sequence of my talking points. At the same time, surreptitiously, I observed my colleagues.

In varying degrees, they displayed an understated nervousness – with one exception. That was Bertie, who kept nodding off and might have fallen asleep altogether had not some inner voice reminded him of where he was and why.

Harry maintained a false stoicism, staring across the room at nothing in particular and continuously drumming his fingers on the arm of his chair in tiny, rhythmic motions. I had the distinct impression that he was wondering why *he* was there. I also wondered the same thing. He had never struck me as the administrative type, preferring to be a go-between; being the Senior Counselor suited him just fine since, if the going got tough, he could always defer to the Director. Now, he had the functioning of the Home thrown unceremoniously into his lap, and he was struggling to keep his head above water. Well, better him than me, I decided. I didn't have any administrative experience either – even at a low level – and I wasn't afraid to admit it. Someday, perhaps, but not under those circumstances.

Maddie chewed her fingernails, a nervous habit I hadn't noticed before (but, then, I hadn't been trying to psychoanalyze my co-workers, had I?) In between chomps, she sighed deeply and audibly. If she had any inkling of what was about to take place, she didn't let on. Yet, of all the staff, I believed she would have become the most alarmed by my report because she had been indirectly involved in some of the events I planned to discuss. Though I had already provided a glimpse into the mind of her late lover, it had been somewhat of a pleasant one; the full story was sure to shock her right down to her toes.

Dante was always nervous (due, I suspected, to an inherent inferiority complex because of his small stature) and whiled away the time by tracing imaginary patterns on the fabric of his chair. It might have been quite revealing to see the sort of doodles he made. Doodling derives from one's unconscious desires, those too embarrassing to put into words. Though doodles are usually associated with children, many adults practice the art, suggesting unfulfilled – and unfulfillable – goals in their childhoods. From the nature of the limericks which he preferred, I had the idea that Dante was still a child at heart, wandering in confusion in an uncaring world.

In sharp contrast to the professional staff, Nurse Michaels presented a picture of cool, calm efficiency – a marked difference to the Michaels I had first encountered. Her previous emotional state may have been the result of her forced relationship with the late, unlamented Nurse Clement. Her changed attitude perhaps now reflected her new status, not only that of Senior Nurse but also as a new participant in the professional staff meetings.

And what of myself? A former angry (and often violent) street kid, now a well-paid professional – what was I feeling? I had sought comfort and routine. I found instead mystery and intrigue. I learned that my idol had feet of clay – and worse, a heart of stone – and the disillusionment was only beginning to sink in. I had experienced fear and anger and disgust and sorrow and resentment – often in combination – but I hadn't had the time to analyze them properly. I was still determined to right all wrongs committed in the Vengtman Home for the Emotionally Disturbed (Illinois branch), whether or not it was my place to do so, and to maintain its good reputation. A naïve attitude on my part, no doubt, but I was stuck with it.

At twenty minutes past nine, Nan walked in. Her appearance shook me considerably. She looked haggard, red-eyed, and disheveled, and she moved mechanically as if it were taking all of her will power to put one foot in front of the other. I rose and took a step toward her in a show of sympathy. She gave me a wan smile and extended her hand. I squeezed it gently. She then pulled away and went to her accustomed seat, falling into it rather than sitting and letting her body go limp.

"Now that we're all here," Harry said (a bit tactlessly, I thought), "let's get started. First order of business: an update on our beloved Director's condition – if you feel up to it, that is, Nan."

"I'm all right, Harry," she responded in a tired voice. "I've been up all night, as you might guess, and I could use some sleep. But, you need to be updated. Uncle Lowell is still on the critical list, though his condition has stabilized somewhat. He lost a lot of blood but, fortunately, none of his wounds involved a major artery. Otherwise, he might not have survived this long...."

Her voice trailed away as if she had no more breath to expend on forming words, and she sat motionless and stared into space. Harry cleared his throat again, this time in embarrassment.

"Um, well, thank God for small favors. And thank you, Nan." He now produced the envelope I had given him. "Now to the main order of business.

"Dr. Vengtman had the foresight to make arrangements for his... replacement should he no longer be able to fulfill his duties. I have here a letter addressed to the Senior Counselor of this facility, signed by the Director and witnessed by two members of the Executive Committee of the Board of Trustees. I'll pass it around for your verification. In effect, I'm the Acting Director until the Board selects a permanent replacement. I've already notified the Board, and they've given me their imprimatur for the nonce."

The letter was short and to the point:

> "To whom it may concern:
>
> Your receipt of this document signals the fact of my inability to carry out my duties or of my permanent absence from this facility. As I have done in the past at other Homes, I am naming you, the Senior Counselor, as Acting Director until such time as the Board of Trustees appoints a permanent Director. By prior agreement, the Board bestows upon the Acting Director full and complete authority to operate the facility as (s)he deems necessary to accomplish the purposes and goals of the Vengtman Homes. I trust you will carry out your new duties with all dispatch."

It passed through our hands quickly.

"Well and good, Harry," Bertie muttered. "but I've been here nearly as long as you have, and I'm damned if I'm going to call you 'Sir'!"

That got a hearty chuckle from all present and served to ease the tension somewhat.

"Anyone who doesn't call me 'Sir,'" the new Acting Director remarked dryly, "will suffer all the torments of Hell. He or she will have to eat his or her ice cream without chocolate syrup." A chorus of mock groans circled the room; even the new Senior Nurse joined in. "If we can be serious again, I'll ask Dr. Maxwell to report on certain information he has recently acquired. Ken?"

All eyes were riveted on me then, even those of Nan, who already knew most of the story. I'd soon learn just how fixed my "reputation" as a *wunderkind* was at the Home. I suspected that it was about to become tarnished.

"What I'm about to tell you," I said by way of preamble, "will astound you. You might not believe any of it. God knows I had difficulty believing it myself. Yet, the proof is right here" – I held up Hinkelman's journal – "for everyone to see. I had planned to write up a formal report for Dr.

Vengtman, until I learned how intimately involved he was in this affair. I may still write that report, but it'll be for a board of inquiry of the APA."

I waited until the expected murmuring of surprise subsided, then proceeded to unburden myself of the whole incredible tale, beginning with my curiosity over Mathias Hinkelman's unorthodox approach to psychotherapy to the strange incidents involving Melissa Waterman, from my discovery of Hinkelman's journal to Melissa's shocking accusations, from the *murders* (loud gasps here) of Nurse Clement and Ray W. to the revelations in Melissa's file and the casual confession of complicity by Lowell Vengtman. For nearly an hour, I gave my colleagues a sterling lecture on the horrors which had been part of the Vengtman Homes for over a decade, a lecture which sounded like nothing less than the latest Stephen King novel.

And, as I rattled on, I continued to observe the reactions of my colleagues. Nan, not too surprisingly, was the least affected, although there were moments when she was on the verge of tears. One might have thought that she would have been the *most* affected – after all, I *was* depicting her uncle as a modern-day Svengali – yet she made no gestures by way of contradiction. Maddie, who also had a personal stake, did give in to emotion and buried her head in her hands, and I felt almost like a heel for exposing her to that dirty business. The others registered varying degrees of shock, incredulity, and anger. Like me, they had believed wholeheartedly in Lowell Vengtman and in his goals; to have the object of their admiration and adulation besmirched and dethroned was stretching their tolerance to the breaking point. Still, they accorded me the professional courtesy of hearing me out. Unfortunately, the grace period ended when I ran out of things to say; as I leaned back in my chair, the onslaught of denial commenced. Immediately, Dante was on his feet.

"Lies!" he shouted. "Damned *lies!*"

"Slander!" contributed Bertie, leaning menacingly toward me. "Nothing but slander! How dare you!"

"Gentlemen, please!" Harry called for order. When he had it, he fixed me with a steely glare. "Once, I might have asked for your head as well. Now that I am in a position of authority and am expected to behave as a referee – as Dr. Vengtman so often did – I am constrained to hold my tongue. You say you have proof of these allegations?" I nodded and held up my stack of documents. "Nan, your opinion?"

"It's all true, Harry, all of it. Oh, God! how I wish it weren't. But I was witness to some of it" – she swallowed compulsively – "especially the

331

worst of it." She regarded me sadly. "I insisted that Ken take me into his confidence. Now, I wish I hadn't."

"Hum. Well, then, I suppose we must accept it, whether we want to or not. Scientific integrity and all that, don't you know? By all means, Ken, write your report, make copies for all of us, and present it at Monday's regular meeting. We'll discuss it in a proper fashion, as Dr. Vengtman would want us to."

I had to hand it to Harry. He was doing his damnedest to cope with an unaccustomed role. And, by invoking the name of Lowell Vengtman, he was attempting to quell the unrest in the others. Both Dante and Bertie were still fuming and working their jaw muscles, but they were not prepared to stage a full-fledged mutiny just yet. They'd give me the benefit of the doubt – or more rope with which to hang myself!

"Now," the new Acting Director declared, "if there's nothing else, we'll –"

He was cut off by the sudden opening of the parlor door. Nurse Blakely burst in, and she looked frightful – wild-eyed, pallid, somewhat disheveled, gasping for breath. She peered uncomprehendingly at each of us in turn, settling at last on her nominal superior, Senior Nurse Michaels. The latter half-rose in response to some silent plea that only women can discern.

"Nurse!" Harry bellowed. "What's the meaning of this intrusion?"

Seeing the terror in her eyes and on her face, Michaels adopted a milder tone.

"What's wrong, Blakely?" she soothed, going to the woman. "Are you all right?"

At first, nothing but whimpering sounds came out of Blakely's mouth. She wrung her hands furiously and stared at Harry like he was a monster come to life. Michaels wrapped her arms about her and hugged her. Blakely buried her head in the other's shoulder and sobbed uncontrollably. It was a piteous sight, and we hadn't the least idea of what had set her off. Presently, having cried herself out, Blakely turned to the assembly.

"I'm sorry, Doctors, Chief, but it was…*awful!*"

"What was?" Michaels asked solicitously.

"*Her!*" the junior nurse whispered. "*She's* out on the lawn – with – with -- Oh, God! it's – it's *horrible!*"

"'She'? Who're you talkin' about?"

"Oh-h-h, I don't want to think about it. You have to see it for yourselves. Hurry!"

One by one, we piled out of the parlor, not bothering to stand on ceremony, and headed for the main entrance. Along the hallway, huddled in two's and three's (for mutual protection/comfort?), other nurses stood as ashen and terror-stricken as Blakely. They beseeched us with their eyes to deliver them from harm. I personally didn't think I could deliver the morning paper just then, least of all act as a savior-figure. I had a fairly good idea of what we'd find out on the lawn, but I said nothing until I had confirmation.

That confirmation came the moment the first of us opened the front door and stepped breathlessly onto the porch. I don't remember who it was, but (s)he stopped dead in his/her tracks, causing a traffic jam/collision. As best we could, the rest of us eased past him/her and spread out along the porch like a battle line. In retrospect, that analogy was quite apt, for we did do battle that day, in a manner of speaking – or least, I did.

For the third time in as many days, I beheld a spectacle I had rather not have witnessed. Blakely had been correct: it *was* awful. It was more than awful; it was *horrendous*! This "savior' felt quite faint at the sight, because he had already seen far too much in too short a time. Nan stood beside me, and we sought each other out and grasped hands instinctively.

The lawn was literally alive with wildlife. Mammals large and small, reptiles legged and legless, birds diurnal and nocturnal – everything that was indigenous to this area and walked or crept or burrowed or flew was represented, each segregated according to its species. Amazingly, there were more creatures present than I had seen in the woods two days before; apparently, most of them had come from off the property in answer to some siren call for some inexplicable reason. As before, none of them moved a muscle or uttered a sound; they all waited – for what? Eerily, they faced the Home (and us) as if they were an audience at a theater. If they expected the humans on the "stage" to perform for them, they were wasting their time; we were as rooted to the spot as they were – perhaps more so – and dared not stir lest we provoke an adverse response from them. I had just established the fact that some wildlife had been the assailants of Ray W. and Lowell Vengtman, and none of us cared to be added to that list. It was a "Mexican stand-off" from start to finish.

Abruptly, time as well as motion ceased to exist in that place. I felt quite detached from the scene, and I imagined I was looking down upon it from a height. All of the creatures below, human and non-human, appeared doll-like; they were mere figurines set in a scaled-down landscape. It was an odd and disquieting sensation, yet I was not afraid. I seemed to drift like a cloud, dreamily, viewing the scene below and pondering the significance of it all. It was most pleasant, and I wished I could stay up there forever. Predictably, I was aware of my "guardian angel's" presence in my mind.

* * *

Beautiful, isn't it, Ken?

Yes. So peaceful – so relaxing. Is this your doing?

Do you need to ask? I've been with you from the very beginning, except that you were never aware of my presence until now.

Why me?

I told you once, my darling. You're a good and kind man who wants to help people. I looked into your mind the day you first arrived and knew you better than you do yourself.

That's cruel, Melissa! Snooping in a person's mind is the worst sort of invasion of privacy. Even if you had his permission, it still wouldn't give you the right to manipulate his thoughts.

Not even for a good cause?

Not even. Besides, you've done terrible things with your power.

I know, and someday I'll be punished for them. But, I hope to do some good to make up for it.

What could you possibly do to even the score?

You'll see. Even Dr. Vengtman never knew the extent of my power – sometimes it scares me *to think of what I can do (if you care to believe that) – and so he never experimented beyond his own selfish desires.*

But you did.

Yes. You've seen some of the results.

I wish I hadn't. I'm going to have nightmares for the rest of my life.

I could fix that, darling.

No! I don't want you whispering in my mind anymore. It's too…monstrous!

I – I'm, sorry, Ken. I just want to help.

You can, but not that *way. Why have you summoned all these animals?*

To demonstrate my power to the others. You and they must be absolutely convinced that I can do what I'm planning to do.

Which is?

Watch.

* * *

As suddenly as the sensation of detachment had come upon me, it departed again, and I found myself back on the porch of the Home, staring at the giant menagerie sitting rigidly on the lawn. I blinked several times in order to re-orient myself. Had I really had a mind-to-mind conversation with Melissa Waterman? Or had I just hallucinated the whole thing? After all I had been through recently, the one possibility was as likely as the other. I cast glances all around to learn if the others had observed my mental absence. Apparently not, for they were still looking straight ahead, fixed on that eerie scene. I took a deep breath and let it out slowly. Beside me, Nan quivered slightly, and I slipped my arm around her waist. She failed to respond to the gesture.

Despite my having communicated (?) with Melissa, I had not seen her anywhere in the vicinity. Was she running this "show" from a distance, using her incredible powers to – as she had stated – convince us of them? When (if ever) would she put in a physical appearance? It probably didn't make one bit of difference if she stood before us or not; still, for the sake of *my* sanity, it would have been gratifying to see her behave somewhat human-like – even if she had gone far beyond the realm of human existence.

While I was considering where she might be hiding, I heard someone down the line gasp sharply. All heads turned in the direction of the gasp, and soon all of us were making sounds of alarm. Incredibly, my four remaining patients were single-filing through the main door with Melissa at their head. The first reaction was concern; the presence of emotionally disturbed people unescorted by staff ordinarily spelled potential danger. Why weren't they in their rooms, ostensibly waiting for the nurses to take them to their "free-time" activities? And what was the nursing staff doing, that they allowed a teen-aged girl to spirit their charges away uncontested? This breach in routine bore further investigation, but it had to be put on hold due to the more immediate problem at hand.

The second reaction was embarrassment. Melissa had reverted to her *au naturel* state, and she exhibited no more self-consciousness about it in this public setting than she had in the private setting of the woods. Yet, no one dared (or was able?) to speak so long as she was present.

And the third reaction was wonder. Ordinarily, the patients displayed varying degrees of negative emotions whenever Melissa appeared in their midst. Not that day. All appeared to be calm and serene, and none seemed to be at all apprehensive by the identity of their "guide" or by the nature of their surroundings, i.e. center stage in front of an "audience" of woodland creatures. Yet, upon closer inspection, I saw not calmness nor serenity, but stupor. The patients' eyes were glazed and unseeing; their arms hung loosely at their sides, and their gait was slow and robotic. Melissa's mental powers apparently had no limits whatsoever. The real question was why she was putting on this demonstration.

This incongruous troop came to a halt in front of the professional staff and, at some unvoiced command, slowly faced us. Melissa regarded us impassively as if to dare us to challenge her actions. Whether in response to that posturing or to a need to re-establish order, Harry cleared his throat and spoke in a tremulous voice:

"Melissa, what's the meaning of this?"

He actually took two steps toward her. I think – no, I *know* – her amethyst eyes brightened slightly. Harry stopped and rubbed his jaw in indecision; then he returned to his original position and said not another word.

And then I had to ask myself: should *I* do something? The girl respected me (in her own queer fashion) and might accede to my wishes. It behooved me to defuse that situation before someone got hurt. But what could I do? Not knowing what she had in mind, I couldn't form a counter-attack; I would be walking into a mine-field, blindfolded.

"Melissa," I began with my heart in my throat, "would you mind explaining yourself?"

"I told you, Ken, I'm going to make up for all the evil I've done in the past. I intend to cure your patients. I know how to do it. It's easy."

I swallowed hard.

"I'm sure it is – for you. It's also unethical. You mustn't tamper with people's minds like that."

"I'm sorry you feel that way, Ken, but this is something I have to do. Don't try to interfere."

I was about to make one last plea when, seemingly like magic, the scene in front of me altered radically. I was no longer standing on the porch of the Home staring at a lawnful of wild animals. Instead, I was in a woods – not exactly like the woods on the grounds of the Home but strangely similar. Melissa, still nude, stood at my side. As I wondered where I was and how the hell I had gotten there, the professional observer in me started to note the details of the scene. The coloring – of the trees, the undergrowth, and even the sky itself – seemed much too rich to be real; it was the coloring of a Sunday-comics page – gaudy, unshaded, and simplistic. I realized instantly that I was seeing, not a real place but another of Melissa's mental re-creations. Once again, she had gone into my mind and filled it with fantasy. What was she up to?

Suddenly, we were not alone. However he had arrived on the scene,

I recognized the figure approaching us. It was my "werewolf," Fred – or, rather, Melissa's interpretation of his physical appearance. He was walking on all fours as a quadruped might, slowly, deliberately, looking from side to side, alert for any danger. If not for the circumstances, I would have considered his behavior ludicrous, but I felt only apprehension at the time. I wanted to speak to him, to ask him what he was doing in the woods, but could not. My tongue was as rigid as cement. I couldn't even move my arms to gain his attention; I was completely paralyzed. And, as "Fred" came closer, I realized that it wouldn't have made any difference had I been able to speak or move. He did not see us, did not know we were there; we were not a part of his surroundings, and so he ignored us. Melissa and I were simply the "audience" in a drama she was putting on. Out of the corner of my eye, I saw that she was smiling. What was next?

Now, new "actors" entered the scene from the opposite direction: four real "wolves" – or rather Melissa's rendition of real wolves. "Fred" halted, sat down on his haunches, and waited expectantly. I had to presume that the newcomers were the "pack" he had mentioned to me during previous sessions. The quartet pulled up before him, sat down on *their* haunches, and eyed him suspiciously.

"Why have you called this meeting?" one of the "wolves" spoke in a quite human fashion.

"I have to report new developments," "Fred" replied.

"Continue," said another "wolf."

"I have learned that our new member – the one who replaced our brother who was killed by hunters – has confronted the hunters and defeated them."

"Defeated them?" asked a third "wolf." "How so?"

"He has taken away their weapons. Now, they are defenseless."

"And how does that help us?" the last "wolf" inquired.

"We are free to do as we please at long last. We no longer have to hide behind lies and deceit. We can be what we were meant to be."

Despite the unreal circumstances in which I found myself, I confess that I was very intrigued by this "conversation" which, undoubtedly, Melissa had scripted. Her methods were reprehensible, of course, but her approach to psychotherapy was the same I would have followed had I been in charge. Had she pulled that approach out of my mind? It was hard to tell. In any event, the first step in tackling mental illness was to have the patient evaluate his illness on his own terms, if at all possible. Melissa had done that by casting Fred as himself in this little drama and making him the principal speaker. The next step was to have the patient doubt that the conditions leading up to his illness were real and convince him that they were merely illusions. Melissa had done that also through "Fred's" report to his "pack." The last step was to have the patient reject the illusions and embrace reality. Would Melissa follow through correctly? I found myself holding my breath.

It dawned on me then that this tableau was not taking place in *my* mind. What Melissa had done was to transport her and me – or rather our consciousnesses – into *Fred's* mind. Specifically, we were in his subconscious where the cause of his psychosis – his abuse of peyote – lay buried. This revelation stunned me as much as, if not more than, anything else I had experienced in the two weeks I'd been at the Home. It was one thing to have someone crawling around in my mind; it was quite another for *me* to be crawling around in *someone else's* mind! I didn't like either situation. But, then, I wasn't exactly a free agent, was I?

"And do you feel free, Fred?" Wolf #1 was asking.

"I think so."

"You *think* so?" Wolf #2 questioned him. "Don't you *know*?"

"Yes, yes. I know I feel free."

"Then stand up," Wolf #3 commanded.

"What?"

"You are a man, Fred," Wolf #4 declared, "not a wolf. Stand up!"

"Fred" peered at each "wolf" in a moment of self-doubt. Then, he assumed a resolute expression, slowly pushed himself upright, and stood before his "pack" triumphantly. I was exultant, in spite of myself. Melissa had made the final connection!

Then the most amazing thing happened. The images of the "wolves" merged into one another and became one. The single image fluctuated, changed shape, and took the form of a human being. I gasped in surprise at who Melissa had conjured up. It was *me* – or at least, her perception of me!

"Congratulations, Fred," "I" said. "And welcome back to the real world."

"Thank you, Dr. Maxwell. It feels...*good* to be back."

In a flash, I was back on the porch of the Home. How long the episode in Fred's subconscious had taken was anybody's guess – a matter of seconds, perhaps, but it had seemed longer. The external world had not changed one iota; all was as I had left it. No, that was not quite true. The real Fred was smiling as happily as he had in his inner world.

The psychotic mind, filled with fears and guilt feelings, seeks relief from them by burying them deep in the subconscious and covering them over with carefully contrived fantasy to which the ego can anchor itself and keep afloat. If the layer of fantasy is threatened, the psychotic mind creates a backlash either to overpower the threat or to destroy it. Therefore, before breaking down the psychosis, one must first deal with the fantasy by convincing the ego of the falseness of the contrivance and then assuaging the fears and guilt feelings that produced the psychosis originally. For, above all else, the psychotic mind wishes to be absolved of all wrong-doing; it wants to believe that it is completely innocent of the cause that led to the psychosis.

What Melissa had done (in her own unique manner) was to place a more positive image in Fred's mind concerning his lycanthropy. First working through Mathias Hinkelman, then through me, and finally through direct contact with his subconscious, she had provided a "solution" to his dilemma, i.e. his addiction to peyote and his guilt feelings concerning it. However much one might deplore her methodology, her approach to the problem had been the correct one. I stood in awe of this demonstration of her power, even while my own mind was still reeling from the incredible experience of being inside another person's mind.

"See how easy it is, Ken?" Melissa said softly. "Would you like to go inside the minds of the others?"

"Uh, no, thank you," I rasped. "Once is enough. Whatever you're going to do, just do it and get it over with."

And now I saw how she did it. She faced the next person in line (old Matt) and concentrated. She became rigid, and her uncanny amethyst eyes glowed like twin fires. Her "subject" also became rigid as the re-creation of the psychosis-producing event took shape. I observed rapid eye movement as Matt's ego "saw" the new imagery and reacted to it; every muscle in his body twitched and spasmed in a St. Vitus dance as his fears and guilt feelings were paraded past the subconscious "eye" and chased out. Then, seconds later, the old man relaxed, and a smile of relief was writ large on his face. Melissa's eyes ceased to glow, and she became animate again. She moved down the line and, in similar fashion, "cured" Terry and Georgina. In the latter's case, "treatment" required less time due to Georgina's prior acceptance of her son's death; what was needed was to absolve her of any guilt feelings. All four of my *former* patients were still statue-like; however, they were smiling statues, existing in a state of purity and innocence. I shook my head in a mixture of amazement and apprehension.

Melissa walked back to my position, inspecting the smiling faces as she went, apparently satisfied with her work. Then she gazed steadily at me. I tensed.

"I could have cured Ray too," she said matter-of-factly, "even though he was filled with hate and violence. He discovered my friends and me communing together and started throwing rocks at us. I couldn't let him hurt my friends, could I? So, I…stopped him."

"I love you, Kenneth Maxwell. I'd gladly give myself to you, but" – here she regarded Nan – "you've already been claimed. I could use my power to cause you to love me, but it wouldn't be the same. This" – she gestured at the four cured individuals – "is my token of affection for you. Please don't hate me too much."

"I – I don't hate you, Melissa," I found myself saying. "I never *hated* you. I only wanted you to be more…*human*."

A faint smile played across her lips.

"We both know that's impossible, don't we? I'll leave now. You won't be troubled by me again."

"Where will you go?"

"Somewhere I can be myself without any interference from those who fear what they don't understand."

"You've got to stay here, Melissa. You'll be safe here."

"For how long, Ken? Everyone here fears me. Even you can't trust me. Sooner or later, someone will try to hurt me, and I'll – I'll have to hurt them. That's what happened to Clement and Ray." A wry smile now. "Besides, you aren't really worried about *my* safety, are you? What worries you is other people's safety."

She had me there. When all was said and done, my main concern was for those in the future who might chance to cross paths with Melissa Waterman, fail to understand her nature, and react in time-honored human fashion. Obviously, she could defend herself; all she had to do was to reach into a person's mind – as she had done with Mathias Hinkelman – and plant a seed of self-destruction. I knew of no defense against a telepath, particularly one who was patently sociopathic, unless it was another telepath. Yes, I did fear for the general populace more than I did for her. But, seen in the light of cool reason, her behavior was the product of negative social conditioning (fostered and encouraged, it must be said, by Lowell Vengtman); and, had she been under the guidance of a more benign individual, she might have become a productive unit in the fight against mental illness, rather than the cause of it. Because of the "Great Man's" monomania, however, she was just a willful child, amoral to a fault, dangerous to herself and to humanity. All the more reason, ironically, to keep her in the Home where she could be "re-conditioned" (hopefully). At the moment, she was beyond reason – despite her personal feelings for me – and she was determined to flee and hide herself away forever.

My failure to counter her argument was probably the convincing point. Her amethyst eyes brightened slightly, and she lifted a hand as a signal to her "friends." As one cohesive mass, the menagerie stirred themselves, poised for action. I swallowed another lump in my throat. Melissa flicked her wrist and, like an animated carpet, the animals turned and scampered, crawled, or flew back to the woods from whence they came. And still they maintained their eerie silence. It was totally unnerving, the way they obeyed Melissa instantly. My personal feelings about her departure notwithstanding, I sure as hell would not miss that unnatural rapport she had with them.

When all the wildlife had scrambled off, the girl approached me, pressed her naked body against me, and kissed me lightly on the lips. She then looked at Nan with knowing eyes. I had (and still have) no idea what message was communicated there, as women have their own language when dealing with each other. A warning? Congratulations? Who could tell? Then, Melissa walked toward the main gate. No one moved to stop her or to call her back – least of all me. In a matter of minutes, she disappeared from sight.

After some semblance of normalcy had been restored, Harry decided to re-convene our emergency staff meeting, for now we had a genuine emergency on our hands. The question was should we report Melissa's absence to the authorities. Technically, she had not been registered as a patient at the Home; aside from the file the Director had kept on her, no paperwork to that effect existed. Legally, she was Lowell Vengtman's ward, a member of his family; also legally, she was eighteen, a new adult who could come and go as she pleased. On the other hand, we could scarcely let her loose upon an unsuspecting world (even though, one of the staff – I won't say which one – was of the opinion that we were well rid of her); we would be remiss in our professional ethics to say nothing. On the third hand, however, who would believe a tale of some rogue telepath wandering about, capable of causing all manner of mischief? Despite all of our impressive credentials, we'd be the laughingstock of the psychological community. Thus, we compromised by filing a "missing-persons" report and prayed that Melissa would keep her word and stay out of sight.

As to the larger question which refused to wait until the regular

Monday meeting, we were in a huge quandary. Should we report the activities which had occurred at the Home, not only during the past two weeks but also during Lowell Vengtman's career? After all he had done for psychotherapy, it might have seemed petty to pick over his faults. Unfortunately, one of those faults had been engaging in an immoral and unethical experiment in which a fellow psychologist had been deprived of his sanity and ultimately his life. To keep silent in order to safeguard someone's reputation was itself immoral and unethical.

As a corollary, to whom should we have reported? The American Psychological Association? The police? The Federal government? This last option sent a chill up my spine as I envisioned some secret security-oriented agency steeped in paranoia and disregard for civil liberties descending upon us to pick – or try to pick – our brains about Melissa and to place – or try to place – us all under wraps. And then there would have been the massive, unrelenting manhunt. Innocent (and perhaps not-so-innocent) people were bound to suffer in this dragnet. None of us wanted to contribute to a police state any more than we wanted to keep the world ignorant of a potential danger. We ended up tabling that issue for a few weeks in the hopes that some new development would take it out of our hands altogether. In retrospect, it was a slim hope.

I spent the rest of the day sitting near the flower garden and meditating on the future – mine, Nan's and mine, and the Home's. All three seemed pretty bleak.

POSTSCRIPT

Lowell Vengtman eventually recovered from his wounds, but his spirit was gone. He never really believed Melissa would develop a streak of independence and turn against him. Her eerie and vicious attack left him emotionally drained and psychologically bereft. Nan, acting in her capacity as power-of-attorney, assigned him a room in his own facility and forbade anyone to interview him. It was probably just as well, since the staff of the Home had decided to sit on the incredible story until after his death. The Board of Trustees named Harry as permanent Director, a post he held until his alcoholism caught up with him. At the request of the rest of the staff, he was replaced by Nan and me, acting jointly. Nan and I married a few months after the events described above. In our spare time, we scoured every newspaper we could lay hands on (and still do) for any reports of a strange young woman who preferred the company of animals to that of humans.

Even now, I am plagued by a touch of paranoia. Whenever I see two or more animals in one place, I look over my shoulder, expecting to see a pair of amethyst eyes peering at me.

And I brace myself for whispers in my mind.